W9-ACC-735

THE STRANGER IN THE ASYLUM

THE STRANGER IN THE ASYLUM

Alys Clare

SEVERN
HOUSE

First world edition published in Great Britain and the USA in 2024
by Severn House, an imprint of Canongate Books Ltd,
14 High Street, Edinburgh EH1 1TE.

severnhouse.com

British Library Cataloguing-in-Publication Data
A CIP catalogue record for this title is available from the British Library.

ISBN-13: 978-0-7278-2307-6 (cased)
ISBN-13: 978-1-4483-1299-3 (e-book)

All Severn House titles are printed on acid-free paper.

MIX
Paper from
responsible sources
FSC® C013056

Typeset by Palimpsest Book Production Ltd.,
Falkirk, Stirlingshire, Scotland.
Printed and bound in Great Britain by
TJ Books, Padstow, Cornwall.

Praise for the World's End Bureau mysteries

"An engaging plot and two richly developed leads"
Booklist on *The Man in the Shadows*

"Industrial London and rural Kent provide the Victorian backgrounds for two fascinating stories of love, hate, and madness"
Kirkus Reviews on *The Man in the Shadows*

"Anne Perry fans will want to check this out"
Publishers Weekly on *The Outcast Girls*

"Mystery and social commentary combine in a heartbreaking and sadly relevant tale"
Kirkus Reviews on *The Outcast Girls*

"Impressive . . . the solid plotting, colorful Victorian settings, and fun detective duo bode well for future instalments"
Publishers Weekly on *The Woman Who Spoke to Spirits*

"Engaging, dark, atmospheric, and, at times, quite charming and humorous . . . A fine choice for all mystery collections"
Booklist on *The Woman Who Spoke to Spirits*

"The author's writing style, likable characters, and intriguing plot will draw in readers . . . Recommended for historical and traditional mystery lovers"
Library Journal on *The Woman Who Spoke to Spirits*

About the author

Alys Clare lives in the English countryside where her novels are set. She went to school in Tonbridge and later studied archaeology at the University of Kent. She is the author of the Aelf Fen, Hawkenlye, World's End Bureau and Gabriel Taverner historical mystery series.

In recognition of well over half a century
of travelling through the better- and lesser-known
parts of France, and thinking with love
of those who travelled with me.

PROLOGUE

They tell him the memories will fade, given time.

They have been telling him this for years. The memories are as vivid as ever, and they haunt him with increasing frequency and intensity.

The memories are terrible; full of violent pictures, and nowadays he seems to hear and smell as vividly as he sees. The sound of metal screaming against brick. The sound of human terror. The sound of his own urine hitting the floor as the greatest fear he had ever known made him lose control of his body. The scream of steam, bursting from its confines. The smell of burning. The smell of blood. The dreadful sense of being hemmed in so tightly with no possibility of escape, nowhere to go. The darkness.

Dead bodies; men, women. Two children, a baby. Bloodied limbs lying unnaturally far from their bodies. The awful knowledge that he too was about to be torn apart and die and there was absolutely nothing he could do about it.

Only he hadn't died, and sometimes – quite often, really – he wishes he had.

He had been a boy. He was travelling alone on the train, going home for the school holidays. He had been with other boys for the first part of the journey. Not that their boisterous company had made any difference, because as usual he had felt alone. He had no friends and the only attention the other boys paid him was when they teased and tormented him and told him he was strange. Odd. Weird. He was no good at the activities they prized, such as playing rugby or doing silly things that made them all snigger or coming up with pranks that fooled the masters and dirty jokes that had the other boys chortling and cruel tricks of the most foul, disgusting vulgarity. The only thing he was good at was drawing. Drawing and painting. And nobody admired him for that.

The last part of the journey was on the little single track branch line. He'd been alone by then; none of the other boys lived very near to him.

And that was when it happened.

They never told him *why* it happened. Because that, he heard them whisper, would only upset him. *But I am already far beyond upset*, he wanted to shout.

So he had to find out for himself.

It was when they were in the tunnel.

The railway men had been doing repairs and a length of rail had been taken up. There were warning signs at both ends of the tunnel but it was foggy, and the daylight had been fading, and the engine driver must have missed them. Nobody knew for sure, because the engine driver was among the dead. He had been crushed by the side of the cab as it finally gave in to the force of the tunnel wall, and then his body had been incinerated when the firebox had burst and the flames had exploded outwards. They said he was already dead when the fire started to consume him; killed by the crushing. But, again, nobody actually knew.

The locomotive's momentum meant that it had run on for some distance after it had hit the place where the rail had been taken up and lurched sideways. It had dragged its two coaches with it. Then it had slammed into the rear of a stationary service train on the far side of the missing rail. It came to a halt with a devastating suddenness that crunched up the boiler and what was left of the cab, destroyed the tender and smashed the first carriage to pieces.

There had been a man in the same carriage. Earlier, before it happened, the man had looked up once or twice and smiled.

It was a nice smile. And the man had kind eyes . . .

He can still see the scene.

Sometimes there are periods of a week, a day, even a month, when it is all he sees. Then the mania drags him down. The only remedy is to work as fast and furiously as he can, the same image over and over again in pencil, charcoal, oils and even watercolours (although they do not really have the power to express the violence that he is trying so desperately to expel from his mind and his memory). If he is left alone – a very big *if* – eventually he finds the place of calm again. Then they come crowding in, those people who say they know what is wrong with him and insist they can cure him, and they justify the petty and the not so petty cruelties they impose upon him by telling him again and again the dreadful things he did while he was under the mania's power.

But for all their supposed medical knowledge and deep wisdom, the 'cure' they force on him is useless. They tell him that by painting his strange, meaningless, nightmare images, he is only prolonging the months and the years of his suffering. And, following their own perverse logic, sooner or later they always make him stop.

If only it would occur to one of them to ask him to explain. To say what it is he draws and paints so obsessively.

Then they would understand.

ONE

Paris, spring 1882

Felix Wilbraham is a very happy man.

This is in no small part because he has been sitting at a pavement café in the sunshine for a long time, watching a succession of very pretty and fashionably-dressed young women pass by (many of whom respond to his frank stares of admiration with smirks, giggles and the occasional suggestive wink) and working his way through several glasses of absinthe.

La fée verte, he muses, gently swirling the liquid round in the sturdy little glass on its thick stem. He has enjoyed watching the skinny young bartender in his long white apron over the black waistcoat deftly preparing each successive drink. First comes the measure of the herb-smelling spirit – Felix has detected mint, fennel, pepper and aniseed – then the placing of the sugar in its perforated spoon over the glass and the careful pouring of the water through it so that the sweetened water mixes with the absinthe and turns it green-cloudy-white.

Felix can't remember if he is on his third or his fourth drink. But he is definitely feeling the effects. And this, of course, is another reason for his sense of heightened wellbeing.

The third reason – which, were he sober, he would appreciate is far more pertinent than watching pretty girls and being intoxicated – is that he has just become a wealthy man.

Wealth is, he knows, a relative term, and the unexpected windfall he has just received is modest by the standards of the historically and habitually rich. Felix, however, has been poor for a long time: very poor verging on desperate for an unforgettably awful few months, although matters have never been so bad again, and now, as work with the World's End Private Investigation Bureau is at last picking up on a fairly permanent basis, he is a great deal more confident that they won't be again.

And now he has his windfall.

Surreptitiously he slips a hand into his pocket and touches the new fine leather wallet that is crammed tight with franc notes. 'Thank you, Solange,' he murmurs.

He is smiling, and he can't seem to stop.

He didn't love Solange Devaux Moncontour, and he never thought she loved him. They liked each other, they were very good friends, they trusted each other, they told each other the truth. They had been lovers – very much to their mutual satisfaction – and Felix had not known another woman who could make him laugh like Solange did, both in bed and out of it.

They were together for four years. Felix enjoyed virtually every day of that time, and he would have put a decent wager on Solange having felt exactly the same.

He was nineteen when they met, and Solange was thirty-nine. He had left Marlborough College two years previously under a very heavy cloud, and early the next year – after a far from festive Christmas and New Year season that had been one long argument after another with his increasingly furious father – Felix had walked out of the family home.

He'd made up his mind not to go back.

He told himself there was no point because his father, and indeed his mother, wanted a life for him that he would not be able to abide. His father proposed special tutoring to get him into Cambridge or, at a pinch, Oxford, and, failing that, a career in the army. Apoplectic when Felix refused, he threatened to beat him and actually picked up his riding crop, which made Felix burst into loud laughter as with ease he wrenched it out of his father's hand. His mother wanted him to marry one of the endless stream of insipid young women she paraded before him, all of whom seemed to share the same dismal characteristics of colourless eyelashes, pale chinless faces, flat busts, large bottoms and no discernible personality.

The trouble with leaving home so precipitously was that he had no plans. And very little money.

He cadged a bed with a succession of the few friends who had accommodation of their own, but since this accommodation was invariably within a university's college, or occasionally in the lodging house where a less academic friend was putting up as he began on his career, sooner or later some irate bulldog, scout, landlord or landlady discovered Felix's presence and threw him out.

He had a few truly brilliant memories of those long months, and many more miserably unhappy ones.

Then he had gone to London, and discovered almost immediately that he was not the courageous, independent and worldly young man he believed himself to be. He was a naïve idiot who couldn't detect trouble when it came hunting for him at full cry, and far too willing to believe those who without doubt did not have his best interests at heart.

He nearly got into trouble with the police during the London times. His narrow escape left him frightened and shaken, as well as hungry, dirty and lonely. Christmas Day 1872 had been his nadir: he had even wondered, as night fell, if he wouldn't be better off jumping from Westminster Bridge and ending his miserable failure of a life.

He didn't.

And two days later he had a stroke of luck.

He spotted a very elegant and expensively dressed man descending from a hansom cab outside the Savoy, and while the man was fumbling for the right money for his fare and a tip and trying to deal with his gloves, he dropped a small coin case onto the slushy, puddled street. Felix skulked in the shadows, keeping an eye on the elegant man while nervously watching the precious little leather case as it lay there right beside a drain, his heart in his mouth and his bowels churning as he prayed that nobody else had spotted it and that one of the elegant man's innocent feet did not carelessly kick it into the drain.

The cabbie clicked his tongue to his horse and the cab moved smartly off. The elegant man caught sight of the friend he was meeting, called out and hurried to join him at the entrance to the hotel. Felix darted out, swooped down to scoop up the coin purse and was back in the shadows in a few heartbeats. Stuffing it in the inside pocket of his coat, he walked away. Down the short road that led back to the Strand, left towards Trafalgar Square, on to the busy forecourt of Charing Cross station, dodging cabs, private carriages and hurrying pedestrians.

He went into the station, and, in a quiet corner, at last inspected his booty.

The little case was tightly packed with coins. Among the florins and shillings there were two sprung holders for sovereigns and half-sovereigns. The one for sovereigns was empty, but the other held four half-sovereigns.

Felix didn't hesitate. With the means now in his pocket, the one thing he wanted to do was get out of England.

He caught the boat train to Dover, crossed the Channel to Calais, and found a room in a dirty doss house close to the port that smelt of urine, garlic, camphor, old fish and vomit. His money was already beginning to run out; he had been so hungry that he'd spent too much on food, so cold in that midwinter season that he'd splashed out too wildly on new undergarments, shirt and jacket. And he had realized – too late – that, beginning with the man who had changed his sterling into francs, everyone had either cheated or vastly overcharged him.

On New Year's Day he was in the railway terminus at Calais, trying with foolhardy persistence to earn some tips by carrying luggage. But the French porters had the place sewn up 'tighter than a cat's arsehole', as he was later to remark to Solange (it was during their first night together, when they had made the delightful discovery that laughter and passionate love-making went surprisingly well together). Enraged at this brash young foreigner trying to poach on their preserve, the porters had set about Felix, who was lucky to escape with a great many furious French oaths but only one accurate punch.

The punch had landed on his eye, and he had doubled over in pain, his eye watering like a leaky hose and the surrounding flesh already swelling agonizingly. He'd been on the platform, where a train was about to depart, its engine building up steam. He heard a window being pulled down and then a woman's voice said in accented English, 'Are you hurt?'

He had been about to reply, 'Oh no, I always stand bent over in a hoop and clutching frantically at my face,' when he looked up and saw her.

She was expensively dressed in a beautifully fitting, dark blue velvet coat with a fur collar, a pretty little hat perched on her thick, smoothly-styled chestnut hair, and her expression was kind. And interested. She wasn't pretty, but there was something about her; she was what he later learned the French called *une jolie-laide*.

'I'm all right,' he said instead. 'Thank you for asking,' he added, managing a smile.

She stood at her window, studying him, her head on one side. Then she smiled too. 'You should come with me,' she said surprisingly.

'Where are you going?' Felix asked.

'Paris. Where else?'

'I have very little money.'

'*Ça, c'est evident*,' she muttered. 'It is of no importance, for I have.'

He held her amused dark eyes for a long moment. Then he climbed aboard.

In their four years together, Solange took Felix to all her favourite places in Europe. Soon after they met, she told him (with startling frankness) the details of her situation: she was a countess, married to a much older man who disliked her almost as much as she disliked him. She had been born to wealthy parents in the Suisse-Normande, her care given over to nurses and governesses from the moment she emerged from her mother, and these strict women controlled her every moment, waking and sleeping, whether she was in the ancient family mansion, the house above the beach at Dinard or the plush Paris apartment recently purchased by her grandfather. In the course of the lively year after she was launched into society – far too lively for her deeply conservative father and her devout mother – she agreed to marry Claud Bertrand de Moncontour because, although he was more than twenty years her senior and had short bandy legs and bad breath, he was amazingly rich and Solange, even at eighteen, already recognized a man who preferred the company of men and would in all likelihood leave her to her own devices and, far more importantly, not demand regular sex (or hopefully any sex at all) once she had provided the son and heir that was his only reason for marrying her.

In March 1853, just before her nineteenth birthday, Solange gave birth to her son and only child, Henri-Josef. The delivery was long and arduous. Claud had insisted that his son be born in the Breton family château; this stubbornness rebounded violently on him (and very much more on Solange) when it became clear that she needed urgent medical attention of a calibre not to be found in a Breton village. She tore, she bled, the baby had to be dragged out of her, and both of them nearly died. Henri-Josef, however, was a strong, sturdy baby – it was his large size that had made the birth so hard – and soon recovered from the ordeal. Put to a large and cheery wet nurse whose calm and generous nature made her ideal for the job, he quickly thrived. Solange was not so lucky. It was six weeks before she was strong enough to resume life outside the sick room, and the damage done to her internal organs meant that there would be no further pregnancies.

Attending the long, depressing and mildly humiliating churching service as soon as she was able, Solange pretended to grieve at this harsh turn of fate while, safe in her own head, she was silently singing a song of triumph.

Henri-Josef was cared for by doting staff in his father's château and sent away to school as soon as he was old enough. He saw his mother only rarely, for she had discovered her love of travel and adventure, and Claud did not care whether she was there or not. When she did come home for a visit, however, she and her son discovered a closeness and a shared sense of humour and fun that boded well for the future, when young Henri-Josef's life would not be so tightly controlled by his father's dictates.

That moment came when Henri-Josef was fourteen. Claud fell off his horse when out hunting and broke his neck.

Solange discovered that much of her late husband's wealth and all of the estates were in trust for his son, although she would continue to receive the allowance she had enjoyed since her marriage, and it was hardly meagre. As for Henri-Josef, freedom from his father's tight grip was at first pure delight, and he set off with Solange during successive school vacations for a taste of the life she loved. But then, in the late autumn of 1872, he turned nineteen years old. Finished with education – rich, delightfully handsome and full of charm – Henri-Josef gently but firmly informed his mother that the past five years had been wonderful, and thanks to her he had learned so much about the world, but from now on he intended to proceed alone.

It was, Felix realized when Solange finally finished telling him this tale, probably entirely due to her beloved son's *merci beaucoup, chère Maman, et adieu* that he was now sharing her life: the chance meeting on the Calais platform had been three weeks after Henri-Josef had set off with a bunch of rowdy contemporaries to spend January and February in the Swiss Alps.

Felix and Solange lived on her money. Whenever his conscience troubled him (which was not all that often) Solange always noticed, and slyly pointed out that he was her companion and her secretary, that she needed his sense, his practicality and his strength to keep her safe in this wicked world that was so full of peril for a poor widow on her own, and – although doubting he had much sense and practicality, even if he was probably all right on strength – Felix always let himself be persuaded.

And life was so *good*.

They paid periodic visits to the rambling old château in the Breton forest, they used the Paris apartment off the Rue de Rivoli and the smart house on the seafront at Dinard, they travelled to Italy, Austria, Switzerland as the mood took them, and once ventured over the Channel for a wonderful summer in a very pretty Regency house in Brighton.

They parted company after four years.

Felix didn't realize that the separation was to be permanent; he had believed Solange when she said she was *un peu fatiguée* and in need of some quiet time being looked after by the staff back in the château.

Three months later, she was dead.

Henri-Josef had told him in a quiet moment soon after he and Felix began travelling together that Solange had known how ill she was, and deliberately kept it from everyone but her two devoted personal maids. In particular, he had said through grief-wracked sobs, she had kept it from Felix, for she wanted her young lover to remember her as she had been at her best.

Felix supported Henri-Josef through the first awful weeks of his grief. They discovered that they liked each other. They got on extremely well, and the pain of loss eased as they set about resuming together the life that Felix, and Henri-Josef before him, had enjoyed so much with Solange. Eventually – inevitably – Henri-Josef had been summoned home to Brittany by his uncle. It was time for him to take up his responsibilities and, as Henri-Josef ruefully said to Felix, 'the two of us are having far too much fun.'

Felix imagined that would be the last of his contact with the Devaux Moncontour family. But after more than two years of not hearing a word, a fortnight ago a letter arrived for him at the World's End Bureau's offices at number 3, Hob's Court, his name and the address written in that highly distinctive and decorative hand that could only have been inscribed by a Frenchman. His cry of surprise made Lily Raynor – the founder of the Bureau – leap up in alarm and come running through from her inner sanctum to the front office.

'What is it?' she demanded urgently, her wide eyes suggesting she was imagining dreadful news of grave sickness or death at the very least.

He couldn't answer for a moment or two, for emotion had got the better of him and suddenly he was flooded with happy, affectionate and profoundly poignant memories.

Then he cleared his throat a couple of times and said: 'Please may I have a few days off to go to Paris? I've just learned that I've been left a very decent amount of money.'

It was Henri-Josef who made the discovery.

He had a new person in his life; neither able or willing to manage alone, he had found, after considerable trial and error, someone whose company he enjoyed almost as much as he'd enjoyed Felix's, but who, unlike Felix, was also highly responsible, trained in the management of large country estates and the intricacies of the legal system, and an expert on inheritance. His name was Clement Toussaint, and, unlike Henri-Josef's callous, unfeeling and greedy family, he actually liked his young charge.

Among his specialties, Clement Toussaint was well-versed in the devious efforts made by impoverished old families to ignore inconvenient bequests to long-lost lovers. Henri-Josef had always suspected that his late mother had remembered Felix in her will, and when he murmured this suspicion to M. Toussaint, the older man agreed that it did indeed seem likely. He shut himself up in his private office in the château, worked away quietly for a few days, sent off quite a number of letters and received almost as many replies, and eventually emerged to announce to Henri-Josef that Solange had indeed left a handsome bequest to '*mon cher Felix, avec qui j'ai passé plusiers ans de gros plaisir et joie*', but that the highly disapproving and crusty old lawyers of the Devaux Moncontour family – undoubtedly alarmed at the "many years of huge pleasure and joy" that Solange had spent with Felix – succeeded in burying it. In response to M. Toussaint's challenge, they pretended that they hadn't noticed the bequest, that they had no idea who Felix Wilbraham was, that they couldn't find him, and that they doubted Solange had been serious anyway.

Each of which objections the coolly efficient M. Toussaint had ruthlessly overcome.

Henri-Josef dispatched his letter to Felix the next day.

Clement Toussaint accompanied Henri-Josef to Paris, and they were both standing at the barrier beaming with delight when Felix stepped off the train. They went to a very discreet and obviously expensive little restaurant for an early supper, over which M. Toussaint revealed the sum of the bequest and apologized for the fact that Felix had been obliged to wait so long to receive it. 'It was not at all what Madame la Comptesse had wished,' he said with an anxious frown, 'because she . . . she . . .' And, lost for words of his own, he extracted a piece of paper covered with Solange's wild and loopy scrawl and silently pointed to what she had written.

All three of them being temporarily too moved to speak, Henri-Josef replenished their champagne saucers and they raised them in a toast to Solange.

Monsieur Toussaint tactfully withdrew after that and left Felix and Henri-Josef to a few days of renewed high jinks of the sort they had formerly enjoyed together. They went to the Folies Bergère (more than once), they took a boat up the Seine, they ate at the most chic restaurants and drank at the bars and cafés frequented by the fickle, restless young people who had money in their pockets. They went shopping, they entertained several very pretty young ladies who took their attentions entirely in the spirit in which they were offered, then they started all over again.

Felix enjoyed each day as it was happening, although late at night, when finally he returned to his modest hotel on the Rue des Beaux Arts, a mood of melancholy often overtook him. This he found unexpected, considering he was usually a great deal more than a little drunk and drink usually made him happy. Quite often he sensed a large and benign (if rather maudlin) presence, and once he was quite sure he heard a low male groan followed by a woman's voice enquiring solicitously, 'Comment va le mal de tête aujourd'hui, M'sieur?' He was not alarmed or even particularly disturbed by these odd manifestations. But then, Felix reminded himself, the drink had a habit of making him woozy . . . He grew quite fond of his unseen companion with the headache and took to wishing him a friendly bonne nuit on settling down to sleep.

Felix and Henri-Josef made the exuberant most of their days together. Then, after a totally splendid week, M. Toussaint came to seek out his charge and regretfully Henri-Josef went home.

Felix has been feeling a little bereft without his lively, cheerful (if slightly dangerous) companion. He has done his best without him, although now he has to admit that the City of Light is not nearly so twinkly without Henri-Josef Devaux Moncontour, and it's no use pretending it is.

Nearly time for me to leave too, he muses now. He is wondering if to order another Green Fairy, but three – or maybe four – is enough. His mind turns to London. To Chelsea, and the offices of the World's End Bureau. To Lily, his cool, intelligent blonde employer, for whom he has developed considerable respect and admiration.

'Is that what we're calling it?' he murmurs aloud. 'Here, in this convivial café on a sunset-lit corner in this beautiful city when I have had rather too much to drink, might we not loosen our stays and admit to other, more personal feelings?'

The inebriated part of his mind says *yes*. The rest of him says, very firmly, *no*.

Abruptly he gets up, squints at the hand-written bills under the saucer, puts the right amount of francs and a free-handed tip in the saucer, then strides away. He makes his way to one of his and Henri-Josef's favourite restaurants and orders a meal, but even though the food is excellent, he has to force himself to eat. He finishes the carafe of red wine, then makes his unsteady way back to the Rue des Beaux Arts and his hotel room.

As he lies waiting for sleep, he senses the vague presence of his large and invisible room mate. 'I believe,' he murmurs, 'that you know all about melancholy.'

But, of course, there is no reply.

Just as he drops off, he thinks suddenly: *I want to go home. One more day, then I'll be on my way. I shall see Lily again.*

And for the first time since Henri-Josef left, he slips into sleep with a smile on his face.

TWO

It is very early on a sunny April morning. A good hour before her usual time for starting the day's work – for sleep has been proving elusive – Lily Raynor sits at her desk in the inner office at the World's End Bureau. As the appetizing smell of frying bacon snakes a tendril through from the kitchen at the rear of the old house, her stomach gives an unladylike growl.

Mrs Clapper too seems to be affected by Felix's absence, and this is manifested in symptoms such as taking greater care of her employer, preparing tempting little meals and snacks for her and – rather annoyingly, from Lily's point of view – arriving at 3, Hob's Court even earlier than her habitual eight thirty start and thus eating into the precious early morning time.

The office is not the same without Felix. Lily has been trying to make a plus out of a minus by thinking to herself: *at least I'll have some quiet days to work undisturbed, with nobody else in the office.*

Mrs Clapper apparently has other ideas.

The smell of bacon intensifies suddenly, accompanied by the brisk military tattoo of Mrs Clapper's booted feet on the hall tiles. She sails across Felix's office and into Lily's and deposits a tray on Lily's desk. Lily only just has time to sweep her notepad and the medical journal she is studying out of the way before her breakfast descends.

'There, now, Miss Lily, you get yourself outside of that, and you'll feel much better,' Mrs Clapper declaims, setting out the plate of cooked breakfast and a rack of toast, with butter, marmalade and an enormous mug of tea.

But I don't need to feel better, Lily wants to say, trying not to grit her teeth. *I am perfectly well.* She respects, however, that virtually everything Mrs Clapper does is out of loyalty to the Raynor family, Lily having inherited her, along with the house, from her grandparents. Since this honourable emotion is almost certainly accompanied by love, of a sort, for Lily herself, she keeps quiet.

Only a fool, reflects Lily, throws love back into the face of the person offering it . . .

'Thank you, Mrs Clapper,' she says, looking up into the thin, intent face with a smile. 'I hadn't realized how hungry I was.'

Mrs Clapper nods curtly, as if to say: *course you didn't, I always say you don't take enough care of yourself*. It is amazing how much she can get into one quick, silent nod.

'I'll clear up in the scullery, Miss Lily,' she says as she turns and strides away, the tray tucked under one arm, 'then gird up my loins and see about tackling *her* rooms while I have the chance.'

Her is how Mrs Clapper refers to Lily's tenant. She always manages to inject a great deal of venom into the word. The tenant is a Russian dancer whose name is somewhat tricky to pronounce and who is always referred to by Lily and Felix as the Little Ballerina. She is probably the most self-centred, self-absorbed person Lily has ever met, and her ideas on personal hygiene leave a great deal – verging on pretty much everything – to be desired. She also totally fails to grasp the concept of keeping her living quarters neat and clean, and she *never* opens a window. The unpleasantly fusty smell, containing overtones of body odour, unwashed clothes, sweaty feet and, for some inexplicable reason, rotten onions, hits out like a clenched fist at anyone who has to negotiate the first floor landing on the way up to their own rooms above. Which, of course, is Lily.

She is longing for the day when the Bureau consistently and permanently brings in sufficient money for a tenant in her house to be unnecessary. But, although she and Felix have been doing much better of late, that day is still not here, nor even on the horizon. So she is stuck with her unlikeable tenant, and Mrs Clapper is stuck with doing the little she can to keep the Little Ballerina's quarters from descending into total squalor.

'I wish you didn't have to do it, Mrs Clapper,' Lily calls out impulsively after her housekeeper's skinny departing back.

'You and me both, Miss Lily,' Mrs Clapper replies without turning round. She mutters something, which it is probably just as well that Lily doesn't catch, although she does pick up the words *slut* and *filthy*.

Lily falls on her food – as tasty as the smell promised – and returns to her medical journal.

So total is her concentration that when she becomes aware of Mrs Clapper's footsteps once again ringing on the hall tiles, she is quite surprised to see that it is half past nine.

Mrs Clapper, she deduces, is responding to a summons from the front door. Listening, Lily hears an exchange – Mrs Clapper's voice and a second female one – and then Mrs Clapper is hurrying across the outer office towards her.

'Young lady wants to see you, Miss Lily,' she says in a harsh whisper that must surely be audible to whoever is standing waiting in the hall. 'Says she needs your help.' Mrs Clapper's eyebrows have gone up in amazement, as if people coming to a private enquiry agency to ask for help is an outlandish occurrence that has never happened before.

'Thank you, Mrs Clapper, please show her in,' Lily replies. She checks that her desk is tidy – her efficient housekeeper came to collect the plates and mug shortly after Lily had finished with them, and Lily's notebook and pen are geometrically arranged – and that her hair is straight. There is a large ink stain on the inside of her middle finger, but there is little she can do about that as it appears to have become a permanency.

Mrs Clapper marches out again, says something to the woman outside and then returns. She approaches Lily's desk, then stands aside and says, 'Here she is. I'll leave you to it, Miss Lily,' and departs.

Lily stands up to greet her visitor. 'I am Lily Raynor,' she says. 'Please sit down,' – she indicates the chair on the opposite side of her large desk – 'and tell me how I may help.'

The young woman studies her intently for a few moments, giving Lily the opportunity to reciprocate. Her potential new client is sturdily built and quite short, perhaps in her early or mid-twenties, and plainly dressed in garments of good quality:

a grey jacket that reaches to her knees, a matching skirt of unfussy cut, a white blouse with a rather masculine collar that is tied with a thin ribbon in an unlovely shade of muddy green. Over the tightly-smoothed brown hair she wears a hat that looks as if it has been crammed back in the cupboard while still damp. Her face is flushed – she looks as if she has been walking hard – and her cheeks are plump above a strong jaw and a very determined chin. Her mouth is set in a firm line and her nose is sort of squashy-looking.

Her eyes enliven her entire face and make her something different: they are large, set slightly aslant, the colour of bluebells and fringed with thick, dark lashes.

Even as she stares at Lily, she is reaching behind her to make sure the chair is there and lowering herself into it.

'My name is Miss Westwood,' she announces abruptly. 'Phyllida Mary Westwood. I live in Rye, in Sussex. I was formerly engaged to be married. In fact,' she adds, a rueful expression crossing her face in which both wry humour and pain are detectable – 'since nobody has thought to terminate the arrangement, one might say I still am. My fiancé, however, is believed by his family to have committed a truly *dreadful* crime, and he has been confined to an asylum. Now another, very similar crime has occurred, and it is almost certain that this too will be deemed the work of my fiancé.' She pauses, and Lily sees her swallow a couple of times.

Then, without warning, the young woman's face goes deathly white, and perspiration sheens her forehead and upper lip. Swiftly Lily gets up, walks round her desk and gently pushes Miss Westwood's head down towards her knees. 'Stay like that,' she says calmly. 'I will fetch some water.'

As she strides off, there is a strangled sound of assent.

'A glass of water, please, Mrs Clapper,' Lily says out in the scullery, 'and would you prepare a well-sugared cup of tea?'

'Faint, is she?' Mrs Clapper responds knowingly, filling a glass from the jug on the cold shelf. 'Poor young lady. Course I will, Miss Lily, and I'll put out some of my shortbread and all.'

Lily thanks her and hurries back to her office.

Miss Westwood has sat up straight again, and her face has

a little more colour. Lily hands her the glass, and she drinks a few sips. 'Finish it,' Lily orders, and, with a swift glance at her, Miss Westwood obeys.

'I am so sorry to be such a fool,' she says as she puts the glass down on Lily's desk. 'I cannot imagine what came over me, for I assure you I am *not* a fainter.'

'I am quite sure you are not,' Lily replies. 'I imagine, however, that you had a very early start this morning and left home without anything to eat, and then you had to find out how to get from the station to Chelsea, and you have just hurried down World's End Passage from the King's Road without pausing to draw breath.' She smiles at her new client. 'The strongest people faint sometimes, under such circumstances.'

Miss Westwood is nodding slowly. 'They told me you were good at your job, Miss Raynor,' she says. 'They did not say that you are also kind.'

Lily resumes her seat, inclining her head in acknowledgement. She wants to know who *they* are, but it is not the time to ask. There is the sound of Mrs Clapper's footsteps – she is clearly trying to walk quietly, without notable success – and she approaches Lily's desk and deposits a cup of tea. There are three little squares of shortbread in the saucer. Lily nods her thanks, and Miss Westwood mutters 'Thank you.'

'Now,' – Lily opens her client notebook at a new page – 'I will write down some details, if I may.'

'Of course.'

Miss Westwood repeats her name, supplies her address and reveals that her fiancé is called Wilberforce Chibb, that he is twenty-seven years old – 'four years older than I, but I do think that such a difference in ages is wise, given that a woman is invariably more mature for her years than a man.' – and that he is an artist.

'Go on,' Lily says, her hand flying across the page.

There is a brief pause as Miss Westwood collects her thoughts.

'Wilberforce comes from a somewhat strange family,' she says. 'His mother saw visions. She thought these alarming sights were prophetic, and she took drastic measures to protect her children from what she believed was to happen. There were originally three of them,' she adds, 'Horatio, who was four years older than Wilberforce and would be thirty-one years old, except that he committed suicide four years ago. He launched himself off Beachy Head,' she adds matter-of-factly. 'And then there is a younger sister, Alexandra Amelia, who is two years younger than Wilberforce. She stays at home, in the care of a private attendant.'

'And the mother?' Lily prompts. Deliberately she keeps her tone neutral; Miss Westwood has recited this fairly alarming set of facts as if she were reading a shopping list, and Lily feels it is wise to control her reaction.

'Amelia Chibb died in a lunatic asylum,' Miss Westwood says. 'She was trying to escape, for she was convinced she must protect her children from imaginary monsters and apocalyptic events, and she fell climbing out of an attic window. Or so I believe,' she adds dismissively.

Lily has the distinct impression that the young lady sitting opposite her has little sympathy for imaginary terrors.

Miss Westwood waits for Lily to catch up, then says in the same business-like tone, 'Wilberforce asked for my hand at Christmas the year before last, Miss Raynor, and I cannot help thinking that it was more to do with the pressure put upon him by his father than for any great passion to have me as his wife.'

Lily glances up, straight into the remarkable eyes. 'And why would that be?' she asks mildly.

'Oh . . . because Frederick Chibb was sick and tired of his difficult family, I imagine, and eager to see one of them off his hands, for he had a mad wife, a son who killed himself, a daughter who is indisposed and Wilberforce, who instead of being sensible and following his father into the family firm – Mr Chibb is an architect and draughtsman, privileged to include royalty among his clients – insists he is going to earn his crust as a painter.'

Lily nods. 'Is he good enough?' she asks. Miss Westwood has been admirably frank, and she feels she should not waste time with polite little circumlocutions and euphemisms.

Miss Westwood shrugged. 'I would have said he was.

Before,' she adds darkly. Lily meets her eyes again, her own asking the silent question. 'May I come to that later?' Miss Westwood asks, and Lily nods.

'So, let me see . . .' Miss Westwood mutters.

'You were speaking of your engagement,' Lily prompts.

'Indeed I was. Thank you. Rather less than two months after our betrothal, Wilberforce suddenly announced that he was going away. Without informing either myself or his father, he had arranged to embark upon a sketching tour with an artist and draughtsman friend of Mr Chibb's, a man called Augustus Cundell Claridge. He has exhibited at the Academy; you are perhaps familiar with the name?'

'I'm afraid not,' Lily replies.

'Ah. Well, Wilberforce had quite made up his mind, and neither entreaties from me nor somewhat forceful persuasion from his father would change it. He and Mr Claridge set off a week later. To begin with all was well. As spring passed and the summer heat started to build, they proceeded in a leisurely way down through Italy towards its toe, sketching and painting, one presumes, as they went.' The slight curl of her lip suggests what she thinks of *that*. 'They then took ship across to Egypt, spending time in Alexandria before venturing south into the desert and putting up in what one can only imagine was somewhat primitive accommodation.'

There is quite a long pause.

'In July,' she announces abruptly and rather too loudly, 'Mr Claridge had to bring Wilberforce urgently home. Wilberforce had become gravely unwell with – er, with a bad stomach,' – *violently ill with diarrhoea and vomiting*, Lily, a former nurse, writes down – 'after which, instead of being sensible and careful while he regained his strength, *very* unwisely he sat out in the hot Egyptian sun and was badly affected with sunburn and sunstroke. Mr Claridge tried to make him keep to his room, but Wilberforce insisted on going out, which was dreadful because he attacked a young woman in the market, cut off quite a lot of her hair, waved his knife around so that onlookers feared he was about to cut her throat, and shouted that he must drag her under a market stall because the sun was going to shrivel her up and the little black crawling thing she would turn into would be consumed by a giant scarlet crow.'

'Dear me, how very alarming,' Lily remarks.

She hears a quiet chuckle from the other side of the desk.

'Back at the family home in Rye,' Miss Westwood resumes, 'Wilberforce was kept *very* secure, and placed under the care of the family doctor. I fear he was not at all competent to treat whatever ailed Wilberforce,' she adds, 'for he is an elderly man, adequate if one has a cold or a cough or a broken wrist, but he was presented with something with which he was entirely unfamiliar and, I believe, too stiff and proud to admit it.' The echo of her angry resentment is evident in her voice. 'Mr Chibb was already faced with more than he could cope with, as I explained earlier, and, possibly because of this long history of stress and anxiety, he had little patience with Wilberforce and readily followed the doctor's recommendation.'

'Which was?' Lily asks when she does not go on.

'Oh . . . Dr Cholley opined that the family should not indulge Wilberforce's strange actions, which consisted largely of opening his window and shouting out to passers-by that they must run for cover because nightmarish birds and beasts were about to descend upon them. If this behaviour were to be ignored, Dr Cholley believed that it would cease, because it was, to quote his own words, "little more than a play for the sort of attention paid to his sister, his late mother and the suicidal brother".'

Wondering what on earth had given an innocent and unworldly Sussex family doctor the confidence for such a pronouncement, Lily writes down his comment.

'Ignoring Wilberforce proved impossible, of course.' Miss Westwood went on: 'The very next day after Dr Cholley had issued his advice, Mr Chibb went up to Wilberforce's landing and spoke to him through the door, commanding him forcefully to stop shouting at people and scaring them because it was not the way a Chibb behaved. Wilberforce broke out of his room, attacked his father and killed him. Oh, I do not believe for one moment that it was deliberate!' she cries, for Lily has been unable to suppress a soft gasp of astonished horror. 'He – Wilberforce – had an open razor in his hand, and I *think* he was trying to drive Mr Chibb away. They were flailing around at the top of the stairs – the ones up to the attic bedroom have *very* narrow treads – and somehow Mr Chibb must have fallen.'

Lily keeps her head bent over her notebook, for she does not want Miss Westwood to read anything in her face. But even as she writes, she is wondering if this stubborn belief in her fiancé's innocence stems more from hope than wise judgement. Twice, according to the loyal Miss Westwood, Wilberforce appears to have gone for somebody with a lethal blade in his hand: first the girl in the Egyptian market, then his own father. To believe that in both cases his intentions were misunderstood is surely a triumph of optimism over logic . . .

She has caught up with all that Phyllida Westwood has said, but she pretends to be still writing – she draws a pretty daisy in the margin – because she strongly senses there is more to come and she does not want to interrupt the flow.

After quite a long pause, Miss Westwood says briskly, 'Wilberforce was forced back into his room, the door was locked and a tough-looking constable was sent up to stand guard. But he managed to escape. We do not know quite how, for the poor young policeman was hit rather hard on the head and has no recollection of these wretched events. The next thing we heard – it was a little over a week later – was that Wilberforce was in France, in the far west of Brittany. I have no idea how he managed to cross the Channel and travel all that way; and it *is* a long way, Miss Raynor, I have consulted my grandfather's atlas.'

Sensing her client's distress, Lily simply says gently, 'All that you have told me speaks of a very disturbed young man, but not necessarily one who has lost the ability to live in the world and deal with its everyday challenges.'

Miss Westwood is a bright young woman, and Lily perceives straight away that she has deduced certain facts from what Lily just said. 'You have experience of the mentally deranged, Miss Raynor?'

'Some,' Lily says. 'Please, go on with your story.'

Once again Miss Westwood takes a few moments for

thought. Then she says, 'He was in a village called Pont-Aven. I am given to understand that it is a place where artists congregate, and some of them were friends of Wilberforce's. They took him in, at first not realizing that he was so dan— that they might need to be wary of him. But then he became violent, attacking a tradesman who asked one of the artists too forcefully for money that was owed. The situation rapidly became unmanageable, and Wilberforce's friends had the good sense to send a telegram to Mr Chibb. Of course that was no good, since he was in his grave by then,' – once again Lily detects a distinct lack of grief for the man who was going to be Miss Westwood's father-in-law – 'and it was his brother-in-law Leonard Bowler, the brother of his late wife, who read the message. He set off immediately for Brittany, discovering on arrival four days later that Wilberforce had been locked in a prison cell in a town called Quimper. Even though Mr Bowler was careful to be *very* sparse with the details, it was only too apparent that poor Wilberforce was being brutally treated.' Her voice breaks, and quickly she clears her throat, a hand up to her mouth. 'Mr Bowler was of course not unfamiliar with the manner in which the insane are treated,' she goes on after a brief pause, 'for it was not only his sister Amelia who suffered from mental illness but also, I understand, an aunt and another sister who died young. Anyway,' – she brushes aside further speculation or explanation with a brisk wave of her hand – 'Mr Bowler was able to contact a specialist in insanity back in England. The specialist recommended a place that was actually in Brittany, in a town called Paimpont, and Wilberforce was transported there from Quimper in a closed and barred carriage and admitted as a patient.'

'And he is there now?' Lily asks. Miss Westwood has stopped for breath.

She nods. 'He is. The authorities in England pressed for him to be brought back, because there is still the question of how Mr Chibb met his death, and whether or not Wilberforce is guilty of murder.' She pauses, frowning. 'It is patricide, I believe, when a son or a daughter kills their father?'

'Yes,' Lily says neutrally.

'Perhaps fortunately for Wilberforce,' the extraordinarily

self-controlled woman opposite says, 'the authorities at the Paimpont asylum stated categorically that for reasons of his insanity, he could not be moved. They said that trying to transport him back to Sussex was fraught with peril, not only for himself but for those who would be guarding him.' She leans forward, her expression intent, and adds in a soft voice, 'It is my belief, Miss Raynor, that although he is Wilberforce's uncle, the very *last* thing Mr Bowler wanted was to be respon- sible for Wilberforce if he were to be returned to England and put on trial. At the least he would be honour-bound to arrange some sort of defence, and that costs money. At worst, from his point of view, were Wilberforce to be found not guilty, spared the noose and freed, he would have had to find a private mental asylum for him, and that undoubtedly costs even more. To speak bluntly, Mr Bowler wanted rid of his nephew and the myriad and costly problems he presented.' Miss Westwood pauses, then adds, 'I deem it highly likely that Mr Bowler offered a sizeable bribe to the doctors at Paimpont to insist that Wilberforce was unfit to be moved, because this was the most economical option.'

Lily nods. She deems it likely, too. She finishes writing; to judge by her aching hand, she has been doing so for a long time. Looking up, she sees the bluebell-coloured eyes watching her intently.

She smiles. 'That was a long tale, Miss Westwood,' she observes. 'I for one am very much in need of a cup of tea. Would you like another?'

'Yes please,' Miss Westwood says promptly. 'Are there more of those delicious shortbread squares?'

Lily smiles to herself as she leaves the office.

'Now,' Lily says when they each have their tea and a plate of shortbread has been placed in front of Miss Westwood, 'you have told me the background story, but you also mentioned that another crime has been committed, and you fear that Wilberforce Chibb will be falsely accused of having perpetrated it.'

'I did indeed,' Miss Westwood agrees, trying to manage a mouthful of shortbread.

Lily waits while she chews and swallows, then says, 'Would

you care to elucidate? And, indeed, to tell me what you wish the World's End Bureau to do?'

Miss Westwood wipes her fingers on a small lace-edged handkerchief, puts it back in her reticule, folds her hands in her lap and says, 'There was a mysterious man in the Paimpont asylum. Some said he was French, others were equally sure he was English. Or Prussian. It is rumoured that in fact he was not mentally ill, although he most certainly was sick in body. They whisper that he was placed in the asylum to protect him from being killed. Assassinated, I should say,' she corrects herself, 'for there was a definite sense that in some manner he was important. Perhaps he was a major political figure; perhaps a very high-ranking military man. Perhaps . . .?' She leaves the thought unspoken, and Lily, who has been wondering the same thing, is fairly sure she knows what Miss Westwood was going to say.

'Perhaps he was of royal blood,' she says softly.

Miss Westwood's bluebell eyes light up. '*Exactly*, Miss Raynor!' she whispers back. 'Now the French do not have a royal family to speak of, or not one that counts for anything, and there is this persistent rumour that the mystery man was English. In which case . . .' Once again, she leaves the sentence unfinished.

And Lily says quietly, 'Yes.'

After a moment, recalling where this fascinating exchange started, she says, 'Am I right in thinking, then, that it is this man of mystery who has been attacked?'

'You are,' comes the instant reply.

'And that Wilberforce is accused of attacking him?'

'Yes. And it wasn't just an attack; the man is dead.'

Lily nods. 'And killed in a way that is very similar to Wilberforce's assault on the girl in the market, and his fatal encounter with his father on the stairs?'

'Precisely so,' Miss Westwood agrees. 'The victim was heard shouting out in the middle of the night, thumping his heels on the floor to attract attention. There was a great cry, the sound of a heavy body falling, and he was found at the foot of the stairs in a great pool of blood, with deep cuts on his hands and forearms and his throat slashed.'

'And where was Wilberforce?' Lily asks after a moment.

Miss Westwood nods, clearly appreciating the fact that Lily has asked the right question. 'In his room, but the door was unlocked. He was in bed, apparently asleep, but there was blood all over the sleeve of his nightshirt. They had to shake him hard to wake him, but they said he was cunning, and only pretended to be deeply asleep in order to allay suspicion.'

Lily nods. She does not want to say so at this moment, but she is thinking that it is very easy to quietly unlock a locked door and dribble blood on a deeply-sleeping man's sleeve.

And how on earth do you decide whether somebody is being made to look guilty or really is? she wonders worriedly.

She finishes making her notes, then looks up. 'You wish the Bureau to find out the truth concerning this mystery man's murder,' she says.

'I do.'

Lily thinks for a while. 'What if the conclusion is that Wilberforce really is guilty? That the madness which drove him to attack the Egyptian girl and gesticulate wildly at his father with an open razor in his hand once more overcame him?'

Miss Westwood eyes her steadily. 'Then you will tell me so, Miss Raynor. I wish to know the *truth*!' she says, making fists of her hands and thumping the desk so that the cups rattle in their saucers and a spoon bounces on to the floor. 'You may think me foolish, when common sense suggests it would be prudent to walk away.' She pauses, and Lily reflects that yes, that is exactly what she does think. 'But, you see, Miss Raynor, when I promised to marry Wilberforce it was because I understood how desperately he needs me, for I am strong where he is frail.' The expression in her bluebell eyes suggests to Lily that being needed, and having an excuse to exercise her strength and undoubted ability, is rather a novelty. 'I love him,' she adds simply, 'and I do truly believe he is innocent.' She frowns. 'If I am wrong and you discover without doubt that he is guilty, then I shall not marry him after all.'

THREE

L ily sees Miss Westwood on her way. She has obtained
the young woman's contact details, made sure she has
made an accurate note of the address of the asylum in
Brittany and recorded all that Miss Westwood can recall of
how Wilberforce's uncle managed to get there. (She wrote
down the name of the village as *Pampon*, but managed to
correct it to *Paimpont* fairly unobtrusively.) She has also
given her new client her scale of charges, taken an initial
payment to cover the first week and the standard sum for
expenses, elevated because this will be a foreign assignment.
Miss Westwood does not appear to be short of money, as
attested by the good quality clothing, shoes and bag; she did
not blanch as she handed over the required sum, in pristine
bank notes.

As she is leaving – almost as if she has forgotten until the
last moment – she delves down to the bottom of her bag and
presents Lily with a sturdy brown envelope whose contents
make it bulge. 'French francs,' she says. 'You will need money
as soon as you arrive in France, and this will save you from
having to search out a *bureau de change* in a foreign country.'

Lily is on the point of thanking her for her consideration
when she adds, 'Naturally, the equivalent sum in pounds,
shillings and pence must be added to my credit column.'

'Naturally,' Lily echoes with faint and, she hopes, undetect-
able irony as she ushers Miss Westwood out on to the street.

Lily goes to the one person she knows who is likely to have
a good working knowledge of cross-Channel steamers and
French railways: Marmaduke Smithers. He is a journalist who
regularly writes angry articles pointing out to newspaper
readers the evils of the contemporary world, invariably
concerning the poor and, more often than not, the female sex.
He is also Felix's landlord, and Lily has always found him

the most charming, kindly, warm-hearted man. Today he is delighted to see her, denies that she is disturbing him even though it's the middle of the working day and listens without interrupting as she tells him she has just taken on a new case which necessitates her going to France straight away to meet Felix in Paris. In answer to her specific query, Marm proceeds to tell her every last fact about the boat train and the ferry to Calais.

'I regret, dear Miss Raynor, that I cannot quote the pertinent train and ferry timetables,' he says, and even as she is protesting that she had never envisaged that he could, he is up on his feet, darting over to his shelves and returning with a small book bound in red, which he hands to her.

'Bradshaw's Illustrated Travellers' Handbook to France, Adapted to All the Railway Routes, with a Short Itinerary of Corsica and Guide to Paris, with Maps, Town Plans and Illustrations,' he quotes from the title page. 'Published in 1873, and so not, I fear, fully up to date . . .?' He looks at her, a slight frown on his lean, lined face.

'Oh, I don't suppose France has changed very much in nine years,' she says brightly, taking it from him.

He still looks uncertain. 'But train timetables alter with frustrating frequency,' he protests.

'Thank you, Mr Smithers,' she says firmly. 'I am quite sure it will be extremely helpful. And,' she adds, in case he is secretly more anxious about her venturing into France than about the times of French trains, 'I'll be with Felix, don't forget, and not only can he speak French but he's also travelled there quite widely.'

'Hmmm,' is Marm's only comment.

Wisely not asking for elucidation, Lily goes on to tell him a little about Phyllida Westwood, briefly describing the reason she has sought the help of the Bureau.

Marm holds up a finger, once again getting out of his chair and this time returning with one of his bulging files. 'Not the Lost Women file this time,' he says with a wry smile, 'but the one devoted to Inadequately Explained Deaths.'

For years Marm has kept a record of women whose disappearances have, in his view, been less than comprehensively investigated. Almost without exception they are working class and very poor. They are often foreign, and frequently had been selling their bodies to keep themselves and their families fed. This record is distressingly huge and growing all the time.

He sits down again and opens the Inadequately Explained Deaths file. 'I remember the defenestration of Amelia Chibb,' he mutters as he flicks through the pages. Then he goes, 'A-*HA*!' so loudly that he makes Lily jump. 'Yes! Yes, here we are . . . of Old Saltway House, Rye, confined to an asylum at the request of husband Frederick Gordon Chibb and on the advice of doctors . . . strongly believed to be a danger to herself and her three children; visions of the devil, the Horsemen of the Apocalypse, whose mounts were all wildly over-endowed stallions with huge swinging testicles . . . I beg your pardon, Miss Raynor, for the indelicacy.'

'That's perfectly all right, Mr Smithers, please, read on.'

'The poor woman was apprehended on the shore near Winchelsea trying to immerse the children in sea water as some sort of divine protection. Perhaps,' he muses, looking up, eyes unfocussed, 'she had in mind Thetis, the mother of Achilles, holding him by the ankle as she dunked him in the Styx?'

'Possibly,' Lily agrees. 'And she died trying to climb out of a window?'

'She did,' Marm agrees gravely. He reads on, turning a page. 'Verdict of suicide, but many disagreed, claiming that Amelia had become too much of a worrisome burden to her husband, who paid the asylum attendants a large sum of money to unfasten a locked window and chase the poor, desperate woman up the stairs.'

'*Oh*!' Lily exclaims.

Marm nods slowly. 'Quite so,' he murmurs. There is a brief pause, as if both of them are having a moment's silent respect for the dead woman, then he says, 'I also recall the Westwoods of Rye; specifically, Algernon Westwood.'

Lily thinks rapidly. 'Phyllida's father?'

'Her grandfather.' Closing the file, he turns to Lily. 'If I recall aright, the Westwoods founded a business at the beginning of the century, importing exotic hardwoods from around

the world. Within a few decades, and certainly by the time
Algernon Westwood was at the helm, this had become specific
to rosewood from Brazil, a commodity that is much prized
for the veneers of good furniture. Algernon's only son
Bartholomew died relatively young, followed within a year by
his fragile wife, and Phyllida, their only child, was adopted
by her grandfather when she was twelve.'

'Was there any reason why you should remember the
family?' Lily asks.

'Oh . . . another inadequately explained death, I expect.'
He flicks back through the file. 'Ah. Not that inexplicable, as
it transpired. I see that I have made a later note that Mary
Westwood, née Miller Marchant, died of food poisoning.' He
looks up and catches Lily's eye. 'Not arsenic, as I had at first
speculated.'

'Oh, that's good,' Lily says, instantly wanting to take the
words back because you're just as dead if you die from acci-
dentally-consumed bad food than if your husband slips poison
into your cocoa, although possibly the death is less agonizing.

But Marm seems to know what she means, because he nods,
smiles and says simply, 'Quite.'

Lily has already paid Miss Westwood's money into the bank.
The last thing she does before she hurries home to pack a bag
and set out is to send Felix a telegram at his Paris hotel. He is
not due to come home for two more days, but suddenly she
is obsessed with the fear that he may be just about to curtail
his trip and set off for England right this minute.

'New case STOP,' she dictates to the clerk in the telegraph
office. 'Involves Brittany so stay where you are STOP Arriving
Paris late tonight or early tomorrow STOP Wait in hotel until
you hear from me STOP L Raynor ENDS.'

She packs clean linen, toiletries, nightdress, a towel and a
change of shoes in a sturdy leather bag shaped like a satchel
that she acquired in India and in which she used to carry
bandages, ointments and medicines when she was travelling.
Copying the nuns, she learned to wrap its long strap round
her ribs with the straps facing downwards, then flip the satchel

over her head so that it sat up on her shoulders. Not only did this make its weight much easier to bear, it also left both hands free; a great advantage when scrambling up and down steep tracks in the foothills of the Himalayas. When in less perilous parts of the world, the bag can be hung on a shoulder or, with the strap shortened, held in the hand.

She asked Marm what he knew about travelling in rural France, and he replied somewhat discouragingly that once one ventured beyond the end of the network of railway lines, it was probably a matter of rustic carts and hiring a horse. Accordingly, Lily decides to wear a generously-cut skirt in fine dark blue wool that will allow her to ride and retain her modesty.

She pauses as she inspects the skirt, brushing off a couple of small mud spots, for the prospect of riding a horse has taken her back to her childhood . . .

Her beloved father's early death when she was twelve and her mother's remarriage to the louche and extremely wealthy man with whom she was having an affair led to Lily being brought up by her paternal grandparents, Abraham and Martha Raynor, and their intelligent and independently-minded daughter, Lily's Aunt Eliza. Grandma Martha was a Derbyshire woman, and her parents – Lily's Owen great-grandparents – still lived on the High Peak farm where Grandma Martha (and indeed Lily herself) was born. Grandma Martha, although contented with her life with Grandpa Abraham and the daily grind of a hard-working pharmacist in Chelsea, nevertheless went home for a visit to the farm in July each year, taking her granddaughter with her and leaving her there to spend the summer with Jonathan and Suzanna Owen. These annual visits had begun when Lily was a toddler, although back then it had been her father Andrew Raynor who had taken her back home. The High Peak farm, with its beautiful location and the unchanging timelessness of life there, had been a great consolation for Lily after Andrew's death.

One of the great joys had been riding; first on a stubby little pony with a belligerent nature and a fondness for tipping the infant Lily into a patch of nettles, then a succession of ponies and horses that increased in size as Lily did.

Initially it had been Great-grandmama Suzanna who had instructed Lily, but quite soon, as Lily became competent, this duty was delegated to whichever farmhand was about. Great-grandmama had muttered about acquiring a side-saddle and teaching Lily to ride like a lady, but the farmhands never bothered to remind her; as a consequence, Lily only knows how to ride astride.

Hence the need for a voluminous and blush-saving skirt.

Trying to keep her tone nonchalant, as if this is an everyday occurrence, Lily tells Mrs Clapper she is about to set out for France. Mrs Clapper's eyes pop out on stalks at this, as if Lily has just announced she's heading for the moon on Jules Verne's space gun.

'*Now*?' Mrs Clapper squeaks. 'This very day?'

'Yes. I will take care, Mrs Clapper,' she adds, affected by the older woman's troubled look. 'I promise.'

'But . . . but . . .' Mrs Clapper splutters, 'they're *foreign* over there! Got funny ways and eat a lot of horses and offal and onions and that, and talk like gibbering monkeys!'

Lily is quite sure Mrs Clapper has never been to France – nor in fact out of England at all – and wonders briefly on what she is basing her impressions of her country's nearest neighbours.

'I will be with Felix,' she adds, hoping that this will reassure Mrs Clapper more than it did Marm Smithers.

Judging from Mrs Clapper's dubious expression, it doesn't.

Later, back upstairs in her own quarters trying to think if she's forgotten anything, Lily stops in her headlong arrangements. There were to have been two more nights until Felix is back, and she had planned to spend this evening with her boatman friend Tamáz Edey.

It is now mid-afternoon. Abandoning her packing – it is done anyway, and it's only anxiety that makes her go on checking and re-checking – she puts on hat and jacket and slips out into the back yard, then makes her way through her grandfather's vast old shed that forms the rear wall of the property and has a door to the street behind. She hurries down to the basin where the boats tie up, praying that she will find him there.

She does.

She goes on board *The Dawning of the Day,* and he takes her hand to help her down the steep little steps into the cabin. The stove is going well, the kettle is coming to the boil, it is cosy and warm and she wishes she was staying. She starts to tell him why she isn't – why she won't be coming this evening – but with a smile he stops her. 'I can tell, *cushla*, that you have an adventure in the offing,' he says gently. 'Go and embrace it,' he bends and kisses her cheek, 'and tell me about it when you come back.'

She stays for a cup of tea – it is too hard, to arrive and to leave again immediately – and she tells him about Miss Phyllida Westwood and poor Wilberforce Chibb, and the mysterious dead man in the remote Breton asylum. He takes it all in, nodding occasionally, not speaking.

But as she is leaving he says, 'Lily?'

Something in his voice makes her turn back. 'Yes?'

'You still have the bottle?'

She pulls it out on its long silver chain from inside her blouse and holds it up to show him.

'Good,' he says softly.

Then he smiles again and lets her go.

The object on the silver chain is a witch's bottle.

As she hurries back to Hob's Court, Lily remembers how strange it seemed when Tamáz gave it to her. It is about the length of a forefinger, and some two fingers in breadth. It contains a long old iron nail, several shorter ones, some barbs, a coil of wire sharpened to a point.

'This is a witch's bottle,' he said softly to her as he removed the bottle on its chain from around his own neck and put it in her hand. 'My grandmother Mary Bridey made it for me when I was small and afraid of the night walkers of the Fenlands. It keeps all harm away.'

The bottle – or, to be precise, the long nail inside it – has already saved her life once.

She worries, as she lets herself into the house, what peril

he has foreseen ahead for her, that he should make sure she will have its protection . . .

It is not a comfortable thought with which to embark on her journey.

She dresses carefully in the accommodating skirt, a couple of petticoats, one of her better blouses and a waistcoat that tones with the skirt, adding a matching form-fitting jacket and topping it off with a newish felt hat that is smart but not fussy. She puts on the stout and very comfortable boots that have a hidden knife in a sheath inside the left-hand one.

On the tram to the station she opens Marm's Bradshaw's again for a longer look. She gleans some useful hints although some are too late, such as the sage words that the less luggage you take, the better (although, bearing in mind that she will undoubtedly have to carry her own bag, she has fortuitously packed the minimum). Bradshaw's suggests half a dozen shirts and a stout pair of double soled shoes; a pair of waterproof sheets are advocated as a precaution against damp beds.

Lily's boots are stout enough, but she does not possess half a dozen shirts. Or a pair of waterproof sheets.

Reading on, she learns that civility and kindness will procure a welcome anywhere, and she is advised that above all things, she should not trouble herself about French politics. Browsing on, she learns that in Caesar's time France was called Gallia or Gaul. It has five principal rivers and, as well as the chief crops, abounds in forests, coal mines and mineral springs. She learns how to ask: *what pretty hamlet is that?* She is briefly mystified by the phrase *donnez-lui une mesure d'avoine*, which means *give him a feed of oats*, until she looks more closely and sees that it is under the entries *il me faut une belle voiture à quartre roues*, meaning *I want a good four-wheeled carriage*, and *j'ai besoin d'un cheval de selle*, which is how you ask for a horse to ride.

When she closes the little book and puts it back in her bag, her confidence about travelling alone into a strange land has definitely increased.

*   *   *

The mail express leaves Charing Cross precisely on time, at five minutes after eight o'clock. Even as it passes through Cannon Street, Lily is already regretting the moment of parsimony that prompted the purchase of a third class ticket, for the carriage is crowded, the upright wooden seats offer nothing in the way of comfort and quite a lot of the passengers appear to have spent the early part of the evening in a pub. There is a smell of whisky and beery breath and the air is thick with tobacco smoke. By the time the train pulls into Dover some two hours later, Lily's hands ache from maintaining the tight grip on the handle of her leather satchel and she is wondering what on earth her cheap ticket will furnish in the way of seating on the steamer that will ferry her over to Calais. She is not at all optimistic.

The crush of bodies on the platform and along the covered ways that lead from platform to quay is almost brutal. She fears that this urge to push for the front signifies that benches for third class passengers on board the steamer will prove to be in short supply. She elbows her way forward, only to be stopped abruptly by the heavy uniformed arm of a French official who seems to be demanding to see her papers: '*Billet. BILLET!*' he snarls, the *b* so emphatic that specks of malodorous saliva burst out of his rat-trap mouth. Lily has her ticket ready in her hand and quickly holds it up in his face; he flinches slightly, and she is almost certain he is disappointed not to have a reason to haul her out of the throng and shut her up in a stinking, windowless cell to hurl incomprehensible questions at her for so long that the ferry sails without her . . .

She hurries along the quay and up the walkway on to the boat. It is elegantly shaped and looks fast; it *is* fast, she thinks, and the timetable that she memorised from Marm's Bradshaw's flashes through her mind. The overnight mail express from London to Paris can take as little as eight and a half hours, a fact that Marm impressed upon her with such pride that its record of speediness might have been his own personal achievement.

She stands on deck, unsure what to do next. She feels like a novice traveller, gauche and unsure; it may not be the first time she has left her native shores, but just now the earlier phase of her life spent in India seems a long time ago. Then, she was with St Walburga's Nursing Services, where nuns and nurses worked side by side (the nuns always in the senior positions) and all were known universally as Swans. Her five years' training under the nuns' rigorous tutelage qualified her as both a midwife and a battlefield nurse; the two divergent areas of medicine co-existed because many of the troops sent overseas to fight Queen Victoria's wars took their wives and families with them.

Now, leaning on the rail of the cross-Channel steamer, a small shaft of her long-buried spirit of adventure reasserts itself. The crowds, the sound of the water slapping up against the side of the ship, the smells of tar and salt, the shouted commands, the lanterns shining out from Dover Castle up on its heights and the dark sea beyond the breakwaters combine to beckon this little shaft out into the open, waxing as it emerges, and she finds she is smiling. Anxieties such as whether she will manage to find the right train to take her on to Paris and how on earth she's going to get to Felix's hotel the next morning begin to fade, and she says quietly to herself, 'Other people manage. So shall I.'

She senses movement and, looking down at the quay, sees that the ship has begun to move. She stays where she is, sometimes looking ahead to the open sea, sometimes looking back at the town. The steamer gathers speed, the bows hit more lively water, and as they emerge from the sheltering cliffs, a salty and forceful north-east wind catches them. Lily's wide skirts billow around her and, but for the ribbons tied firmly under her chin, she would probably have lost her hat. Spray like cold, fine rain hits her face, and, glancing down, she sees that tiny droplets have already settled on her jacket.

Much as she has been enjoying the open deck, it is probably time to seek shelter inside. She looks up and down the deck, off which doors open into various public spaces. The door at the far end has been propped partly open, and the fug of smoke emerging on to the night air, together with the noise, suggests this is where people with third class tickets must go.

With a sigh of resignation, she heads along towards it.

As she passes one of the other doors, it crashes open and
a small, slight figure emerges, moving far too quickly to stop
and running straight into Lily. Lily grasps her arm – it is a
young woman – and a cry of anguish bursts out of her, followed
by a rapid stream of French with a few English words thrown
in. Catching the gist, Lily perceives that the young woman
feels sick and is trying to reach the rail so that she can avoid
vomiting over herself or anybody else.

Lily moves her grip from the young woman's arm and puts
it around the tightly-corseted little waist.

'Come along with me and sit down,' she says slowly and
calmly. She takes the young woman – she really is not much
more than a girl – to one of the wooden benches set along
the deck, in the lee of the ship's superstructure. 'There,' she
says when they are seated, 'now, sit back – that's right – and
fold your arms across your stomach.' The girl, after a dubious
glance at Lily, does as she's told. 'Look back towards the
shore – there, that way – and fix your eyes on the line of lights
along the sea front.' The girl obeys, but even as she does so,
Lily senses she's about to protest, to insist she needs to throw
up. 'The sea is really quite calm,' Lily goes on, keeping her
tone smooth and reassuring, 'and you probably only noticed
the motion because we have not long left harbour. Keeping
your eyes on something that does not move allows your body
to adjust.'

She can hear the soft voice of Sister Teresa saying the same
words after the troop ship left Portsmouth and, as it cleared
the Isle of Wight, hit the swell out in the Channel; the wise
advice had helped then, and, as Lily watches her companion
closely, it appears to be doing the same now.

After a short time, the girl takes a deep breath and says,
'*Merci*. Thank you. I do not any more wish to spew forth.'

Lily tries and fails to suppress a chuckle. The girl picks this
up and, turning to look at her with wide brown eyes, says
anxiously, 'It is not right?'

'It expresses what you mean' – rather eloquently, Lily adds
to herself – 'but I think I might say, *I no longer need to be
sick*.'

The girl repeats the phrase several times. Then she bestows

a beaming smile on Lily (who notices she really is very lovely) and says, 'I am Séraphine. I go to France with my 'usband of not long for we must stay *chez ma grandmère* in the good country air of Normandy. I am *très excitée depuis plusieus semaines* and many mornings I am sick, just like now, for to be in France and at home is *good* for me, and—'

At that moment the door through which Séraphine emerged opens again and a tall, handsome, very well-dressed and clearly worried man of about forty emerges. He looks each way along the deck, his frown deepening, and clearly does not see Lily and Séraphine on their bench.

'*Monsieur!*' Lily calls, for she is sure she knows what, or rather who, he is looking for. She struggles to remember the right words, and adds, '*Nous sommes ici.*'

The man spins round, spots them and his face floods with relief. In moments he has run along the deck and is crouching down in front of the beautiful young woman, taking her hands between his and murmuring to her. Lily cannot understand the words, but the meaning is clear: *where have you been? I've been so worried about you! Thank God you are safe.* From the tone in which they are delivered, he clearly loves the young woman very much.

Séraphine interrupts the outpourings and says something, also in French, indicating Lily and grasping her hand. When she has finished, the tall man gets to his feet and gives Lily a bow, his right hand on his heart.

'I am Hector Gordon-Ross,' he says. He sounds English, and his name implies he probably is.

'Lily Raynor,' she responds.

He nods. 'How do you do, Miss Raynor? My wife tells me that you stopped her from falling over on the deck and also cured her seasickness. You have my heartfelt gratitude and I am deeply in your debt.'

'It was nothing,' Lily replies modestly. 'Common sense, really.'

Hector Gordon-Ross is studying her closely. 'My wife's hands are cold,' he says, 'and both of you will grow dangerously chilled sitting out here. Shall we go inside?' He points to the door he came out of. 'The cabin is warm and comfortable, and there is plenty of fresh air coming in.' He pauses. 'Unless you think that going within will make the – er, the indisposition return?' He shoots a nervous glance at his young wife.

Lily, who has an idea that Séraphine's sickness had nothing to do with being at sea and rather more to do with the marriage to the new 'usband, says that she does not think it will.

'Then, shall we?' Again he indicates the door to the cabin.

And Lily, embarrassed, says in a rush, 'Yes, of course you must go in. I'm afraid, however, that I cannot come with you, for my ticket does not permit it.' She feels her face flush, and she hopes it is not apparent in the dim light.

Séraphine, who has clearly understood, shoots a rapid stream of protesting French at her husband, who puts up a pacifying hand and says calmly, '*D'accord, ma chérie*.' Turning to Lily, he says with charming diplomacy, 'It is an unnecessary luxury to travel first class, and I understand that hard-working people wisely elect not to waste their money on such fripperies. However, I wished to indulge and spoil my wife,' – he shoots a glance at Séraphine which even in the darkness shines like a bright light – 'and so we journey as lords and ladies do. If you will permit me to make the necessary arrangements, Miss Raynor, will you be our companion for the remainder of the journey?' Leaning closer, he adds softly, 'My wife is nervous and apprehensive, and your presence clearly calms her.'

'Of course,' Lily replies, and at the thought that she will not have to endure third class accommodation for the rest of the night, her face breaks into a smile.

'Excellent!' exclaims Hector Gordon-Ross. 'Oh – you are going all the way to Paris, I assume?'

'I am,' Lily confirms.

And all at once the prospect has become infinitely more appealing.

They head for a corner of the first class lounge. As Hector Gordon-Ross strides over to it, two older people dressed in formal dark clothes stand up, worried expressions on their faces. One is a man of perhaps fifty, very thin, very upright, with a pale face shaved so close it gleams and hair liberally oiled to keep it firmly in place. The other is a woman a few years his senior; she too is thin, with a look of wiry strength. Her hair is all but invisible under her severe black hat, so tightly has it been bound into its little bun. The pair are clearly very relieved to see Séraphine safe and apparently unharmed, and the woman leaps forward with a shawl, a blanket and two pillows, which she begins arranging as soon as Séraphine has sat down.

Lily discovers that the seats are very comfortable. Their little area is set apart from the remainder of the passengers – not that there are many – which provides a degree of privacy. Two uniformed stewards appear, bearing a tray of tea and another heavy with plates of delicate little sandwiches and plain biscuits. Having ensured that his wife and Lily have all they need, Mr Gordon-Ross disappears and presently returns, smiling, to quietly inform Lily that she is now officially a first class passenger.

The steamer docks at Calais in the early hours of the next morning.

Lily discovers rapidly that travelling first class is so far removed from cramming into third class accommodation that it is hard to see it as the same activity. Her well-worn leather bag is whisked away with the large amount of Gordon-Rosses' luggage by a trio of porters, and she can only hope that the insouciance of her companions implies that she will definitely see it again at some point. They are ushered down the gangway and along to the waiting train by more uniformed men, who ruthlessly shove lower mortals out of the way and, very quickly, Lily and the Gordon-Rosses are installed in a private compartment with deep seats, cushions and a lavatory along the corridor. The thin man and the severe woman go into the compartment next door.

Mr Gordon-Ross and his young wife had been chatty on the steamer, eager to tell their new acquaintance the tale of their meeting, their marriage and their hopes for the future. It is clear that he is a very wealthy man and that he and Séraphine have married for love. Nevertheless, and for all it remains unspoken, Lily has the clear impression that the young woman is expected to conceive an heir in the near future, and that, as she had surmised, the visit to the Normandy grandmother – during which Séraphine will eat good food, breathe good country air, be pampered and indulged far from the dirt, crowds and the busyness of London – is intended to encourage this happy event.

Listening, covertly studying Séraphine, drawing on all the experience of her nursing career, Lily is now all but certain that it has already been brought about.

But, of course, it is not up to her to say so.

Now, warm and comfortable on the train, Séraphine is drowsy, and Lily leans forward to tuck the blanket round her. Watching her, she stifles a yawn: seeing someone relax into sleep often has that effect. Mr Gordon-Ross notices, and says kindly, 'Why not try to sleep too, Miss Raynor? I certainly intend to, for it is more than five hours until we arrive in Paris, and I always find the rhythm of the train most soporific.'

Rather to her surprise – for she is in the company of strangers, and surely it is foolhardy to be so trusting? – Lily finds herself arranging her limbs in a comfortable position, positioning the pillow and drawing up the blanket, and shortly afterwards falling into a profound sleep.

FOUR

Paris in the early morning of a bright springtime day is a joy to behold.

Lily has never been here before, and she is astounded to find that although, like London, it is a capital city on a river, there the resemblance ends. The architecture looks as if someone has gone round all the streets with a huge cart full of decorative finishing touches: balustrades of elaborately-worked metal, brightly-painted shutters, window boxes full of healthy-looking spring plants, flower stalls that dazzle the eyes with the brilliance of their colours and the geometrically perfect arrangement of the blooms.

And the people! Although it is early still – not yet eight o'clock – the pavements on either side of the wide boulevards are bustling with activity, and Lily avidly studies the fashions of the women. Stripes seem to be popular, as do ridiculously huge upper sleeves and extremely tight corseting. On the roads themselves, carts and wagons are outnumbered by omnibuses, cabs and carriages, all determinedly forging their own route with not very much regard for anyone else's.

Lily bade an affectionate farewell to Hector and Séraphine Gordon-Ross at the *Gare du Nord*. There were carriages waiting for them and the two servants, and, after hugging and thanking Lily yet again, Séraphine was helped into the first of them with such care that she might have been a parcel marked *Extremely Fragile*. Mr Gordon-Ross had courteously offered to take Lily to her destination, but, thinking that arriving in a convoy of very classy carriages would hardly foster the anonymity that is a private enquiry agent's prime concern, equally courteously she refused.

'But do you know where you are going?' he asked her, frowning worriedly; perhaps, Lily thought, he considered all women delicate and unworldly and totally incapable of looking after themselves. Then, castigating herself because really, he was only trying to be kind, she smiled and assured him that she did. All the same, he would not abandon her until he had summoned a cab, although, once again in the interests of anonymity, she waited until his cortège had clattered off before giving the cabbie the address of Felix's hotel.

Now the cab is heading into a maze of much smaller streets. They have just crossed the glittering Seine, and she has spotted what she is sure from Bradshaw's Guide must be the cathedral of Notre Dame, over on the left on its island in the river. Lily spots a street sign – Rue de Seine – and then the cab swings to the right into an even narrower street and the cabbie shouts out something that sounds like *V'la, nous sommes arrivés*, and Lily looks out to her left and sees a small and somehow apologetic hotel sign on a white building with black-painted double doors and little balconies with low wrought-iron rail-ings on the first floor. Craning her neck, she sees several more storeys extending upwards, culminating in a mansarded roof.

Briefly wondering what she will do if Felix has not received her telegram and is already on his way back to London, she dismisses the worrying thought, pays off the cabbie and walks purposefully through the doors.

She is absorbing the rapid succession of first impressions – narrow reception area, tall counter, fat frowning woman looking up from a huge ledger, smell of polish and coffee, posy of flowers in a vase on the counter – when a voice from behind her says quietly, 'Lily, you're here. *Bienvenue à Paris.*'

And, spinning round so fast that her neck creaks, she sees Felix.

He looks wonderful. He is dressed very smartly in what must be a new coat and trousers in fine pale grey wool and undoubtedly of Parisian manufacture, an immaculate starched white shirt visible beneath a startling waistcoat, and his narrow black boots shine with recent polishing. His dark blond hair has been trimmed, he has clearly had a very recent shave, and he smells of something that brings to mind lemons and bay leaves. Before she can comment on any aspect of his rather surprising appearance, he has moved right up to her and has his warm hands on her shoulders, drawing her close and kissing her resoundingly on both cheeks.

'Good morning, Felix,' she says, withdrawing slightly and feeling herself blush. 'You – er, you look well.'

He grins, trying to control it, and she is quite sure he is suppressing his amusement at her depressingly unoriginal remark. 'You do too,' he says. 'I had expected you to be haggard with weariness after a night on the ferry and the train, but here you are looking daisy-fresh!'

Fearing that he is about to kiss her again, she takes another step backward. Really, he has been in France for less than a fortnight and here he is dressed in dandy's clothes and adopting risqué foreign habits! 'Thank you, but I slept for several hours on the train from Calais to Paris,' she says repressively.

He is still struggling not to laugh. 'We will ask Madame Martin if we may leave your bag in my room', – he glances enquiringly at the fat lady behind the counter and she nods – 'and perhaps you would like to rest up there for a while?'

'I am not in the least tired,' she replies. She notices that the fat woman is watching with evident amusement: *just what is it they are finding so funny?* Lily thinks crossly. 'But I would indeed like to leave my luggage,' she adds, speaking slowly and clearly and holding up her leather nursing satchel, pointing to it with her free hand.

'Of course, Madame Raynor,' the woman replies in perfect but heavily accented English. 'In addition, after a night spent travelling, I imagine you would welcome a jug of hot water. I will have one sent up so that you may refresh yourself.'

And, mortified that she has addressed this cosmopolitan and obviously multilingual woman as if she was a field worker, Lily meekly follows her up the narrow stairs to one of the first floor rooms with the little balconies that she spotted from the cab.

Felix, Lily observes, is clearly a tidy man in his personal life as well as at work, for the room shows scant evidence of his presence other than the leather valise on top of the wardrobe – a huge construction made of heavy dark wood – and his boots standing neatly beside the door. Apart from the alarming wallpaper the room is plain, but it is more than adequate: iron bed frame, plenty of pillows, blankets and an eiderdown, bedside table with chamber pot, screened-off corner with wash-stand, slop basin and the promised jug of hot water. There is also an oval-shaped basin on a low stand, and, after a puzzling moment, she recognizes it from Bradshaw's Guide as a bidet. She is cross with herself for blushing (again) as she also recalls its purpose, for such an object is practical and hygienic, and she approves. She makes use of the lavatory along the corridor – it is the squat and straddle type and she is instantly reminded of her quarters in India – and returns to the room to wash her hands and face, neaten her hair and take a couple of minutes for some deep breaths to calm herself. Then, leaving her bag beside Felix's boots, she goes downstairs.

Felix is waiting for her. He is still grinning. He says, 'I haven't had breakfast yet. I thought I'd wait for you, and we could have it together. Coffee and croissants at the café on the corner?'

It is such a thoughtful and welcome suggestion that as she says, 'Yes please,' she is struggling to hold back foolish tears.

'I guessed,' Felix says, 'that you wouldn't want me to book a room for you because we'd be setting off on our way to wherever we're going.' He has ordered two *café complets*, and he and Lily are watching the waiter behind the bar preparing them.

Lily has been staring round the bright, busy little café with wide eyes. Felix has been both amused and touched at her manner, which seems to combine an almost child-like wonder at this different world she has so abruptly arrived in with a very English determination to disapprove of virtually every-thing. Yet she is hardly some sheltered, stay-at-home spinster, he reminds himself: she has nursed in India and—

But she has recovered herself and is replying to his remark.

'Quite right,' she says, and he detects that she is resuming her normal working demeanour. 'We have to go to Brittany, and it appears from the guidebook that we need to catch a train from Montparnasse station to a place called Rennes.'

'Gare Montparnasse is not far,' he says. 'Rennes is a big town, so I dare say trains are quite frequent. We can go and—'

'There is a departure at half past ten,' she interrupts.

He glances at his pocket watch. 'Plenty of time. Now, tell me all about this mysterious new case.'

Her eyes light up, she reaches into her small bag for her notebook, places it on the table before her and has just opened her mouth to speak when the waiter brings their breakfast. She frowns in irritation, then manages a smile and a somewhat stiff *merci*. Returning to the notebook, she takes a sip of coffee and a smile of surprise crosses her face.

'Try dipping the end of your croissant in it,' Felix advises.

She does, and for some moments he watches as she turns her full attention to the food and the coffee.

'Goodness, that was delicious!' she says, wiping her finger-tips on the checked napkin.

'Another?' he suggests.

'One is sufficient,' she says primly. Then she presses the notebook open and for the next few minutes talks almost without pause.

She has given him a great deal of information in a short space of time, he reflects when she has finished, but such is her ability to extract the bones of a case and summarize them that he thinks he has a pretty clear picture.

'So . . . the fiancée, this Miss Phyllida Westwood, would rather you prove Wilberforce did not carry out this deadly attack in the asylum, but if we discover that he did, she will calmly walk away and leave him to his fate?' he says when it's clear she has no more to say.

'I cannot vouch for her being *calm*, but in essence, yes.'

Miss Westwood, thinks Felix, is a coolheaded young lady.

'Do you think Wilberforce Chibb is a murderer?' he asks.

She ponders the question, frowning. 'The attack on the young woman in the market in Egypt could very well have been due to a temporary state of confusion and disorientation after the sunstroke,' she says slowly. 'Such symptoms were common when I nursed in India, where it proved difficult for many of the British troops to deal with the heat. And the death of Mr Chibb Senior might have been from the fall down the stairs, and thus an accident rather than murder, although it is hard to overlook the fact that Wilberforce had a razor in his hand.'

'He might have been shaving when his father came storming upstairs to remonstrate with him,' Felix suggests. He is not unfamiliar with fathers like that.

She nods but does not comment. 'As for whether the blood on his nightshirt cuff is incontrovertible proof that he killed the man in Paimpont, that' – she looks at him, her face full of excitement – 'is what we are going to Brittany to find out.'

Back at the hotel, Felix runs up the stairs to pack his bag. Before he does so, he changes out of his very smart new garments, folds them carefully and puts on his familiar black coat and trousers. It is quite a sacrifice to put away the vivid waistcoat, but it is hardly a garment for someone who wants to be unobtrusive. He also hesitates over his footwear: he really loves his new boots, but in all honesty they are too narrow; already he has a sharp pain in his left foot and is developing a blister on the heel. He picks up his hat, grabs Lily's bag and his own and hurries downstairs to pay his bill.

Madame Martin gives him a sardonic smile. Glancing at Lily, waiting just outside the door, she says, '*Un peu froide, la jeune femme, n'est-ce pas?*' and, leaning closer, '*Il vous faut trouver un moyen de l'exciter, eh?*'

He wants to say that Lily isn't chilly, she's nervous, and rebuff the saucy comment by explaining that it would be highly inappropriate for him to find a means of stimulating her. He smiles – discouragingly, he hopes – thanks her for a comfortable stay and hurries out to join Lily.

The train leaves Gare Montparnasse only three minutes late by Felix's watch. He had been going to ask Lily how she knew the times of the departures, but on the short cab ride from the Rue des Beaux Arts she had taken a Bradshaw's Guide out of her bag, a piece of paper marking the page, and frowned down at it.

'Good idea to buy that,' he had remarked, peering over her shoulder.

'I didn't. It belongs to your landlord,' she replied. Glancing up at him, she added, 'I knew he'd be able to give me a great deal of valuable information about trains and ferries and France in general, and indeed he did. This,' – she waved the Bradshaw's – 'provides the details.'

Now, sitting side by side in a reasonably comfortable second class carriage, with Lily by the window, Felix settles back to enjoy the journey. And, if he is honest with himself, Lily's company. It seems she believes she has told him all he needs to know about Wilberforce Chibb for the time being, and for some miles she bombards him with questions about the French way of life, asking him to teach her some handy phrases. 'There is quite a comprehensive selection in here,' – again she indicates the Bradshaw's Guide – 'and I am confident that I will be able to command a carriage or a pair of well-fed riding horses once we are beyond the scope of the railways.' She tries out a few words, much to the amusement of the woman sitting beside Felix, who he can feel shaking with silent laughter. Trying not to smile, he gently corrects her.

'I remember,' she says once he is satisfied that she has improved as much as she is going to, 'you said you spoke French the day you came for your interview.'

'Did I?' He has forgotten.

'Yes. You told me you had Latin and some Greek, and that although your spoken French was good, you were not so capable when it came to reading and writing the language.'

He thinks back to that day.

He had seen the advertisement for a clerical assistant. He'd had little conception of what such a post entailed, no idea what work the World's End Bureau did, and he'd assumed that its proprietor, L. Raynor, was a man. Thankfully Lily hadn't held any of these drawbacks against him. Two years later, he does not have a single regret and he hopes she feels the same. The impulse to apply for the job had been prompted by desperation – he had been almost out of money and very hungry – but it had turned out to be one of his better decisions.

She is looking at him expectantly, and he realizes she is expecting him to comment. 'Oh . . . well, the reading and writing have advanced considerably in the last week or so, since I've had so many papers to read and sign, and spending so much time with dear old Henri-Josef has helped with the speaking too.'

The expectant look is still there. *She wants to know about my inheritance*, he thinks suddenly, *but she's too polite to ask.*

'My friend the Countess – his mother – left me a generous bequest,' he says, leaning closer to her and lowering his voice. He explains how Solange's cunning and parsimonious family and their lawyers had decided to keep this fact to themselves, and that it was only the inexorable determination of Henri-Josef's new companion and advisor that had led to the uncovering of the truth. 'It has been a great pleasure to have money in my pocket that I don't have to be careful with,' he concludes, 'and I've had something of a spending spree.'

'So I noticed,' she replies wryly. 'It's wise, however, to have put aside your Parisian fashions for the time being.'

He grins. 'Henri-Josef persuaded me to buy the waistcoat,' he admits. *And the shoes*, he thinks. His heel gives a throb.

Lily, he notices, is fiddling with the clasp of her bag. He guesses there is more she wishes to say, and he thinks he knows what it is.

Leaning down to her again, he says, 'Henri-Josef is a delight, but he has little concept of what constitutes sound financial good sense. His companion Monsieur Toussaint, however, appears to know more or less everything, and with his help I visited a very impressive Parisian bank and managed to transfer the majority of my new wealth to my London account.'

She looks at him, relief in her face, and then, blushing, lowers her eyes. 'It is really none of my business, Felix,' she says stiffly. 'It's just that . . .' Her voice trails off.

Just that you would have been horrified if I'd thrown the whole lot away on wine, women, fancy waistcoats and uncomfortable shoes, he finishes silently. She is right, it *is* none of her business. But all the same he is touched that she cares.

The train makes a longer than usual stop at Le Mans, and Felix, who has been getting increasingly hungry for the last hour and a half, takes the opportunity to descend to the platform and buy food and drink. He barges his way through the dithering, chattering crowd and homes in on a stall selling *baguettes* cut in half and filled with luridly-coloured sausage; noticing paper bags full of small, sweet pastries, he buys one of those as well. Two large mugs of coffee from the station buffet – a notice advises that the cups may be left on the train – and he strolls back to the carriage.

Lily is peering anxiously out of the window. 'There were ominous clanking noises, and just now a great release of steam,' she says, eyeing his purchases eagerly, 'and I was afraid the train would set off without you.'

'I was watching out,' he says, but in fact he had been far too intent on foraging for food to notice what was going on behind him.

They settle in their seats and almost immediately the train begins to move. He hands her a *baguette*. She eyes it dubiously. 'What's that smell?'

Which particular one? he wants to ask, for the *saucisse* is powerfully redolent of pig, with a tang of blood and a base note of the earth, and the most dominant element is garlic. 'I expect it's the herbs used in the cooking,' he says casually. She needs to eat, he reflects, because she's been travelling for hours and she's only had one croissant all day. The last thing he wants to do is put her off the good, solid – if slightly malodorous – offering he has found for her. 'They use quite a lot of garlic.'

Her expression brightens. 'I've heard of garlic,' she says. 'I understand it is good for the blood.' This is obviously reassurance enough, and she takes a huge bite of the filled *baguette*. He watches her while trying to pretend he isn't; she chews, frowns, gags slightly (she puts up a delicate hand and spits a piece of gristle into her half-closed palm) and then swallows and instantly takes a second bite.

'Do you like it?' he asks.

Her brows draw together as she considers her answer. 'I don't *not* like it,' she replies eventually. 'It's – er, it's a very strong flavour, isn't it?' He agrees that it is. 'I suppose,' she adds thoughtfully, 'that this is the sort of food we'll be eating over the next few days?' He nods. 'In that case, I shall get used to it.' And she glares down at the last half of the *saucisse* in its bread coating as if it was an enemy to be overcome.

He relaxes in his seat, making short work of his own food. The bag of little pastries is an unqualified success, and he has to work quite hard to ensure he gets his share. The mug of coffee, which Lily seems taken aback to discover is served without milk and hair-raisingly strong, is clearly something else she is going to have to work at.

'Thank you,' she says when they have finished. 'I hadn't realized how hungry I was.'

'It can be tricky to find food when travelling overnight,' he observes. 'Especially when you're not familiar with the journey.'

'Very true,' she agrees, 'although I was fortunate in that I met a couple on the steamer who were far more experienced than I, and they, in particular the husband, were most helpful.'

He listens as she recounts her meeting with Séraphine Gordon-Ross, her suave and sophisticated husband and the two servants. Every time she says *Mr Gordon-Ross* he is torn between smiling and wincing.

'Is that what you called him?' he asks when she has finished.

'I beg your pardon?'

'You addressed him as Mr Gordon-Ross?'

'Of course I did,' she replies, irritated. 'That was his *name*.' But she has noticed his smile, and hisses, '*What*? Why are you finding that so amusing?'

'Hector Gordon-Ross is the second son of Lord Strathcraich,' he says. 'His elder brother was killed in a mountaineering accident a year ago. His father died last autumn.'

He watches her expression change as she works it out. 'So he's not Mr Gordon-Ross. Not Mr anything.' Her eyes are wide. 'He's a *lord*!'

'He is indeed. He—'

'I *wondered* why the two old attendants looked so scandalised!' she exclaims. 'They were probably aghast at my lack of respect! Oh, dear, and he was so very kind!'

'You had been attending to his wife,' he points out, 'and no doubt he was grateful.'

But he doesn't think she heard. 'Why on earth didn't he say?' she asks with some asperity. 'And the silly man introduced himself as Hector Gordon-Ross. How was I supposed to know he was really a titled lord?'

'He probably imagined you'd have heard of him,' Felix says

mildly. 'Most people have. He and his wife frequently appear in the society pages, and a couple of months ago I read a long piece about the glories of their Scottish estate.'

She mutters something about being far too busy with Bureau work to read the society pages, and he can't help thinking that given the time, there is other reading matter she would opt for. The muttering stops abruptly and she says, 'Why is there so much press interest?'

'Oh – the common view is that old Lord Strathcraich was devoted to the older son, heartbroken when he was killed, and probably died of grief.' She nods, and he can see she is listening intently. 'When Angus – that was the older brother – died, Hector, of course, became heir to the title, and pressure was put upon him to abandon his carefree ways, find a wife and quickly set about assuring the inheritance for a further generation. You said they were going to France for Séraphine's health?'

'Yes. They are going to stay with her grandmother in the good Normandy countryside.'

He nods slowly. 'And everyone will be praying, no doubt, that when Lord Strathcraich takes his young wife back home, she will be with child.'

Lily starts to say something, then very firmly closes her mouth. She turns away, suddenly fascinated by the countryside racing past. And Felix, remembering that she was once a nurse and a midwife, silently draws his own conclusion.

It is the middle of the afternoon when they disembark at Rennes. Aware that his companion did not have the advantage of a full night's sleep last night, no matter what she says about setting down comfortably on the train from Calais to Paris, Felix is covertly watching Lily for signs of fatigue. She is not showing any.

They emerge on to the busy concourse, and he sees a wide area full of people where omnibuses are arriving and departing. She has reminded him of the name of the place they are bound, and, mentally bracing himself, he walks over to where a trio of uniformed men stand in deep conversation and asks, without a great deal of hope, if any of the omnibuses are going that way.

As with working men everywhere, the straightforward question elicits a spate of earnest and slightly fractious conversation between the three, little of which Felix picks up because they all speak so fast and the local accent is strong. After what seems at least five minutes but is undoubtedly much less, the youngest of the three, a good twenty years his colleagues' junior, turns to Felix and explains somewhat disparagingly that the old grey-beards will be arguing till bedtime but he reckons the best way is to catch a tram to the western fringes of the town, then take the omnibus to somewhere called Plélan-le-Grand, which apparently necessitates two different vehicles and a couple of changes along the way. Obligingly he writes down the names of the villages where they will change, although his writing is flowery and full of loops and Felix is doubtful he'll be able to make it out. He hopes the map in Lily's Bradshaw's will provide elucidation.

'*Et Plélan-le-Grand à Paimpont, c'est loin?*' Felix asks hopefully.

The young man shrugs and says the distance is five, six kilometres, which Felix mentally translates as three and a half miles.

'*Et on peut trouver des logements à Paimpont?*' Now he has his fingers tightly crossed, for if there are no hotels or rooms where he and Lily can stay, he is not quite sure what they'll do. And it will be late by the time they arrive . . .

But the young man is smiling. He nods, '*Oui, oui,*' (only his accent is so strong that it sounds like *wah, wah*), and explains that Paimpont is *un lieu de pèlerinage*, and *beaucoup de monde* go there.

Felix thanks him, shakes his hand and hurries back to tell Lily that they'll have to take at least two omnibuses and perhaps walk the last three miles, but the good news is that they're sure to find somewhere to put up because Paimpont is a place of pilgrimage and the world is just queuing up to pay a visit.

She looks up at him, a dubious expression in her eyes. Then she says brightly – and he can't but admire her courage – 'Let's be going then.'

FIVE

Lily is at last alone. She sits down on the bed – straw mattress, and the bedlinen crackles with starch – and with a groan of mingled pain and pleasure, removes her boots and her stockings and puts her feet into the bowl of hot salted water on the wooden floor before her.

The relief is so great that it almost hurts.

She sits quite still for some minutes. Then, slowly, being gentle with herself, she unbuttons her jacket and slips it off, then her waistcoat and shirt, laying the garments carefully on the bed beside her. She unfastens the waistbands of her skirt and petticoats, takes them off over her head – she cannot bear to take her feet out of the wonderful hot water just yet – and then unhooks her corset. The joy of sitting there in her chemise after almost twenty hours in her clothes is so great that she finds she is humming gently.

The journey by tram and omnibus from the railway station in Rennes to Plélan-le-Grand had been challenging, to say the least. She knows she could not have done it without Felix, and silently sends him her renewed thanks. The bus service was haphazard, and that's putting it generously, and Felix gathered from several disgruntled people also attempting the journey to Plélan-le-Grand that transport being late or failing to turn up altogether was what one had to expect living out in the country, and the locals often resorted to begging a ride from a passing farmer on his cart.

There had been no vehicle of any description to take Lily and Felix on to Paimpont. She had watched with increasing pessimism while Felix did his best, and when he finally gave up and told her they were going to have to walk, he'd looked so dismayed that she had said she didn't mind and exercise was just what she needed after sitting for so long.

There was no need for him to know that her stays were digging into her hips and her left knee hurt.

They had found a place called *un relais* in the little village. Felix said he thought the word translated as a stopping place, but the long, low building facing the road was much more than that. They had gone inside to a smiling welcome, a fire in the main public room, a wonderful smell of food and a bar where a crowd of people were cheerily imbibing a wide range of alcoholic drinks that included wine, cider and cognac. She and Felix were ushered up to small but adequate rooms on the floor above – the squat and swarthy boy who took them up actually carried their bags – and they had paused only briefly before hurrying back down for, first, a drink, and second, a large meal of four courses that began with vegetable soup served with chunks of fresh bread and pats of golden butter, went on to fish and then pork with fried potatoes and cabbage and ended with a strange dessert called a *kouign-amann* that appeared to be a multilayered dough pudding rich with butter and caramelized sugar.

It was hardly surprising, Lily thinks now, that it had been an almost sensual delight to take her corset off.

Presently she stands up, dries her feet and, going over to the washstand, pours out another bowl of water. Standing in a second, shallower bowl, she has an all-over wash. Then, dry and clean, a smell of lavender permeating the air from an unknown source, she gets into bed.

It had been her intention to review the events of the day and start to think how she and Felix could best proceed with the investigation in the morning. But it is very quiet – people in the village seem not to keep late hours – and there is a sweet smell of the country night coming in through the partly-open window. She plumps up her pillow, releasing another gentle waft of lavender. Outside an owl hoots, long and low, and is answered by a second. There is the yelping scream of a vixen from somewhere in the thick forest that encloses the little town.

In moments she is asleep.

She dreams of a pale, plump face with intense dark eyes set amid fleshy pouches. She hears a great howl, sparking fear and anxiety so that, even deeply asleep, she emits a soft cry of distress. The deep, sombre note of a huge bell rings out, as if for a funeral. Or an alarm.

She wakes to pale early light and thin ribbons of mist creeping in through the window. Her dreams are still vivid in her mind; they bring back in unpleasantly sharp detail a person, a place[1], and madness, watchful but unseen, abroad in the night.

Briskly she shakes the dreams away. She has a quick wash – someone has left a jug of water outside her door – and dresses for the day. She has the strong sense that she and Felix will be moving on today, and packs her leather satchel ready for a swift departure. As she hurries down the stairs, she notices with relief that her knee no longer hurts.

Felix is already seated at the table where they ate last night. 'Good morning,' he greets her. 'I have ordered coffee and *baguettes*.'

'Good morning.' She glances over to the door that leads to the kitchen. She can smell the coffee, and the delicious aroma of warm bread.

Turning back, she sees that Felix is leaning across the table towards her. 'Did you hear it?' he whispers.

'Hear what?' The response is automatic; she fears she already knows what he is referring to.

'The abbey bell started tolling, at about three o'clock this morning.'

So it had been real, not a dream memory . . .

'I did,' she whispers back. Then, in a rush: 'I thought it was part of a dream. I was back at Shardlowes,' she admits with an unconvincing little laugh, 'and the bloodhounds were baying.'

'I didn't hear any baying,' he says reassuringly. 'But in other respects, your dream was pretty accurate.'

He waits while she thinks it through.

'Something happened at the asylum? Where Wilberforce Chibb is a patient?' she asks very quietly. There are other people at the breakfast tables, although nobody is very close.

Felix nods. 'I imagine the bell in the night is the accepted signal for an emergency.'

[1] see The Outcast Girls

And, God knows, she thinks, they have had one of those in the very recent past. She hears Phyllida Westwood's voice: *A great cry. A pool of blood. Found at the foot of the stairs with his throat cut. Blood all over the sleeve of his nightshirt.*

'Do you think there has been another attack?' She is almost mouthing the words, so softly is she speaking.

Felix shrugs. 'Possibly. It could be the signal for summoning help, although I would have thought they would be fully equipped to deal with – er . . . to deal with such disturbances.'

Lily senses someone behind her, and with a cheerful *bonjour* a young woman unloads a tray of jugs, cups, plates and food on to their table. Now she understands Felix's sudden change into less emotive language and, while it is highly unlikely the serving girl would understand English, it's better to err on the cautious side.

'There is, of course,' she says as she pours out steaming black coffee and hot milk into their two large green cups, 'another possibility.'

And as she meets his light hazel eyes, she is sure he can see it as clearly as she can.

Half an hour later, they have left their bags behind the reception desk and settled the bill. 'Best, I think,' Lily says as, hatted and coated for the morning is chill and the mist is still obscuring the sun, they set out from the Relais, 'if, here in the village, we do not display overt interest in the asylum and whatever is going on there.'

'Agreed,' he says promptly.

'You said that this is a place of pilgrimage?'

'Yes. There's an old abbey down beside the lake,' – he points through an archway opposite, down a little street lined with terraces of houses and a few shops – 'and a grotto in the woods where services of thanks are held. For people who have been healed by the intercession of the saints and the Blessed Virgin.'

'I see.' She refrains from further comment. She and Felix have hitherto kept their spiritual beliefs to themselves, and she has no desire to disturb that sensible reticence. 'We can

therefore pose as visitors to the abbey and this grotto without
arousing suspicion?'

'I imagine so,' he agrees.

She stops suddenly, and he walks on a couple of paces
before he realizes. 'What is it?' he asks.

She smiles sheepishly. 'I don't know precisely where the
asylum is,' she admits. 'Miss Westwood merely said Paimpont.
And if we are to be discreet, we can hardly ask someone.'

'No.' He frowns. 'Well, it doesn't seem to be a very large
place. Let's act like the itinerant English people pursuing an
interest in old abbeys and grottos that we're pretending to be
and start wandering around.'

In the absence of a better plan, she agrees.

They set off under the arch and along the narrow street. At
its far end it opens into a wide square, and the abbey is before
them to their right. Beyond it is a lake: wide, dark khaki-green,
bordered on its further shores by thick forest. It ought to be
beautiful, Lily thinks, and it *is*, one cannot deny it; yet . . .

'Sinister, isn't it?' Felix whispers.

'Yes.' She fumbles for the word that best describes it and
mutters, 'Secretive.'

They stroll on past the long frontage of the abbey. At the
far end a low wall with trees behind it hides a steeply-sloping
bank that falls to the lake. They turn right, and presently
regain the road. Turning left, they walk over a low bridge that
marks the end of the lake. To their right, narrow streams flow
away down snaking little valleys.

At the far end of the bridge a path turns off to the left, in
among the trees. There are several people walking along it,
singly and in pairs or groups. All are smartly dressed, and one
of the women carries a pretty lace-edged parasol. Lily and
Felix follow. After perhaps half a mile, they emerge from the
shadow of the trees into a wide open space. There is a little
chapel at the far end, and an opening in the rocks soaring up
behind it on which there are numerous china plaques that all
read a variation of *merci*.

Most of the other strolling people stop here. Lily and Felix
stride on.

Back on the road, they see a sign that points off into the denser forest on the far side. The sign reads *Institut Hugues Abadie*. There are other words beneath, too small to make out until they are closer: they read *Asile d'Aliénés*.

And Felix murmurs, 'I think we've found it.'

They walk for so long down increasingly narrow and over-shadowed roads, lanes and paths that wind through the thick forest that Lily starts to think they have missed their way. Echoing the thought, Felix says suddenly, 'Perhaps it's a clever trick to mislead the curious, and the Institut Hugues Abadie is five miles in the opposite direction.'

'I really hope you're joking,' Lily replies.

Some two hundred yards further on, a small hamlet comes into view: lines of low dwellings built of reddish granite, a pond, a blacksmith's forge, a shrine with a statue of the Virgin. A track leads off to the left; checking to see that nobody is watching – the place appears strangely deserted – they take it.

More of the low houses, many with their shutters tightly fastened. A cock crows once, twice, then stops. A dog is barking in the distance. There are no human voices, no sound of birdsong. The mist is swirling along the track between the trees.

They round a corner.

And there is a large, square, forbidding building straight in front of them. It is stone-built, three storeys high and there are windows – barred and shuttered – set in the steeply-sloping slate roof. Iron railings surround it, topped with spikes. The gates are closed and a heavy chain padlocks them together. Beyond the gate there is a little hut fashioned like a sentry box. A man leans into the open doorway, and he is speaking to someone within.

Moving in step, Lily and Felix slowly creep back under the shadow of the trees. The men are now barely visible through the mist.

But in the deep silence, their muttering voices can be heard.

Lily glances at Felix, who is listening intently.

Then the uneasy quiet is abruptly broken; from somewhere

beyond the big building comes the clatter of horses' hooves, the rumble of wheels on hard ground. The men at the gates hurry to open them and push them out of the way just in time for a group of six mounted men and two vehicles, one a cart with barred windows and the other a small, closed carriage, to race through.

Lily and Felix have already moved deeper into the trees. Nevertheless, as the cortège rattles past, Lily is close enough to see the heads and the open, drooling mouths of three blood-hounds pushing their noses out with worrying eagerness through the bars of the carriage.

Quiet descends again. The gates are closing, the second man has gone and the guard is alone.

'The search party?' Felix suggests.

Lily nods. 'Yes. But who, I wonder, will they be searching for?' He shrugs. 'Do you think that carriage with the bars was a police vehicle?'

He frowns. 'It could be from the asylum. If it is the police, then it implies that this emergency is rather serious.'

Lily is thinking hard. So far, they have not declared them-selves, which gives them the protection of anonymity. But unless they find out what has happened, they will be wandering in the dark in regard to finding Wilberforce Chibb and fulfilling the task which Phyllida Westwood is paying them to do.

'We must go in,' she says firmly, making up her mind.

He looks at her. 'I believe you're right,' he says. 'Do we say who we are and state our business?'

She thinks again. 'No. We should not reveal that Miss Westwood is questioning the truth of Wilberforce's guilt. We'll say we have come on behalf of the family. I'm sure I can tell a convincing tale, for she told me plenty of details.'

He waits. She always appreciates these moments when he does not interrupt but simply waits for her to decide on the next move.

'I will tell them that I am a close friend of Miss Westwood's and that, prostrate with distress at her fiancé's incarceration, she is deeply worried that he is not being cared for properly.'

'And has sent us to check?' He sounds doubtful.

'Sent us to explain that it is not certain that he really did kill his father,' she says firmly. Sensing he is still unconvinced, she adds, 'Since that is largely the case that Miss Westwood put to me, I am sure I shall sound credible.'

Felix looks at her for a moment longer, then gives a slight shrug – which she doesn't think he meant her to see – and says, 'Let's go in, then.'

Going in is not as straightforward as simply walking through the gates. These have been barred and chained again, and now there are four men on guard. Side by side, Lily and Felix approach.

She waits as Felix addresses the older man who steps forward to hear what they have to say. She listens intently, picking up quite a few words while closely watching the guard's expression. Initially he shakes his head and barks out a long stream of words beginning with *non, non, c'est impossible*. But Felix persists, his demeanour more authoritative now, and the guard turns to confer with a couple of the others. One of them hurries up to the house, disappearing inside.

They wait.

After a surprisingly short time, the man appears again, and he has a woman with him. She is tall, broad-shouldered and carries herself very well. She is dressed in a black gown that looks like a nurse's uniform or even a nun's habit, over it a starched and immaculate apron. Her headdress, also stiffly-starched, fits closely around her firmly-boned, handsome face, fanning out behind her. She walks right up to the gates, stares at Lily and Felix for a long moment, then says: 'I am Mrs Choak. I am told you represent Wilberforce Chibb's fiancée.'

She is speaking in English, the words spoken tonelessly and carefully enunciated.

'We do,' Lily says. 'Miss Westwood urgently requires reassurance that he is being well cared for and treated for his – er, his mental confusion.'

Mrs Choak watches them for another silent eternity. Then she nods curtly to the senior guard, the gates are opened just a crack and slammed shut immediately after Lily and Felix have gone through, and Mrs Choak has already turned away and is striding back to the house.

'We will go in here.'

Mrs Choak leads the way to a small office that opens off the vast hall. She sits down behind a large desk. Lily and Felix sit down opposite. She starts to speak, but Lily forestalls her.

'We wish to speak to whoever is in charge,' she states. 'I do not wish to give offence, but I must insist that Miss Westwood's concerns are properly addressed.'

Mrs Choak rests her elbows on the arms of the chair and clasps her hands in front of her. 'The director of the Institute is unavailable. I am his senior assistant, and, as the person responsible for the foreign patients, best equipped to speak of Wilberforce Chibb.'

Once again, Lily notes the very deliberate delivery. But she must not get distracted . . . Leaning forward, she says, 'In that case, what have you to tell us?'

Mrs Choak has very dark eyes, round and slightly protuberant. She does not seem to blink; suddenly Lily realizes that the woman reminds her of a snake.

Mrs Choak draws a breath and says, 'Recently one of our patients was attacked.' According to Miss Westwood, rather more than attacked, Lily reflects, glancing at Felix. 'There are grounds for believing that it was Wilberforce Chibb who attacked him,' Mrs Choak goes on carefully, 'and the matter has been the subject of a thorough investigation.' She pauses. Lily wants to leap in and prompt her to go on, but, apparently realizing, Felix clears his throat quietly.

Lily forces herself to keep silent.

And Mrs Choak says, 'As a suspect in this regrettable incident, Wilberforce was under close guard. However, it appears that one of the guards permitted himself to be persuaded, or bribed, to assist him. During the night, some two weeks ago, somebody unlocked the door. Wilberforce has fled.'

He's gone, Lily thinks. *He's run away. Oh, goodness, what on earth do we do now?*

'*Two weeks* ago,' Felix is saying, and there is a chilly note of dismay in his tone. 'And you have not seen fit to inform the family?'

'The matter is in hand.' Mrs Choak snaps out the words, her mouth closing like a steel trap when she's finished.

'His disappearance was not the cause of last night's alarm?' Felix persists. Shooting a glance at him, Lily is impressed with his impersonation of a worried and angry family representative.

Mrs Choak looks at him sharply. 'You heard it, then. No,' she adds firmly, 'that concerned a different matter.' Before either he or Lily can comment, Mrs Choak begins on what appears to be a prepared statement. She sounds both authoritative and forceful, and as she talks, she is getting to her feet. 'The search for Wilberforce Chibb is in hand. Both the Institute's security force and the police are out hunting for him, as of course they have been since he fled. He will not have got far,' she states, with the absolute certainty of someone announcing that the year has twelve months. 'You will appreciate that finding our patient and bringing him back to the security of the Institute and the treatment that he requires must be our sole concern.' *And we have no time to waste on the likes of you and your footling questions*, seems to be the silent addition. 'Rest assured, however, that, before he decided to leave us, Wilberforce was not only well cared for but was also beginning to respond to treatment.' Now she has walked round the desk and is clearly intending to usher them out. 'I trust that these reassurances will calm Miss Westwood's fears. Perhaps you should inform her that, until the moment Wilberforce decided to flee, he could not have been in a better place. When he is once more safe within the Institute, this beneficial treatment will resume.'

Lily and Felix have also stood up. Since there is little choice but to obey the very obvious dismissal, they go out into the hall, and then suffer Mrs Choak to escort them back to the gates.

The sound of the chain clanking against the iron gates and the heavy click of the padlock is still echoing in the gloomy shadows under the trees as they head off down the track.

'Do you think they'll catch him?' Lily says. She tries to sound business-like and unsentimental, but she knows she hasn't been very successful. 'That search party we saw flying through the gates seemed very threatening and efficient.'

'It did,' he agrees. 'But if Wilberforce escaped two weeks ago, would they still be hunting for him so urgently? More likely they were after whoever caused last night's alarm.'

'Hmm.' Lily isn't convinced. Then she says, 'If Wilberforce thinks he's about to be tried and hanged for murder, you can see why he'd flee.'

'I think it's the guillotine in France,' Felix replies. 'And executions are carried out at three o'clock in the afternoon.'

She contemplates that chilling fact. Before distress can cloud her thoughts, she forces herself to be practical and says, 'If Wilberforce has any sense, he'll be miles away by now, and we have absolutely no idea where he's gone.'

Felix takes her arm, and together they walk back towards the village. 'Absolutely no idea *now*,' he concedes.

She waits. When he does not go on, she says impatiently, 'And? Are we going to wait for divine inspiration, or have you something more down to earth in mind?'

He releases her arm, and they increase their pace. 'We have learned little from the tight-lipped Mrs Choak except that Wilberforce escaped two weeks ago and she confidently expects him to be found and brought back any moment,' he says. 'Which is no more than you'd expect since it's undoubtedly the Institute's policy to reveal as little as possible about what goes on within its high walls and locked gates. I doubt, however, that its secrets are as closely guarded as its doctors, attendants and management would wish. We—'

But she has picked up what he means. 'They probably employ local people,' she puts in, 'not in medical roles, but as orderlies, cleaners and groundsmen, and in addition there will be regular deliveries of supplies.'

'Yes,' he says, 'and—'

She interrupts him with an exclamation. 'I've just thought of something else we need to know!' She clicks her tongue in exasperation. 'I should have asked Mrs Choak, although she probably wouldn't have told us . . .'

'Asked what?' he prompts.

She looks up at him. 'The mystery man. The *dead* man,' she whispers. 'Did you notice that Mrs Choak only said he'd been attacked, and nothing about him being found in a pool of blood?'

'I did,' Felix says.

'We already know quite a lot about him . . .' She is trying to recall Miss Westwood's description. 'He wasn't mentally ill, but he was certainly suffering from some physical afflic-tion. He might have been English or Prussian, and the rumour-mongers thought he was a high-ranking military man or a politician or—'

'Or royalty,' Felix finishes softly. 'That's what you said.' Then, eagerly, he goes on, 'You also told me Miss Westwood said the asylum was alive with whispered rumours, so surely all we have to do is ask a few discreet questions. Undoubtedly, they'll all be in the habit of gossiping, even when there haven't been thrilling and alarming occurrences such as murders and escapes. And, with Paimpont the only settlement where these orderlies, cleaners and groundsmen could come from, a little discreet and well-judged questioning of quick-witted locals may well provide the clues we so urgently need.'

The Relais is humming with people. Many are dressed in the hard-wearing garb of labourers, although there is also a group of five smartly-dressed men and women, some of whom Lily recognizes from the little chapel beside the lake. There is also a party of priests, who, Lily observes, seem to be making more noise than the rest. It is midday, and food is already being served; Lily is surprised to see that most of the diners (including – especially – the priests) are accom-panying the plates of hearty beef stew with large glasses of red wine. Hoping that the alcohol will make everyone conven-iently loose-tongued, Lily takes her food to a long table where a group of three men and four women are leaning towards each other and deep in what seems to be a very absorbing discussion. Felix is beside her. 'Don't sit down just yet,' he whispers, 'let me see if I can hear what they're talking about and if it concerns us.'

She nods curtly, trying not to let her impatience show. He leans down, pretending to check to see if there is room for two. He listens for a few moments, then turns to Lily. 'This man in front of us is saying something about it being a scandal for a dangerous killer to be still on the loose after a fortnight,' he whispers, 'and the authorities need to increase their efforts and catch him before they all get murdered in their beds.'

'Tell him we want to sit down!' she hisses back.

He nods, asks a polite question of the man, and as he shifts along, Felix and Lily take their seats.

The meal seems to go on forever. Lily, trying desperately to work out whether the intense discussion actually has any relevance to their search, meets with little success. Whoever prepared the list of useful French phrases in Marm's Bradshaw's Guide clearly had not envisaged a traveller trying to find out about a violent murder in an asylum and a runaway killer who has fled a scene of bloody violence.

Felix is half turned away from her. She can tell by the tension in his broad shoulders that he is listening intently, and she knows better than to distract him. More food is served: a big platter of cheese, plates of a sweet and solid batter pudding stuffed with prunes, tiny cups of coffee. By now Felix has joined in the fast-flowing talk, and a woman sitting opposite has held forth for some minutes about *le mystérieux inconnu*, all the time with a large spoonful of pudding poised a few inches from her mouth.

Finally the group get up and leave.

Felix lets them disperse, then takes Lily's arm and says, 'We'll go outside and find somewhere we won't be overheard.'

She very much hopes the excitement glittering in his eyes signifies that he's made some useful discoveries.

It does.

They follow a little track branching off behind the Relais, which leads through a narrow belt of trees to a field. Felix stops beside the gate, checks to see nobody is about, and says, 'We were right, they were talking about nothing else.'

'I heard that woman talking about the dead mystery man,' Lily says, unable to restrain her impatience. 'What did she say?'

'He was quite poorly and had to spend regular spells in bed,' Felix replies. 'She said – and they all agreed – that he was young to be so feeble, because even when he was up and about, he had a big fellow who used to look after him.'

'And was he English?'

'They didn't agree. He spoke both English and a little French and also German. And the pool of blood in which he was found was no exaggeration, apparently. It sounds as if he'd tried to fend off his attacker with his bare hands, because there were slashes across his palms and forearms which must have been viciously deep because they bled profusely too, as well as the fatal cut to the throat.'

After a short pause she says, 'What else? Who do they think killed him?'

'They said the murderer is foreign, he's extremely dangerous, he killed an Egyptian princess and his own father, who was an English lord, and he cut the mystery man's throat with a scythe. Or maybe a saw – the man speaking used the word *scie*, and I'm not sure how to translate—'

'Frederick Chibb wasn't a lord,' Lily interrupts, 'and the girl in the market, who Wilberforce didn't actually kill, incidentally, wasn't a princess. But—'

'But the details are far too close for it to have been anyone else,' Felix supplies. 'They all seemed to think that Wilberforce was responsible, although nobody said why, and I wondered if it could be because that was the Institute's official view. Then I heard one of the men say he'd heard from his *beau-frère* who's a cleaner at the asylum – that's brother-in-law – that the murderer was an artist.'

'Yes, we *know* that,' she begins impatiently.

'Wait! The brother-in-law reported that Wilberforce kept turning out really strange and disturbing paintings, the same subject over and over again. And that's not the best of it,' he hurries on, not giving her a chance to ask why the paintings are so disturbing, 'because apparently he – Wilberforce – has friends who are concerned about him, and recently one of

them came all the way from somewhere called Pont-Aven to
see how he was.'

'Pont-Aven! *Yes!*' Lily exclaims. 'Miss Westwood said
Wilberforce had friends there. He'd been staying with them
after he fled from England – I'm sure I told you – and they
didn't mind at first, only then he threatened some local
tradesman with violence and they all got scared and
Wilberforce ended up in a police cell in Quimper.'

'I remember,' Felix says. 'Then his uncle, this Bowler
fellow, came to fetch him and deposited him in the Institut
Hugues Abadie.'

'It sounds as if the Pont-Aven friends were stricken with a
collective bout of conscience,' Lily observes, 'which, since
their panic at the attack on the tradesman resulted in poor
Wilberforce being shut away in an asylum in one of the
remotest regions of Brittany, is hardly surprising and—'

She stops suddenly as a thought strikes her. Looking at
Felix, she says, 'I bet that's where he's gone! If he knew one
of them came enquiring after him, he might have thought it
meant they were regretting having been so hasty, and he'd—'

'He'd conclude that they might welcome him and hide him
if he went back!' Felix finishes.

She frowns. 'Do *you* think they would?'

'No,' he says bluntly. 'If we're right to assume they're
English, like Wilberforce, then I very much doubt they'd hide
a runaway murderer who has escaped from an asylum. For
one thing, it'd be the first place his pursuers would look – who
else does Wilberforce know in the area? – and for another, as
foreigners they're highly unlikely to risk getting into trouble
with the French authorities. They'd be breaking the law in
sheltering an escaped murderer,' he goes on in case she hasn't
understood, 'and—'

She waves an impatient hand. 'Yes, yes, I know.' She is
thinking; going back to something Felix said just now.

'What is it?' he asks eventually.

'You said the man with the brother-in-law who's a cleaner
mentioned disturbing paintings?'

'Yes.'

'Why were they disturbing?'

Felix doesn't reply straight away. She senses he is reluctant, as if he too has been affected by the strangeness.

Then he said, 'Wilberforce Chibb paints cats. Cats' heads, with grey or black or brindled fur, long whiskers and unnatural smiles on their faces.'

'That doesn't sound all that odd,' she says, 'animal paintings are very popular, I understand, and people love a portrait of their pet, and probably pay extravagantly for the privilege.'

'I don't think any such practical or financial considerations are behind Wilberforce's choice of subject matter,' Felix mutters. Then, turning to stare at her, he says, 'Whether grey, black or striped, Wilberforce's cats have one common feature: they all stare out of the canvas with strange and disconcerting human eyes.'

SIX

As they walk back towards the Relais, the sound of loud and cheery voices floats out to greet them through the thinning trees. Emerging on to the road, they see a group of half a dozen men all clad in black. 'The priests!' Lily whispers, pointing to the men in black. 'They were eating at the Relais earlier.'

He nods, grinning. 'Sounds as if they enjoyed it. They'll have been visiting the abbey, or that grotto out by the lake,' he adds.

'How can you know—' She stops. 'Yes. The pilgrimages. Do you think they—' she begins, but he doesn't hear the rest because he has marched over to one of the priests and is talking to him. In English, she notes with surprise. She hurries after him.

The priest is a large man in late middle age, with a bald head, a ready smile and a clear blue-eyed glance that turns to Lily as she approaches. Sensing her beside him, Felix says, 'Lily dear, this is Father Michael. Father, may I present my sister, Miss Lily Wilbraham?'

The priest turns and says, 'Delighted to meet you, Miss Wilbraham, and to encounter some of my own countrymen in this distant place!'

Lily detects the accent of the north-east. 'You're a Northumbrian, Father!' she says. And he bows. And then she realizes what Felix has just said.

Felix says, 'I was asking the Father if he could suggest how we might journey on to our next destination on our exciting itinerary, and he said he and his companions are returning to Lorient and they will have room on the *char-à-banc* for us. Isn't that splendid?' he adds encouragingly when she doesn't immediately reply.

He has half turned away from the priest, and he is looking at her with particular intensity. Her mind working rapidly, she understands that they are posing as brother and sister, they are on a tour of Brittany, and Felix hasn't divulged to Father Michael precisely where they are going next. Fighting the innocent reaction that surely you can trust a priest and couldn't they tell him the truth, she arranges her face into a suitable expression, turns to Father Michael and says, 'That is *most* kind, Father! I confess we were slightly at a loss as to how we should proceed, and here you are coming to our rescue!'

'It will be a pleasure to have your company, Miss Wilbraham,' Father Michael says gallantly. 'Now, let me introduce you to your travelling companions.'

He has got as far as Father Connor from Liverpool, Father Eric from London, Père Loïc and Père Hervé, who are Frenchmen, when there is the sound of hooves and iron-shod wheels. Leaving the last priest unnamed and looking slightly annoyed, Father Michael leaps out into the road waving his arms just as a team of horses appears round the corner, a high wooden vehicle bouncing along behind.

'*Ici! Nous sommes ici!*' Father Michael calls to the driver, adding, surely unnecessarily, '*Nous sommes les prêtres, et nous allons à Lorient!*'

Even Lily can tell that his French accent is appalling.

Felix disguises his dismay at the sight of the *char-à-banc*. It is a large conveyance with a seat for the coachman at the front and an open space at the rear lined either side by two long benches, each provided with a rudimentary back rest. It is uncovered, and Felix has learned from recent experience that the tracks and roads of rural France are always either very muddy or very dusty. Lily, so smart in her navy blue London clothes and, as he knows, fastidious about her appearance and determined at all times to look professional, is going to suffer, whatever the weather does. For now the day is fine, and he hopes it will stay that way; apart from any other considerations, mud always makes for slow going, and they have a long journey ahead.

He watches as the priests politely stand back to allow her to be first to climb the flight of steps at the rear of the vehicle.

It is short but vertical and the treads are narrow, and she accepts
Felix's steadying hand under her elbow with a tight little smile.
She sits down at the far end of the bench on the left, and he
settles beside her. They tuck their bags under their legs.

In the flurry of activity as their six companions find a place
and sit down – there is quite a lot of lively discussion over
who sits where – she takes the chance to say quietly to him,
'How far is Lorient from Pont-Aven?'

'Only about twenty miles or so,' he murmurs.

'*Only* twenty miles!' she echoes.

He guesses she's thinking that if twenty miles is a short
distance, then how far can it be from here to Lorient?

Sure enough, she asks him.

'Sixty miles, Father Michael says,' he replies.

And the dismay in her face strongly suggests she's not too
happy at the prospect of sixty miles on a hard wooden bench
on top of an unsprung wooden cart.

'Don't worry,' he says, trying to cheer her up, 'we're not
going all the way today. We'll be stopping at a jolly wayside
inn especially designed to cater for the needs of weary and
hungry travellers.'

'Weary, hungry travellers with very sore bottoms.' She
speaks very quietly, but he still hears.

The rural roads are rudimentary, clearly designed mainly for
local farm traffic. Quite frequently the *char-à-banc* has to
pull to the side of the track to allow some monstrous agricul-
tural vehicle lumbering along behind a team of oxen to go by.
The weather does indeed stay fine, and the afternoon sun has
some heat in it, although there is, as Felix had feared, a lot
of dust. Presently he reaches down into his bag and extracts
a large square of silk with a swirling pattern of blues and
greens; it is something called a *foulard*, and, encouraged by
a decidedly tipsy Henri-Josef (well, to be honest he'd been
tipsy too), he bought it in a fit of whimsy in a very expensive
shop off the Rue Saint-Honoré. Lily eyes it with the suspicion
he might have expected from a down-to-earth Englishwoman,
but nevertheless she accepts it with a brief thank you and ties
it over her hat, pulling the edges forward to shield her face.

Felix looks at their fellow passengers. The dark garments of the priests are already covered in pale dust, as if they have been sprinkled with a liberal coating of flour. The bench seat feels harder by the mile, and his muscles are becoming sore from tensing himself against the sudden lurches as one of the vehicle's wheels jolts down hard into a pothole. Lily's tense expression suggests she is finding the journey equally uncomfortable.

Observing her reaction after a particularly violent jolt, one of the French priests leans towards her and says, '*Pouf! Les nids de poules, eh?*' laughing as if being thrown around on an unyielding bench with nothing to hold on to is quite hilarious.

She gives him a polite smile, then as he turns back to his neighbour, whispers to Felix, 'Why on earth is he talking about hens? I thought *poule* meant chicken?'

He murmurs back, 'Hens' nests. That's what they call potholes.'

And she murmurs back, 'I wonder why I didn't think of that?'

Taking advantage of a moment when all six priests are deeply engaged in a discussion that seems to be about arrangements for some feast day – the fast chatter is mostly in French – Lily leans close to Felix and says, 'What did you think of Mrs Choak?'

'Typical employee of a place like the Institute,' he replies. Strangely, he's just been thinking about the woman at the Institute too. 'Highly protective of whatever activities go on behind those walls, and so discreet that she gave nothing away we couldn't have found out for ourselves.'

'Quite,' Lily replies. 'She was wearing the uniform of a matron and she claimed to be the director's senior assistant, which explains why those gate guards were so wary of her. Was she English?'

'I was wondering that,' he agrees. 'Her English was almost too perfect, as if she was trying too hard.'

'Did you pick up any hint of a different mother tongue?' Lily asks.

He frowns, and after a pause says, 'I thought perhaps she might be German.'

They travel on. Despite the discomforts and the depressing fact that there is a great deal of this journey still ahead, nevertheless Felix is surprised to find that he's enjoying it. The countryside is beautiful. Fields, woods, low hills and green valleys spread out endlessly all around, and regularly they pass through villages, hamlets and isolated farms, the latter usually advertised well in advance by the smell of pig dung. Or cow dung. Or both. They stop a few times for the horses to take on water, and there is a longer stop at a place called Josselin where a fresh team is attached. They have drawn up outside an old stone inn, and a large and square-shaped woman emerges with a huge tray on which are small glasses of wine and chunks of bread. Felix thanks her, enjoying his new confidence in speaking French and adding a pleasant remark about the weather. The woman responds with a hard stare, her expression unchanging.

He has already observed that the Bretons are a taciturn race.

The priests, however, are the complete opposite. Their presence provides another of the journey's pleasures, for they are generally cheerful, chatty and given to breaking out into song now and again. Some of these are English folk songs, and Felix is amused by Lily's look of surprise at the robust earthiness of some of the lyrics.

'I don't think that verse features in the original,' she says disapprovingly to Felix at one point. He doesn't think so either, grinning as the words *she lifted up her apron and I saw her little . . .* prompt a great chortle of delight from Father Connor, who clearly knows exactly what was under the apron.

'It depends which version you're familiar with,' Felix says. He smiles at her. 'I don't imagine they sing like this in the course of their usual lives,' he adds. 'But they're on holiday, and nobody's listening.'

The overnight accommodation is considerably better than Felix had feared. He hurries ahead into the inn and manages to acquire a very small room for Lily. It has a narrow bed and a minute window, but it has a wash hand stand and a jug of hot water and she has it to herself. It is, however, the only single room available; Felix will have to sleep in a sort of dormitory with the priests and whoever else of the male sex is putting up overnight. He resigns himself to a restless night, for without a doubt at least one of his room-mates will snore.

They are served a hearty evening meal in a large public room that has a blazing fire at one end. They sit on forms either side of a long oak table dark with age and pitted with ruts, cracks and deep scratches, some of which seem to contain an interesting residue from decades, if not centuries, of past meals.

'Mrs Clapper would shudder in horror and hurry to fetch a scrubbing brush and a pail of hot, soapy water,' Lily remarks.

He glances at her, concerned. He's about to ask if the robust attitude to hygiene is going to put her off her food, but then, noticing that she is busy devouring everything that is put before her and happily eating her bread straight off the ancient table just like everyone else does, he doesn't bother.

As later he settles down to sleep, pleased to be lying between stiffly-starched sheets that smell intriguingly of both lavender and garlic, he thinks about Lily. This is all new to her, he reflects, and at times he can almost hear the thoughts racing through her head as she studies and absorbs life in this deeply rural society, so different from the endless onslaught of London's bustle. Her disapproval was so evident at first, but already she is adapting.

Which is just as well, he thinks, as they still have a long way to go.

The next morning they are on the road early. The countryside is changing, Felix notices, pointing out to Lily that there appear to be more settlements today, some of them large enough to qualify as towns. The roads are better, their speed is faster and the horses are changed more frequently.

'We're making good time,' Father Eric from London observes. He is sitting opposite Felix and Lily today. 'We'll be in Lorient in fine time,' he adds.

Lily responds with a nod and a smile.

'And where are you and your brother bound next?' the priest goes on.

Lily shoots Felix a glance, and, as clearly as if she'd spoken aloud, he hears the words: *I have absolutely no idea how to answer him, so you'll have to.*

She has obviously decided that it would be wise not to mention their true destination of Pont-Aven, and, thinking quickly, he says, 'My sister and I are fascinated by the local archaeology. It is our intention to travel on to Carnac, and then—'

One of the French priests – it is Père Loïc – has been listening, and on hearing the word Carnac he leans over and interrupts, pouring out a long stream of rapid French that appears to be a list of places they must see. Felix frowns as he tries to understand; Père Loïc has a very strong accent, and now that he has got into his stride, shows no sign of stopping and apparently doesn't feel the need to draw breath. When finally the torrent of words stops briefly – Père Loïc is clicking his fingers impatiently as he tries to remember yet another place that he insists they visit – Felix grabs his chance, and, turning to face Lily, says firmly, 'Père Loïc has given us such a lot of information! Isn't that kind of him?' and, picking up her cue, she replies that it is and immediately goes on to discuss where they think they should go first.

Once Père Loïc has safely turned his attention to his neighbour, Felix says softly, nodding towards the priest, 'He seems to be a local man, and very proud of his region's history.'

'Evidently,' she replies.

He grins. 'He says we must not miss the Gavrinis, whatever they are, and to allow a full day for the stones at Carnac.'

'Shame we're going to Pont-Aven, then,' she whispers.

'I picked up some useful information when I was talking to Père Hervé,' he says. She raises her eyebrows enquiringly. 'There's a train service from Lorient to Quimper, and there's a stop on the way that's only a few miles from Pont-Aven.'

'Hmm,' she says doubtfully. Then: 'Won't the Father wonder why you asked about trains to Quimper when we've told Père Loïc that we're going to Carnac?'

'We'll just have to hope they don't compare notes,' Felix

replies, more confidently than he feels. Then, sensing she is unconvinced, adds, 'Come on, Lily! I've solved our next dilemma even before we've come to it! By train most of the way, and we'll find horses to take us the rest.' He nudges her and adds, 'Didn't you have a useful phrase about wanting to hire a saddle horse who's had a good feed of hay?'

She suppresses a chuckle. 'Oats,' she says.

'Oats?'

'It was oats, not hay.'

It is mid-afternoon by the time they are bidding farewell to their travelling companions in Lorient. At Lily's prompting, Felix offers to pay a contribution towards the cost of the *char-à-banc* hire, but the priests all say no need, they were travelling anyway and it was a pleasure to have some fresh company.

As soon as Lily and Felix have rounded the corner and are out of sight, Felix asks the proprietor of a pavement café for directions. Shortly afterwards, they are hurrying into the railway station and Felix is enquiring about the next train to Quimper.

As they sit opposite each other on the train – more very hard wooden seats – Felix senses that Lily has something on her mind. He waits, but when she does not speak – she has her head bent over the Bradshaw's – he says, 'Are you all right?'

'Yes! No,' she replies. Then, the words pouring out, she says, 'Felix, what if Wilberforce Chibb really did murder his father? Even Miss Westwood would not say for certain that he was innocent! She *believed* him to be because she loves him, but she also said that she would not marry him if we discover he's guilty, which surely tells us that she at least thinks he might be. And if he killed his father,' she rushes on before he can comment, 'then perhaps he murdered the mysterious foreigner at the Institute too, and—'

'And here we are rushing across north-west France as fast as we can to confront him,' he finishes. 'Yes. I admit, I do wish we had an independent opinion on the likelihood of his guilt.'

'Both the Institute and the police are hunting for him,' she whispers. 'With a closed, barred carriage and bloodhounds.'

And some of the men in the search party were armed, Felix recalls. 'You accepted the job,' he says, careful not to sound critical. 'I'm sure you considered the possible danger, yet still you—'

'I felt so sorry for him!' she says in a suppressed wail. 'Miss Westwood's account left much in doubt: his father's fatal fall down the stairs was just as likely to have been because *he* attacked Wilberforce, who understandably fought back, and the evidence for saying he killed the man at the Institute seems *extremely* dubious.'

'I think,' he says after quite a long pause for reflection, 'that we have no choice but to go on. For one thing, you have accepted the case, and, I imagine, Miss Westwood's advance payment.'

'Yes.' She nods.

'For another, I agree with you that Wilberforce Chibb's guilt is by no means certain. I reckon that, if he is captured and charged with murder here in France, it will be very hard for him to prove his innocence. If he is innocent,' he adds. 'I believe,' he concludes, 'that we ought to hear *his* version of everything that's happened.'

'What if he's dangerous?' she whispers. 'What if he has another of his fits of madness, and comes flying at us as he did with the young woman in the Egyptian market?'

'Again, we need to ask Wilberforce why he did that,' Felix says.

And, her face lighting up, Lily says, 'Yes! Yes, you're right, because I remember now, Phyllida Westwood said he'd had sunstroke, and that he claimed he was trying to save the girl and get her out of the sun because it was going to shrivel her up and she'd be devoured by a red crow!'

'Good grief,' Felix mutters. Then, seeing from Lily's face that this is not the most compassionate of reactions, adds, 'It sounds as if he needs understanding and help, not a prison cell and a trial in a foreign land. We'll find him, and we'll try to help him.'

'And if he becomes angry and attacks us?'

'Then I'll put you safely behind me and fend him off with my bare hands,' he says flippantly, trying to lighten the mood.

She is looking at him intently, unsmiling, her expression unchanged and he doesn't think she's taken in what he said. He's just thinking it's probably just as well when to his surprise she reaches down and raises the generous folds of her voluminous blue skirt and the assorted underskirts. She extends her left leg, clad in a sturdy boot that comes up over her calf, and says very quietly, 'I can always lend you my knife.'

And from a sheath sewn inside the boot she draws out a long, thin boning knife with a brass handle bound in red leather.

Not knowing if he is more alarmed by Lily's concealed weapon or the suddenly-revealed lower leg – admittedly clad in a decidedly unfeminine boot – he leans forward and says, 'I think you'd better hide that.'

Meeting her eyes – *now* she's smiling – it strikes him that neither of them know if he's referring to her knife or her leg.

As he is watching Lily rearrange her skirts, Felix is suddenly aware that the train is accelerating. And, indeed, that it has just been stationary. With growing dismay, he leaps up and looks out at the station receding behind them. And at a small enamel sign that says *Quimperlé*. Sitting down again, he announces to Lily that they have just missed their stop.

She is clearly very angry, but, he observes, fair-minded enough to realize that the error is as much her fault as his. All the same, when she asks how far the next stop is, and how much further it will be from Pont-Aven, he can see she is trying very hard not to shout at him.

'I don't know,' he admits. 'I only asked which was the closest station to where we're going. I didn't bother with where the train goes next. But I imagine it'll be Quimper.'

She already has her Bradshaw's open at the right page. 'Yes, you're right,' she says. She looks up and meets his eyes. He shrugs.

They sit in an uneasy silence for ten minutes or so. Then the train starts to slow down. And goes on slowing down. Leaping up, Lily says excitedly, 'We're stopping!'

He goes to stand beside her. The train has virtually stopped, and a long hose is being extended from a metal arm towards the engine.

Lily is bending down, picking up their bags. Shoving one under her arm, she opens the door and says, 'Come on!'

'We're in the middle of nowhere!' he protests.

She is urging him forward. 'But I know where we are, I've studied the map. Pont-Aven's situated at the mouth of a river, and there's a river over there, we've just gone over it on that bridge!' She waves her arm back down the track. 'Oh, come *on*, Felix, you've got to go first because it's quite a long drop and you're much taller than me!'

He can appreciate her logic. With the definite sense of throwing wisdom and caution out of the window, he lowers himself down through the door and on to the ground, reaching up his arms first for the bags and then for Lily. Then he slams the door and they hurry away from the train.

They find a narrow lane that runs along beside the track and follow it back to the river. They clamber up on to the bridge and turn in the direction the water is flowing.

He is still almost sure they've made a big mistake.

But they haven't. The river is steadily growing wider, they start to see isolated houses and clusters of cottages beside the road, and less than half an hour after they have left the train, they are walking into Pont-Aven.

The water is right beside them, loud now as it flows swiftly towards the sea. There are long rows of houses either side of the street, stone-walled and slate-roofed. Fires have been lit against the encroaching chill of night, lamps glow behind small shuttered and curtained windows, delicious smells of cooking creep out of warm, cosy homes.

Presently the river widens. Its bed is littered with rocks and large boulders, and the sound of rushing water is loud in the evening quiet. There is a mill on the far bank, and on this side, they round a gentle corner and find a square opening up before them. Unlike the outskirts of the little town, the square is lively with activity, there are several places advertising themselves as *crêperies* and more than one sign saying *Hôtel*.

'I hadn't expected it to be so busy,' Felix says in surprise.

Lily is forging ahead, marching in the direction of a modest but homely-looking *pension* at the far corner of the square, and he hurries to catch up. 'It's an artists' colony,' she says. 'They started coming here about twenty years ago because the light was good and it was much cheaper than Paris.' Felix is about to protest that this sort of busy commercial activity doesn't fit with the image of struggling, half-starved artists when she goes on, 'But then the railway from Paris was extended to Quimperlé, which as we both know is quite close,' – she shoots him a vaguely accusatory look, which he thinks is unfair because it really was as much her fault that they missed their stop – 'and that made the journey much easier. Some landscape painter exhibited a painting of Pont-Aven at the Paris salon in 1864 and then American artists started coming, after which the colony really began to thrive.'

He grins at her. 'Bradshaw's?'

She smiles back, nodding. Then, pointing towards the window of the *pension*, says, 'What does it look like inside?'

He understands why she has asked. The lower half of the window has a stiffly-starched, thick lace curtain hanging on a narrow brass rod, and she isn't tall enough to see over it. Stretching up, he looks inside at a large room with white-painted stone walls and ancient heavy beams, a high desk at one end that seems to serve as the *pension*'s reception, some tables covered in blue and white gingham cloths, several benches and a quantity of chairs. One end of the room is formed by a wide fireplace, the hearth set up on a stone platform some two or three feet high. The fire is alight, the flames dance cheerfully and Felix reckons he has seen enough.

'It looks fine,' he says. And, opening the door, steps aside to let her go ahead.

By the time they have been shown into two pleasantly-appointed rooms, dumped their bags and been talked at for some time by the *pension*'s large and enthusiastic proprietor – a squat and powerfully-built man who resembles a square box on rather short legs – it is getting on for eight o'clock. Felix has managed to inform the proprietor that he and Lily need to find something to eat – the man has already informed them the *pension* does not do evening meals – and he tells them they must hurry up, hurry up ('*Dépêchez-vous! Dépêchez-vous!*') because the cafés and restaurants will soon be closing. Which, as Felix remarks to Lily, is ironic considering it is he who has been holding them up.

They find a *crêperie* that still has half a dozen occupied tables, and a waiter shows them to an empty one by the window. Observing what other people are eating, Felix suggests a savoury buckwheat galette followed by a sweet crêpe, accompanied by a jug of cider. Lily, he observes, looks dubious.

'It smells good,' he says reassuringly, 'and they're all enjoying it.' He nods towards the nearest table, whose jolly and flushed occupants have clearly put away at least one carafe of cider.

She smiles at him. 'I'm so hungry I could eat almost anything,' she replies.

But when their *galettes* arrive very shortly afterwards, only a couple of bites serve to inform her that what's on offer tastes as good as it smells.

They have cleared their plates and are finishing off the cider – drunk out of coarse earthenware bowls that are apparently called *bollées* – when she leans close to him and whispers, 'The six men at the table in the corner are speaking English. One of them sounds American, but I think the others are English.'

He nods. As the restaurant has gradually emptied and the noise level has gone down, he too has been listening to the men in the corner. 'They've been talking about someone who's doing a painting of the port,' he begins, 'and—'

But just then one of the men – short, lightly built, fine brown hair and narrow dark eyes – abruptly pushes back his chair, puts a handful of grubby franc notes on the table, crams a soft, wide-brimmed black hat on his head and hurries out of the *crêperie*, pulling the door shut with such violence that the little bell jingles wildly and the lace curtains flap like sails.

'What's the matter with Howard?' one of the others enquires, gazing at the still-trembling bell. 'He's hardly said a word all evening.'

'God knows,' says another voice; it sounds like the American. 'He's left more than his share of the bill, so who cares?'

Another man starts to say something about their companion having been preoccupied and withdrawn for some time, but then the American mutters something under his breath that makes all the men break out into loud guffaws of laughter, and one of them, still chuckling, says, 'D'you think they'll bring us another jug of cider if we ask really nicely?'

Lily leans close again and, her expression intent, opens her mouth to say something, but Felix is already pulling out his wallet. He looks at the bill, folds several notes inside it and stands up. 'I agree, we should go after him,' he says.

And, both of them smiling at this evidence that they have been thinking the same thing, they get up and unobtrusively ease their way out of the *crêperie*.

'Of course,' she pants as she hurries along beside him, 'there are all manner of reasons for this Howard person to be preoccupied.'

Felix has caught sight of the slim man in the hat, walking away up the path that runs beside the river. Grabbing Lily's arm, he increases their pace. Many of the lamps have been extinguished now, and the moonlight is intermittently cut off by clouds. 'I know,' he says, 'but we have to start somewhere. And, like most of those men, Howard is English, like Wilberforce, so surely, it's possible that he or one of the others knows him, or at least knows *of* him?'

She seems to accept this.

The man in the hat suddenly darts down an alley leading off to the right. Lily disengages her arm and says urgently, 'You're faster than me, go on, see where he goes!' and he sprints off up the track.

Once he has taken the turning to the right, the darkness closes in. Slowing – he can't see where he's going – he listens. Nothing: the night is silent. He can hear Lily behind him, obviously treading carefully, and waits for her to catch up.

And then the darkness is riven by a wedge of light that suddenly spills out, gone as quickly as it appeared.

'Someone just opened and closed a door,' Lily says. 'Come on!'

They reach the place where the light has just beamed out. Standing in front of a doorway set down a step and deep within stone walls, they can see a faint outline of light around a low, narrow door. Felix is about to knock when Lily puts up her hand and hisses, '*Listen!*'

And, close together, they go down the step and lean forward, ears to the door.

'. . . *told* you not to do it!' a woman's shrill voice hisses.

'Hush! *Hush*, damn you!' a man's voice responds.

'I *won't* hush!' the woman cries. 'You've brought this trouble on us when life was bad enough already, and now I'm in danger as well as you, and *it's all your fault!*'

'He's my friend,' the man protests, 'and I was raised to help my friends when they need me, especially in a foreign land where we do not know the intricacies of the law and—'

'Friend? You barely know him!' the woman fires back. 'Murder's murder, wherever you are,' she goes on, 'and if you're too much of a fool to realize that I'm not staying. It's obvious I matter so little to you that you won't even *consider* how I feel, and as far as I'm concerned, you can face what's coming on your own!'

There are sounds of movement from within, and Felix takes Lily's hand as they turn away from the door and hurry back up the track. They slip into a noxious little alley between two rows of huddled houses, and presently the door opens and a woman carrying a cloth-wrapped bundle appears. Turning back towards the room, she fires off her parting shot – 'You can find yourself another bloody model!' – and strides off down the track in the opposite direction. Shortly afterwards there is the sound of an angry fist banging on a door and the distant mutter of voices.

'I think we can assume she's found a bed for the night,' Felix says softly as silence descends once more. 'Shall we go and talk to Howard?'

'Yes,' she says. 'We'll tell him the truth,' she goes on as they return to the low door, 'and try to persuade him we're here to help Wilberforce, not harm him.'

They are back outside the door.

And all at once there is noise: shouting, someone sobbing wildly, the sound of running feet.

It is coming from behind them; from the road that runs beside the river.

They race towards it but stop just before breaking out of the cover of the darkness in the alley. Felix draws back into the concealing shelter of a doorway, and Lily huddles beside him into the deeper shadow. Cautiously they lean forward to see what is happening.

There is a crowd of people milling around and a buzz of alarmed, frightened chatter. Three burly figures are none too gently shoving the onlookers back, and there is a sudden outburst of angry shouting as a thick-set man is pushed too hard.

'What is it?' Lily whispers.

'No idea,' Felix replies. 'But those three men are armed and the crowd's beginning to disperse, so if we wait, we'll be able to see what they were all so agitated about. I don't imagine it's—*Christ!*'

He wishes he'd been quick enough to grab Lily by the shoulders and turn her away so that she didn't have to see. He wishes he didn't have to see what is lying on the road either. And he really wishes he'd had time to hold a hand-kerchief to his nose, because if he had, he wouldn't now be breathing in the iron-heavy, unmistakable smell of fresh blood.

A great deal of it; the cobbled street running between the houses and the river looks in the half-light as if someone has spilt a barrel of red wine.

And the body of a man lies prone, legs straight out behind him, arms at his sides. His canvas satchel has spilled its contents, which appear to be artists' materials. The face is turned away so that Felix and Lily are looking at the bony, bloody remains of what used to be the back of his head.

SEVEN

'We *couldn't* have knocked on Howard's door tonight, not with the town stirred up like a broken wasps' nest!' Lily says. 'We would have made ourselves conspicuous and probably aroused the suspicion of whoever will be investigating the crime, especially when everyone else eventually did what they were told and went home.'

'Yes,' Felix agrees dully.

She can tell both by his expression and his tone of voice that he is as frustrated as she is at not paying a visit to the man in the hat. Especially as this Howard may well take fright and flee once he finds out someone has been brutally murdered not fifty yards from his front door.

They are sitting in Lily's room, Felix on the hard little chair by the tiny desk, she on the bed. She has noticed – and she's quite sure he has too – that the floorboards on the landing give off creaks like gunshots even if you tiptoe along the edges. The stout proprietor wished them a civil *bonne nuit* as they came in, but Lily has no doubt that he is fully aware they are both in her room and will be listening out to make quite sure Felix returns to his own before too long.

He eases his position in the little chair, which creaks almost as loudly as the floorboards. 'The victim was killed by a bullet fired from a large calibre revolver,' he says.

'How do you know?' she demands. 'I wasn't aware you had such detailed knowledge of firearms and bullets.'

He shrugs. 'I've picked it up here and there,' he says vaguely.

She doesn't pursue it, merely puts it to the back of her mind to ask about another time. It reveals a hitherto unsuspected side to her colleague . . . Making herself return to the matter in hand, she says, 'Was it Wilberforce?'

He frowns. 'How old did you say he was?'

'Twenty-seven,' she replies promptly.

'Then I don't think so. I'd have said the victim was older, because what you could see of his hair was streaked with grey. Sorry,' he adds. 'I didn't mean to make you visualise the corpse again.'

She shakes her head. 'No need to apologize, I was already doing so. The next thing to think about,' she goes on, determined to be businesslike and not let the image of a shattered skull take over her thoughts completely, 'is whether this sudden violent murder is connected with Wilberforce.'

'It must be,' Felix says. 'I can't imagine this little community of artists is often disturbed by such horrors, yet in recent weeks they've had a fugitive wanted for murdering his father trying to hide here, they've seen him taken away and locked up in an asylum, we believe he's come back because he's suspected of another murder, and now a man's been found with his head blown to bits. Good grief, Lily, this is a peaceful little Breton town full of painters, not revolutionary Paris!'

She nods. 'Yes, I agree. Do you think, then, that it means other people are hunting for Wilberforce, and one of them shot the dead man because they thought they'd found him?'

'We already know others are on his trail,' Felix replies. 'The asylum guards and the local police.'

She pauses, thinking whether to go on. She does. 'But neither of them would have *shot* him. Would they?' she asks quietly.

He turns to stare at her. 'They might if he'd been threatening them.'

'Felix, the only weapon he uses – and he may not even have used that one – is a razor. Someone armed with this heavy calibre revolver you speak of wouldn't have needed to shoot him dead, he could have shot him in the arm, or the leg. Somewhere non-fatal,' she finishes impatiently.

But he is nodding. 'You're right,' he says. 'It's not professional to shoot a runaway patient dead, whether you're a policeman or an asylum guard.'

'He was shot in the back of the head,' she begins, 'and—'

'He wasn't,' Felix interrupts. 'That great wound was where the bullet emerged. It would have gone in round about the middle of his forehead.'

'More knowledge you've picked up here and there?' she says very softly. But her mind is leaping on. 'Murdered by someone who was a marksman, then, unless it was a lucky shot?'

And, ominously, he says, 'That's what I was thinking.'

She doesn't believe it is necessary to speak aloud the disturbing thought that follows in the wake of this: that whoever is also on the trail of Wilberforce Chibb brings with him a whole new level of determined brutality that neither she nor Felix had hitherto suspected.

Lily sleeps more soundly than she expected to. She had anticipated a noisy night full of police activity, with officers detailed to remove the body and search for clues, bystanders pulled in to answer harsh questions, and undoubtedly house to house enquiries to see if anyone witnessed the shooting. Strangely – and as she wakes, she realizes that it really is strange – there was nothing.

This morning it is quite an effort to shake off the after-effects of deep sleep and get out of the high, generous bed. The morning is chilly, and she hurries through a swift wash; the jug of water left outside her door was probably hot half an hour ago, but it isn't now.

She finds Felix in the big room downstairs, a basket of croissants and slices of bread in front of him, little pots of butter and apricot jam arranged round his plate. The smell of coffee wafts up to her as she sits down beside him.

'I think we should present ourselves to Howard as our real selves, explain that Wilberforce's family are very concerned about him, but not mention that it is in fact Miss Westwood who has engaged us,' she says through a mouthful of hot croissant.

'Why?' he asks.

'Oh . . .' She pauses. 'It seems to me in hindsight that it is in fact rather odd that it is Phyllida Westwood who is so anxious for news and not the uncle.'

'Because it's Leonard Bowler who arranged Wilberforce's release from the Quimper gaol and deposited him in the asylum,' Felix says, 'and therefore it seems logical that he would be the one who came this time too. Yes, I agree. We'll tell this Howard that Leonard Bowler hired us.'

They set off for the little cottage along the alley as soon as they have finished eating. They pass by the site of last night's shooting: there is not a single sign that anything happened. 'They've covered it up surprisingly quickly,' she says. 'Do you think they've caught the killer already?'

Felix stares down at the place where the dead man lay. 'I shouldn't think so,' he replies shortly. He looks at her, and she can tell from his expression that he has the same worrying misgivings that she has. 'A great deal more to discover about that, I believe.'

They walk on.

Daylight does not improve the place where Howard lives, and it is now revealed as little more than a hovel set in a row of even more dilapidated dwellings. There is one small window to the left of the door, and another even smaller one set in the slate roof.

'If he's a painter,' Lily says, glancing up at the tiny rectangle, 'I cannot think he will achieve very good results in there. Aren't artists' studios meant to have a good northern light?'

'Yes,' Felix agrees. 'I believe it's because the north light is less changeable, being the one direction from which the sun doesn't shine. There's probably a studio somewhere that they all use,' he adds.

'Mm,' Lily murmurs. She has stepped down to the door and now raises a fist and knocks.

They wait.

They hear the sound of slow, dragging footsteps, and a voice says, 'If that's you, Agatha, you can go away again.' There is an unpleasantly self-pitying, whining tone to the words.

'It isn't Agatha, it is Miss Raynor and Mr Wilbraham of the World's End Bureau,' Lily replies crisply, 'and we are making enquiries about Wilberforce Chibb, who we believe is—'

She gets no further. The door is flung open and a slim, slight man almost entirely enfolded in a thick blanket reaches out, grabs hold of her wrist and pulls her inside. Too vigorously; Felix, standing close behind her, throws himself forward, right at the muffled man, shoving him so forcefully away from Lily that he cannot step back quickly enough, loses his balance and sits down hard on the bare stone floor.

He lets out a wail of anguish, already reaching down a hand to rub at his backside.

Felix closes the door and leans against it. 'Did he hurt you?' he asks Lily anxiously.

'Not in the least,' she replies. 'There was no need to be quite so rough, Felix,' she adds in a hissing whisper, 'you're twice the size of him and it would have sufficed to tell him to let go of me.'

Felix mutters something about having been taken by surprise, but nevertheless reaches down to the man – it's Howard, as they can see now that he has removed the swathe of blanket over his head – and helps him to his feet. 'Sorry about your bottom,' he says.

It seems to Lily that Howard is taking an unnecessary amount of care fussing over himself and straightening his garments, and she suspects he is giving himself time to work out how to reply to Lily's announcement of their purpose. She is not going to afford him that time.

'Wilberforce has been here, hasn't he?' she says, fixing Howard with a hard stare. 'We have been told that he has a friend, or friends, here in Pont-Aven, and it was to them that he fled when he needed sanctuary after the death of his father.'

Howard is clearly having an internal struggle between reticence and anger. Anger wins, and he says in a burst of furious words, 'We took him in! We didn't know he'd been accused of *killing* his father, we had absolutely no *idea*, I give you my most solemn word! We cared for him, we let him share the studio, I even gave him canvasses and let him use my *oils*, the devil take him, and what did he do? He took against the man who supplies our groceries and he really *went* for him, *hitting* him, merely because the man had demanded we give him the money we owed! Truly, it was *terrifying*,' he rushes on with, Lily observes, unseemly eagerness. 'Wilberforce seemed to change right before our eyes into someone else, and a very frightening someone else it was too, and although it is true we had all been good friends, you must believe me when I tell you we had no choice!' He darts nervous glances at Lily and Felix. 'We honestly feared he was going to *kill* somebody, either the groceries man or, more likely, one of his friends who were trying to restrain him, and I am willing to admit it was nothing but the most enormous relief when officers of the law arrived and took him away!'

He stops, panting, wiping spittle from his lips. He is sweating and red in the face, the blanket has slipped off to reveal a dirty vest and a pair of shabby trousers held up with string, and it is clear from the stench coming off him that it is some time since he had the benefit of soap and water.

Lily is still absorbing what Howard has just said; it is Felix who breaks the silence.

'You would have us believe that the only emotion you felt as your friend was bundled into a closed conveyance and taken off to a prison cell was relief,' he says neutrally. 'Yet we are further informed that you went all the way to the Institut Hugues Abadie to enquire after him. Which leads me to conclude that you are not as indifferent to his fate as you make out.'

Howard stares up at him. Watching closely, Lily believes she can see conflict again: *He wants to agree so that he appears to us as a good, compassionate man who will not desert his friend*, she thinks. *Yet he is worried that if he does, we will ask him to help us in some way; to become involved again.*

She already knows what Howard is going to say.

And when presently he mutters sulkily, 'That wasn't me. Me and Agatha only took him in because he needed a room and we needed the money. It's Jasper Geary who was the friend,' she suppresses a smile.

'If you want to know more, you'll have to go and talk to him,' Howard is saying, trying to push Felix towards the door and not meeting with a lot of success. 'He'll be in the studio. Down the alley, turn left and it's in front of you. Good day to you both.'

Felix has relented and left the hovel of his own accord, and Lily joins him out on the track. The door slams and they hear bolts being shot across.

He turns to Lily. 'He stank like a rutting goat,' he says. 'The sweat of blind fear, do you think?'

'Exacerbated by fear, maybe,' she replies, 'but from the general state of the man and the room, I imagine he always smells like that. Let's find this studio.'

The dank little alley winds its way around a few more bends, tightly-packed hovels on either side and a deep groove down the middle that appears to be the outlet for the sort of household waste that Lily prefers not to think about, and then abruptly opens out into a broad track. They notice for the first time that the sun has come out and is actually providing some warmth.

Down to the right there are houses of a better quality than Howard's, and beyond them the bustle of the little town begins, with a baker, a butcher, a hardware store, several cafés and a wide-fronted establishment where paintings are displayed for sale. Directly in front across the road is a wide, lofty building that looks like a barn, except that it has more windows. The doors stand wide, propped open with large chunks of granite. The sun is striking minute sparks of light from the stone.

What really draws Lily's eyes is the big wooden sign that stands beside the open doors. The background has been painted the same bright blue as the springtime sky, and there is a border all the way round which, looking more closely, she sees is made up of dozens of little images, each beautifully painted: wild flowers, a circlet of oak leaves, a wizard with a staff, several different cottages which she suspects are drawn from life, a witch with a black pointed hat riding a broomstick, a bowl of ripe apples, a cauldron, a trio of cider *bollées* and a man's face painted deep green with foliage emerging from his open mouth. The little paintings are clearly done by a variety of hands, but the overall effect is deeply pleasing.

The wording, in a beautiful italic script, reads simply *L'Atelier*.

'The studio,' Felix says beside her. 'Shall we go in?'

They step through the doors. Inside, the old building is full of light: there are the big windows they observed from outside and, looking up, Lily sees that several very large openings have been cut into the roof. Two people are at work, a man and a woman. The woman is red-faced and plump, dressed in a patterned blouse and a heavy wool skirt with a rough and rather grubby smock worn over the top, and looks to be in her early thirties. She is standing at an easel and has two paintbrushes stuck through her untidy bun. The man is bending over one of the two long benches set either side of the central space. A ladder leads to a half-floor above, where finished works hang on display. Judging from the echo of footsteps, there are people moving about up there.

It is the man at the bench who looks up from his task and sees Lily and Felix in the doorway. He says with a smile, 'Can I help you?'

He is in his thirties, perhaps a little older. He has dark hair, neatly trimmed, he is clean-shaven, wears a canvas smock over a shirt and trousers and he presents a pleasant contrast to Howard.

Lily moves towards him, Felix beside her. She has one of the Bureau's cards ready in her hand, which she gives to the man. He reads it, then looks up. 'A private investigation bureau,' he says. His light brown eyes hold Lily's. 'And the two of you have come all the way from Chelsea. I believe I know why. Follow me if you would.'

He mutters something to the woman, who nods distractedly, then leads the way to the far end of the big barn. Half concealed behind an enormous oak post that appears to support the entire end of the building is a small door. The man pushes it open and courteously stands back to let his visitors precede him into the small room beyond. This too is full of light. It contains a wooden desk and chair, a battered old sofa and row on row of shelves containing ledgers, books and bundles of loosely-tied paper. There are paintings hung on the walls wherever there is space between the shelves. One of them – a small, square oil – briefly snags Lily's attention and for some reason makes her think of Alice in Wonderland, but then, her eyes moving on, she is taken aback by an explicit male nude. She turns her gaze to the large ginger cat that is lying on a blue rug in a pool of sunshine. The room is filled with a wonderful smell of coffee.

'Please, sit down,' the man says. 'If I have guessed aright

the reason for your visit, then I believe it is I you wish to talk to. May I offer you coffee?'

'Yes, please,' Felix says promptly. Lily has noticed his new fondness for black coffee and so far has not seen him pass up a single opportunity to have a cup.

'I am Lily Raynor,' she says. Quite often when people read the Bureau's card, they assume that *L. G. Raynor, Proprietor* is Felix because he is the man. Something tells her that Jasper Geary would not have been among them, and she rather wishes she'd given him the chance to prove it.

When they all have their cups of coffee, Jasper Geary sits down behind his desk and says, 'Wilberforce Chibb was a good friend. We knew each other when we were boys and discovered that we shared a passion for painting. Neither of us was encouraged by our families to pursue this, our fathers having in common the attitude that young men from backgrounds such as ours should enter one of the worthy professions and, best of all, follow a life path that walked precisely in their own footsteps. We remained friends, each of us very pleased that the other had remained true to his calling.' He pauses, taking a thoughtful sip of coffee. 'I like to think that it was because of our long friendship that Wilberforce sought me out after the death of his father, although logic informs me that it was probably because I live a long way from Rye.'

It sounds to Lily rather like a prepared speech. She glances at Felix, but he is intent on Jasper Geary. 'Did you consider that—' she begins.

But Felix interrupts. 'He was on the run when he arrived in Pont-Aven,' he says. 'He was wanted for murder.'

The stark word sounds harsh in this calm little room.

'For patricide,' Jasper corrects mildly. 'Indeed he was, Mr . . .?'

'Felix Wilbraham,' Felix supplies.

'Mr Wilbraham. Wilberforce told me exactly what had happened. On the orders of the family doctor, he had been locked in his attic room and left entirely alone. He was deeply disturbed; he described terrifying visions in which vast flights of creatures out of myths and legends descended on the town, claws extended to tear out the eyes and the hearts of its citizens, yet when he repeatedly tried to shout out warnings, his father withheld food until he desisted. After three days of nothing but water, which they were slipping into his room while he slept, he was desperate. His father came up to speak to him, unlocked the door and drew back the bolts, and poor Wilberforce, thinking himself free, burst out on to the landing. He had a razor in his hand, for he had been attempting to shave, and his father took it as a threat and tried to wrest it from him. They struggled, and his father missed his footing and fell down the stairs.'

It is, Lily thinks, largely the same tale that Phyllida Westwood told her. She is about to comment when Felix says, 'Did you believe him?'

Jasper turns to him. 'I did, Mr Wilbraham.'

'Why?'

Jasper thinks for a while. 'Frederick Chibb had a long history of misunderstanding his son,' he says eventually. 'He was not, indeed, a man gifted with insight. He dispatched both his sons to boarding school as soon as he could find an establishment that would take them, and he shied away from any suggestion of closeness or intimacy with them. His daughter was permitted to stay at home, and that is where she will remain for the rest of her life. The elder son committed suicide; Wilberforce's sorry story you already know.' Jasper pauses, gazing down at the ginger cat. 'I am entirely convinced that Mr Chibb died because he failed to understand his son's state of mind. Wilberforce would no more murder his father than I would stamp on dear old Marmalade down there.' He gives the cat a fond smile and, as if in response, the cat springs up and settles itself on his lap. 'Wilberforce struggled all his life for some sign of his father's approval and, even more, of his affection,' he concludes, stroking the cat in long, slow gestures that soon have it purring like a small engine. 'It is inconceivable that he would have killed him, for up to the point of Frederick's demise, no sign of any such intention had been forthcoming.'

You are truly his friend, Lily thinks. And the argument for Wilberforce's innocence is convincing; she looks forward to discovering if Felix agrees. 'Did you ask him if—' she begins, but once more Felix speaks over her.

'You say you thought Wilberforce came to you because of your friendship, yet—'

'In fact I said it was more likely to have been because I live in Brittany,' Jasper corrects politely.

'Yet you summoned the police and watched as he was taken away to prison,' Felix ploughs on. 'His trust was misplaced, wasn't it?'

Jasper sighs. 'Yes, I did indeed feel that I was betraying him. However, the poor man was in a dreadful state. The visions of flying monsters were back, he could find no peace, he wasn't sleeping and when he attacked Monsieur LeClerc, who supplies our groceries, we – I – realized that it was not safe to allow him to remain. Wilberforce believed he was rescuing Monsieur LeClerc from a cloud of harpies,' he says very firmly. 'The wounds were purely accidental. Do either of you speak French?' he asks surprisingly.

'I do,' says Felix.

'I have been trying to recall the French word for harpy,' Jasper says.

'*Harpie*,' Felix supplies. 'Feminine noun.'

'Ah, yes, I should have tried that. I wanted to explain to Monsieur LeClerc, you see, that there was a rationale behind Wilberforce's actions, but sadly he was not amenable to reason. Well,' he adds, 'one can understand that since he was bleeding quite heavily.'

Silence falls. Lily knows there are important questions she should be asking, but such is the effect of Jasper Geary that she can't seem to bring them to mind. As if he senses her mental efforts, he turns to her and says, 'You were about to ask me something, Miss Raynor, when your colleague forestalled you?'

The words are polite, and his tone is conciliatory, but nevertheless Lily realizes that Jasper had just given Felix a mild reproof. From Felix's sudden tension, he clearly thinks so too.

'Er – well, one thing I would like to ask is whether it was you who went to the Institut Hugues Abadie to ask about Wilberforce?'

'It was,' Jasper agrees. 'I managed to gain admittance,

but I was told very firmly that visits to patients were not permitted under any circumstances. I was assured that Wilberforce was being well looked after and that regular reports were being sent to his uncle. Then I was shown the door.'

'Leonard Bowler,' Lily murmurs. 'Yes, it is understandable that the Institute authorities would report to the man who committed Wilberforce to their care.'

'You are well informed, Miss Raynor,' Jasper observes. He raises his eyebrows, clearly inviting her to reveal her source. She doesn't.

'The doctors at the Institute believe he murdered a man there, another patient,' Felix says. 'By the same method he employed when he killed his father.'

'But he did not kill his father, Mr Wilbraham,' Jasper says. 'Which, if the similarity of the murder method is the only reason for the doctors' assumption of his guilt, rather undermines it.' The tone is soft but his expression as he stares at Felix is steel-hard.

'The victim was killed with a razor,' Felix says, his rising irritation evident, 'and Wilberforce was found covered in blood.'

'Razors are commonplace,' Jasper says calmly, 'and it is easy to smear blood on the clothes of a deeply-sleeping man.'

'Did he come back here?' Felix demands, leaning forward. 'Did he once more make his way to the only friend he had, tucked conveniently away in the far corner of Brittany? Is he here now? We want to *help* him!' he cries, the mounting frustration very evident. 'Lily – Miss Raynor – and I are far from convinced of his guilt, but in order to prove his innocence we *have* to speak to him!'

His voice has risen to a shout, and Jasper does not answer straight away; it is as if, Lily thinks, he can see the jagged zigzags of Felix's anger dancing round the room and is waiting for calm to descend before he speaks.

'I believe you, Mr Wilbraham,' he says eventually. 'Were I able to, I should try to convince Wilberforce to put his trust in you. However,' – he shrugs, and the cat momentarily stops its purring – 'Wilberforce is not here and has not been back since the distress of his removal by the police.'

He resumes the stroking, and the cat starts purring again.
Lily finds herself watching the smooth, rhythmic strokes. After
a few moments, and quite absurdly, she realizes she would
quite like to close her eyes and have a little nap.

She jerks back into reality, standing up in a hurried, ungainly
movement. 'We must be going,' she says, her voice too loud.
'Come along, Felix, we have taken up enough of Mr Geary's
time.'

'Jasper, please,' Jasper says pleasantly.

Felix too appears to be not quite in control of his movements. He lurches to his feet, tries to put his empty coffee cup
on the desk and misses. It bounces on the edge of the cat's
rug, and fortunately does not break.

'No harm done,' Jasper says, retrieving it.

Lily finds herself being gently but firmly escorted back
through the barn and out on to the track. 'Goodbye, Mr – er,
Jasper,' she says. Her voice doesn't sound quite right.

'Goodbye, Miss Raynor.'

Felix is blinking in the sunlight. 'You'll inform us if
Wilberforce returns,' he orders.

Jasper smiles very quickly, so quickly that Lily almost
misses it. 'Of course, Mr Wilbraham.'

As they stride away, she turns to look back at Jasper Geary.
And she is sure he gives her a discreet wink, as if to say: *How
do you imagine I would be able to inform you of anything
when you have neither told me where you are staying nor
where you are going next?*

And she is left with the very uncomfortable sensation
that every moment of that interview was totally in Jasper
Geary's control.

EIGHT

As he and Lily walk away, Felix has a strange sense of coming back to himself, and almost straight away he realizes he's angry. Stopping – Lily turns to look at him in enquiry – he says, 'I don't know about you, but I reckon he was hurrying us away. Now that we're out of that weird office of his, I'm remembering all the things we should have asked him. First of which is, where does he think Wilberforce has run to if he hasn't come back to Pont-Aven? As far as we know, this is the only place where he had friends – where he *thought* he had friends – so are we now to think he's fled into the wilds of rural France entirely on his own? Knowing that he's suspected of two murders, one here in Brittany, and for all he knows has the police forces of two countries hunting for him, not to mention the guards from the Institute? Dear God, Lily, it's not a position I'd like to be in! I'm beginning to feel quite sorry for him.'

She says in a small voice, 'I've been sorry for him since we saw the bloodhounds in the search wagon. Probably before that, indeed, when Miss Westwood said so bluntly that if it transpired he really did kill his father and the mystery man in the Institute, she wouldn't marry him.'

Felix nods slowly. Then, because this is now the question that is pushing most insistently for an answer, says, 'Do you think Jasper Geary was telling the truth? When he said Wilberforce hadn't come back?'

Lily frowns, the expression deepening. After some moments she says, 'When he told us, I believed him. I didn't doubt him for a second. But that was then.' Slowly she shakes her head. 'But now . . . oh, I can't explain, but it's as if I'm seeing more clearly now, and it strikes me that if they really are old friends, then saying Wilberforce isn't there and hasn't been since the first visit is just what Jasper *would* do.'

'To get rid of us?' Felix demands. She nods. 'But we explained that we wanted to *help* Wilberforce!'

She shrugs. 'Maybe we didn't convince him.'

The morning stillness is abruptly broken by someone calling out: 'You! You people from London! Wait!'

He looks at Lily, grinning, 'I think that must be us.'

They turn towards the source of the voice. The woman from the studio is trotting down the road towards them, her face even redder from the exertion and the bun even messier. 'I want to speak to you,' she pants as she comes up to them. 'Not here – go back to the river, cross it and there's a church on the far side. Wait for me there.'

Giving them no chance to question her, she turns and trots back the way she came.

Lily says, 'Well, I suppose there's nothing else pressing that we should be doing . . .'

They take the next alley on the right and stride back towards the river.

'I'm called Cora, Cora Todd,' the woman says not long afterwards. Felix and Lily located the church, and they have made their way through the long grass around it to emerge on the edge of the field beyond. Now the three of them are standing in the shade of a little orchard of apple trees, nicely hidden from the eyes of the curious.

'Why did you want to speak to us, Mrs Todd?' Lily asks.

The woman smiles, making apples of her plump cheeks. 'Call me Cora,' she says. 'I used to be a wife, but that was long ago and in another place.' Felix would quite like to query that enigmatic statement but restrains the impulse. 'I've been here for years. I love it – it's the freedom I always dreamed of, and I paint all the time.'

'We noticed the display of paintings,' Lily says. 'Do you – er, are you a professional artist?'

Cora laughs. 'If you're asking if I make money from my work, then go ahead and ask, don't be coy about it! Yes, I do,' she goes on, 'largely thanks to Jasper, and he's helped me look after my earnings so I've been able to put a bit by and have some security at last.'

'Does he—' Felix begins, but Cora is in full flow and he doesn't think she notices the interruption.

'He looks after us so well,' she is saying earnestly, 'and in truth most of us only make anything at all because of him. He keeps all the records, he makes sure we're paid what we've been promised, he arranges exhibitions and that to promote our work and—'

'I noticed the shelves of ledgers in his office,' Lily breaks in. 'He's—'

'Yes, that's right! Like I say, he's a really good administrator and . . .' Frowning suddenly, her voice trails off.

Suspecting she has sought them out to speak privately to them because she has something to say about this really good administrator that she would rather Jasper Geary did not hear, Felix says gently, 'Did you hear what we were talking to him about?'

The grateful look she flashes at him confirms that he is right. 'Oh, I wasn't eavesdropping! I just happened to be nearby, and I couldn't help hearing all that about Wilberforce Chibb.' Now her brown eyes are round with the shocked fascination of people who witness a distressing event but are not personally involved. 'I *said* it was a mistake to shelter a murderer the first time he turned up,' she hurries on, 'but the rest said he was Jasper's friend and he was on the run and it wasn't right to condemn him without knowing what really happened with his father, and I was outvoted.' She pauses, then adds, 'We're a community, see. We don't have leaders and that, but if there's a big decision to take, like if we should harbour a wanted man, then we talk about it and have a vote. Me and a couple of others voted no – that Agatha who lives with Farrington Howard was one of them, only I reckon *she* only voted no because Wilberforce was lodging with them and she didn't like the extra work – but, like I said, the majority said yes.'

'Why did *you* vote against Wilberforce staying?' Felix asks.

Cora purses up her mouth. 'Well, most of us here aren't French. There's us English, a big group of Americans and a few Dutchmen to start with, and we're strangers in a foreign land when all's said and done, and we don't have any *idea* what the law here says about sheltering a fugitive wanted for murder! We could all be arrested and flung into jail and they could keep us there as long as they liked, and there'd be nobody, not a bloody soul, to help us and plead our case, and none of them worries like I do, and there's Jasper sitting there stroking that bloody ginger cat and *that's* another thing, he treats it like it's an old friend and it's less than a fortnight since it sauntered in off the street, and he treats it like he *loves* it, and it's *me* who—' She stops. Closes her mouth firmly.

Felix and Lily wait, but she folds her arms and compresses her lips.

Then, watching Lily, Felix sees something odd happen to her expression. Her eyes open wide, she gives a soft gasp, then she smiles with what could be relief or satisfaction. He waits, still staring at her, eyebrows raised, but almost imperceptibly she shakes her head.

And presently she says gently, 'You just referred to the *first* time Wilberforce Chibb came here.' Rapidly Felix thinks back over Cora Todd's most recent outpourings and realizes Lily is right; he's cross with himself for missing it. 'That of course implies,' Lily is saying, 'that there was a second time.'

Cora stares at her, brows knotting in a worried frown, hands clenching and unclenching. 'I . . . It's not . . .' she begins. Then, her face angry now, she blurts out, 'Well, even if he did come back, *I* didn't bloody ask him, it's not *my* fault!'

'I expect people are scared,' Lily says in the same gentle voice. 'As you rightly said, when you're in a foreign country and you're not familiar with the law, it's very brave to help someone who is on the run from the authorities.'

'Brave, is it?' Cora cries. 'I'd call it stupid, and it's not fair, it's all of us who'll suffer if they find out, and I'll end up losing what small amount of security I've found at long last and I won't let that happen, I *won't*!'

Lily puts a consoling hand on Cora's arm but she throws it off. 'Will you tell them?' she asks plaintively. 'Will you say I helped you, told you the truth?'

'We have no influence at all on the French authorities,' Lily begins, but Felix doesn't think he should let her finish in case she undermines Cora's resolve.

'When did Wilberforce come back?' he asks.

Cora looks at him, guilt all over her face. 'I shouldn't be telling you . . .' Felix waits, praying that Lily doesn't interrupt.

And Cora whispers, 'It must be a week, give or take. He'd been on the run for ages, he was all thin and his clothes torn and filthy, and when he turned up at the studio Jasper just *took him in* without asking us!' Her face is full of angry resentment. 'He was wild, twitching with nerves and although he barely stopped talking – ranting like a maniac, he was – he didn't make much sense but just kept saying they were after him and he didn't do it. The studio was busy that day and the artists were all scared of him because it was plain to us all that something was deeply *wrong* with him.' She pauses, eyes wide and unfocused. 'Well, you could tell something dreadful had happened – something else dreadful, I should say – but Jasper, he wouldn't hear any of my – any of our arguments and he went on and on about innocent till proven guilty, and then that blasted ginger cat that haunts the office got up on Wilberforce's lap and Jasper said it was a sign because cats don't take to bad men and I said that's a load of old tosh because my old Gran had a black tom that'd go to anyone for a couple of pilchards' heads, even the worst of villains!' She stops, panting.

'How long did he stay?' Lily asks quietly.

'Oh—five, six days? I can't say for sure – one day he was there, then he wasn't.' Now she sounds surly, and Felix thinks they'll have to be quick if they want to learn any more from her before her conscience wins and she hurries away.

'You won't, of course, know where he's gone,' he says, making his tone rueful. 'I'm sure he wouldn't have mentioned something so sensitive to anyone but his friend Jasper.'

Cora bridles and puffs out her generous chest like a ruffled hen. 'Well, that's all *you* know,' she says rudely. 'I *do* know because it was me who looked after him, bathing all his cuts and scratches and sewing up the tears in his trousers! He's got this great-auntie, only he calls her Aunt, Aunt Eulallie or something, she lives down in the south in a spa because she's got dicky lungs, and Wilberforce reckoned he could touch her for a few francs because he said she'd always liked him. Don't

suppose he'll tell her they think he's killed two men, though
– *I* wouldn't.'

'A spa,' Felix repeats, trying to sound as if his interest is
purely academic. 'There are health spas all over France, aren't
there?' He glances at Lily, who replies somewhat frostily that
she believes this is so. 'Did Wilberforce say where this one
was?'

'He did, and I remembered because I used to have a cousin
of the same name,' Cora says, her aggrieved tone suggesting
she hasn't forgiven Felix for the assumption that she was of
insufficient importance to be let into Wilberforce's secrets.
'It's a place called Aurelie-les-Bains – that's baths, see. My
cousin was actually called Aurelia, but it's near enough and
that's why it stuck in my mind.'

'And where is this spa?' Felix asks, fighting the strong
temptation to shout.

'Oooh, now you're asking . . .' Cora frowns again. 'It's in
those mountains.'

'The Alps?' The words snap out of him.

'No. I think it began with a R . . .'

Felix is on the point of yelling that there aren't any bloody
mountains in France beginning with R when suddenly Cora
shouts triumphantly, 'Pyrenees! That was it! The Pyrenees!'

Felix feels a sharp nudge in the ribs and, glancing at Lily,
sees that she is making none too subtle hurry up signs, briefly
jerking her head in the direction of the river and the town
beyond. Looking, Felix sees a party of men and a few women
walking towards the church, chatting and laughing. Cora sees
them too, and nervously draws back further under the apple
trees.

Lily is right, he thinks, it's time for them to melt away.

'Thank you very much, Mrs – er, Cora,' he says, 'you've
been very helpful. Good day to you.'

Lily nods to Cora, and the two of them start to walk away.

'Wait!' The word is a harsh whisper. They turn back.

'Something to add, Cora?' Lily asks politely.

'You're going to go after him, aren't you?' Cora says softly.
Neither of them answer. 'Well, I'm quite sure you'll try,' Cora

goes on. 'In which case you should be aware that you aren't the only people looking for him.'

Felix senses Lily go tense. 'Are you quite sure?' he says.

Cora leans forward, lowering her voice so that they have to strain to hear. 'For some reason the authorities are trying hard to cover it up, but someone was shot and killed last night,' she mutters. 'Back of his head blasted away.'

'Do you know who he was?' Lily asks.

'Of course I do!' Cora's tone is scathing. 'I know all the painters in the community, I've been here since the start.' Her face crumpling, she says, 'But *he* was new here. He said his name was Piet, and he came from Belgium or Poland, some place like that, and although he had plenty of enthusiasm, that was about all he had, poor man.'

'Why would anyone kill him?' Felix muses. He hadn't meant to speak the words aloud, and, sure enough, Cora gives him a look of deep derision.

'They didn't intend to kill *him*!' she hisses scathingly. 'Whoever shot him thought they were shooting Wilberforce!' She stares from Felix to Lily and back again, face in a rictus of anxiety as she waits for a response.

'But why—' Lily begins.

Cora tuts impatiently. 'Piet was dirt poor and didn't have any paints or nothing. Jasper took pity on him and gave him Wilberforce's old canvas satchel. Nobody here would have killed him, or Wilberforce either,' she goes on, her voice stronger now. 'It was *them*, it must have been. And he was shot, poor sod,' she goes on, 'and who here in this artists' colony do you imagine has a revolver? For one thing most of us are pacifists and for another, we don't have the money to go wasting it on *guns*.'

'"It was them",' Felix repeats. 'Who do you mean? Did you see these people? Do you know who they are?'

Slowly Cora nods. 'Posing as art lovers, they were,' she mutters. 'Several of us spotted them hanging around the studio, and they bought a couple of little oils from the shop in the town, one of the church, the other of three old Breton women sitting on a bench by the sea.'

'Did you tell them where Wilberforce was going?' Lily asks urgently.

Slowly Cora shakes her head. 'I most certainly did not,' she says very quietly. 'I didn't like the look of them. Didn't like it at all.' She pauses, and once again her eyes seem to stare back into the recent past. 'He was a tough one, that's for sure. He always wore immaculate black and he had pale, cold eyes that looked everywhere, for all he tried to pretend he was here for a nice little holiday.' She pauses. 'As for her . . .'

'*Her*?' Felix and Lily say together.

'Thought that'd surprise you,' Cora says, smiling smugly. 'Yes. The other one was a woman. But apart from the fact that she was shorter than her companion, I can't tell you anything about her because she always wore a veil to keep the dust off. Oh, and there was one more thing.' The smile intensifies. 'I know where they were putting up, because it's where one of the Americans who works in the studio lodges, and *he* didn't like the look of them either.'

The young man who opens the door to them at the lodging house tells Felix that it's his aunt's establishment, he's only there to serve the breakfasts and do jobs like clearing out the gutters and he doesn't know anything about the guests, but when Felix mentions a man in the company of a woman who habitually wore a veil, his expression changes from benign amiability to one of righteous indignation, and immediately a burst of angry French bursts out of him. Felix, trying to keep up with the rapid flow, mutters '*Ah, oui*?' and '*Mon dieu*!' periodically, but the young man doesn't really need the encouragement; in fact Felix finds it quite tricky to extract himself.

When he and Lily are outside on the road once more, she says eagerly, 'What did he say?'

'They said the pair were a Mr Joseph Clark from Harrow and his wife Hilda; they were here on holiday and they set off early this morning to go on to Quimper.' He grins. 'The young man *really* didn't take to them. They were rude, she snapped her fingers when she wanted more coffee and then complained because it was *tiède* – that means lukewarm – and the man had very cold eyes, never said *merci* and didn't know how to smile. And, although they claimed to be married, my young man was up doing his gutters early one morning and saw through the window that someone had been sleeping on the floor. Oh, and he overheard them muttering when they didn't know he was there and he reckons they were speaking German.'

They have returned to Lily's room and resumed their seats, he on the chair, she on the bed.

'You played that woman like a fiddle,' Lily says.

He knows he did, and he feels slightly guilty over the way in which he got Cora to reveal where Wilberforce was heading. Only slightly. He replies shortly, 'But I found out what we need to know.'

And she has no answer.

'And how about you? What made you push her like that?' he demands. 'You went all vacant, and then all at once it was if you *knew* Wilberforce had been back, and that made you force her to admit it.'

'I did know, or I was pretty sure I did,' she replies. 'It was when we sat down in Jasper Geary's office. I was looking at the paintings on the walls and there was one of a ginger cat. Remember?' She looks at him expectantly but he shakes his head.

'Well, Jasper's got a ginger cat,' he says tersely. 'He seems very fond of it, so there's no reason why he shouldn't paint it.'

'None at all,' she agrees eagerly, 'except he didn't. That painting wasn't Jasper's work.'

'How—'

'The cat had the wrong eyes!' she cries. 'It had eyes like a man, and that's what *Wilberforce* does! *You* told me that – the man at Paimpont with the brother-in-law who cleans at the Institute said Wilberforce's cats *always* have human eyes.'

'Yes, but he could have done the painting when he was here before, after he ran away from Rye, and—'

But then, of course, he understands.

He lets Lily explain, however, because it really is her discovery and it's only fair that she should have her moment.

'*No he couldn't,*' she says triumphantly, 'because Jasper didn't *have* the cat then!'

'Oh, well *done!*' he says, genuinely impressed.

She waves a dismissive hand. She bends down to take her Bradshaw's out of her bag, but he has already spotted the fetching rosy blush in her cheeks caused by his praise.

'We must search for this spa called Aurelie-les-Bains in the Pyrenees,' she says, her voice brisk. 'There are several pages of maps . . .' She thumbs through till she finds the right place, then tries to hold the book so that he can see too. 'Oh, come and sit on the bed,' she says shortly when this proves impossible.

He does as he's told.

They pore over two pages displaying the Pyrenees before Felix spots Aurelie-les-Bains. '*There!*' he shouts, right in her ear.

'Thank you, Felix,' she murmurs.

The spa town is a very small dot on the map, situated at the western end of the great range of mountains that separates Spain from France. It lies about a third of the way between St-Jean-de-Luz, on the coast to the south of Biarritz, and St-Jean-Pied-de-Port up in the mountains.

Felix points at the black line that goes all the way down France's west coast as far as Bayonne and Biarritz. 'That's very good,' he says brightly, for he can see that Lily is dismayed at how far they are going to have to travel.

'Why is it good?' she mutters.

'That black line is the railway,' he says. 'We'll be able to go by train almost all the way.'

She has flipped back through the maps to the first one, showing France in its entirety.

'But it's such a long way!' she says. 'And, remember, we won't be travelling alone – there are two more people hunting for Wilberforce and they have a gun. A *revolver,*' she adds in a whisper.

I'm not likely to forget, he thinks.

He shares her apprehension; the idea of possibly sharing a train – a carriage, even – with two killers is indeed a daunting one. Then he remembers that Cora Todd hasn't told anyone but him and Lily where Wilberforce is going.

'It would be an extraordinary and unlikely coincidence if they decided to look for him in the Pyrenees,' he says confidently. Unless, he adds silently, someone other than Cora knows about Wilberforce's ailing aunt . . .

He studies the map, in particular the coast.

Then he says, 'Lily, I've had an idea.'

NINE

The Basque Country is nothing like Lily's mental picture of it. In the light of her admittedly limited experience of France, she is expecting something akin to the flat and fairly featureless lands that surround Paris, or the deeply rural fields, woods and soft hills of Brittany, dotted with ancient stone cottages with slate roofs and redolent with the smells of agriculture, primarily pigs. As they reach St-Jean-de-Luz and finally leave the small ship that has brought them all the way down the west coast of France – not a moment too soon for Lily, who has had to battle with seasickness once or twice – she looks inland as the morning sea mist clears and sees a vast mountain range rearing up in front of her.

Felix marches them off to a smart little café on the pretty waterfront that is in the process of putting out tables and winding out a red and white striped awning. Lily doesn't think she could face anything to eat or drink – the wind had whipped up quite large waves as they came into port – but the delicious aroma of coffee and freshly-baked bread works like a charm and soon she is tucking in as enthusiastically as Felix. Her mouth full of hot bread, yellow creamy butter and smooth, golden honey, she grins at him. *He really does have some good ideas*, she thinks.

She is reflecting not so much on his proposal that they find somewhere for breakfast but of the whole experience of their two-day journey down to the Pyrenees by sea. When Felix suggested it, at first she had been full of protests: they would have to find a port and a boat going that way, how would they know where they should be heading, and what if the other people hunting for Wilberforce had the same idea? Calmly he had countered each one: 'We're in a town on the mouth of a river and the sea is less than a mile away,' he'd begun, 'we'll simply use our eyes and look for a suitable ship and if we

can't find one we'll ask; we've already found the location of
Aurelie-les-Bains on your Bradshaw's map and we'll ask for
directions and find out how to reach it once we're down there;
and finally, the other people after Wilberforce don't know
where he's going.'

He had managed to assuage most of her doubts, but she
still found herself anxiously checking their fellow passengers
on each of the successive craft that bore them south to see if
she could spot anyone behaving suspiciously. She didn't, but,
as she thought worriedly the first night on board the first boat,
if they were on a secret mission then they would know how
to present themselves as ordinary people going about their
day-to-day lives.

Back in Pont-Aven, a fisherman friend of their hotel proprietor had ferried them from the mouth of the river below the
little town to the much larger port of Concarneau. Lily had
protested to Felix that they were going the wrong way – north-
west when they should be heading south-east – but he
shrugged and replied that he'd simply asked the fisherman to
take them to somewhere where boats sailed down the coast,
and presumably the man was aiming for the nearest suitable
port. It was fortunate, Lily thinks now, going back over the
journey in her mind, that the first part of the voyage was
the worst. The small coaster that took them from Concarneau
to La Rochelle might have been grubby and totally lacking in
comforts, but at least it wasn't like the fragile little fishing
boat open to the elements, tossed about viciously by the waves
as if it was a piece of driftwood, that bore them out of the
harbour below Pont-Aven to Concarneau. The final leg, from
La Rochelle to St-Jean-de-Luz, was almost luxurious by
comparison to what had gone before . . .

They have both finished eating, and Felix has just asked for
more coffee. Patting her lips and brushing down her bosom
with a napkin – croissants may be delicious but they make so
many crumbs – she says, 'I expect Miss Westwood was reassured by my telegram.' Lily sent a brief message to her client
when they were in La Rochelle, merely reporting that the
subject had fled to the Pyrenees, they had an address and were
pursuing him. 'She paid me a large sum of money before I

left London,' she continues, 'and undoubtedly, we shall be claiming a great deal more in expenses. I must make sure she feels we are giving good value.'

'She signed the contract,' Felix says bluntly. Lily glances at him and sees that he is frowning; he was not in favour of her sending their client the latest information on their progress, she recalls, saying they'd surely do better to keep it to themselves.

Lily had overridden him.

'She did indeed,' she replies, turning to the maps at the back of the Bradshaw's. 'Now, we are here,' – she points to St-Jean-de-Luz – 'and Aurelie-les-Bains is here.' It is only about eight miles away, roughly two-thirds of the way along the route to somewhere called St-Jean-Pied-de-Port, but she notices with a faint sinking of the heart that those eight miles appear to take them right up into those great soaring mountains.

Felix has apparently noticed this too. 'You'd expect a health resort to be high in the mountains,' he says reassuringly. 'And also,' he adds before she can comment, 'if lots of sick people go there, then there must be some easy means of getting to the place that doesn't involve walking up the side of a mountain or riding a frisky horse up a track with a precipice on one side, or negotiating any other hazards unsuitable for those in need of long-term medical care.'

He is right, and she sends him a grateful smile. 'Now we just have to find this easy means,' she remarks, 'and hope it isn't for the exclusive use of spa patients.'

She uses some more of Miss Westwood's francs to pay for breakfast, and they set off into the heart of the town. Felix has just said he'll find someone to ask when Lily spots a smartly-dressed middle-aged couple standing beside a bath chair, in which sits an elderly man tightly wrapped in blankets, shawls and a large muffler, pointing towards the mountains with a crabbed and shaking hand and complaining loudly and continuously that he is hungry and where's his lunch?

Complaining, Lily notes, in English.

She nudges Felix, but he has already seen the trio. 'Go and ask them,' he murmurs.

Lily takes a moment to adopt the persona of a nervous

Englishwoman adrift in an alien place, puts on a tremulous smile and walks up to the couple beside the bath chair. 'Oh, you're English!' she gushes. 'How relieved I am, for my command of the French language is proving to be utterly inadequate, and I am forced to admit that I am at a loss what to do!'

The man has his hat off already and is looking concernedly at Lily. He is about forty, well-dressed in good clothes and there is a heavy gold Albert chain with a large fob stretched across his smart waistcoat. 'How may we help?' he asks. 'The name's Robinson, Jeremy Robinson, and this is m' wife.' He turns to include the woman in the conversation; she is staring at Lily, her smile slightly less in evidence than her husband's. Like him she looks to be around forty, and wears a beautifully-tailored gown in dove grey, over it a cloak a shade or two darker.

'I must travel to Aurelie-les-Bains,' Lily says, 'to see a—'

She gets no further – which is just as well since she hasn't decided whether to mention the great-aunt with the dicky lungs – because Mrs Robinson says loudly, 'Aurelie-les-Bains! Why, that's where *we* are going!'

Lily tries to temper her delighted surprise – for surely Mr and Mrs Robinson must appreciate that being in the company of a pale and fragile old man in a bath chair is a broad hint that they are bound for a health resort – and says, 'Are you really? Oh, that *is* fortunate! Perhaps you might be so kind as to tell my brother and me,' – she turns to indicate Felix, who courteously doffs his hat and bows – 'how best to get there?'

'We will do better than that, won't we, Helena?' Mr Robinson says to his wife. 'We await a conveyance that we are assured will be dispatched from the spa, and we shall all travel together!'

The old man says loudly, 'Eh? What's that you're saying?' He cups a hand behind his ear. 'I want my lunch!' he adds plaintively.

'Hush, Father,' Mrs Robinson says vaguely, with the air of someone who has said the same thing a hundred times and has little faith in being obeyed this time any more than the last ninety-nine.

'That is most generous,' Felix says, adding, in what Lily sees as a move to cement the arrangement before anyone can change their mind, 'I have our bags here; we only have one each!' Mr Robinson casts a rueful glance at their own large pile of bags and cases.

Mrs Robinson is telling her father in a firm and long-suffering voice that they will soon be on their way, that luncheon will be served when they get there and he's only just had breakfast, when a very elegant pair of matching greys come trotting smartly towards them pulling a large, closed carriage. Lily stands back while Mrs Robinson helps the old man on board; Felix helps Mr Robinson fold the bath chair and hand it up to the coachman, who ties it and the trio's bags on to the luggage rack, and then they too take their seats. The carriage sets off, and very soon they are at the foot of the narrow little road that leads away from the coast and up into the mountains.

Lily is so entranced by the scenery that once or twice she has to remind herself what she and Felix are doing there. The mountains are already steep and formidable, and she can see snow on the peaks. In the sheltered valleys the pasture lands are green and lush with spring grass, and there are vast flocks of sheep, the clonking of the bellwethers' bells making a pleasing and harmonious sound. The track is narrow but busy; they pass one or two other carriages, a number of carts and wagons, riders on horseback and even a few people struggling uphill on foot. These are the lower slopes of the Pyrenees, she realizes, and a sizeable population lives and works here, mostly involved in sheep farming and its products, to judge by the number of signs she sees for *fromage de brebis*, and also in viticulture; she spots a large building called a *cave* that advertises a wine called *Irouléguy*, which she hopes nobody will ask her to pronounce. There are several villages dotted along the track, all of them featuring the same very distinctive architecture of low, wide, white-painted houses with steeply-sloping roofs of red pantiles. The protective nature of these roofs, combined with the pitch and the deep eaves, suggests that heavy snow is likely in the winter.

Arriving at yet another village, the carriage slows to a crawl. The slope has increased suddenly, and Lily attributes their crawling pace to this. She is about to say as much to Felix, but silently he points out of the window. They are going through a pair of tall, black-painted wrought-iron gates set between high railings, beside which a sign reads *Spa Hydro de St Roc*, and underneath in much larger capitals, *PRIVÉE*. There is a lodge set just inside the gates, and two men in navy blue braided uniforms stand on guard.

'Aurelie-les-Bains looks just the same,' Mrs Robinson announces to the carriage in general. She points a slim hand clad in a close-fitting calfskin glove at a half-ruined shed of some sort just inside the gates. Frowning, she adds, 'As does St Roc; I note they *still* haven't removed that eyesore, although M. Dupont promised faithfully that it would be gone by the start of the season.' She sighs, shaking her head as if in despair at the unreliability of this M. Dupont. 'And one pays enough,' she mutters darkly, shooting a less than charitable glance at her father, now snoring in his corner with his mouth open and drool hanging off his chin. She turns to her husband, muttering something that sounds like a complaint, and Lily takes advantage of this to whisper to Felix, 'We ought to get out and hurry on inside as soon as the carriage stops.'

He nods, instantly understanding. 'Yes, it'll take them a while to get all the baggage off, not to mention the old man. With luck we can say a cheerful goodbye and thank you, then melt away before they ask us anything we don't want to answer.'

Clutching her bag, Lily nods.

And presently, as the carriage draws to a stop beneath a generous porch with shallow stone steps leading up to an imposing pair of doors, they do just that. 'Thanks very much for the ride,' Felix says as the attendants come forward to meet the carriage, 'we'll get out of your way now.'

Mr and Mrs Robinson are still finishing their farewells as Lily and Felix sprint up the steps and through the slowly opening doors.

The hall is wide and elegant, with a geometric pattern of

black and white marble tiles, a corner in which there is a sofa, three chairs and a low table, and several tall *torchères* on which stand heavy pottery pots containing various healthy-looking foliage plants. There is a sweeping staircase leading up to the first floor and double doors set in the rear wall, at present closed. To the left of these doors is a high reception desk, behind which a man and two women stand, the women dressed in the sort of full, starched white headdresses that suggest they are nurses. All three are looking at Lily and Felix; if their expressions are not exactly hostile, Lily observes, they are not far off.

Felix strides up to the desk and, in the loud, clearly-enunciated accents so typical of the Englishman abroad, says, 'My sister and I have travelled from Rye in England to see our Aunt Eulallie. Perhaps one of you would be so kind as to show us to her room?'

Lily is just wondering why he hasn't announced them in French when the man begins a murmured conversation with one of the women and she sees Felix lean forward almost imperceptibly to listen to the rapid French. She goes to stand beside him, tapping her fingers on the desktop in a mime of impatience.

She hopes these staff members will not ask them to provide Aunt Eulallie's full name, because they don't know for certain which side of Wilberforce's family she is on. For herself, Lily would guess she is a Chibb; she has a strong suspicion that this is entirely a Chibb matter . . .

The staff are still conferring. The woman says something that catches Felix's attention: Lily senses sudden tension in him. She is on the point of risking everything by saying something on the lines of, 'You *must* know who we mean! Miss Eulalia Chibb, of Rye in Sussex! Come along, we have travelled a *very* long way to see her!' but Felix leans close and murmurs, 'It's all right, they believe me.'

And then the man walks out from behind the desk and, smiling pleasantly, solemnly shakes both their hands. In immaculate English, he says, 'I will show you the way myself. Welcome to Spa Hydro de St Roc.'

*   *   *

'How is she?' Lily asks as they are shown through the double doors and escorted along a corridor. It is a likely question for a visiting relative to ask, and she was asked it herself a hundred times during her nursing career. 'She always used to find the cold weather extremely trying,' she adds, 'but then of course the English winters can be so very *damp*.'

The man replies politely but reservedly that Miss Chibb – yes! she *is* a Chibb! Lily was right – has indeed found some of the weeks in the winter just past a little trying, adding with a smile, 'But, as with each one of us, both her spirits and her health improve as the spring comes!'

They proceed up a staircase that is far more business-like than the one leading up from the hall – serviceable drugget covering the carpet, cream paint above the dado rail and green below, all high gloss for easy washing-down – and go on to the far end of another, narrower passage. Here the man – is he a doctor? Lily wonders – pauses outside an imposing oak door on which a painted enamel sign reads *Miss Eulalia Marguerite Avis Chibb* and taps on it softly.

A voice says loudly 'You may enter,' managing even in three short words to sound both imperious and condescending.

The man opens the door and says, 'Visitors for you, Miss Chibb! Here are your nephew and niece from Rye,' standing back to let Lily and Felix go in. He follows Felix through the doorway, but Miss Chibb's commanding tones ring out again: 'Thank you, Monsieur Hervé, that will be all.'

As the door closes behind him, Lily glances all round the large, bright room. Sunlight pours in through the window, illuminating pale walls, a beautiful blue Persian carpet on the light oak floor and some elegant and expensive-looking furniture. She stares at the elderly woman sitting straight-backed in the pretty, deep pink velvet chair placed beside the window. She has silver grey hair pulled back from her face and wound in a bun. Two braids have been detached and arranged from a centre parting to wind around her ears before being fastened to the bun; Lily has seen images of the Queen with such a hairstyle, but they were painted in the 1840s or 1850s. The gown dates from the same decade; it is made of heavy, costly silk in a shade of deep blue with lighter blue bands let into the very full, wide skirt. The bodice with its big sleeves is high-necked and very close-fitting, suggesting some fairly rigid corsetry; Miss Chibb's waist is drawn in to a tiny circle, and it's no surprise that she is sitting up so straight. Lily's swift inspection of the old lady's attire complete, she looks up into the bony face with its firm chin and thin, hard line of a mouth and sees a pair of narrow steel-grey eyes staring into hers.

There is silence in the room apart from the tread of M. Hervé's retreating footsteps. When even this sound fades, Miss Chibb says softly, 'Now I only had the one nephew, and he is dead. He, however, managed to sire three children on that pale, frightened, unworldly woman that he married before she threw herself out of a window. One is dead – he followed his mother's example and also leapt from a height, in his case the rather more dramatic location of Beachy Head – and although I understand his sister is still alive, I am told she is cared for at home. If ever she nerved herself to go out, by no stretch of the imagination would she have the wit or the courage to travel right through France to the Pyrenees.' She stares at Felix for a moment, then the intelligent gaze returns to Lily. 'I deduce, therefore, that you are not who you claim to be. I am, however, intrigued to discover who you really are.' She glances at a pretty little gold fob watch attached to a bar brooch on her bosom. 'You have three minutes to explain yourselves. If I am not satisfied, I shall ring my bell,' – she points to a large brass handbell on the small table beside her – 'and you will be quite taken aback at the alacrity with which several burly attendants will respond.' Again, the quick darting glance to Felix and back. 'Well?' she says sharply. 'Speak up!'

Lily delves into her little bag and extracts one of the Bureau's cards. 'We have been engaged by Miss Phyllida Westwood to find Wilberforce Chibb and determine whether or not he is guilty of the murder of his father Frederick and that of another victim, who was a fellow patient in the asylum in Brittany. I am Lily Raynor,' she continues as Miss Chibb raises a lorgnette and studies the card, 'and this is my associate, Felix Wilbraham.'

They wait. Lily risks a quick look at Felix, who stands quite still, staring impassively in front of him.

When at last Miss Chibb speaks, it is not what Lily is expecting. Staring up at Felix, the ringing voice says, 'So you work for a woman, Mr Wilbraham. You do not look like a timid, emasculated type, so I conclude that you took the post out of necessity.'

Felix stares straight back. 'Yes, Miss Chibb,' he replies. 'When I saw the advertisement for a clerical assistant at the World's End Bureau, I was almost penniless, I had but the one suit of clothes, I was hungry and living in a grim little room above a filthy yard that stank of human waste, and I would have taken *any* job.' He pauses. He shoots a look at Lily, and adds, 'In the two years that I have worked for the Bureau, I have come to like and admire Miss Raynor very much, and now I cannot think of any work I would rather do.'

Miss Chibb nods. 'An unexpectedly full and frank answer,' she observes. Then she says sharply, 'Why do you believe I have any relevance whatsoever to your search for my great-nephew?'

'When he escaped from the asylum he returned to his painter friend in Pont-Aven, where he had fled before,' Lily says. 'The colony there, however, feared the consequences and could not allow him to stay. Someone told us he said he was coming here.'

Miss Chibb nods slowly. 'It was prudent of these artists to fear the repercussions of concealing a foreigner wanted for murder,' she remarks, her tone suggesting merely detached interest. 'I imagine several official bodies would have been on the trail of such a person: the asylum staff, the local police and perhaps also the English authorities, since you report that my nephew is accused of murdering his father and I assume that took place at the house in Rye.'

'It did,' Felix says. 'Although there is some doubt that it was in fact murder.'

But Miss Chibb does not appear to have absorbed his comment. She has turned to gaze out of the window – there is a glorious view over the gardens and to the mountains beyond – and she is shaking her head. 'Old Saltway House is the most beautiful building,' she says, and now she sounds almost dreamy. 'My grandfather purchased it early in the 1700s, and it was old even then; Jacobean, and they understood how to build for eternity back then. It was my home for nigh on sixty years, and I loved every brick, tile and stone of it. It was mine, you see; Father made sure of that, and when the terrible decade began in which I lost my parents, my last surviving brother died of typhoid and the man I was to marry proved faithless, I became the house's guardian and chatelaine, and it was at my indulgence that my nephew Frederick was permitted to live there.' Her expression tightens and Lily has the impression that she is fighting down an old anger. 'But Frederick was a greedy man, just as he had been a greedy boy, and once he had wed that feeble, fancy-ridden wife of his and she began turning out her pale little whelps, he wanted Old Saltway House for his own. I was taken ill with consumption, and I attribute it solely to my *wretched* nephew's insistent, *ceaseless* nagging and worrying at me!'

Her voice has risen almost to a shout. Lily, noticing a tray on a side table, pours a glass of water and silently hands it to her. Miss Chibb takes it with a curt nod.

'He cheated me,' she goes on, and now her tone is icy. 'I was in the sanatorium, feverish, not in possession of myself at all, and he took advantage and made me sign certain documents. When I returned to my senses, I discovered what he had done.' She pauses dramatically, fixing first Felix and then Lily with a hard stare. 'He took my house,' she whispers. 'He found some unscrupulous lawyer and somehow arranged to have the title changed from my name to his. When I protested – and believe me I did – he had the nerve to tell me I had seen sense whilst I was unwell, realized that such a big house was far too much for a woman no longer young and in frail health, and that it was I who proposed that he take the responsibility from my shoulders.' Her voice shaking with fury, she shouts, 'Can you *believe* it?'

All too easily, Lily thinks sadly. 'I am so sorry, Miss Chibb. Your nephew acted appallingly.'

Miss Chibb nods. 'Indeed he did, Miss Raynor.'

'Could you not have engaged a lawyer of your own to put matters right?' Felix asks.

She looks at him sadly. 'I tried, Mr Wilbraham. But . . .' She pauses. 'Regrettably I was not in my right mind. After wasting a considerable amount of money in my pursuit of what was rightfully mine, I left. I abandoned the field of battle.' She smiles grimly. 'Not without my favourite goods and chattels, however,' – she glances round the room – 'for in his haste to have me sign away the house, Frederick forgot to include the contents. With a large amount of the best of the Old Saltway House treasures following on, I sailed for France. I travelled the length and breadth of the country; I learned the language. I lived for some time in hotels and boarding houses, but then, tiring of looking after myself and, indeed, not in the best of health, I came here to St Roc and installed myself. I have been here ever since.'

Lily very much wants to ask how she pays for it, but even after such a frank outpouring, she senses this is a step too far.

Miss Chibb, however, reads her mind. 'Frederick might have robbed me of my house, Miss Raynor, but not of my fortune. That remains in *very* safe hands, and, soundly invested as it is, affords me an income that is more than adequate for my needs. Which is why I—'

Abruptly she stops.

Lily, hungry to know what she was about to say, glances at Felix. He frowns, then slowly nods. A smile spreads across his face.

'Which is why you were able to help your great-nephew when he came to you in desperation?' he asks very softly.

She stares at him and he gazes steadily back. Lily, watching, finds she is holding her breath.

'Why should you assume that?' Miss Chibb whispers.

'It was a remark that Monsieur Hervé made to one of the women at the reception desk,' he replies. 'When I told them that Miss Raynor and I were your niece and nephew, he observed that you seemed to have quite a lot of young relations calling on you at the moment, and maybe they were worried you were planning to change your will.'

Miss Chibb is looking at him with a strange intensity. 'But he would have spoken in French. Those women who take turns at the front desk do not speak English . . .' She pauses, then exclaims, 'You clever man! You understand French, but they did not know that because you spoke to them in English!'

And Felix says modestly, 'I did.'

Silence falls once more.

After some time Miss Chibb says, 'Wilberforce was the only one I liked. He was bright, he was artistic, like me, and he disliked his father almost as much as I did.' She smiles grimly. '*I* could have attacked Frederick with a razor and pushed him down the stairs, but I can assure you that Wilberforce could *not*. If this was how Frederick died, then the fall was an *accident*.' She utters the word so loudly that it echoes round the room. 'The dear boy was only nine years old when my home was stolen from me, but nevertheless he tried to stand up for me. He told Frederick that it was unfair to take my house, and Frederick boxed his ears and sent him up to that isolated attic room and wouldn't let the poor boy out until he had apologized. Shortly afterwards I left the land of my birth forever, but already Wilberforce and I had developed a bond, and I felt there was true affection between us. And that,' she adds acidly, 'let me assure you, is a rare commodity in my family. He used to write to me,' she goes on, 'such a correspondence we had, the two of us, and because he wrote so fully and vividly, I believe I am in a better position than anybody else to know the truth about him. My nephew failed utterly to understand his younger son, he tried to force him to be something that he was not, and the catastrophic result was far more Frederick's fault than that of Wilberforce. As one disaster succeeded the one before, the fatal chain of events began to appear almost preordained.' She stops, once more gazing out at the distant mountains.

Lily and Felix wait.

'Wilberforce did indeed seek me out,' she says eventually. 'He told me everything, and my heart went out to him. I tried to persuade him to stay here under my protection, and I undertook to engage good lawyers to plead his innocence.' Slowly she shakes her head. 'But he refused.' Her expression is bleak. 'He said he felt safer on his own. On the run.'

Lily thinks she has finished. She shifts slightly, stiff from standing still for so long. Miss Chibb must have sensed the little movement. She looks up and straight into Lily's eyes.

'I would have engaged the best,' she says softly. 'I like to think I would *not* have supported a man I believed guilty of two murders, no matter how much I cared for him.' She sits up very straight. 'Fortunately, I was spared that dilemma. Wilberforce did not murder either his father or the man in the Paimpont asylum. He is innocent of these crimes, and I will happily swear to it in a court of law with my hand upon the Holy Bible.'

TEN

Lily has the strange sense that the sudden wave of emotion set off by Miss Chibb's impassioned announcement must be given time to dissolve and disappear.

Pushing the idea firmly aside, she says briskly, 'What is Wilberforce planning to do next?'

Miss Chibb gives a frustrated sigh. 'He has no plan, other than run away and hide. He—' Abruptly she shuts her mouth.

'He must have known you would offer to help him,' Felix says. 'He came here from Brittany because he knew he could trust you.'

'He did not know anything of the sort,' Miss Chibb corrects him firmly. 'He *hoped* he could trust me, and he discovered that his hope was justified.' She smiles slightly. 'He came here for one reason. An elderly woman such as I – and I *am* elderly, I shall be eighty in November – can offer little practical help to a young man running from the forces of law and order. But I could and did give him money.'

Into the short silence that follows, Lily says quietly, 'You claim to know, Miss Chibb, that your great-nephew is no murderer.' Miss Chibb's head jerks up and her steely eyes fix on Lily's. 'How can you be so sure?'

She thinks at first she has unleashed a furious outpouring, for Miss Chibb's lean face works violently and her pale cheeks flush. But then, subsiding, she says, 'It is, I suppose, a logical question.' She is still gazing at Lily, her mouth a hard line. 'I have just explained: I understand the character of my great-nephew. That must suffice.'

Into the uneasy silence Felix says, 'Where is he now?'

Miss Chibb fixes him with a hard stare but does not reply.

After a moment she sighs. 'One thing I must tell you: Wilberforce is *very* afraid.'

Lily looks at Felix, who nods almost imperceptibly.

'We believe he has reason to be,' she says. She pauses,

wondering if what she is about to say will prove too much for an elderly woman in a health hydro. But there seems to be no option. 'A man was shot in Pont-Aven,' she says bluntly, 'and it seems whoever killed him thought he was Wilberforce.'

Miss Chibb draws a sharp breath.

'Whoever it was cannot know where he is now,' Felix begins, 'and I'm sure—'

But Miss Chibb isn't listening. She is staring at Lily. 'You will of course continue your pursuit of my great-nephew, for that is what this Miss Westwood is paying you to do. In addition,' – Lily has the uncomfortable feeling that the old woman's intelligent gaze is penetrating through her skull and into her mind – 'I believe you and your associate will provide Wilberforce with the help and support that I cannot. But you must be *careful*!' And, clenching one hand into a fist, she thumps it three times on the table beside her.

'Miss Raynor and I are professionals,' Felix says.

But Lily is watching Miss Chibb's face. 'You didn't mean that, did you?' she says softly.

'No,' Miss Chibb says with a wry smile.

'You meant we must be careful how we search, because if we let our vigilance slip, we might lead others to him.'

'I do not question your determination and your diligence,' Miss Chibb replies curtly. 'But you two are young and have not had the rigorous training and the many years of experience of the ruthless men who are ranged against you.'

Felix, clearly stung by the implication that he and Lily are not capable of the task, says rashly, 'What do *you* know about them?'

Lily can hear all too clearly his unspoken comment: *you're an old lady sitting in luxury in a health spa, you can know nothing of the outside world and its perils.*

Looking at Miss Chibb, it's quite clear that she can too.

There is a brief silence that seems to crackle with unspoken anger. Then Miss Chibb says, 'I have seen them, Mr Wilbraham. A pair of strangers. They scare me, although I cannot say why. Perhaps it is their utter stillness; the air they have of maintaining a very intense focus . . .' She pauses.

'Did you see them in the village?' Felix prompts.

'It is worse than that,' Miss Chibb replies. 'They were right here, in the grounds of the Hydro. They were standing just down there, on the paved terrace behind the house that leads down to the lawns and the gardens.' She points with a sudden violent gesture, and Lily and Felix hurry to look out of the window. Below is the terrace, with a row of wicker chairs set out in the sunshine, two of them occupied by people wrapped in blankets. Beyond the terrace a long lawn stretches down to a copse, and on each side there are wide borders of flowers and shrubs that will soon be showing a lot of colour.

The iron railings that entirely enclose the grounds look capable of keeping a cavalry charge at bay. The rails are twice the height of a man, sturdy and set close together. There are no cross members to provide toeholds; each one is tipped with a quartet of sharp spikes. In addition, this metal barrier stands in isolation; no trees offer the possibility of climbing up on either side, no shrubbery offers concealment.

'Do the railings enclose the front garden as well?' Felix asks.

'They do,' Miss Chibb confirms. 'The only opening is the gates through which you came in. They, as you will have observed, are watched by the men in the guard house and kept locked.'

'So how did the people you saw down there get in?' Lily asks. Miss Chibb shrugs.

'Are you absolutely sure they were not legitimate visitors?' Felix demands.

Miss Chibb turns to stare at him. 'Quite sure. They did not behave in the way of visitors. Before you ask, let me assure you that they were not residents or staff, either medical or domestic.' She frowns, clearly thinking hard. 'They stood perfectly still, staring intently up at my window as if they had every right to do so. The first time I saw them, I indicated that they should desist – I made it *absolutely* plain, they cannot possibly have mistaken my meaning – and they ignored me. One of them touched his hat and smiled up at me; an unpleasant, supercilious smile.' She pauses. 'They returned, of course. More than once. Their aim is to unnerve me; to frighten me into some act that will reveal what they want to know.'

'Can nothing be done to keep them away?' Lily demands.

Miss Chibb utters an angry '*Pah!*' She shakes her head. 'I ordered Monsieur Hervé to get rid of them and ensure they did not return, but he said he had tried in vain to verify what I'd told him and concluded that I had been mistaken because there were no signs that anyone had been there, nobody else had observed them, and for anyone to obtain unauthorised entrance to St Roc was quite impossible.' Bristling with indignation, she adds, 'He gave the strong impression that he thought the whole matter was nothing but a figment of my imagination – he even said, curse the man, that I'd probably awoken from my afternoon nap and still been half-asleep!'

Lily waits a few moments for Miss Chibb to regain her composure. Then she says, 'You do not think that they could be policemen, or have come from the asylum in Paimpont?'

'Of course not,' Miss Chibb says witheringly. 'Such men would have announced themselves and been brought up by Monsieur Hervé to speak to me. They would hardly have felt the need to skulk about in the garden disappearing like a genie in a pantomime when anybody went out to look for them.'

She's right, Lily thinks.

Then Felix says softly, 'You said they are trying to make you reveal something they want to know. Would that be the whereabouts of your great-nephew?'

But Miss Chibb turns her head away.

'Who are they, Miss Chibb?' Lily asks quietly. 'Why do they frighten you?'

Miss Chibb does not reply immediately. Her stiff posture makes Lily wonder if she is about to deny that she was frightened, but then she slumps a little. 'I know who I *think* they are,' she mutters, the words barely audible. Then, pointing a peremptory finger at a stack of neatly-folded editions of *The London Times* beside her chair, she says in a very different voice, 'I have the newspaper delivered regularly.' She sends them both a challenging look. 'Not only do I read, I *reflect* upon what I have read, I try to fill in the spaces between the lines, to supply by means of my own reasoning the information that the journalists are not permitted to state openly. I

have friends in London with whom I am in regular correspondence, and they—' She stops abruptly.

'And what have you concluded?' Felix asks.

'We live in perilous times, Mr Wilbraham,' Miss Chibb
replies. 'The inhabitants of powerful countries such as England,
France and Germany believe themselves to be safe within
their firmly-governed borders. They put their faith in those
who, either through royal blood or election to power, have
governance over them. However, such faith is to an extent
misguided, for the security of these countries is less perfect
than their governments would have us believe. There are many
dark forces at work underneath the surface, and the wise are
becoming aware of them.'

Lily glances at Felix, who is looking as bemused as she is
feeling. 'But—' he begins.

Miss Chibb ignores him.

'I do not expect you to know, but in France, England and
Germany, new branches of the police and the military are in
development. The French already have their *Deuxième Bureau*,
and they always like everyone else to believe they are ahead
of the game. These new organisations all have the same exclusive purpose, which is to seek out, watch, pounce on and
eradicate the enemies of the state. The English—'

'I know something about this!' Felix exclaims softly.
Turning quickly to Lily, he mouths *Marm*. She nods. 'There's
talk of a new section of the Metropolitan Police whose sole
purpose will be to watch and report on the Irish question.'

'So I believe.' Miss Chibb nods. 'And there are other matters
that require some secret and clandestine new body to counter
nebulous and imperfectly understood threats.'

'But why on earth should such an organisation be interested
in Wilberforce?' Lily demands. 'He's accused of killing his
father, although none of us believe he is guilty, and—'

But Miss Chibb interrupts. 'You have forgotten the man
who was murdered at the Paimpont asylum, Miss Raynor.'

'No I haven't,' Lily protests, 'I was just coming to him,
although we know nothing except that he was found covered
with blood at the foot of the stairs with his throat cut.'

'I can tell you more,' Miss Chibb says quietly. 'For, unlike you, I have the advantage of having talked at length to the poor innocent young man who was accused of the murder, and whose nightshirt cuffs were soaked in blood in order to prove his guilt.'

Lily looks quickly at Felix and sees her own excitement in his face.

'He was called Louis,' Miss Chibb begins. 'He was a few years younger than Wilberforce, and in poor physical health. He was born to a woman already approaching middle age, and she did not survive the birth of her only child. He was pale, thin and disinclined to eat the good, nourishing food that was pressed upon him. He was frail, he preferred to stay in his room and would not mix with other patients; he was well-read and, on good days, permitted Wilberforce to go in and talk to him. He was in dire need of a friend, for, as he told Wilberforce, his life had been full of betrayals and he did not know who he could trust. But Wilberforce was English, do you see' – she leans forward eagerly – 'which, of course, made it likely that it would be safe for Louis to confide in him.'

'In the asylum they referred to him as the mysterious foreigner,' Felix says.

Miss Chibb affects not to hear. 'But then, of course, the poor boy was killed,' she says. 'Wilberforce knew nothing of the brutal slaying until he was roughly woken from profound sleep to discover armed men in his bedroom, a doctor and two very well-built nurses bending over him, voices shouting, someone screaming and the stench of blood in his nostrils. The lamps were lit, and Wilberforce discovered the source of the blood.' She shudders, briefly closing her eyes. 'He thought at first that it was his own blood; that either he or someone else had slit the veins in his wrists. But then he understood.'

'The blood was spilled on his nightshirt cuffs to make him look guilty of Louis's murder,' Lily whispers.

'Yes,' Miss Chibb says. 'And however hard he tried to protest his innocence, to swear he had been fast asleep and nowhere near the stairs Louis fell down as he died, nobody believed him. The forces ranged against him were too powerful,' she mutters darkly, 'and he was left in no doubt that he was about to be arrested, put on trial and executed for murder.'

'Leaving him with no option but to flee,' Felix says.

Miss Chibb nods.

'So the mysterious foreigner was called Louis,' Lily says after a brief silence. 'Was he French?'

'French?' Miss Chibb's tone is derisive. 'No. Use your logic, Miss Raynor! If he was French, the staff at the Paimpont asylum would hardly refer to him as a foreigner, would they?'

'No,' Lily admits.

'He was German.' Miss Chibb says the last word so softly that it is only just audible, as if she fears eavesdroppers at the door and must make quite sure they do not hear.

Lily is quite sure that the mystery man's nationality is somehow significant. But, at a loss to see why, she turns to look at Felix. He gives a shrug.

Abruptly Lily's irritation rises, hotly and irrepressibly. 'Enough, Miss Chibb, of clandestine government agencies, of your hints at things we ought to know but we clearly don't,' she says spiritedly. 'Let me summarize what I think: Wilberforce came to you for help, and you gave him money, probably a great deal of money. He refused your offer of a lawyer, and when he could come up with no alternative plan but to lose himself in the depths of rural France, you told him not to.' She pauses. Miss Chibb is watching her very closely, her body tense. 'He's still here, isn't he?' Lily says quietly. 'You said you would take care of him. You said, I expect, that you'd think of something. You promised to save him.'

Miss Chibb suddenly looks every one of her almost eighty years. 'I did,' she whispers. 'God help me, I did, and I have been trying. I am considering a letter to one of my London friends . . .' She stares up at Lily and Felix, her face anguished. 'But he's in such a state!' she cries. 'He was never very practical – I have no idea how he managed to travel here from Pont-Aven – but the strain is destroying him. It is *pitiful*.' She pauses, visibly collecting herself. 'And,' she adds, dropping her voice, 'as he always does when threatened, he is retreating into the world where he feels secure. He draws endlessly, obsessively, and always the same disturbing image.'

'We have seen an example,' Lily whispers.

Miss Chibb nods. 'The cat. The *eyes*.'

And she shudders.

'Where is he, Miss Chibb?' Felix asks quietly.

For some moments she doesn't answer. Then, with a deep sigh, she says, 'He is near. I told him to be on his guard against the two strangers who have been watching me.' She stops. Then – and it is as if her resistance has finally crumbled – she murmurs, 'He will be looking out for help that comes from me, for I promised, although I was not envisaging a pair like you.' She gives a grim smile. 'Wilberforce will find you.'

'Do you think she was right?' Lily asks as she and Felix stride away from Spa Hydro de St Roc. 'About sinister agents from some government's secret force watching her?'

Felix has been thinking of little else since they left Miss Chibb's room. 'Yes. I can't think why but I do.'

'But it seems so unlikely!' Lily protests.

'I know,' he replies. 'I'd say the same, except that Marm mentioned something very similar.'

'Ah!' she exclaims. 'You mouthed *Marm* at me when Miss Chibb was talking. What did he say?'

Felix thinks back. 'Much the same thing that she did, except he didn't glean it from some subtle reference in *The Thunderer.* Someone he knows in the Metropolitan Police mentioned it.'

'But he doesn't like the police,' Lily protests. 'He—'

They are walking along beside a high wall, overhung by the branches of a row of lime trees. Suddenly a small gate set into the wall opens a crack and an urgent voice hisses, '*Over here!*'

Felix starts to move towards the little gate, but Lily catches his arm. '*No!*' The sound is a suppressed cry. 'Felix, we have no idea who—'

'Come on! *HURRY!*' The insistent voice is louder now. '*He's armed!*'

Felix looks over his shoulder.

Two men, dressed alike in long, dark overcoats. One is running, his hat in his hand, and he has fair hair. The other's face is concealed by his hat brim, but Felix has a fleeting impression of a fulsome, dark brown moustache.

This man has a gun in his hand.

Felix lunges forward, grabbing Lily's hand and dragging
her with him. He drops his shoulder and shoves the gate further
open, pushes Lily through and instantly turns to shut it again.
But there is a thin, gangly young man beside him doing exactly
that, dropping the latch into place, sliding a bolt and turning
a big key in the lock. Spinning round to face Felix, who is
trying to shield Lily, he says urgently, '*Run!*'

A narrow, overgrown path runs along inside the wall, veering
sharply away under the trees after a few paces. The gangly
young man is pointing frantically and Lily is already running.
Felix thunders after her, the young man right behind.

As they reach the bend, the sound of a gunshot smashes
the spring stillness. And, as they spin round in horror to look,
a few inches above the lock the solid wooded panels of the
door are smashed into splinters.

Felix takes Lily's hand again and all three of them race in
beneath the trees.

The path through the trees is little more than an animal track,
and it twists and turns to no obvious purpose. Lily, in the lead,
pauses at a place where it diverges, and is pushed quite hard
out of the way as the thin young man forges past her.

'I am so sorry,' he pants, giving her a quaint little bow, 'I
did not mean to be discourteous, but I know the way.'

He dives off down the right-hand track, moving swiftly,
shoving branches aside, glancing round regularly to make sure
Felix and Lily are close behind.

Another shot rings out. Felix assumes – hopes – their
pursuers are still trying to get the gate open. Fleetingly he
wonders why they don't just pepper the wood around the lock
with bullets, then he thinks: *they're on the edge of a village.*
One or two shots might be unremarkable in an area where
people undoubtedly hunt, but a whole fusillade would attract
attention and require explanation.

The trees grow thin and the gangly young man stops, putting
up his hand to halt them. Felix stops close behind him and
sees that they are on the edge of what appears to be an
overgrown garden. 'Where are we?' he says quietly.

The young man turns. He is tall; almost Felix's height,

but so skinny that he appears taller. He is wearing what looks like an ancient military overcoat and has a schoolboy's leather satchel on his back. His shock of dark hair flops over his damp forehead, and he brushes it away. His cheeks are flushed, but otherwise his skin has an unhealthy, yellowish look. His cheekbones stand out sharp and stark in his long, thin face and his well-shaped nose stands proud like the prow of a ship. His eyes, brown with golden lights, are watching Felix intently.

'I have led you to my hiding place,' he says. 'These are the grounds to a big house that burned down and is virtually a ruin. It's uninhabited. I have made a camp there,' – he points across the wilderness of coarse grass, straggly shrubs and self-seeded trees – 'in that little building.'

Felix looks. The building seems to be a pavilion, situated halfway down the long side of a flattish rectangle of finer grass which was clearly once a tennis court. The walls of the house are over to the right.

'We can't use it,' Felix says. 'If those men follow us this far, they'll see it and guess that's where we are.' He thinks rapidly, then turns to the right. 'This way.'

He turns back into the trees and pushes a path through the undergrowth. After perhaps fifty yards, he steps out on to what must once have been a terrace. Now the fire-devastated old house is right in front of them. He runs on, and two pairs of footsteps follow. Round the side of the house, across a wide semicircle of forecourt, down the short drive, overgrown now and almost indistinguishable from the undergrowth on either side. A pair of gates appear before him, as tall and forbidding as those of the Spa Hydro de St Roc. These gates too have a lodge, and the door looks fragile. It responds to Felix's kick, and he stands back to let Lily and the gangly young man go inside. He checks swiftly to make sure there is a second exit – there is, there's a window in the tiny second room which gives on to a tangled, bramble-ridden hedge – then turns to the young man.

'Wilberforce Chibb?' he asks.

And with a smile that crinkles the brown eyes and illuminates the thin, haggard face, the young man says, 'Who else?'

Lily reaches out a tentative hand. 'We've been looking for you,' she says gently. 'We've travelled from London, and we've just come from talking to your great-aunt.' She smiles, and Wilberforce does too. 'We know what happened. You'd been accused of murdering your father, and we believe that when that poor man was murdered in the Paimpont asylum, someone took pains to make it seem that you killed him too.'

'I didn't! I haven't killed *anyone*!' The protest is an agonized cry. 'It is true that I had my razor in my hand when Father went for me, but they only said I was going to attack him with it because of the girl in the market in Egypt, only I wasn't trying to hurt her, I was trying to *save* her! But *everyone* thinks I'm some terrible razor murderer, and when they wanted to get rid of poor Louis, it was the easiest thing to use those awful rumours about me and make it look as if I had done it! But I *couldn't* have done, I couldn't kill anybody, especially not Louis because he was my *friend* and I *really* looked after him and all those times when he was too sick and in too much pain to leave his bed it was me he wanted to be with him and I used to read to him and he said it was nice and it helped him sleep and—'

His distress has been growing as the hot, hurt-filled words spill out of him, and now his tears threaten to choke him. Mutely he shakes his head, his thin shoulders slump and he sobs as if his heart is breaking.

Lily gives a soft sound of distress. 'We believe you,' she murmurs. Felix can see she wants to comfort him – to hug him, even – but wisely she holds back. Felix has noticed how stiffly the young man holds himself, the rigidity of his thin body putting an almost visible barrier around him. Briefly he gives into his fear and drops his head into his dirty hands, and a muffled sob breaks out of him. Then he straightens up, wipes the back of his hand across his nose and cheeks, gives Lily a polite smile and says, 'I apologize for my loss of control.' He turns to Felix, giving the formal little bow again.

'No apology necessary,' Felix replies. He too is deeply sorry for the young man. He wonders what sort of a state *he'd* be in after being wrongly accused of patricide and the murder of someone he cared about, locked up in three different places

– one of them his own attic bedroom – and escaping from each one, then fleeing first across Brittany and then right down the west coast of France with a couple of determined gunmen after him. *I don't think I'd break down in tears and wish I could cling on to Lily*, he thinks honestly, *but it'd be a close-run thing. Especially the clinging on to Lily.*

As if she senses he's thinking about her, Lily turns. Seeing that he is smiling, she smiles back.

'We can't stay here,' he says decisively. 'You did well to find such a good hiding place, Wilberforce,' – the young man looks delighted at the compliment – 'but those two men know where we are now, or, at least, they know we've entered the grounds of this old house and very soon they'll start searching it.' *If they haven't already*, he thinks.

'This gate house is well hidden,' Lily says, looking at Felix. 'How on earth did you know it was here?'

'Lucky guess,' he says modestly. 'Now, we need to move, and—'

'But where?' Wilberforce says rather wildly.

Of course, Felix thinks grimly. *He has no plan; Miss Chibb told us that.*

It was going to be up to him and Lily to come up with one.

'What about going home?' Lily ventures. 'Back to Rye, where your family will look after you.'

'*No*,' Wilberforce mutters. 'Anyway, there is only my sister Alexandra now, and it would be more a case of me looking after her than the other way round.'

'Your uncle Mr Bowler was involved in your care,' Felix points out.

Wilberforce's face darkens. 'Uncle Leonard put me in the asylum,' he says coldly. 'He refused to believe I was innocent, and he . . .' He stops. His expression changes, and he looks wildly at Lily and Felix, the soft brown eyes darting to and fro. 'You say that you come from Great-Aunt Eulalia, but who *are* you?' he hisses.

There is a weird look on his thin face. Against his will, Felix hears the echo of Miss Chibb's words: *He's in such a state.*

Instinctively he moves closer to Lily. But, unconcerned, she has reached in her little bag and is presenting Wilberforce with a World's End Bureau card.

Wilberforce reads it. Stands perfectly still and studies it.

Finally he looks up. 'You are both from this private investigation bureau?'

We are *this private investigation bureau*, Felix wants to say. But he merely nods.

'Did my great-aunt hire you?'

'No, we—' Lily begins, but he interrupts.

'Then somebody else wants to find me,' Wilberforce murmurs. He frowns, and Felix wonders if he is running through his list of people who might have done such a thing. 'Who?'

'Your fiancée!' Lily replies with a happy smile. 'Miss Phyllida Westwood,' she adds. Felix suppresses a grin; despite all his harrowing experiences, it is hardly likely Wilberforce has forgotten the name of the woman he is proposing to marry.

He notices that Lily has stopped smiling and is gazing at Wilberforce, her expression concerned. Felix studies him.

And he realizes why Lily is looking anxious. Because instead of being full of joy at learning that one, at least, of the people back in England who are meant to love him actually cares enough to hire private investigators to go and find him, he is slowly shaking his head.

'Phyllida,' he whispers eventually. Just for a moment, he gazes up at the dirty, cobweb-decorated ceiling and a beatific look crosses his thin face. But then he shakes his head again.

'Dear Phyllida,' he says quietly. 'That would have been lovely,' he murmurs, and briefly holds a hand up to his eyes. 'But I am afraid I cannot believe you.'

ELEVEN

'But she engaged me herself!' Lily protests. 'It is her advance payment that is funding our search! She—' Then she stops, holding up her hand.

And Felix hears what she has just heard: voices. Not close, and the exchange is very brief; just a name, softly called – it sounds like *Hamilton* – and a response of *Here*.

'We must go. *Now*,' he says urgently.

'Best to go back the way we came,' Lily says. She frowns, and Felix guesses she is envisaging the journey. 'Then Bayonne, which has good connections and where we could board a north-bound train, that would be quickest, and—'

'The quickest route is the most obvious,' Felix interrupts, 'and the one they'll expect us to take, because they'll calculate we'll head for England. No – we must leave here unseen and take off in an unexpected direction. Lily, have a look at the map.'

But she already has the Bradshaw's open.

She has marked the page and has her finger on Aurelie-les-Bains. 'Here's a place with roads or tracks going in and out from many directions,' she says, moving her finger. 'Look. It's over to the south-east and high in the mountains.'

'St-Jean-Pied-de-Port,' Felix reads. He's heard of it: he screws up his eyes as he tries to remember. 'It's something to do with pilgrims.'

Lily is flipping back through the pages. 'It's ancient,' she says. 'It was on the old pilgrimage routes from France and the rest of Europe to Santiago de Compostela, at the north-west tip of Spain.'

Wilberforce is looking from one to the other of them, eyes round with fear. 'I don't want to go to Spain!' he whispers.

'Neither do we,' Felix says reassuringly. 'But look, if we aim for the south of this place, St Jean de whatever it was, we can pick up the track going into the town from the border.'

'How will that help?' Wilberforce asks desperately.

But Lily has understood. 'Because it's spring, the weather is good and it's likely there will be people walking the path,' she says. 'Our pursuers will be looking for a party of three, but we might be able to blend in with a larger party, and thus, even if they suspect we have gone that way, which I doubt, confuse them for long enough for us to rest and purchase provisions. Then we shall head for Pau, which is on the railway network – I've just checked – and from there we can get to Bordeaux or Toulouse, both of which have train connections to virtually everywhere.'

Felix catches her eye and almost imperceptibly shakes his head; it's exactly what he has in mind, but somehow when Lily outlines the plan, it seems wildly over-optimistic . . .

Something in her confident tone, however, seems to have reassured Wilberforce. He is nodding, looking eager now. 'There's a lean-to attached to this side of the house,' he says. 'It's full of boots and jackets and waxed coats and everything's covered in dust and cobwebs but it's sound, and it's where I found this.' He grabs at the sleeve of his greatcoat. 'We can find similar garments for you.'

Felix doesn't want to. He wants them to get out now and head off to the south, where the mountains soar up. Lily goes over to the door and listens for a moment. Then suddenly her face is full of alarm and she cowers back inside the room.

And all three of them hear the sound of running feet on the hard surface of the road on the other side of the gates.

Felix slips out and, keeping to the undergrowth, crouches down. Slowly he straightens up until he can see the road through the iron bars of the gate. One man is striding away towards the centre of the town, the other is running to catch him up.

He pauses, perfectly still.

I can't swear those two are the pair who shot at us, he thinks, *I didn't manage a good enough look at them.*

But surely they must be . . .

For a moment he is frozen with indecision.

Then he goes back into the gate house.

'Come on,' he says. 'We'll adopt Wilberforce's sensible plan and equip ourselves for a hike, and we'll set off that way.' He waves towards the mountains.

Lily whispers, 'Was it them? The footsteps in the road?'

And he says firmly, 'It was.'

As well as banging the dust of decades off a couple of long, waxed, high-collared old coats from the dilapidated lean-to, Lily and Felix help themselves to stout walking staffs, as does Wilberforce. Hanging on a peg is a compass in a cracked leather case. Wishing she had thought to bring one from home, Lily appropriates it and hangs it round her neck. Consulting it in combination with the Bradshaw's map, determinedly she sets off across the grounds of the ruined house, over the wooden fence to the rear and down a track that leads roughly in the right direction. After half a mile this intersects with a narrow dirt road heading south-south-east, and unerringly she takes it.

For the moment, it seems, they have shaken off their pursuers. Striding along, trying to get into a rhythm, Lily becomes aware that something is nagging at her, and after a few more paces she identifies it.

Yes.

Not now, when they have far more important concerns to deal with such as escaping from men who tried to shoot them, but at some point where they feel safe, she must ask Wilberforce why he doesn't believe Phyllida Westwood engaged the World's End Bureau to find him.

The first few miles are downhill and relatively easy.

But then they stop descending and start climbing.

There is plenty of daylight left, she tells herself bracingly, for the sun is still many degrees above the horizon. They have water with them, for Wilberforce has a metal bottle in a canvas holder and Felix remembered to fill the canteen he purchased in St-Jean-de-Luz. But it is a very long time since breakfast, and that wasn't a substantial meal such as they would have eaten in England but a mere confection of buttery pastries and bread that was full of air holes.

She stops thinking about baguettes and croissants because it makes her mouth water and greatly increases her hunger.

The path is even steeper now. Lily has no idea how far they have come; it feels like at least twenty miles, but it can't be because they haven't been walking that long. They reach an obvious halting spot some three-quarters of the way up the shoulder of the mountain, and Lily straightens her back, putting her hands on her hips to allow her lungs to expand. As her breathing slowly returns to normal, she notices that Wilberforce is delving into his school satchel. He pulls out the end of a large, long loaf: 'It's gone rather hard and there's nothing to go with it,' he says apologetically, 'but would you like some?'

It's only good manners that stop Lily from fighting Felix off it and tearing it out of his hands.

The last quarter of the climb is agonizing. Lily cannot bear to look ahead, for it is too discouraging. Instead she keeps her eyes on the path and counts silently in her head to a hundred, only then raising her eyes to see how far there is to go. At last, they reach the summit.

They celebrate with sips of water, and then Lily looks at the map. The track winds down a short way and then joins a wider one coming up from the south, and even from where they stand, they can see tiny figures moving along the larger track. Lily glances at her two companions. They nod, and without another word she sets off down the narrow, winding path.

'Around here they refer to it as the Roncesvalles Pass,' the woman in tweeds and sturdy shoes says to Lily, 'but of course *we* know it from history as the Ronceval Pass.'

The woman speaks like a schoolteacher and has the air of authority so often demonstrated by the English abroad, as if they alone are appraised of the true facts of history and it is their duty to share them with these ignorant locals.

'Of course,' Lily murmurs. She hears Felix, walking along beside her, give a soft chuckle.

'Battle of the Ronceval Pass, AD778, where the hero Roland led the rearguard and defended Charlemagne's army from the ambushing Basques, bravely standing their ground so that the vast majority of their comrades in arms made it to safety,' the tweedy woman continues, with a disapproving sniff at these cowardly tactics by the enemy.

'But wasn't the Basques' action in retaliation for Charlemagne's attack on Pamplona?' Felix asks innocently. Lily nudges him quite hard; they are depending on their unwitting saviour and her five companions to give them safe passage into St-Jean-Pied-de-Port, and it really isn't wise to antagonize her.

The tweedy woman mutters something disparaging about underhand foreign tactics, and as Felix opens his mouth – Lily is absolutely sure he's going to point out that Charlemagne was foreign too – Lily says loudly, 'Is that where you have been today? To the Ronceval Pass?'

'It is indeed!' the woman replies cheerfully. 'We are on a walking holiday, putting up at St-Jean-Pied-de-Port, and it is a long, challenging walk to the Pass and back. But we fortified ourselves in the little rest house at the Pass and none of us is a jibber!' She glances round at her four companions with steely eyes, as if challenging any of them to contradict her, and a nervous-looking man replies: 'No, Miss Perry, we're not!'

'Is your accommodation good?' Lily asks. 'My brother, his friend and I are in need of somewhere to stay tonight.'

Miss Perry gives another of her sniffs. 'We stay in what purports to be an ancient hostel for pilgrims, and one is left with the impression that the mattresses have probably been on the beds since Charlemagne passed through.' She looks at Lily, and, possibly reading Lily's dismay, adds, 'It is clean, there is a good fire in the evening, the food is a little surprising but plentiful and, although one sleeps in a dormitory, the sexes are *very* rigidly segregated.'

'Would there be room for us?' Lily asks.

'I'm sure there would,' Miss Perry replies.

Too soon they are descending the narrow, stony path into St-Jean-Pied-de-Port. Lily has politely detached herself from Miss Perry's side, and now walks between Felix and

Wilberforce. 'Do you think they are here?' she says softly. There is no need to say who *they* are.

'Unlikely,' Felix replies. 'But just in case, we should not walk together. Wilberforce, go and start talking to that pair of young men at the back. *Don't turn round!*'

Wilberforce forces himself to look ahead again. 'What shall I say?' he whispers plaintively.

'Ask them what they plan to do tomorrow,' Felix says shortly. Glancing at Wilberforce, he adds, 'And do at least try to look like someone enjoying a carefree walking holiday.'

Wilberforce swallows nervously. 'I'll try.'

'I've struck up a conversation with the man just in front of us, who is Miss Perry's brother,' Felix goes on, nodding towards a broad man with a barrel chest who sports a soft hat with a feather and, like his sister, is dressed in tweed. 'I'll walk with him, and Lily, you go up ahead and join Miss Perry and the woman with the paisley scarf.'

'But they're right at the front,' she says. 'I'll be very visible as we enter the town.'

'You will, but for one thing, I don't imagine our pursuers saw you clearly enough to know what you look like, and in any case, now you're wearing the old coat from the lean-to, you'll look different anyway. For another, walking in the lead is the last place someone would be if they were hiding.'

His logic is unanswerable. Lily increases her pace, moves up until she is on Miss Perry's left and is just in time to hear the woman with the paisley scarf say in a nervous undertone that she is sure she has picked up a flea under her corset and has Miss Perry any powder in her luggage?

The hostel is in the narrow main street of the little town, on the far side of an ancient arched bridge over a fast-running river. Lily has found it challenging to keep up her conversation with Miss Perry and the woman in the paisley scarf whilst at the same time trying to look in every direction for signs of anybody watching out for them. She can hear Felix's laughter from further back up the street, and she hopes he is managing to keep an eye on Wilberforce.

The hostel can accommodate them, and Lily breathes a sigh

of relief. Felix and Wilberforce follow the four men of the party along to the mens' quarters, and Miss Perry leads Lily off in the opposite direction, the woman with the paisley scarf trailing along behind and still muttering about flea powder. They follow the dark little corridor for some way, then take two steps up to the left and, going through a stout oak door with iron bolts on the inside, emerge into a room with four narrow single beds at one end and a set of bunk beds at the other.

'Miss Brownlow and I are here and here,' Miss Perry says, pointing an imperious finger at the two beds nearest to the iron stove in the middle of the room. 'I suggest you take that one, dear. There will probably be a draught, for the shutters do not fit well, but at least you will be apart from the cheaper accommodation over there.' She gives a ladylike shudder as she contemplates the bunk beds.

'Thank you, this will suit me very well,' Lily says, shrugging off her leather bag and firmly placing it in the middle of the bed right under the window. It is in fact the one she would have chosen, for there is indeed a soft breeze coming in through the shutters but it is most welcome, since the rest of the room is stuffy and smells of dirty clothes. 'Is there – er, can one wash?'

'Of course!' Miss Perry says indignantly, as if shocked at the implication that an Englishwoman in tweeds and sensible stout shoes could permit herself to stay in a place that did not offer bathing facilities. 'On down the passage and it is the door at the end, and Miss Brownlow and I will follow directly. I should hurry, if I were you,' she adds, 'because there is never enough hot water.'

Felix is awake again. It is not proving to be a comfortable or a peaceful night, and, despite his ability to sleep virtually anywhere, he has discovered that this does not include the bottom level of a pair of bunk beds where the gangly young man on the top one is restless with fear and anxiety and, even when he does drop off for brief periods, mutters in his sleep and is repeatedly hurled back into wakefulness suppressing a scream and writhing as if in great pain. The bunk beds are flimsy and even a small movement makes the wooden supports and the imperfect joints creak as if about to split apart.

The men's dormitory has only seven occupants. They are Felix, Wilberforce, the four men from Miss Perry's party and a large, sweaty youth who appears to be employed at the hostel. At Wilberforce's frightened insistence, he and Felix are sleeping in beds set a little apart from the rest. As he lies open-eyed in the profound darkness just before dawn, Felix reflects that this was the other men's good fortune.

This is at least the fourth time that Wilberforce has woken up in terror. With weary resignation, Felix gets out of his narrow bunk and, standing up, leans over Wilberforce and whispers, 'It's me, Wilberforce. Felix. Would it help to talk?'

After the initial jolt of alarm that makes the bunk beds set off another volley of shots, Wilberforce takes half a dozen steadying breaths and then, in a remarkably calm voice, says softly, 'Wilberforce is a very cumbersome name. My friends call me Will.'

'Will,' Felix repeats. He is touched at the realization that even after so brief an acquaintance, Wilberforce – Will – seems to be looking upon Felix as a friend. He can't help concluding that friends have not been numerous in the young man's life.

'I'm sorry if I'm disturbing you,' Will goes on. 'I tell myself we're safe here, and that I'm very lucky to have met up with you and Miss Raynor, but it's dark and I can't light a lamp which means I can't *draw*, and as soon as I drift off, I see—' But his courage deserts him and he can't make himself describe the night horrors that haunt him.

Felix thinks for a few moments. Then, in what he hopes comes across as the voice of cool reason, he says, 'I cannot deny that you are in danger.' *As are Lily and I*, he adds silently. 'I don't believe you are guilty of murder, but nevertheless you ran away from the asylum, and it is not surprising that the authorities there are eager to recover their patient, nor that the police of two countries wish to establish the truth about the deaths of your father and the mysterious foreigner.'

'But they *shot* at me!' Will's voice squeaks with fear on the word shot. 'You were there, you *saw* them!'

I did, Felix thinks. He has only a vague image of the two

men, the one called Hamilton and the other one. And he remembers, back in Pont-Aven, Cora Todd telling him about a pair of pursuers who she didn't like the look of at all: *He was a tough one, that's for sure. He had cold eyes that looked everywhere, for all he tried to pretend he was here on a nice little holiday.* This description could apply to Hamilton or his companion; Felix didn't see them well enough to judge. But chillingly he knows that the men currently on their trail must be another pair altogether, because one of the Pont-Aven couple was a woman.

One thing he can be sure of, however. He doubts very much whether either the French or the British police would open fire on a fugitive out on the street when he was unarmed, and they surely wouldn't if this fugitive had two other people with him. It is equally unlikely to be the sort of behaviour of men employed as guards at an asylum.

Which leads him straight to the worrying conclusion that whoever these people are who are so keen to hunt down Wilberforce Chibb, they are ruthless, dangerous and probably won't hesitate to kill him.

Not a word of this can be breathed to poor Will, though. Trying to rid his thoughts of men in dark coats with side arms, Felix says gently, 'Yes, they shot at you. But they did not hit you, Will. The three of us escaped, we got out of Aurelie-les-Bains and lost our pursuers in the mountains. They do not know we are here, and the hostel has a stout door that has been secured for the night. Try to sleep,' he concludes, lying down in his bunk, 'and we will move on in the morning.'

He has little faith that his soothing words will have much effect. He lies awake, listening to Will turning over a couple of times. He waits for the next bout of muttering, the next suppressed howl and loud creaking from the bunks as Will wakes to terror once more.

But the sound that presently drifts down to him is quite different: Will is snoring gently, deeply asleep.

Lily has sat down at the long dining table before them the next morning. It is still early, and none of the other guests are about; they requested this six o'clock breakfast the previous evening, saying that their little party had a long way to go today. As Felix and Will sit down on the bench either side of her, Felix observes that she has a map spread out on the old, scarred table. She's also pink in the face, and he guesses she has been out to take the morning air.

'Good morning!' she says brightly.

They return the greeting, and Felix looks at the legend in the top corner of the map: *Following the Old Ways through the Western Pyrenees.*

'Miss Perry was telling me last night all about her map,' Lily says quietly – the sweaty youth has stumped into the room and is unloading a tray with a coffee pot, a jug of hot milk and three mugs – 'and when I said it was exactly what the three of us needed and where did she purchase it, she said she brought it with her from London and acquired it from some special walking club she belongs to where, in her own words, they like to do things *properly.*'

'Then where did you get this one?' Felix demands.

Lily smiles smugly. 'From Miss Perry. Her brother also has a copy, they only have one more day of their holiday and they are doing a local walk today.'

'That was most generous of her,' Will says.

Lily snorts. 'It wasn't generous at all! She made me pay for it, and despite the fact that it's well used and has a black-currant jam stain on the corner,' – she stabs her finger crossly at the top right-hand corner – 'she charged the *full price!*'

Felix smiles at her indignation. 'It's worth whatever you paid,' he says. He too is pointing at the map, moving his finger along a dotted green line that enters St-Jean-Pied-de-Port from the south and leaves to the north-east. In tiny letters it is marked *Ancient Pilgrimage Route.* 'If we compare this map with the one in Marm's Bradshaw's,' he goes on, 'I'm all but certain we'll discover this path goes to Pau.'

Lily has her smug smile back on her face. 'I've already checked,' she says. 'It does.'

TWELVE

I t is not long after half past six when they leave the hostel. Lily has settled the bill – she is surprised at how modest it is – and they are standing in the dark recess of a doorway as Felix carries out a reconnaissance. Her young companion has just invited her to shorten his name to Will – 'I said the same to Felix last night.' – and she has remarked that the abbreviation is indeed more convenient.

She is making polite conversation in a not very successful attempt to calm him, for he is tense with nerves and trembling gently.

Felix is back.

'All clear,' he says softly. 'I didn't see any signs of activity, either in the private houses or the other hostels.' He grins reassuringly at Will. 'Doors still closed and barred, windows firmly shuttered,' he adds. 'I'm pretty certain nobody except the fat boy who chucked our breakfast at us knows we're leaving, and I doubt he'll remember once everyone else comes down.'

'But—' Will begins.

Lily touches his arm lightly. 'We will not improve matters by crouching here and speculating,' she says kindly.

'I agree,' Felix says bracingly. 'And I have excellent news: I believe I have found our path! If I could just have a look at the map, Lily,' – she has it folded to the right place and hands it to him – 'I can verify it. Yes!' He gives the map back to Lily and strides out over the bridge, turning off to the right down a narrow little lane lined with modest little shops. Lily and Will follow. The lane twists and turns a few times before emerging on to a wider road, which he crosses before heading down a track. They go over an old stone bridge that humps up over a fast-running stream and continue for a few hundred yards before coming to a place where three tracks meet. Here he pauses. 'We need to go north-east,' he mutters. 'Lily, have you the compass handy?'

She has, but she doesn't need it.

'It's that way.' She points up the right-hand path, the least distinct of all, which looks more like an animal track.

'Are you sure?' He is frowning, and Will looks anxious again.

'Absolutely certain.' She moves over to the side of the path, crouching down to move grass and foliage away from a stone set in the earth. It is covered in yellow lichen, deeply pitted and looks as if it has stood there a very long time. She looks up, meeting Felix's quizzical eyes. Then she points to some marks that have been carved into the surface of the stone. They form a cross with equal arms, and they each end in a three-branched design like a little trefoil.

'It's the Cross of St James,' she says. 'In Spanish he's called *San Iago*, which contracts to Santiago.' When neither man replies, she hurries on. 'There has been a pilgrimage trail to Santiago de Compostela for centuries, ever since the head of St James was found there and they built a cathedral to house it. People used to come from all over Europe, and they travelled on tracks and paths like this one. It was long before the days of maps, and people were probably illiterate anyway, so the trails were marked with a sign that everyone would recognize.' She traces the arms of the cross.

Felix smiles. 'Well done,' he says.

'Miss Perry told me,' Lily admits. 'She recognized me as someone totally ignorant in the history of the pilgrimage, and she didn't stop lecturing me until even she could no longer pretend not to see me yawning.'

She straightens up, brushing grass and earth from her hands. 'This way,' she says determinedly, and strides off up the path.

To begin with, the going is quite easy and they make good progress. They are still close enough to St-Jean-Pied-de-Port for there to be hamlets and isolated settlements on the trail, and they purchase bread, a round of cream goat's cheese and two rather dry onions and pack them away for their midday break. Gradually, however, the little farms and the single houses peter out. At times it is very hard to find the marker stones. At one place where the track divides into two just beyond a narrow old bridge, where both paths are roughly the same size and both go more or less in the right direction, it takes them almost half an hour before Will gives a shout of triumph and finds the Santiago cross, carved into the parapet of the bridge on the right-hand side.

The climb has been gentle but continuous. Lily's legs are aching when they stop at midday to eat, and she is careful not to show what a relief it is to sit down. Hungrily cramming food into her mouth, she catches movement out of the corner of her eye. Turning, she sees Will, his bread and cheese in one hand and in the other a piece of charcoal. He is bent over something resting on the school satchel on his lap, deeply involved in whatever it is he is doing.

She opens the map and studies it. She is dismayed to see that it shows a range of mountains in front of them, enclosing their current position in a gentle curve to the north and the east. Pau is on the far side of the summit, and it looks as if they have no choice but to scale the great natural obstacle rearing up right in their path.

She notices Felix watching her and makes herself smile. 'We are making good progress,' she says brightly. 'Judging by the scale of the map, and assuming I have correctly pinpointed our present position – and I'm sure I have because we just crossed that stream down there – I calculate we have walked twelve miles or more since we left St Jean.'

'We should make halfway by nightfall,' he replies.

She nods. She knows he meant to be encouraging, but his mention of nightfall has reminded her of what she is trying hard not to think about: where they will spend the night. They have saved half of their food, so there will be supper of sorts. But they are in the Pyrenees, and it is not yet May: it will be very cold.

Packing away the bread and the cheese, taking a sip of water, she reflects miserably that taking this ancient and discreet trail over the mountains might be keeping them safe from men with guns who are trying to hunt them down, but that will be of negligible benefit if they all die of cold.

*   *   *

The path becomes steeper. The mountain now looming ahead looks to Lily like the side of a tall building. She is already weary, and now she has to pause every time they reach the top of the steeper inclines to rub the cramp out of her thigh muscles. They go on, up the most savage little slope that they have yet encountered, and she is just wondering how to ask if they can have a short rest stop when Will, who is taking a turn in the lead, turns round to Lily and Felix clambering up behind him and, with a beaming face, cries, 'Look! *Look*! Oh, come and look at this!'

His excitement is a spur, and Lily gathers up her skirts and hurries up the last few yards of the climb. He grabs her hand to haul her up beside him on his shelf of rock, and she follows the direction of his pointing arm.

And lets out a cheer of delight.

The mountain still stands like a barrier in front of them. But the path turns abruptly to the left, then to the right, twisting and turning as far as the eye can see. And instead of climbing, it stays level, following the contour around the side of the mountain's lower slope rather than heading straight up over it.

Felix comes puffing up to join them. He too sees what is making Lily and Will so happy; he too grins. When he has got his breath back, he says, 'The path looks dry, as well as level. I had a school friend at Marlborough College who liked walking the old routes. He told me that you come across many routes called Dry Hill Lane, or Dry Hill Road, and they originated with our distant ancestors who first walked the land and who, just like us, preferred to reach their destination without soaking their footwear. They learned from experience which tracks stayed dry, and hence the name.'

'If I had a glass of wine in my hand,' Lily remarks, 'I would raise it in a toast to our ancestors and thank them for the fact that they avoided steep climbs wherever possible too.'

As the afternoon wears on, Lily can no longer deny that the light is starting to fade. They are heading almost due east now, along the long summit of one of the foothills, and she does not have to watch the sun slowly sinking in the west.

But the growing chill in the air is unmistakable.

They are all adequately dressed for the daytime, and they have the heavy old coats they took from the lean-to behind the ruined house. She has a growing dread, however, that these are not going to be anywhere near adequate for the coming night.

They reach another bifurcation in the path. The marker stone is right on the junction, but Will has to peer at it in the dim light before he can make out the cross. Sensing that she is not the only one to feel apprehension, Lily looks at the map, does another of her calculations and says, as cheerfully as she can, 'Thanks to the fact that the path stayed fairly level, we have made very good time and we are well over halfway.'

'Good,' Felix says, and she can tell from the enthusiasm with which he speaks the word that he too is worried about the cold and the night to come but trying not to show it. 'We'll go on while the light lasts, and then—'

'Then stop to eat,' Lily finishes. 'Food will hearten us!'

But neither Felix nor Will answers.

They cover another mile, perhaps two. It is growing darker. Felix is now in the lead, and his pace has slowed. As Lily anxiously watches him, she sees him come to a halt.

'What is it?' she asks.

'It's . . .' He pauses. 'I'm surely mistaken, but I thought I saw a light ahead.'

She hurries forward to join him. She peers into the darkness. For a moment she can almost make herself believe she too can see a light, but then it's gone. She senses Will, coming to stand beside her. After a long moment, he says very softly, 'I can't see a light, or I don't think I can. But I can smell woodsmoke.'

Together Lily and Felix take a great sniff of the chilly air. And they both shout, 'So can I!'

They hurry on, down a short slope, around a bend. They are in a narrow valley, and there is indeed a light ahead, and the smell of smoke is now accompanied by the rich aroma of simmering meat: someone is cooking a stew. Felix is running, calling out encouragement but none is needed, for

Lily is right behind him and Will is pounding along at her heels. They can make out the source of the light now: there is an oil lantern hanging from a hook outside a simple wooden construction that is little more than a hut. But beside it there is a tiny stone chapel.

There is a hand-painted sign in front of the hut, and written in black capitals is *MAISON DE BONNE ESPÉRENCE*. Someone must have heard their approach, for the sturdy door of the hut is opening to reveal a very small man dressed in a monk's habit with a bald head circled by a band of greying brown hair. He is extending his hands towards them in welcome, and he is smiling as he addresses them in French.

Lily, listening to Felix's response, tries to understand. But then the monk gently takes her hand and leads her inside. A fire is burning brightly in the hearth, an ancient iron cooking pot bubbles on the stove, another monk is cutting bread and turns to give them a cheery wave with the hand holding the bread knife, a third monk busy building up the fire says something that makes the others laugh.

Felix turns to Lily, and she can read the huge relief in his face. 'This is the House of Good Hope,' he says. 'The monks have been running it for centuries – well, not these three, obviously, their predecessors – and it was put here on the pilgrim trail because we're roughly halfway between St-Jean-Pied-de-Port and Pau.'

'Why were they laughing?' Lily asks, wanting to laugh herself for the sheer joy of warmth and light, shelter from the dark and the imminent promise of food.

Felix is laughing too now. 'Because the brother by the fire just said it never fails, they open a window to let out the smell of Brother Luke's mutton stew and people *always* turn up.'

The monk who invited them inside is saying something else. Felix says, '*Oui, oui, s'il vous plaît, c'est très gentile,*' and the monk smiles and nods.

Lily looks enquiringly at Felix. 'He just asked if we'd like accommodation for the night. I said yes please.'

The monks retire early. Soon after the evening meal has been eaten, cleared away and the pot, crockery and cutlery washed and stacked on the shelves, the three of them go over to their little chapel for the last office of the day, and then return to say courteous but brief good nights. Brother Michel – the small monk who welcomed them in – apologizes for absenting themselves but explains that they must be up at dawn for the first office of the new day. Felix tries to think how to say *please, there is no need to apologize* in French, but he is too weary, and has to be content with renewing his heartfelt thanks and saying yet again that the food was delicious and he's sorry that he and his companions all gulped it down so fast.

Finally the door closes on Brother Michel and his fellow monks. They sleep in a little dormitory next to the chapel, he has told Felix, but the guest accommodation is through a door at the back of the hut. The privy, he adds, is out in the yard. As the monks' footsteps fade, Lily jumps up and goes to inspect their overnight quarters. She returns with what Felix identifies as a brave smile.

'What is it like?' he asks.

The smile wavers a little. 'Oh – one small room with straw-filled mattresses along the wall. There's an old sheet hung over a length of cord that divides the space in two,' – she is blushing now – 'so I imagine one side is for men and the other for women. There are pillows in proper pillowcases and blankets folded on the beds,' she goes on, 'and although they look rather heavy and coarse, I'm sure we shall be warm enough.'

By no means for the first time, he admires her spirit. Faced with the prospect of sharing a room with him and a near stranger and only a sheet to separate them, she can still find something to be cheerful about.

Will, sitting with his back to them in front of the fire and facing the flames, is intent on whatever he is doing and does not appear to have heard the conversation. Felix notices Lily staring fixedly at him and raises his eyebrows in query. She jerks her head towards Will and mouths *Miss Westwood*.

He raises his hands, palms upwards, to imply he doesn't know what she means. With a tut of impatience, she swoops down to sit beside Will and says, 'Will, there is something I've been meaning to ask you.'

He jerks out of whatever anxious thoughts have been occu-
pying him, and his face is still wearing the worried expression
as he says, 'What is it?'

Equally curious, Felix goes to join them on the floor.

'When I told you back in Aurelie-les-Bains that it was
Phyllida Westwood who had engaged Felix and me to seek
you out and help you, you said you couldn't believe me. Now
I must assure you that she did; she came to the Bureau's office
in Chelsea, she told me the whole story and she said she
wanted us – er, she wanted us to prove your innocence.'

Felix knows this is not precisely what Miss Westwood said.
According to Lily, Miss Westwood told her quite firmly that
she wouldn't marry Wilberforce if Lily's enquiries discovered
he was guilty, which, as Lily had observed, strongly suggested
Miss Westwood had not entirely discounted the possibility.

Now, he thinks wryly, is not the moment to mention this
to Will.

'She did, Will,' Lily is saying, 'truly, she did. She sat right
there in my office, and what's more she gave me a more than
adequate initial payment, plus a considerable amount of money
in francs because, as she rightly said, I would need local
money as soon as I arrived in France and having some already
would save the necessity of finding a money changing office.'

Will is slowly shaking his head. He is muttering to himself,
but Felix can't make out the words and, from the way Lily is
frowning, neither can she. Then Will turns to look at Lily, and
it is a searching, burning stare. 'Phyllida is a dear, sweet, kind
girl,' he says. 'I am not sure if I can honestly say I loved her,
but I liked her, and when my father made it plain that he
expected me to wed, and not to take too long about it, I thought
that marrying Phyllida would be all right because we've always
said good morning and exchanged a few words when we've
met coming out of church, or found ourselves at the same
little tea parties and concerts that the ladies of the town
organize. So I asked her, and she said yes, but then I started
to understand that being married to her would mean being
together all the time, and that we'd have to – well, you know
– and I didn't think I'd be able to do it after all. When Papa's
friend Mr Claridge said he was going on his sketching tour,

I asked him if I could go too, and I think he thought it was my final fling as a single man and he was amused by that and kept making little jokes that I didn't really understand. When he said he'd take me with him I was *so relieved!*' he adds fervently.

For a moment the thin, pale face lights up. But then Will's expression changes. 'Then, of course, there was all that bother in Egypt, and Mr Claridge had to bring me home again.'

Felix glances at Lily. He can sense her distress at Will's outpouring, and her pity for the poor young man is almost tangible.

'You were telling us that Miss Westwood is a kind, gentle young woman,' he prompts. 'Would that not make it very likely that she would want to hire investigators to find you and help you? She must have been deeply worried about you when you were placed in the asylum; but learning that you had been accused of a second murder must have made her all but frantic.'

Lily shoots him a glance. Frowning, she says, 'Miss Westwood most certainly did not appear frantic when she came to the Bureau. Quite the opposite, in fact; she was composed and self-assured.'

'But that's just what I *mean!*' Will exclaims, waving his hands around violently. 'Phyllida's not the sort of girl who would *do* that. And as for having a quantity of French francs ready to give you, for one thing I'm not sure she even knows what sort of money they use in France, and for another, she would have absolutely no idea how to go about acquiring any.'

'She was determined to help you, Will,' Lily says. 'And she had agreed to marry you, so of course she cares about you and wants to help you! Strong emotion can make people do things they never thought they could, you know.'

'She's spent her whole life in Rye,' Will replies stubbornly. 'She's utterly unworldly, she doesn't know *anything!* When I said Mr Claridge and I were going to Italy and on to Egypt, she thought Egypt was in *India.*'

'But she knows *you*,' Lily says firmly. 'She told me your whole story. She described your father, she explained how you had lost your mother and your elder brother, and she said your sister leads a quiet life at home. She told me all about the mystery man in the Paimpont asylum too, and both of us speculated on whether he might be a politician, or an important military man, or even a member of one of the European royal families, and—'

She stops dead.

Felix is wondering if the same thought that has struck him has just occurred to her.

It has. She whispers, 'How could she know all that? About the mystery man?'

And Felix murmurs quietly, 'How indeed?'

Lily has recovered herself. Back straight, eyes intent on Will, she says, 'The young woman who came to the World's End Bureau saying she was Phyllida Westwood was short in stature, well-built and told me she was twenty-three years old. She was dressed in plain but good quality garments: a grey jacket and skirt and a shirt tied with a green ribbon. Her hair was brown and wound into a small bun, and she wore a rather shapeless hat. Her face was round and quite plump, she had a strong chin and a button nose. Her eyes were a very beautiful shade of blue and set at a slight slant.'

Will, who was looking bemused even as Lily began on her description, is now shaking his head in increasingly wild denial. 'No, no, *no!*' he cries as Lily stops speaking. 'Phyllida is tall, slender and fair-haired, and she's always very fussy about her clothes and tries to copy the sort of garments that rich London ladies wear in her magazines. She loves fashion, and gossip, she's not at all resourceful but naïve and not terribly clever, and she hasn't got beautiful slanting blue eyes but round, pale brown ones that are set too close together!'

His voice has risen to a shout, and he is panting, beads of sweat on his forehead.

Round, brown eyes set too close together, Felix thinks. It's hardly the sort of description a love-stricken young man would apply to the woman he intends to marry.

He meets Lily's worried glance. He knows even before she speaks that she's going to blame herself. He is wondering how he can persuade her not to when she says dully, 'Who was she, then? Who was the woman who came to the Bureau and

said she was Phyllida Westwood and engaged me to find her
fugitive fiancé?' Before Felix or Will can reply she adds in a
wail, 'But she *fainted*! Almost immediately after she'd told
me who she was and what she wanted, she went deadly white
and I had to push her head down and ask Mrs Clapper to
fetch a glass of water and a cup of well-sugared tea! You can't
fake a faint!' She looks desperately at Felix. 'Can you?' she
adds in a small voice.

He wants very much to reassure her. To take that self-
accusatory look off her face. 'I've known schoolfellows
manage a very creditable imitation,' he says. 'Usually by eating
something foul that made them puke.'

'Miss Westwood did not vomit,' Lily says, her expression
reproving as if she thinks he has been vulgar. 'And I'm a
nurse, Felix, or I was! I shouldn't have been taken in!'

He doesn't know what to say, so he reaches out and silently
takes her hand.

After a moment Will says, echoing Lily's anguished words,
'But who *was* she if she wasn't Phyllida?'

Neither Lily nor Felix can give him an answer.

They retire to the dormitory.

Lily, behind the sheet that divides the room, lies down on
her bed. Her thoughts are far too hectic to allow her even to
think she might go to sleep, and instead she simply relaxes
her tired body. Her legs ache, and she tries to massage her
sore muscles. The movements, however, make the straw of
her mattress rustle, so she stops.

Felix has extinguished the lamp, and now the room is in
profound darkness. She lies looking up into it. She knows she
should undress, for it will be even harder trying to get to sleep
in her corset. There is silence from the other side of the divide;
presently she hears someone snoring gently. She undresses
down to her chemise, then reaches into her leather bag and
extracts her nightgown and shawl, quickly putting them on.
The dormitory is quite warm; the stove in the other room backs
on to the wall behind the row of beds. She reaches down and
unfolds one of the thick blankets. It smells of lavender
and goat.

She lies down again.

Then from somewhere very close she hears a whisper: 'Lily? Are you awake?'

Felix. It's Felix!

Quickly getting up, she wraps the blanket round her and pulls aside the sheet. 'Yes,' she whispers back.

'Shall we go into the other room?' He is beside her, his mouth is almost touching her ear and his breath is warm. 'Will's asleep.'

She nods. There is a line of orange light around the door into the main room, where the fire is still glowing. Felix takes her hand and very quietly opens the door, and they go through.

They resume their places in front of the hearth.

'She knew about the mystery man,' Felix says straight away. 'That's what I keep thinking.'

'She knew exactly what had happened in the asylum,' Lily adds. 'About how Will came to be accused of murdering the man.' She glances at Felix. He is staring into the fire. 'I know I should have asked myself how she could have known so much,' she whispers. 'All I can say is that the woman who said she was Phyllida Westwood was totally convincing. Not only that,' she goes on, 'she was consistent. Whatever version of Miss Westwood she had invented – and we have to admit it *was* an invention – it was nothing like the real woman.'

'But she knew you could not know that,' Felix says, 'and also that you would not find out. There wouldn't be time because you'd be setting out for France straight away.'

She nods. It's generous of him to try to mitigate her fault, but it isn't really making her feel better. Suddenly she gasps.

'Hush! What is it?' Felix whispers.

'Marm,' she whispers back. 'He knew all about the Chibb family misfortunes, but he also recognized Algernon Westwood's name. Phyllida's grandfather,' she adds impatiently as he mutters, 'Who?'

'It all added to why I believed the woman really was Phyllida,' she hurries on. 'Well,' she adds honestly, 'it didn't even occur to me that she wasn't. And when Marm told me about this Algernon's antecedents founding a business importing hardwoods, and how his son died young and the son's wife succumbed to food poisoning and he – Algernon – adopted Phyllida when she was young, it made the whole story seem so true.'

'That's because it *was* true,' Felix says. 'It was the story of Phyllida Westwood's life and family, and the details were all totally accurate. It just wasn't the story of the imposter who engaged you to find Wilberforce Chibb.'

'Why?' Lily asks softly. 'What reason could anyone have for wanting us to find Will unless they were his family, or someone who cared about him?'

Felix is silent for some time. Sensing he is thinking, Lily keeps quiet.

Eventually he says, 'What would happen if Will were to be found guilty of murdering the mystery man?'

'He'd be hanged,' she replies. 'No, it's the guillotine in France, you said so.' A wave of nausea floods through her. It's all very well to speak of hangings and the guillotine in the abstract, but this is in connection with Will. And she realizes she has become rather fond of him.

No. She pictures his thin, earnest face. Quite a lot more than *rather*.

As if Felix has read her thoughts, he says softly, 'Lily, for now let's not worry too much about why this imposter woman wanted us to find Will. Instead, we'll agree that he's a lonely and frightened young man who's innocent of the charges against him. We'll go on spending the false Miss Westwood's money, but instead of meekly delivering Will to her door for whatever she wants him for – and I really don't think it'll be anything to his advantage – we'll do everything we can to keep him safe from her. Agreed?'

And as she murmurs a fervent '*Yes*,' Lily feels as if a huge weight has fallen off her back.

THIRTEEN

Felix is dreaming.

Solange is dancing in her corset and stockings, a scarlet feather boa wound round her head like a fluffy turban. He is watching her from a vast four-poster bed and through the open windows come the sounds of the countryside: the chatter of hens, the sound of a pitchfork's tines scraping on a stone floor. Solange is pretend-angry with him because he forgot to post a parcel for her and it was important because it's a present for her son, her beloved Henri-Josef, to make up for his old dog dying and now Solange is whispering urgently and telling him to wake up which is silly because he's not asleep, he's watching the end of the feather boa brushing against her breasts and . . .

It's not Solange. It's Lily. She's leaning over his mattress, her face very close so that Will won't hear and wake up. 'Felix! *Felix*!' she hisses. Now she's shaking his shoulder. 'Wake up, I *must* talk to you!'

He slides out from under the blanket, clutching it to him – he is sleeping in his underclothes – and, trying to be as soft-footed as Lily, follows her out of the dormitory and into the main room. He has a quick look outside; the eastern horizon shows a line of pale pink sky, and the room is illuminated by a dull greyish light. The fire is almost out, and it is very cold. Lily, he notices, is fully dressed and, like him, wrapped in her blanket.

'What is it?' he says.

'I've done something really stupid,' she says. She looks furious, and he guesses from what she just said that the anger is directed firmly at herself.

'That doesn't sound like you,' he says lightly. 'What did you do?'

She takes a couple of breaths, then, with the air of someone rushing at an obstacle before they lose their nerve, says very quickly, 'When Miss Westwood left, she was agitated because she would have no way of knowing how the search for Will was progressing, and I offered to keep her informed about our movements. You *must* understand,' she hurries on, 'I wanted only to ease her very evident distress, to comfort her!'

'Of course I understand,' he says. 'And I know you sent a telegram from La Rochelle.'

He is still half-asleep and, as realization dawns, he attributes his slowness to this; he is, he knows, a great deal kinder to himself than Lily is.

'Yes, I did,' she is saying, her fingers frantically braiding and re-braiding the fringe of her blanket. 'Which would have been perfectly all right if she was Miss Westwood, but she *isn't*. Felix, she was so convincing! I didn't for one moment think she was anything but who and what she said she was: Miss Phyllida Westwood of Rye, engaged to Wilberforce Chibb and so desperately concerned for him that she was prepared to seek out a private enquiry agency in Chelsea and pay a great deal of money for their services.'

He is barely listening. There is a very important question he must ask her: halting her rush of words with a hand on her arm, he says, 'Lily, did you send her another telegram?'

She drops her head. Will not look at him. Very slowly she nods.

In the privacy of his own head he says one of the more extreme expletives, several times. Then, when he is fairly sure she won't pick up any tinge of accusation, he says, 'When did you send it and what did it say?'

'From St-Jean-Pied-de-Port, yesterday morning. I went out before you and Will came down, and although the *bureau de poste* wasn't open, there was a man there who opened up when I knocked and I said it was a vital message and please would he send it straight away and he agreed.' She stops for breath. 'I just said *Subject located STOP heading for Bordeaux or Toulouse STOP.*'

The confession seems to be over. He turns to look at her. Her green eyes are wide open, her expression apprehensive. He says in what he hopes is his usual voice, 'Have you got the map handy?'

'Yes!' She extracts it from inside her jacket and spreads it out on the floor.

'Assuming the worse, that in some way we haven't yet fathomed the woman posing as Phyllida Westwood is in touch with those who are hunting for Will, then we must accept that the pair who shot at us in Aurelie-les-Bains know we reached St-Jean-Pied-de-Port, because that's where the message was sent from, and that we're now going to Bordeaux or Toulouse, and have Will with us.' He is studying the map intently as he speaks, trying to read it from a pursuer's perspective.

'Felix, I'm *so sorry*,' Lily says passionately. 'I can't believe I was so foolish, that *not one single thing* about blasted Miss Westwood warned me that she was an imposter.'

Even as she's speaking, Felix notices a change in her expression. He hears her say very softly, '*Oh!*' And just for a moment she smiles.

But this is not the moment to ask her to explain. He says, 'We'll take it that the telegram was received yesterday morning and acted upon straight away. Which means they knew then that we'd be making for Toulouse or Bordeaux, and they'd undoubtedly assume we're going to get on a train as soon as we can, which either involves heading from St Jean back to Bayonne' – he points – 'or on to Pau.' She nods. 'Now there are two of them – again, assuming it's the pair from Aurelie-les-Bains – and I imagine they'd almost certainly have split up.'

She says apprehensively, 'Which means one of them has followed us through the mountains.'

'Even if he has, it doesn't mean he's going to find us,' Felix replies. *Or that this very moment he's crouching outside the door with his gun in his hand*, he adds silently. 'Anyway, it's by no means certain the pursuers were anywhere near St-Jean-Pied-de-Port when – *if* – they received a message sent in response to yours. And where would the imposter woman have sent it? Must we assume she has some sort of messaging network that covers all of France? Imagining the worse – that somehow the message did reach them, and one is now behind us on the pilgrims' trail – we must have a good start on him. If we hurry, we'll get to Pau before him.'

'He could have gone on walking all night,' Lily says.

'No he couldn't,' Felix says very firmly. 'Lily, we had trouble finding the marker posts in daylight! He wouldn't have risked missing one in the darkness. He'll have stopped somewhere, found what shelter he could and hunkered down to wait for daybreak.'

Daybreak.

He spins round to look out of the window.

Daybreak has come.

The monks are coming out of their little chapel as Lily, Felix and Will leave. Brother Michel says they *must* stay for breakfast, only a fool goes off walking in the mountains with an empty belly, but Felix insists they must be off. Shaking his head at such folly, Brother Michel dispatches Brother Luke to fetch some supplies, and he returns with bread, cheese, some withered little apples and three thick slices of ham wrapped in an old piece of cloth. Lily gives Brother Michel some of her francs, and he says he will put it in the poor box. They are still thanking the monks for their hospitality as they stride away up the track.

Lily is trying to walk fast and study the map at the same time. Will, restored after a night's sleep, is up ahead, almost at the top of the first, very steep slope and at the point where the path turns a sharp corner and disappears behind an outcrop of rock. 'Lily, the path is too steep not to watch your footing,' Felix says.

'But we have to hurry!'

'I know, but we won't be going anywhere if one of us falls and turns an ankle.' *Or worse*, he thinks. 'Look, Will's rounded the corner and he's out of sight of anyone following. We'll catch up with him, then look at the map.'

She nods curtly and, gathering her skirts, increases her pace.

As they struggle on, at times gasping for breath, Felix says quietly, 'How do you think he's doing?'

She risks a quick glance at him. 'Will?'

No, the Prince of Wales. *Of course* Will, he wants to say. He nods.

A pause while they negotiate a huge boulder right on the

path. Then she says, 'He's frightened, but then so am I, and I dare say you are too.' Felix makes a non-committal sound. 'But for now, I think it *is* just fear; the very natural fear of someone in our predicament.'

He waits for her to explain. She doesn't, so he says, 'And?'

She smiles, a quick little expression, there and gone in an instant. 'You always *know*,' she murmurs. Before he can ask her to explain that too, she says, 'It seems to me that our poor Will frequently struggles with fear of a very different nature, as if he can see unnatural darkness and dangers swirling round him . . . Or maybe he knows these terrible threats are inside his own head, which I suppose must be even worse, especially if the rational part of his brain tells him they are not real . . .'

They climb on for ten or twelve paces. Felix, who hasn't thought any more or any less about mental illness than the next man, which probably isn't very much, is about to pursue Lily's interesting observation when, pausing for breath, she says, 'It's when Will is fighting very hard against his inner demons that he gets out his sketchbook and starts drawing those wretched cats. You can tell how deeply he's disturbed by how fast his hand moves and how hard he presses down with the pencil or the charcoal.' She gasps another couple of breaths. 'The most recent sketch was truly alarming – the cat looked more like a tiger about to pounce, with its fur on end and its huge claws extended, and, with those awful human eyes, it was just . . . just *haunting*.' She shudders at the memory.

Then, bracing herself, she sets out determinedly on the last slope of the climb. For a moment Felix stands quite still. He is trying to visualise Will doing a drawing and at first sees absolutely nothing. Then an image of Will by the fire last night springs into his head. The young man had been absorbed in some activity, making notes or something . . . No. He'd been drawing. Very fast.

And once that image has come into focus, Felix sees another, and then another, and understands that Lily is quite right.

Cursing himself for his lack of observational skills – and he calls himself a private investigator! – he hurls himself at the ascent.

*   *   *

Shortly afterwards he and Lily join Will at the turn in the path. He has stopped in the shade of the rock outcrop, and, drawing his companions close, is staring down into the valley they have just left. He has a hand up to shade his eyes.

Felix is hot from the exertion but all the same feels a chill. 'What are you looking at?' he asks.

'There's movement on the track we came down yesterday,' Will replies. He points.

'An animal?' Lily says hopefully.

'A horse, I think, or maybe a mule.' Will turns to look at them. He has gone pale. 'But it won't be travelling along the path to please itself.'

Lily already has the map spread on a shelf of rock. 'We are here.' She points. If she's afraid, Felix can't detect it in her voice. 'This is where we are bound.' She stabs at the letters *PAU*. 'The monks said that the Maison de Bonne Espérance was halfway between St Jean and Pau, but in fact it is quite a lot closer to Pau, which I believe is no more than fifteen miles away.'

'Fifteen *miles*!' Will bursts out. 'And he's on a mule!'

'Fifteen miles on the main track, which is this one,' – Lily runs her finger along a solid green line – 'and which in all likelihood is the only track shown on most maps. Thanks to Miss Perry, we are guided by an older and much more detailed map, and this is the path we shall be taking. As you'll see, it follows one side of the triangle as opposed to the other route, which follows the remaining two, and I estimate that this probably cuts the distance to about—'

She is still working it out when Felix says, 'Ten miles, or probably less.'

Will does not look reassured. 'But he's going faster, and he'll follow us up the shorter track!'

'Not on a mule.' Felix is pointing up the narrow little path. 'I know they are good at climbing, but they can't suddenly lose half of their width.'

Up ahead, where the track abruptly steepens to a short climb they'll probably have to do on hands and knees, it turns sharply to the left, and the rock walls narrow to form a dark and sinister-looking tunnel. Even Lily will have to go through sideways, and Felix thinks Will will probably have to shove him from behind.

The tunnel is even more unpleasant than Felix anticipated. As well as being narrow it is low, and Felix is tall. So is Will, but he's not nearly as broad as Felix and he's skinny into the bargain. Lily leads the way, Felix follows her and Will brings up the rear.

She has to feel her way because the light fades to virtually nothing as soon as they have gone round the first curve. She calls out as she goes: 'Path going steeply upwards. There are steps but they are very rough and – *ouch*.' And, later: 'The roof is sloping down. *Really* down, much lower than just now. Felix, you may have to crawl, you too, Will . . .'

After what seems an age, the light begins to wax and then they are out again. They stand looking at each other. Lily and Will are grinning broadly, and Felix is sure he is too. They bash the dust and the cobwebs and the gritty bits of rock off each other, have a drink from the replenished water canteens, and Lily consults the map.

'I think,' she says after a moment, 'that is almost all the climbing. Other than a ridge just this side of Pau, it looks as if it's downhill all the way.'

She is right.

They stop after an hour to eat – Felix has been increasingly embarrassed by his rumbling stomach – and the good, nourishing food, together with the easy downward slope of the gently-curving path, lead to a definite increase in their pace.

By noon, they are low down in the foothills and Pau is ahead.

The town is set up on the heights above the Gave de Pau, and the railway runs along the deep valley carved by the river. The station is set amid trees, and on its facade are advertisements for the attractions of the town above. They stop under the trees to study the map and the Bradshaw's.

The trains can take them in one direction to Bayonne and on to Bordeaux, or in the other to Toulouse, on east to Nîmes and then north to Clermont-Ferrand and Paris. Will and Lily are for avoiding the more direct and therefore more obvious route to the west and instead opting for Toulouse. But Felix thinks they are safe: 'There's no sign that anyone's watching us,' he says, 'so let's take the direct route to Bayonne and Bordeaux.'

A large, colourful poster depicts a wide boulevard offering a spectacular view of the Pyrenees. Glancing at it idly, Lily notices groups of very smartly-dressed people sauntering along, the men depicted in top hats and the women holding dainty little parasols. She glances at her companions and hastily ushers them towards the rest rooms.

'We urgently need to tidy ourselves!' she hisses. 'Yes, Felix, I appreciate that we must hurry, but in our present state we are horribly conspicuous, and people will be much more likely to remember us if anyone asks!'

He starts to protest, but then nods curtly and grabs Will's arm. As they go through the door marked *Hommes*, Lily slips into the ladies' waiting room. She uses the lavatory, then hurries over to the wash basins, nerving herself for what the large looking glass will reveal.

She is horrified by her appearance. Much of her fair hair has escaped from its tight bun and clouds around her face. Her chin and forehead are filthy, and her cheeks are pink from a combination of exertion and sunshine. The left shoulder of her jacket is covered with grass stains and soil from where she fell on a down slope. Her hands are covered in scratches and dried blood. She takes off her jacket, fills a basin with warm water, grabs the soap on its metal spur between her hands, lathers up and embarks on a very thorough wash of every part of her that she can decently uncover. Then she takes off her hat and unwinds her hair, brushing it thoroughly and then re-braiding it and fastening it into a bun. She bangs her hat and her jacket against the wall to remove the dirt, then puts them on again. Staring at herself in the glass with critical eyes, she decides she looks neither smarter nor shabbier than the average passenger. She nods; it will do. It will *have* to.

Outside on the concourse, Felix and Will both show the benefits of a visit to the rest room. Felix is holding a bunch of tickets. 'We've bought three tickets each for Bayonne and

Toulouse,' he says, leaning close and speaking softly. There are a lot of people around, Lily observes, but no-one seems to be taking particular notice of them.

'But—' she begins.

'Lily, *listen*,' he says urgently. 'We're safe for now. There's been no sign of the man on the mule for half a day, and I'm sure we lost him when we took the narrow path. But he, or his companion, will undoubtedly be here before too long, and they'll ask at the ticket office about three English people, two men and a woman, and when the clerk tells them we bought tickets for both directions, they—'

'They won't know which way we went,' she finishes.

Will is grinning. 'That was my idea,' he says. 'I bought the Bayonne tickets with some of Aunt Eulalia's money, and Felix bought the others.'

Lily makes herself smile and says, 'Well done!'

Catching Felix's eye, she perceives that he doesn't rate it as a delaying tactic any more highly than she does.

But it's nice to see Will smiling.

They go through on to the platform. Moving steadily through the crowd, they make their way towards the far end, stopping while there are still people around them. Felix goes to stand behind a heavy iron stanchion supporting the roof, inclining his head towards a second; Lily moves towards it. Will follows. As cover, the stanchions are not very substantial, but she too feels the need to keep out of sight as they wait for the Bordeaux train.

A large locomotive puffs into the station on the other line; the one heading east. They watch it, and Lily leans towards Will and is in the middle of an innocuous comment about not many people going that way because the four carriages are half empty when something pings off the metal support just to her right and there is the sound of a gunshot.

Will goes deadly white and moans in terror. Lily looks wildly around. There is a curved footbridge over to the left and she can see a tall figure in a long dark coat standing perfectly still right at the apex.

Then she is jerked violently forward and dragged to the edge of the platform. Felix has grabbed her arm, and Will is hanging on to her other hand. Together they jump down on to the line and sprint across to the train just starting to pull away from the opposite platform. Another shot blasts large splinters of wood from one of its carriages. Felix lets go of Lily and reaches up, jumping once, twice and on the third attempt and with a huge effort, managing to grab the handle of a carriage door. He wrests it open and as it bangs back against the side of the train, the momentum jerks him violently forward. He stifles a cry and, taking Lily round the waist, lifts her and throws her into the carriage. Will is already clambering up, head and shoulders already inside and blocking the doorway, and Felix pushes him hard to get him clear.

The train is accelerating, great billows of smoke rising from the engine and the deafening *puff-puff-puffs* coming louder and closer together. Felix is running now, one arm hanging at his side, the other reaching up to the open doorway. Will and Lily grab him, hand over desperate hand working their way up his arm, his shoulder, his upper body, his waist, his hips and then he is lying on the carriage floor and Will is leaning right over him, out into the perilous opening to catch hold of the door handle. As he crashes the door closed, two more shots ring out, followed by another. But they are moving quickly now. The platform slopes down gently and then disappears under a short length of tunnel. As it emerges on the far side, the track curves away down the river valley and the station is left far behind.

FOURTEEN

Lily is sitting on the floor, slumped against the front of the seat. Will is sitting on the seat opposite, leaning back with his eyes screwed shut. Lily is wearing her leather bag slung across her body, and absently she reaches down to check the straps are fastened, afraid suddenly that all the contents have been lost in the frantic struggle to get on the moving train. No, it's all right, the satchel is still fastened. Oh, that's good, she thinks, because the treasured old hairbrush that Aunt Eliza gave her when she was twelve is right at the top and she'd hate to have lost it because it has little flowers made of mother-of-pearl set in the wood of the back panel and . . .

She hears someone moaning.

She can feel a weight across her legs.

With a sort of snap, she is back in the moment.

Felix is lying with his head on her thighs. He is curled up and his right hand clutches his left shoulder, so hard that the knuckles are white.

In a series of rapid flashes she sees him grabbing the door handle and it being almost torn out of his hand as the door swung away from him. He'd gasped in pain but held on. And now all three of them are safe.

In a rush of deep gratitude mixed with profound affection and tenderness, she gently removes his clutching hand and feels inside his jacket.

'I'm afraid you have dislocated your shoulder,' she says, momentarily proud that her voice sounds calm and matter-of-fact.

He grunts.

Moving cautiously, she gets out from underneath him. 'Will, help me get him up on to the seat,' she says briskly.

Will doesn't answer and, turning to look at him, she sees his eyes are still tightly closed.

'Will!' she repeats, sharply now. 'It's over, we're out of danger,' – *for now*, she adds silently – 'and Felix is hurt. Oh, come along, I need your help!'

Will opens his eyes, swallows, nods and says, 'I'm sorry. What should I do?'

'Felix has dislocated his shoulder,' she says, trying to sound unconcerned and as if such mishaps are a normal occurrence when travelling. 'Reducing the dislocation – putting the shoulder back – is straightforward if it is done quickly, before the surrounding tissues swell, and we must act immediately. Help him up – no, don't hold his arm, hold him round the waist! – and we'll sit him well back on the seat with his back supported.'

Felix subsides on to the seat. His face is ashen, and his lower lip is bleeding from where he's been biting it. He looks up at Lily, and the trust in his eyes almost makes her falter because she knows and he doesn't just how much this is going to hurt.

'Will, stand there, in front of him on my left,' – she shoves him into the position in which she wants him – 'and put both hands on his right shoulder. Lean your full weight against him because I need him to stay very still. Can you do that?' She catches Will's eyes and stares at him intently. 'It's all right, I used to be a nurse and I know what to do,' she adds, trying not to sound as impatient as she feels. His expression changes: he had been looking very anxious and slightly sick, but now, as if forcing himself to rise to her challenge, he raises his chin and says, 'I can do it.' Then, smiling at Felix, he says bracingly, 'I'm here, I'll look after you.'

Lily sees Felix's mouth quirk briefly in a swift smile.

'Now, Felix, I'm going to open your jacket and put my knee into your left armpit.' She does so. 'By exerting a gentle, pulling and turning pressure on your arm' – she takes his wrist firmly in one hand and his forearm in the other – 'the head of the humerus will go back into its cavity. I shall count to three, and on three I shall begin.'

She gives him a reassuring smile.

Before any of them have time to think, she says clearly, 'One, two,' but as she says *two*, she pulls firmly and powerfully on his arm, twisting it in the precise, subtle little movement that was demonstrated to her in the foothills of the Himalayas by a nun who was a natural teacher and whose methods made sure no pupil of hers ever forgot a lesson.

Felix gives a great roar of agony.

His eyes full of involuntary tears, he glares up at her and says furiously, 'You said you were going to do it on three!'

'I know,' she replies. 'I'm sorry. You'd have tensed up, and it goes back more easily when you're relaxed.' She is kneeling beside him, her hands inside his shirt on his warm flesh, fingers feeling all around the shoulder joint. The area is swollen, but as far as she can tell, the reduction has been successful.

She straightens up, removing her hands. He is looking at her, and there is amusement in his hazel eyes. '*What*?' she demands, discomfited and not prepared to work out why.

'I was just about to tell you to unhand me, but then you did,' he murmurs.

Just for an instant they are the only people there. Something flashes in the air, sparkles and is gone. And she says in her coolest professional voice, 'How does it feel?'

He frowns, then the frown clears. 'Better,' he says.

Noticing Will, still obediently pinning Felix back in the seat, Lily says, 'You can stop now, Will, thank you. All done.'

Will jerks away from Felix as if someone has prodded him. Not for the first time, Lily observes how he dislikes and avoids human contact, and a rush of compassion floods through her.

'You did well,' she says to him.

Will beams. 'I know how it feels because I had a dislocated shoulder when I was a boy,' he says in a rush. 'I can remember how much it hurts, and the pain is a hundred times worse when it's put back.'

'Decent of you not to tell me that just now,' Felix murmurs. He has his eyes closed.

'But mine took *ages*,' Will says. 'Father said we didn't need the doctor as he could do it, but he tried and he couldn't and when Doctor Cholley was eventually summoned, it took him four attempts before he was done.'

Lily, disgusted at such parental behaviour, mutters, 'That was *very* poor treatment,' and Felix, clearly imagining how it would feel to experience the agony Lily has just put him through several more times, goes pale again.

'We need sustenance,' Lily says decisively. 'A draught of water and our remaining bread and cheese, but first,' – she is delving in her satchel – 'we shall each take a little nip of this.' And she pulls out a small hip flask.

She gives it first to Felix, and then Will takes a cautious sip. He makes a face. 'What is it?'

'Brandy,' Lily says shortly. She drinks, swallows and feels a wonderful warmth spread down through her.

Felix still has his eyes closed, but his colour is better.

'I've always said it is a good idea to have a nurse with you when you try to board a moving train and dislocate your shoulder,' he says. He opens one eye and looks at her. 'Especially one who hides a hip flask full of the finest cognac in her luggage.'

'It is good for shock, and we have all had quite a severe one,' she says reprovingly. Then she unpacks the scant remains of Brother Michel's provisions and starts handing them round.

The train keeps up a fast speed and it does not make many stops. For some time after tending to Felix's injury, Lily has been preoccupied with watching him while trying not to let him see, and urging him to eat his share of the food, and she has not had time to worry about very much else. But now the afternoon is well advanced, Felix has been asleep for ages, Will is sketching again and, from his expression, deeply, compulsively absorbed. *Poor Will*, she thinks.

Moving almost imperceptibly, she shifts so that she can see the sketchpad on Will's knee. She tries to make sense of what he is drawing, and as soon as she does, jerks away again; a sharp, involuntary movement entirely prompted by the sight of what he is committing to the page.

It is like something from a nightmare.

This time the cat's head takes up the entire page. It is huge, and the way Will has drawn it makes it seem that the creature is forcing its way from the paper out into reality. Its dense fur is darkly shaded so that it looks dark grey or black, and has the suggestion of faint stripes, or brindling. Its mask of a face is stark white, its mouth is open in a great snarl of violent fury and it looks totally, frighteningly wild.

And the eyes – those human eyes – bear an expression of such deadly, ominous malice that Lily fears she will see them in her dreams.

She turns away, gazing out of the window, in case Will looks up before she can hide her reaction.

The train is slowing down to pass through a station. She makes out letters – M, U, R, E, but then someone gets in the way and she misses the rest. She gets out her Bradshaw's and finds somewhere called Muret that is a short distance south-west of Toulouse.

Their tickets only take them as far as Toulouse, and, as far as she can tell, that must be the next station.

Should they get off? Should they stay on beyond Toulouse, and hope they can pay the difference when they finally disembark?

She leans forward and taps Will on the knee. He starts violently and looks at her with a face full of fear, one hand going automatically to cover his sketch.

'Nothing to worry about,' she whispers, 'but we must decide what to do when we arrive in Toulouse, and I don't want to disturb Felix.'

The way in which Will is mutely opening and closing his mouth suggests he does not have an opinion to offer, but fortunately Felix opens his eyes and says, 'I'm not asleep. How far are we from Toulouse?'

'Next station,' she replies shortly. 'And that's where our tickets run out.'

Felix frowns, and she guesses he is disorientated by the combination of the pain and the long, deep sleep. 'What do you want to do?' he asks her.

'I don't think I want to risk getting into trouble for travelling without a ticket,' she says slowly.

'I agree,' he replies. 'We'll get off, then, and find somewhere we can hide out of the way while we decide what to do next.'

She tries to compose herself as the train covers the miles to Toulouse. Too soon – she has been soothed into an illusion of safety by the long journey – their speed begins to decrease.

Then they are drawing to a halt at a long platform in a busy, crowded station. She helps Felix to his feet – the movement clearly hurts, but he does not make a sound – and picks up their bags. With a curiously old-fashioned little bow, Will takes Felix's from her. 'You have enough to do with caring for your patient,' he whispers right in her ear.

They are ready. Will is preparing to open the door and climb down first when abruptly he gasps and draws back, away from the window. He points. Following the line of his arm, Lily sees a tall man in a dark overcoat standing at the back of the platform about ten or fifteen paces further along, half hidden by a porter's trolley piled high with baggage.

'Are you sure it's one of them?' Lily whispers as they all move back from the door.

'Absolutely certain,' Will says. 'It's the man on the mule. I'm sure of it, because he held his head slightly to the left and so does that man.' He points a trembling hand towards the platform.

She does not know what to do.

Felix says softly, 'Lily, we must put our trust in Will. He's an artist, and artists study people in a particularly intent way.'

And, glancing at Will, she sees a strange expression cross the young man's gaunt face: very briefly, he looks as if he's been illuminated from within.

They wait, moving right to the far side of the compartment, crouched down, barely daring to breathe.

Along the train, doors are being opened and slammed shut.

Is it just passengers embarking and disembarking?

Or is it the man in the dark coat, looking into every compartment with his gun concealed in his hand because he *knows* they are on this train?

A whistle blows.

With a series of exhalations the train starts to move.

They keep hidden until they are moving swiftly again and Toulouse has been left behind.

'Where are we going now?' Felix asks.

Lily is studying the Bradshaw's. 'The main line goes on to Narbonne, Béziers, Montpellier and Nîmes, and after that there are different lines going on east to Marseilles, north-east to Avignon and Lyons, or north to Clermont-Ferrand and Paris.'

Paris.

I wish we were in Paris now, she thinks miserably. *I wish we were about to board the boat train and were heading back to England and safety.*

She suppresses the traitorous little moment of fear and goes back to the map of the railways. Will, sitting beside her, is looking at it over her shoulder.

'There's no doubt anymore that they know where we are,' Felix says. 'We should think about— what is it, Will?'

For Will has tentatively put his hand up.

'Miss Raynor only said where the main lines go,' he says. Leaning closer, he puts his finger on the map. 'What about this one?'

Lily looks. 'Millau, Figeac,' she mutters. 'I've never heard of those places. And anyway that line goes in the wrong direction, it won't help us – *yes it will*!' She raises her head, full of delight. 'It goes on to Limoges, and there it intersects with the main line from Bordeaux to Paris! Oh, well *done*, Will!'

'Where does this line leave the one we're now on?' Felix asks.

Lily gets up and goes to sit beside him so that he can read the Bradshaw's map with her. 'Béziers,' she says. Then, anxious suddenly, she adds, 'It's a long way. And we only had tickets as far as Toulouse.'

He looks at her, and she notices an expression in his eyes that she doesn't think she's seen before. 'Don't worry, Lily,' he says gently. 'At the next stop I'll get off, seek out an appropriate official in an important cap and tell him we've made a mistake, we now want to go on to Béziers and please can we buy three new tickets?'

Afternoon is turning into evening when they get off the train at Béziers. Lily and Will disembark together, straight away joining on behind a crowd of women and small children and hoping to pass for members of the same group, and Felix follows a few moments later. They keep apart while Felix goes to the ticket office and purchases tickets for the journey on to

Limoges. While he does so, she hurries over to a small open-fronted shack that sells baguettes and hastily makes a purchase. Turning back to watch Felix, Lily sees him fleetingly hold up a hand with two fingers extended: it is the sign for the platform number.

She goes on watching as he climbs up the steps of a foot-bridge and descends to the far platform. A party of rowdy young men go up after him, and again she and Will tag on to the group. Felix is waiting about halfway along the platform; Lily and Will go past him, careful not to look at him.

As they wait for the train, Lily reflects that their attempts to disguise themselves from anyone searching for them are pretty puny. She glances at Will. His thin face is taut with anxiety. She leans closer and whispers, 'Courage! France is a very large country, and it's highly likely that we are not where they expect us to be.'

He gives her a faint smile, but she doesn't think he is any more reassured than she is.

The train draws in. Even to Lily's uneducated eyes, the locomotive looks smaller than the one that drew the main line train, and there are only two rather basic-looking carriages.

Will hurries forward and flings open the nearest door. Lily is about to protest that they are not entering the same carriage as Felix when she sees that in fact they are, because he has just taken a few rapid paces to his right. She clambers aboard behind Will, her heart pounding so hard that she feels slightly sick. He reaches round her to close the door, and they hurry along the carriage to join Felix.

He is staring intently out of the window. 'What is it?' Lily asks. 'What have you seen?'

'I'm just keeping an eye,' he replies. Before she can ask on what, the train lurches a couple of times and starts to pull away from the platform. She is thrown back on to the hard wooden seat, and Will sits down beside her. Slowly Felix sinks into a seat opposite.

None of them says anything for a while. The carriage is about half full, but nobody is sitting close enough to overhear; Lily realizes, however, that it isn't this that keeps the three of them mute. It's sheer weariness.

Presently she takes the Bradshaw's out of her bag and once again checks the map. 'There are a lot of stations on this line,' she says, 'but I don't imagine the train will stop at every one. Oh.'

They have come to the first place, and the train is in fact stopping.

Felix grins at her. '*Oh* indeed. This journey will take some time, I fear, so we may as well try to rest while we can.'

She watches as he leans his head into the corner between the window and the back of the seat and closes his eyes.

They have been travelling for almost an hour when Will nudges Lily gently in the ribs and says, 'I'm worried.'

The two words seem to hit her like hurled stones.

'What about?'

He hesitates. 'It's probably nothing.'

'Tell me anyway.'

'There's a man in the next carriage who keeps looking this way.'

'Do you recognize him?' she demands. *Oh, please say you don't . . .*

'I–I'm not sure. He's dressed differently, not the long dark overcoat but what looks like a workman's blue jacket and cap.' He shakes his head. 'It's the *way* he's looking. It's so – so *relentless*.'

She reflects on how many little halts there are on this line.

And she thinks she knows why this watchful man in the workman's clothes is keeping such a close eye on them.

She turns to look out of the window. Casually, disinterestedly. It is dark outside, but not dark enough that the watchful man won't see them if they get off at the next station. Where would they go, anyway? They seem to be right out in the countryside now, and, other than the little villages and the hamlets where the train stops, the area is very thinly populated.

Besides, they would almost certainly be leaving the safety of the train for no good reason. The man in the workman's clothes is probably just that, a workman, and he's on his way home, as tired as the three of them and not really watching them at all.

Only she can't quite believe it.

The train is slowing down for yet another station.

Making up her mind, Lily whispers to Will, 'Watch him closely. I'm going to try something. Do exactly what I do,' she adds.

He looks at her worriedly but nods.

The train comes to a stop. A few doors open and close. She waits. Waits some more. And, just as the train begins to strain forward again, she gets up and lurches towards the door, and Will copies her. But she doesn't open it; she simply wipes her forearm across the window as if clearing the condensation to peer out and then after a moment sits down again.

She waits again. She can feel Will's tension, emanating from him like the warmth of a fire. Presently she whispers, 'Well?'

'He got up too,' Will whispers back. 'The instant you did. And his face darkened like a thundercloud.'

She nods.

Oh, God.

She looks across at Felix, deeply asleep. She hates to wake him up because the sleep will be helping his body to heal. But there is no option.

Leaning forward, she says softly, 'Felix.' And puts a hand on his knee. He slowly opens his eyes, focuses, stares at her. 'We have to leave the train.'

He frowns. 'You're sure?'

'Yes.'

To her huge relief, he doesn't ask for an explanation. 'How?' he mouths.

'We'll wait for the next stop. The train builds up speed quickly – I've been checking – and we'll need to act almost as soon as we've left the station.'

'But he'll follow,' Will whispers. 'He'll see us and jump off straight after us.'

'No he won't,' she says with a lot more conviction than she feels. 'I'm going to give him something else to think about.'

'But that means you'll be too late to jump after us because the train will be going too fast!' Will's voice is anguished.

'*Please*, Will!' she hisses.

Felix is staring at her. 'You're sure we have to do this?'
She nods.
'Very well.'
And she leans forward to explain what she is going to do.

Lily feels as if she has entered a dream state. She is clear in
her head what she must do, but it seems so unlikely: what is
she doing here in the depths of the southern French countryside, planning something so risky and with no certainty that
it will work? As she sits quite still, waiting for the train to
start moving again and draw away from the station, an image
flashes through her mind of Felix and Will running off and a
man with a gun holding it up steadily as he takes aim.
Stop that, she tells herself firmly.
She waits.
The train begins to move. She puts her bag beside Will and
stands up, blocking both the door, and Felix and Will, from
the line of sight of the man in the workman's jacket. She walks
between the rows of seats, letting the irregular motion of the
accelerating train send her jerking from side to side. As she
reaches the man in the blue jacket, she lurches right across
him and instinctively he puts out a hand to stop her falling
on him. Instantly she lets out a piercing scream and, drawing
back her arm, slaps him hard across the face. '*Monster*!' she
screams, as loud as she can. It is close enough to the French
word, and already heads are turning, and two men are out of
their seats. '*Scélérat*!' one yells. '*Enlevez-vous vos mains*!'
She screams again, thrashing and struggling as if trying to
fight him off, and now the two men have been joined by two
more and a fat woman, and someone is yelling for the guard,
and as the man in the blue jacket tries to throw off those
restraining him, a powerfully-built young man sits on him and
Lily slips away, hurries back up the carriage and clambers out
of the same door that Felix and Will just used, flinging it
closed as she jumps down after them.
The train isn't really moving very fast yet. But as she flies
through the air and into Will's waiting arms, she screams
in terror.
Then she is on the ground.

And she isn't dead after all.

She wants to catch her breath, to check herself for damage, to ask urgently if the leap has further injured Felix's shoulder, but he and Will are either side of her, Will has grabbed her arm and they are all running, running over the short springtime grass and plunging off into the darkness.

As she runs, she takes a quick look over to her right.

The train is already rounding a bend and disappearing into the night.

'I have no idea where we are,' she says.

They have crossed what felt like an endless field, and now are under the spreading branches of trees that form the edge of a stretch of woodland.

'We were going north, if I remember the map aright,' Felix says. She thinks he sounds remarkably calm, and if there is a tinge of anything in his voice, she suspects it is exhilaration. He is pointing up into the sky. 'That's the Pole Star,' he goes on, 'so while we have neither daylight nor lamplight with which to study the map and find out where to head for, we should go on heading north.'

'Pole . . . Oh, the North Pole!' Will says. *He too sounds as if he's on an adventure*, Lily thinks. Perhaps it's simply relief.

'Go on, then,' she says to Felix. 'Take us north.'

After far too long spent struggling through the wood they come to a track. Emerging from the shadowing trees, the night seems very bright; there is a large slice of silvery-white moon high in the sky. The track runs roughly north-south, and they turn north. The land is deserted. Sometimes they see lights in the far distance which could be farms or hamlets, but the track leads them through deep, uninhabited countryside. Its surface is rough, and there are three deep, continuous ruts with grass growing between them. 'It's an old cart track,' Felix says, noticing her looking down. 'Two ruts for the wheels, one for the horse, and it's not much used, to judge by the grass.'

Will mutters something that sounds like *wish we had a cart now*.

They have been walking for a long time when a structure

of some sort looms up ahead. The darkness is confounding:
it is hard to tell scale and distance. They walk on, and presently the scene clarifies. Through the trees there is a massive
wall, and it continues for some way to the right and the left,
curving away as if encircling something protected within.

Felix says softly, 'There are lights in the distance. Beyond
the walls – look.'

Lily and Will look.

'What are they?' Will is gazing up at the wall ahead.

'Let's go and see.' Felix strides on.

A round tower becomes visible as they go on through the
trees. Beside it there is an arched opening. Lily thinks she's
dreaming again. They go through it and find themselves
standing in an open space between buildings. There are no
lights showing, no smell of woodsmoke, no aroma of cooking.
The place, whatever it is, appears to be deserted.

Over on the far side of the open space there is a steep stair
leading up the side of a tall building, and at the top is a partly-
open door. They climb up the worn stone steps. Will pushes
the door further open and they go inside. The stone floor is
dusty and there are sticks of old broken furniture stacked in
the far corners. A stubby candle sits on a plate. There is a
huge stone hearth set in the wall to the left.

Felix takes out a small silver vesta case depicting an image
of a woman with abundantly-flowing hair. *That's new*, Lily
thinks absently. A Paris purchase, no doubt. He strikes a flame,
putting it to the candle's wick. The light seems very bright
after the darkness. Lily looks around, and Felix says, 'I think
we should use some of that old furniture and light a fire.'

Some time later, sitting on old sacks in front of the blazing
fire, thick chunks of bread split and filled with fresh butter in
their hands, Lily reflects that the situation could be a great
deal worse.

FIFTEEN

Lily creeps over to Felix in the night and in the light of the fire he watches her crouch down beside him.

'Felix?' It is barely a whisper.

'Yes?'

'Are you all right?'

'Yes.'

'Are you in a lot of pain?'

'Some,' he admits – which is an understatement, but what can she do about it? – 'but it's better than it was.'

'I wish I could make you more comfortable,' she says.

'That's the trouble with deserted old buildings,' he says lightly, 'not much in the way of luxury. But the fire is very welcome,' he adds, as her face falls.

'You should sleep,' she tells him. 'Get all the sleep you can while we're here and we're safe.'

'I slept for most of the afternoon,' he reminds her. 'I'm wide awake now and I'd rather talk. Unless you want to sleep?'

She shakes her head. 'I can't. Too much on my mind.' She shoots a sideways look at him. 'That's why I came over,' she admits. 'Well, and to see if you were all right.'

'I am. What did you want to talk about?'

He waits while she collects her thoughts.

'I've been thinking. In Pont-Aven we saw someone killed. Shot through the head, and if we had arrived a short time earlier, we would have witnessed the murder. He was killed because someone thought he was Will, and straight away two people who said they were Mr and Mrs Clark from Harrow melted away, but they weren't English because the young man in the lodging house heard them speaking German.'

'Yes, and we know that—' he begins, but she is well into her stride now and ignores him.

'Then we followed Will's trail down to Aurelie-les-Bains,' – she sends him an apologetic look for not letting him speak

– 'and immediately after we had spoken to Will's Great-Aunt Eulalia, someone shot at us several times and we only got away because Will was watching out and took us to safety. Ever since, our steps have been dogged by *another* pair, these two men dressed in long, dark coats, who we must assume not only carry guns but are perfectly happy to use them, which one of them did at Pau station.' She stops for a breath. 'These two men *have* to be in contact with someone watching over the whole operation, or whatever you call it, because it's just not credible that they could keep on finding us and trying to kill us purely by chance.'

'Yes,' he says when he is sure she has stopped. 'And what we have to ask ourselves is why does this someone want to kill Wilberforce Chibb, and why is it so important that they're quite happy for you and me to be killed too if we are silly enough to get in the way.'

She gives a soft gasp as he says that. Then, recovering herself, she straightens her shoulders and says, 'All afternoon on the train while you were asleep, I kept going over and over everything I know. Why would one German pair and one English pair – assuming they *are* English – want Will dead? What has he done? Since I couldn't come up with any satis-factory answer to that, I went back to the fact of this Joseph and Hilda Clark from Harrow being German. And I remem-bered the mystery man at the Institut Hugues Abadie.'

'Who was also rumoured to be German,' Felix says softly. 'Yes. I've been thinking about that too.'

'Felix,' she says, and he can hear the mounting excitement in her voice, 'supposing someone wanted the mystery man dead? Supposing he'd been hidden away in the Institute to get him out of the way, but then something happened and keeping him hidden was no longer enough, and so he was killed in the way everyone said Will had killed his father – only of course we know he didn't – so that it would be really easy to say Will had killed the mystery man too because he'd also had his throat cut with a razor? And they were all set to have poor Will arrested, tried and executed for the murder of the mystery man, only Will didn't kill him either so if he didn't, who did? And why did they want him dead?'

Her voice has risen in her excitement and they both hear a faint rustling from the corner where Will is asleep. They wait, but all is quiet again.

'Will said his name was Louis,' Felix says. 'We should have tried to find out more about him in Paimpont. I bet that formidable Mrs Choak would have had plenty to tell us.'

'Huh! We wouldn't have got a word out of *her*,' Lily says scornfully. 'Besides, back then we didn't know we'd need to know about him, if you see what I mean.'

'I do,' he says. 'Too late now to go back to the Institute. And I have no suggestions whatsoever as to who else can tell us about the mystery man.'

There is silence for a few moments.

Then from out of the darkness a voice says quietly, 'I can.'

And, wrapped in his greatcoat, Will comes shuffling over the dirty floor to join them in front of the fire.

'He wasn't such a mystery to me,' he adds, 'because we used to talk to each other. A lot.'

And Lily is silently berating herself because they *knew* this already: Miss Chibb said Will was the one person whom Louis allowed near him; Will himself had cried out in distress *Louis was my friend.'*

She says gently, 'Tell us about him, Will.'

'He was a boy, really, for all that you've been calling him the mystery man,' Will says dreamily. 'He wasn't much more than twenty, he was thin and he hadn't grown or matured properly, and he was always very pale. He'd lived a very sheltered, protected life.' He stops, his face sad. 'We had a lot in common,' he goes on presently. 'We both lost our mothers when we were young. Mine died when I was fifteen, but I hadn't been allowed to see her for years before that because she was in the asylum. Louis's – that was his name, I told you, Louis Eduard, and he had a long German-sounding surname – Louis's mother died when he was born. And another way in which we were similar was that his mother was English, or at least half English, and she'd been born in London. She was sickly, and was an invalid like him, and he said once someone had been really cruel to him and told him his mother should never have married, nobody expected her to, and after she did they ordered her not to have a baby because she was far too feeble and it would kill her, and then she did and it did – having Louis *did* kill her – and so he felt terrible about that too.'

There is a brief silence. Then Lily says – and Felix can tell she is trying to sound as if it is only a casual enquiry – 'I don't suppose you ever drew a picture of Louis, did you, Will?'

He leaps up and hurries over to his pack. He returns with his sketch book in his hands, flipping back through the thick clutch of pages. 'Of course I did.' He has found the right page and he is gently stroking it. After a moment's reluctance, he holds it out to her.

She turns it so that the light of the fire falls on it. Felix twists round to look.

Will's drawing shows a thin, very pale young man with a broad face and a weak, rounded little chin. His hair is fair and smooth, his eyes hooded and slightly prominent.

Presently she says in the same light tone, 'You said he was sickly and pale, and that really shows up in your drawing. It's very good, Will.'

He holds out his hand and she gives the sketch book back to him. 'You can't really judge because you didn't know him,' he says quietly. Then, looking up at Lily with a smile, he adds, 'But it's nice of you to say so.'

She looks at Felix. She is quite sure he knows exactly what she is thinking, for he must have seen it too.

'Er – do you know why that was, Will?' She tries to make it sound as if it were a matter of only minor interest. 'Why Louis was sickly?'

But she has pushed too hard: Will shakes his head, abruptly turns away and stumps off back to his corner.

Their sleeping place in the serene old building gives an illusion of safety, but when Lily wakes in the faint early light, her first cogent thought is to wonder what happened to the man in the workman's jacket and whether he managed to get off the train and is even now scouring the countryside in search of them. She slips out from under her coat and gets up, looking round to see if she has disturbed Felix or

Will. Both are asleep. She goes outside and stands at the top of the steps.

It has clearly been raining hard in the night. In the distance she can hear the sound of water, and moving towards the nearest gate she sees a wide stream pouring off the hillside. Rivulets have found their way inside the ruined settlement and are rushing and gurgling along the alleyways. The sun is climbing higher now, and she can see their strange surroundings properly in the strengthening light. Slowly she lets her eyes move over the scene. It seems to be in a ruined fortress, with a curtain wall all the way round and several round look-out towers. There is nobody about, although, judging by the terracotta pots of well-tended herbs and flowers on the door-steps, some of the old habitations appear to be in use. Beyond the enfolding walls, the land rises up in a series of hills and valleys. It is a harsh environment; she can see no fields full of burgeoning crops, and the only signs of life on the nearest hillside are a large flock of sheep and a pen full of goats. Melodious bells clonk gently on the morning air, and overhead large birds – buzzards, perhaps? – circle lazily watching out for prey.

She descends the steps and walks on through the old fortress. Presently she comes to another gate, and beyond, not far from the walls, she sees a little hamlet. The smoke from morning fires and cooking stoves rises, and she can smell frying onions. Drawn by these signs of ordinary human activity, particularly the smell of frying – which is making her stomach growl alarmingly – she goes on. She comes to a house with its door wide open, and inside a cool kitchen she sees a squat, fat woman in rolled-up sleeves and a volu-minous white apron standing before a stove cooking a large pan full of bacon, eggs and onions. Lily taps on the door frame and the woman turns round. Her eyebrows are raised in mild enquiry, but she doesn't look particularly surprised to find a stranger on her doorstep.

'*Madame?*' the woman says. '*Vous voulez quelque chose?*'

Vouloir is want, Lily thinks. *She's asking me what I want.*

'Er – *quelque chose à manger, s'il vous plaît,*' she replies. '*Pour moi et mes deux hommes.*'

She hopes she has just asked for food for herself and her two companions, but the woman's smile suggests she hasn't got it quite right. But she says '*Bien sûr*' anyway, and, cutting three generous portions of fresh bread, slices them open and piles in bacon, onion and eggs. While she is doing so, Lily looks around the kitchen. More bread – a lot of bread – and some little glass jars containing a richly-coloured oil of some sort and small round pieces of cheese. Pointing to them, she asks, '*Madame, c'est quoi?*' and the woman, glancing, says '*Le fromage du brebis avec l'huile d'ail.*'

Understanding little but *fromage*, Lily asks for three of the little jars. Then, having paid what seems a very small amount of money for such a feast – her mouth is watering so copiously that she has to keep swallowing – she thanks the woman and heads back into the ruined fortress.

Will and Felix fall on the hot rolls, and Lily, devouring her own just as swiftly, waves her free hand in acknowledgement of their appreciation. When they have taken the edge off their hunger and can talk again, Felix says, 'Where is this place? Did you ask the woman?'

Still chewing, she shakes her head. Then, having swallowed, she says, 'We could go back and ask, I suppose. She had more provisions too – I restricted my purchases to the jars of cheese only because I couldn't resist them, they looked so intriguing.'

Will is looking doubtful. 'I'm not sure we should,' he says. 'Supposing she's in league with the people hunting for us? She might even now be hurrying off to tell them where we are.'

It is a disturbing image. Lily looks at Felix, but he is still calmly working his way through his breakfast. 'It's possible, Will,' he says. 'But from what Lily just said, it would appear her woman is busy preparing food for a number of people, so I think we can assume she's not much concerned with what goes on outside her village.'

'The people in the village must be used to passers-by,' Lily says. 'She didn't ask me what I was doing here, or where I was going or anything.'

Felix has finished. Standing up and putting on his coat

– Lily notices how the movement makes him wince – he says, 'We need to find out where we are and how best to proceed with our journey. Lily has established a contact in the village, so I suggest we go and ask her.'

Lily looks at Will. He still looks uncertain, but nevertheless he gathers his belongings, puts on his greatcoat and follows Felix out.

The woman is still in her kitchen, and now there are several men standing around outside. There is a rumble of quite animated conversation, and all of them are eating. One of them looks up as they approach. He is sturdily built and wearing a blue workman's jacket.

Will gives a low moan. 'It's all right, Will, he's nothing like the man on the train,' Felix says quickly.

'He's just like a male version of my woman,' Lily adds. 'He's probably a relative – a brother, perhaps.'

Nevertheless, Will hangs back as Lily and Felix go inside.

The woman looks up and gives Lily a grin. '*Vos hommes*?' she says, jerking her head towards Felix and Will.

Felix starts to speak to her. Lily, trying to make out what he is saying, guesses he is complimenting her on the rolls. She nods, and he asks something else. Now the conversation flows fast, and at one point the stout man outside is summoned to give his opinion. He and the fat woman bicker amiably for a while, then the woman shoos him outside again and addresses Felix, wagging a finger for emphasis and saying several times, '*Figeac, oui. Figeac.*' Then she adds, '*Puis c'est la ligne pour Clermont-Ferrand, et après ça, Paris.*'

Felix expresses his thanks by purchasing one of practically everything the woman has for sale on her shelves.

'What did she say?' Lily demands as Felix leads them away from the village.

'The place where we stayed last night is an ancient fortress built in the days of old,' he begins, 'but hardly anybody lives in the ruins because they are haunted by dead Knights Templar who were tortured and put to the fire back in the early 1300s. She and her fellow inhabitants live in the later village, which is quite separate and presumably beyond haunting range. This is the *Causses* region, and as we have surmised, it is pretty remote and the people are far from rich. They farm sheep and grow chestnuts, and the wildflowers are beautiful in the spring, and—'

Lily has heard enough. 'Lovely, Felix, but where are we going now? I heard you talking about Paris, and a *ligne*, which I very much hope means a railway line, so dare I believe that we are heading for a station?'

He grins. 'You may. There's a halt about five kilometres away – that's about three miles – and we have to take the train to Figeac, then there's a connecting line that takes us to Clermont-Ferrand and we can go from there direct to Paris.'

Will says in a frightened whisper, 'But what about the man in the blue jacket? Won't he be looking out for us to reappear and catch another train?'

Felix puts a hand on his shoulder. 'Not today, Will. There was a bit of excitement last night. That's what the men outside were talking about. The fat woman's brother said there was a man on the train from Béziers last night who assaulted a woman,' – he grins at Lily – 'and when some of the locals set on him, he pulled out a revolver. The guard had already been called, and the man was overcome, his gun was taken off him and they locked him in one of the animal pens at the rear of the passenger carriages until he could be taken away by the police when the train stopped at Limoges. I don't think he'll be troubling us yet because he won't be released until he's explained why he was carrying a loaded pistol.'

Will is plucking nervously at a loose button on his coat. 'But there's another man,' he mutters. 'More than one, probably. What about them?'

Lily watches Felix trying to restrain his impatience. He isn't very successful: 'Dear Will,' he says tersely, 'we can either stand here all day quaking in our boots about what might or might not happen, or we can proceed with a decent plan which, if not one hundred per cent foolproof, with any luck at all will see us in Paris by the end of today, and after that we're only a boat and a train ride away from home.' He shifts his bag higher on his undamaged shoulder. 'I'm going on, I'm fairly sure Lily is too, so unless you want to stay here by yourself, you'd better start walking.'

The straight talking has heartened Will, Lily observes as they board the train at the little local halt. He persists in his habit of repeatedly staring all around him in a series of jerks of his head, and his eyes still widen periodically whenever he sees something he thinks is suspicious, but he hasn't made any further protest.

He's brave, she thinks suddenly as she and Felix settle side by side on a hard wooden bench with Will sitting opposite. Her thoughts run on. Will is obviously full of fear, he knows people want to kill him, he faces two murder charges, one in France and one in England, but he seems to have put his trust in Lily and Felix, and in their ability not only to get him safely home but also to prove to the police and the legal systems of two countries that he is not a murderer.

It is a tall order, she reflects anxiously. She hopes very much that she and Felix are up to the challenge.

She watches Will make himself comfortable. Presently his eyelids droop and soon he is asleep.

'That's good,' Felix says softly, nodding towards Will. 'I don't think he had much sleep last night.'

'We'll have to wake him up when we change trains at Clermont-Ferrand,' she replies, 'but after that he can sleep all the way to Paris.'

Felix yawns. 'I might join him.'

'Before you do,' she says, 'I've been thinking.'

'Not again,' he says resignedly. 'Come on, then, tell me.'

She smiles. 'Well, I've had what I think is quite a good idea. Yesterday morning, when I had the awful realization that I'd been giving away our movements to the woman I thought was Phyllida Westwood, it seemed like the most dreadful mistake. Well, it was,' she corrects herself honestly.

'I'm fairly sure it's the first serious mistake I've ever known you make,' he says gently.

She says tersely, 'Don't be kind to me, I don't deserve it.' She glances at him. 'Especially when I caused you such pain yesterday afternoon when I put your shoulder back in.'

'It hurt like the devil, I agree, but as soon as it settled down again, there was a distinct improvement.'

'How is it now? Shall I look at it?'

'No. It's not too bad, and you'll make the other passengers stare if you start fumbling around inside my clothes. Tell me about this good idea.'

'Oh. Yes.' Cross with herself for the hot blood flushing her cheeks at his flippant remark, she sits up a little straighter. 'The false Miss Westwood will not realize that we now know she isn't who she says she is.' She turns a beaming face to him.

'Yes?'

She clicks her tongue impatiently. 'Which means she will go on believing that my messages are sent in ignorance of the true facts. *And we don't know she's an imposter,*' she hisses when he still looks blank.

But in an instant, he is smiling too. 'So we can feed her false information.'

'*Yes*! And I've thought it out. Supposing I tell her that the subject – that's Will – has got it into his head that we don't believe him? That he believes we think he really did murder his father and the mystery man, and that we're taking him back to England as fast as we can to hand him over to the authorities? And all that has made him so terrified that he's escaped, and we can't find him?'

'Ye-es,' Felix says slowly.

'I'll tell her we're heading home to London,' she hurries on, 'but I'll say it's by some route other than the one we're really going to take. She'll be completely thrown because that's not what was meant to happen. We were *meant* to lead that pair who shot at us to Will, and they were meant to kill him and—'

'How do you know she sent them?'

'Because it *must* be what's happening! It's how they always know where we are! She's passing on the information I'm sending to her and her agents, or whatever they are, act on it.'

'And the other couple? The man and the woman in Pont-Aven?'

'I don't know,' she admits. 'I was hoping we managed to lose them back in Brittany.'

He is quiet for so long that she is quite sure he's going to come up with a list of objections to her suggestion.

But then he leans close to her and murmurs, 'I think it's a good idea. But there's one way in which we could make it even better, although I don't think you're going to like it.'

She mutters back, 'Tell me anyway.'

He looks across at the sleeping Will. 'If you confess you've lost him and he's running wild somewhere in the middle of France, she and her gunmen are simply going to redouble their efforts to locate him. Because, assuming we're right and Will really is to be made a scapegoat for murder, they don't want him lost. They want him dead.'

'But . . . you're saying I tell Miss Westwood he's *already* dead?' she says in a horrified whisper. *I can't! I can't*, she thinks wildly, the very suggestion flooding her with a powerful atavistic dread that if you pretend someone is dead then they really will die and it is you who will have brought it about.

Felix waits. It occurs to her suddenly and vividly that he knows exactly what's going through her head and he is giving her the chance to deal with it.

He does know, she thinks. *I'm quite sure he does.*

The realization gives her an odd feeling deep in her chest.

Then she realizes Felix is speaking.

'You could say he was fatally injured as we jumped off the train,' he says. 'The man in the blue jacket saw us jump; he'll verify that Will *could* have been killed in the fall.'

'I don't think I can . . .' she begins.

'Dearest Lily, we wouldn't be taking this drastic step with the intention of harming Will,' he says gently. 'We'd be doing it because it's the only way I can think of that has a chance of saving his life.'

She gasps. 'You really think they'll try to kill him?'

He sighs. 'Lily, I know they will. They have already done so.'

SIXTEEN

As they change trains at Clermont-Ferrand, Lily sends a telegram to the imposter Miss Westwood informing her that *the subject has been fatally injured in a fall from a train*. She had hastened to the telegraph office under the cover of going for fresh provisions, since, without discussing it with Felix, she is quite sure he would agree that they can't mention this tactic to Will. Her assumption is borne out by the fact that, as she returns to the station, she finds Felix engaged with Will in a conveniently distracting conversation about the beauties of Paris.

The journey north from Clermont-Ferrand seems interminable. The day wears on, the seats get more and more uncomfortable, and they appear to be stopping at every single station. As the light fails, they find themselves at a major junction between two lines, shunted into a siding, apparently waiting for a fast train from Brest to precede them on towards Paris. Felix goes to lean out of the window in the hope that he can pick up something relevant in the conversation between three railway employees standing on the platform.

'There has been an incident on the line to the west,' he reports, turning back to Lily and Will. 'Nobody seems to know how long we'll be held up here.'

'Can't our train go on ahead?' Lily demands.

'You'd think so,' Felix replies. 'Apparently not, because our train stops everywhere – much as it has been doing all afternoon – and the fast train doesn't.'

Lily sits fuming for a few moments. Then, standing up, she says, 'We'll get off. Find a hotel – there's bound to be a Hôtel du Gare, there always is – and have a meal, a proper wash, a good night's sleep, then set out in fresh clothes early in the morning and go on to Paris.'

The alacrity with which Felix and Will grab their belongings and jump up from their seats suggests it is one of her better ideas.

An hour or so later, adequately if not imaginatively fed, Lily stands naked in a wide bowl in front of the washstand in her tiny room. She has a large jug of very hot water, two more of cold water, a washcloth and a small, clean towel. Slowly, almost sensuously, she washes every part of herself from the crown of her head to her toes, wrapping her long, wet hair in the towel once she has finished drying herself. The little room smells of roses: leaving Hob's Court, she included a small tablet of rose soap in her bag and this is the first chance she has had to indulge herself and use it.

She looks at Tamáz's witch's bottle, hanging on its silver chain round her neck. With a rueful smile, she reflects that he was right about this journey having more than its share of dangers, and even without having to think about it, once again she sees herself being shot at and leaping from an accelerating train.

Tamáz. For a moment he fills her mind. She sends him a brief mental message to tell him she is safe.

'So far,' she adds aloud.

She puts on a crisp nightgown. She has fresh underwear for the morning, but after that she has no more clean clothes.

'But I shall not need any,' she says firmly. 'Tomorrow we shall be heading back to London.'

She goes downstairs very early the next morning to find that Felix has ordered breakfast and he and Will have almost finished.

'Eat yours while I settle the bill,' he says as soon as she appears. 'There's a fast train leaving in fifteen minutes.'

She wolfs down the dry end of *baguette* with apricot jam so fast that she has to suppress burps all the way to the station.

The train is not only faster but considerably more comfortable than yesterday's. Lily watches the stations as they pass through them: Chartres, Orsay, Versailles. She is lulled into a half-asleep state; last night she slept deeply, but the proximity of the station meant that sudden explosions of steam, squeals of brakes and clanking of chains from shunting engines kept jerking her awake.

When Felix leans close and says quietly, 'We'll soon be arriving at Gare Montparnasse,' it takes her by surprise.

She sits up straight. 'How do I look?' she mutters back.

He gives her an appraising stare and smiles. 'You look daisy-fresh.'

She glances down at herself. 'Wearing those coats we picked up in Aurelie-les-Bains has kept my clothes reasonably clean.' She and Felix abandoned them before boarding this morning's train. 'You look fine, too.'

He nods. 'It's good to have left them behind. They weren't what you'd call fragrant. And, having helped us to blend with our fellow passengers up till now, in Paris they would do the precise opposite.' Lowering his voice, he adds, 'Which of us is going to tell Will?'

She looks over at Will. He is still hunched in his greatcoat and, since the morning is already pleasantly warm, looks decidedly pink in the face. The coat is dirty, torn and very shabby. The sleeves cover Will's thin hands, which are clutching his canvas satchel tightly to his chest. Even as Lily studies him, his hand slides inside the satchel and he starts to pull out his sketch book and the little soft leather case in which he keeps his pencil and charcoals.

'Will,' she says, leaning towards him with a smile, 'I don't think there's time for a drawing, because we shall soon be arriving in Paris, where we'll have to cross the city to the Gare du Nord for the train to Calais. I think—' She hesitates. 'Felix and I have dispensed with our topcoats, and perhaps you should too?'

He looks at her with panic in his eyes. 'It's my protection,' he whispers, so softly that she can only just make out the words.

'Yes, I agree, the coats have served us very well in the country areas, but we shall be mingling with the smart Parisians soon, and we—'

His expression has turned mulish. 'I can't take it off,' he

mutters. 'They'll try to shoot me again, and if I'm not wearing my coat, they'll succeed.'

'Do you believe it has magic powers, then?' she asks, laughing as if to imply that he can't possibly be thinking anything so absurd.

But he must do because slowly and solemnly he is nodding.

The train is starting to slow down. They are passing through the outer *banlieues* of Paris now and they haven't got long.

'Leave it,' Felix murmurs. 'He's as terrified as a kitten, and if he thinks a magic greatcoat's going to protect him, it won't help if we make him take it off.'

Montparnasse station is busy with a cross-section of Parisians so totally absorbed in business of their own that the presence in their midst of a presentable couple accompanied by a white-faced, thin young man who looks like a tramp or an army deserter barely raises an eyebrow.

Felix marches ahead through the barrier. Will is beside him. Lily is just behind, and she can see Will is shaking with dread. Felix hands over their tickets, indicating Will and pointing over the intervening heads to Lily. Then the three of them are separated by a crowd of excited schoolboys in the care of two burly young priests, the boys pushing through with such force that Lily almost falls. The voice of one of the priests rings out sharply, the boys fall into line and there is the sound of two stinging slaps as the ringleader has his ears boxed. The other priest has hurried to Lily's assistance and sets her on her feet again as if she weighed no more than a small suitcase. '*Merci, merci,*' she says, '*pas de–pas de—* I am perfectly all right!'

'Ah, but you are English!' the priest exclaims. 'How I adore your country – your Oxford, where I studied, your so beautiful York, where I briefly was in a seminary, your—'

Before he can think of any more English places for which to express his adoration, Lily thanks him again, excuses herself and stares anxiously round for Felix and Will.

Felix is standing on a luggage trolley, eyes roaming over the station concourse. She runs over to him and he jumps down. His face is tense.

'Where's Will?' he demands, grabbing her by the shoulders. 'Isn't he with you?'

Felix mutters a long stream of oaths under his breath. 'No,' he says.

She takes his arm and hurries him out of the station. She knows in her bones that something awful has happened, and they are far too public where they are. The pavement outside is heaving with people and she lets them carry herself and Felix along for a few yards before diving off down a side alley.

'What happened?' she demands.

Felix is rubbing his face hard with both hands. '*Bloody* Will! He was almost hysterical with fear as we reached the barrier, and then when those blasted schoolboys shoved us apart, he gave a muted shriek as if it was an assault and I thought he was going to be sick with terror. I tried to call out to him and tell him it was nothing to worry about, but he was too far away to hear and in any case, I think by then he was a long way beyond listening to any voice of reason.' He stops, his breathing slowing down. 'I'm sorry, Lily,' he says quietly. 'All this way, over all these endless miles, we've cared for him, kept him safe, reassured him, only to have him bolt like a rabbit at the penultimate hurdle.'

He looks so woebegone that she doesn't stop to think but puts her arms round his large, powerful body, draws him close and simply holds him.

After a time – a long time, a short time, she's not sure – he says, 'Delightful as this is, my dearest Lily,' – and she can *hear* the amusement in his voice, and something else besides that she doesn't identify – 'it isn't going to help us to find Will, herd him to the Gare du Nord and see him safely back to England.'

And very gently he unwinds her arms and steps away.

'Did you see what scared him so badly?' she says, and even in her own ears her tone is far too brisk and she sounds like a middle-aged spinster who has just been horrified at a lewd suggestion.

Whereas the very opposite is in fact true . . .

Stop it.

'He was already terrified,' Felix replies, and he still sounds as if he is finding this funny. 'I was looking all round to see if something in particular had unnerved him when you came up to me.'

She nods. Then edges forward so that she can see out into the street. Hoping she is concealed by the mass of passers-by, she stares up towards Montparnasse.

And leaps back into the alley as if she's been prodded with a red-hot pin.

'*What*?' Felix hisses.

'It's the couple from Pont-Aven!' she whispers despairingly. 'The woman in the white veil and the black-clad man, the ones who pretended to be English!' She struggles to remember their names, fighting down the panic. 'Mr and Mrs Joseph Clark.'

And the small achievement of dredging up the memory amid this sudden confusion calms her a little.

Felix is moving round her to look where she was looking. 'I can't see them,' he says. 'Oh – yes, I can. She's gone ahead, she's turning back, beckoning to him impatiently, and she . . . *there's Will*!'

Grasping Lily's hand, he uses his undamaged shoulder like a battering ram and shoves a space in the crowd out on the pavement, then pulls her after him as he races to catch Will before the woman known as Hilda Clark and her husband do.

Will is ahead. Running fast, dodging and weaving, stepping into the road apparently unaware of the danger from horse-drawn traffic. Along a wide boulevard, and then, clearly aware he is too visible, dodging right – straight across a surge of vehicles that miraculously part for him so that Lily wonders if the magic coat really is protecting him – but unfortunately not on to a quieter street but an even wider, busier one. Then he goes left, darting so fast that Lily and Felix almost miss him. Then, flying along alleys, passages and dark, impossibly narrow gaps between rows of buildings, suddenly he emerges into the open, and they are not far behind.

Then there are black-painted railings and beyond them, just on the other side and tantalizingly near, is a wide green space, with grass, paved paths, benches, old men playing chess in the sunshine, shrubbery, tall trees, *places to hide*, and now Lily is gasping for breath and she can't open her lungs enough because of her corset, and Felix's hand on her wrist is like a manacle and she tries to cry out '*I can't go any further*!' and he is running harder now and then he's up in the air, hauling her after him and something very sharp and hard digs into her left side but it hits a whalebone in her corset and she tries to cry out but she hasn't got the breath and then she is tumbling, falling with Felix, falling *on* him – he suppresses a cry of pain – and they land in a huge pile of last autumn's leaves and it has broken their fall.

He gasps out urgently, 'Are you hurt?'

She puts a frightened hand to her rib, where whatever it was dug into her. The fabric of her gown is not torn, and there is no dampness from a spreading pool of blood. She draws in a cautious breath: the area around the rib hurts like the devil but everything seems to work.

So she says, 'No. But what about you?'

He grunts.

He is getting to his feet, holding out a hand to her. She takes it, and he helps her up. 'We must move away from here,' he says. 'They aren't far behind, and they won't know we got in this way if they don't see us; they'll assume we came in via the next gate and they'll hurry on to find it.'

Her legs trembling, she trots off beside him and they take a path that dives in among the trees. As the dense planting beneath the trees rises to head height and cuts off the view of where they've just come from, she takes a look back.

Somehow Felix has managed not only to scale the very high iron railings of the fence surrounding the park, he also pulled her up with him. And picked the one place where there was a huge pile of leaves on the far side. Yes, she has been stabbed quite hard by the spike at the top of one of the railings, but it's only a bruise and it will soon stop hurting quite so much.

For now, they are safe.

And Will—

Will!

'Felix, where's Will?' she pants. They are running faster now.

And, as they come to a gap between the thick trunks of a stand of chestnut trees, she can see Will up ahead.

A sign reveals that these are the Luxembourg Gardens. Felix and Lily move as fast as they can through the groups of sauntering people, trying not to bump into anyone, although once Felix almost takes a sprawling dive when a toddler wanders into his path, only correcting himself with a swerving twist of his entire body worthy of a full back on a rugby pitch. Lily, gritting her teeth against the pain that has now spread right through the ribs on her left side, forces herself to run, run and not lose sight of Felix.

Or Will.

They catch him up at the big gates on the north-east corner of the Gardens. He is frantic: as Felix grabs him hard by the shoulders to hold him still, he freezes. His eyes are wide with fear, his deathly white face is wet with sweat and he is staring back over the grass, the shrubs and the trees, his lips moving but no coherent sounds emerging.

'*Will!*' Felix shouts. 'Come on, we have to move!'

And Will lifts his arm and with a trembling hand, points at a place about a hundred yards away where a narrow little path emerges from the chestnut trees. A man and a woman are hurrying along it. The woman has a wide white veil tied around her hat.

Out through the gates and into the Boulevard St Michel. Will's terror still grips him tight, and now he runs right beside Felix, at times almost tripping him as he tries to match his pounding feet to Felix's fast pace. The Boulevard St Michel goes on over the river on its own *pont*, but Felix turns to the left before the road begins to rise, and they are running along the Rive Gauche, and now the meandering crowds getting in the way are leisurely sightseers browsing the second-hand book stalls but, thinks Lily furiously, they are just as annoying and frustrating whatever they are doing. A well-dressed man in a top hat stands right in front of Felix and says in a plummy English voice, 'I say, is this the way to Notre Dame?' and Felix, clearly sharing Lily's frustration, waves an arm to point and pants, 'No, you idiot, it's there, soaring up right behind you!'

The man spins round to stare goggle-eyed after Felix's retreating form and is just remarking loudly and plaintively that manners are not what they used to be when Lily shoves him out of the way.

They come to a complete blockage and skid to a stop. An unruly crowd of elegantly-dressed people and a scrum of small boys are milling around on the quay, chattering and laughing, queuing loosely by a gangplank and full of excited anticipation at the novelty of what they're about to do. Tied up on the river beside them is a wide, flat boat with two tall funnels and a huge wheel at the stern.

'Good grief, it's an American sternwheeler!' Felix says in surprise. 'What is it doing here? I thought they belonged exclusively to the Mississippi.'

Lily, taking advantage of the enforced halt to bend over, hands on hips, and catch her breath, nods towards a large, colourful advertising poster. *River trips on the SS New Orleans*, it reads, *promise a unique and unrepeatable experience, so hurry, hurry because this offer is for the duration of one spring and summer only!*

And suddenly Will gasps, 'Oh, *God*!'

The man and the woman they know as Joseph and Hilda Clark are ruthlessly pushing their way into the crowd of people at the back of the queue.

Up ahead, a man in a uniform moves forward, preparing to halt the flow of passengers up the gangway. The *New Orleans* is almost full and about to depart.

Felix grabs Lily, Will pushes ahead and the three of them forge a way over the gangway just as the cord that forms the barrier is put in place behind them.

They run round the superstructure of the boat to the open observation deck at the stern, all three of them searching the crowd on the quay for Joseph and Hilda Clark. The high walls of the Île de la Cité soar up beside them as the boat pulls out into the stream, dark and sombre with damp, dirty water dribbling out of drainage pipes, moss on the ancient bricks. The *New Orleans* catches the fast-flowing current and its speed begins to increase even as the huge wheel at the stern starts to revolve, faster, faster, sending up great arcs of water that sparkle and glisten in the sunshine.

Then Lily points.

Back on the quay the two figures, smaller now, have raced along to a cordoned-off area of the riverside where there are small craft for hire. They are grappling with a light skiff, which is already out on the water. The woman releases the mooring rope, and the black-clad man is shouting and gesticulating at the attendant in the striped shirt and the dark beret who is remonstrating with him. Lily, Felix and Will are too far away now to hear what is being said, but the altercation ends with Joseph Clark landing a heavy punch on the boat attendant's jaw. He tumbles into the water and Clark pushes off with his foot so that the skiff shoots out into the river.

It is worryingly apparent straight away that Joseph and Hilda Clark know exactly what they are doing. The sternwheeler is moving fast now but the light little skiff, expertly handled, is faster. Lily and Felix look on horrified and helpless as the gap narrows. Will is moaning in fear.

'We're safe,' Felix mutters, 'they can't reach us, and we'll see if they draw a weapon and we'll take cover, and there are no steps, no way of climbing on board . . .'

The skiff is right astern of them now, immediately to the right of the great wheel, now rotating so fast that its gaudy, blue-painted blades are a blur. There is a wooden frame that surrounds, guards and anchors the wheel, and, even as they watch, aghast at the peril, the woman stands up in the skiff, reaches out and grabs hold of the support's upper bar. She holds on tight, grasping it with her other hand for extra stability, and looks over her shoulder at her companion, who is trying to keep the skiff steady and in position. She starts to say something – she is shaking her head, and shouting *nein, nein* – but the skiff, light as a leaf on the surging wash created by the pounding wheel, is suddenly caught in a cross-current and it seems to leap into the air and away to the right. The woman is left with nothing to stand on, holding on by her hands, desperately trying to twist her body so that she can get her feet on to the rail she's clinging to.

On the deck, Felix and Lily can see what is about to happen. They race from the observation deck to the stern rail, but the wheel is below them, too far away for them to reach the woman. Felix grabs a coiled rope and unwinds it, flinging it out to her, but she does not see and, tangling itself up in the wheel, it is jerked violently in Felix's hands and he only just lets go in time.

The woman's strength is failing. She gathers herself for one last huge effort but her legs fall back. She tries to hold on, but her garments are drenched and heavy, the support is soaking wet now and more water is being splashed up all the time, blinding her. She removes one hand to brush the water off her face and from her wide-open mouth but her other hand isn't strong enough to hold her.

There is a loud, horrified cry from the man in the skiff, who makes a last effort to draw close enough to the fast-turning wheel for her to drop back into the little craft. But he is too late, for with a scream that soars above the noise of the wheel and the water and the happy laughing passengers as yet bliss-fully unaware of what is happening so close behind them, the fingers of her remaining hand uncurl and she falls into the wheel.

It turns, once, twice, three times, quickly now. On the first turn there is scarlet in the white foam and something human-shaped is draped on the blades. On the second turn, half of the shape is no longer there. On the third turn, what looks like a long white veil is tangled around a quarter of the wheel's circumference.

On the fourth turn there is nothing left.

The skiff, which came too close on its final approach, is matchwood on the churning water.

And the man has disappeared.

SEVENTEEN

Excited voices herald the arrival of the *New Orleans*'s passengers, alerted by the dead woman's scream and pushing each other roughly out of the way in order to obtain the best view of the drama. Lily, with a glance at Felix, moves unobtrusively to merge with them. She has firm hold of Will's hand; he is bolt-eyed and white with terror, he looks as if he's about to be sick, and she knows she must move him somewhere quieter before people start demanding to know what is wrong with him. She is managing to make headway against the flow of avid passengers and into the salon that they have just vacated when a man in a navy coat with brass buttons and a peaked cap says, '*Madame?*' adding something in rapid French and eyeing Will suspiciously.

'I cannot understand you,' Lily says loudly and clearly.

The man tuts in irritation and says in halting English, 'What is wrong with the young man?' He jerks his chin at Will. 'What did he do?'

Lily bridles with feigned indignation. 'My nephew has done nothing!' she says. 'How dare you accuse him? There has been an accident at the stern of the boat – I heard somebody say a woman had fallen overboard. We did not see, for my nephew was already feeling unwell and I wished to bring him into the salon for a glass of water.' She eyes the officer. 'Perhaps you would be good enough to fetch it for him?' she adds imperiously.

The man emits an angry *hrummmph!* noise and shoulders his way through the door and out on to the deck, muttering under his breath. Lily suppresses a smile; she can clearly see that her deliberate insult has hit home, and the officer really isn't happy at being taken for a lowly orderly.

'We shall sit here,' she says calmly to Will, helping him to a sofa seat by a window that looks out forward and has no view of the stern. 'Presently I shall fetch a hot drink. Felix will join us soon, I expect.'

There are raised voices, sounds of alarm and quite a few screams from the stern. Then Felix appears, and magically he is holding a small tray on which there are three large cups of coffee. 'Here,' he says, handing one to Will. 'There's plenty of sugar in it, and I bought you a *madeleine*. Eat, drink, and soon you'll feel better.'

He hands a second cup to Lily. She raises her eyebrows, and he shakes his head minutely. Then, glancing at the door to the foredeck, he says, 'We'd better go out there and find somewhere out of sight. It'd be sensible not to be seen together.'

They move outside, closing the salon door behind them, and sit down on a bench largely obscured by the bulky foundations of the funnels.

Will slurps some coffee, dribbles, shoves half the little cake in his mouth and, chewing swiftly, swallows. Then he stares up at Felix and says, 'Are they going to kill us now?'

Slowly Felix sits down on his other side. Both Will and Lily turn to look at him. Lily has the strong sense that he is thinking, choosing his words very carefully.

'Will,' he says, his voice soft, 'nobody is going to kill us. Nobody is even going to try, for now anyway.'

'But he . . . she . . .'

'Both of them have perished,' Felix says gently. 'The woman died on the stern wheel, and the man's body has just been recovered.'

'He's not going to kill me?'

It is obvious to Lily that Will is in deep shock. Taking his hand, she wraps it round his cup and encourages him to drink again. He doesn't even seem to notice her.

'He's dead, Will.' Felix's voice is kind. 'I have just seen his corpse. The captain of the *New Orleans* brought out a blanket and they covered him up. Now we are going to proceed to a place where the boat can moor – on the left bank, beyond the Pont Neuf,' – Will nods eagerly as if he's familiar with the details of the boat's itinerary – 'and we shall all be allowed to disembark.'

Will nods again. He drinks more coffee, gulps down the

remainder of the *madeleine* and then, a hand flying to his mouth, leaps up and runs for the door that leads to the lavatories.

Felix leans back on the bench, stretching out his long legs. He sends a dispassionate glance after Will. 'He bolted that cake as if he thought I was going to take it away.'

She nods. 'Poor Will,' she murmurs. 'He has had a dreadful time.' Felix doesn't reply. 'Is it – do you think it's nearly over?'

He shrugs. 'Well, Mr and Mrs Joseph Clark from Harrow won't be troubling us again, but we mustn't forget the other sinister pair who dogged our steps in the south. Even if, when we last heard news, one of them was in custody somewhere between Figeac and Millau.'

'I haven't forgotten them,' she murmurs.

He frowns. 'Judging by the fact that Joseph and Hilda were at Gare Montparnasse watching every trainload of passengers from the Clermont-Ferrand direction, I'd say your Miss Westwood was keeping the Clarks informed of Will's movements too.'

'The German couple,' she murmurs. 'They're dead.'

She feels rather odd. Perhaps, she muses, she too is in shock.

'On that subject,' he says tentatively.

Oh, dear Lord. 'Yes?'

'I'm not saying anybody actually witnessed that you, Will and I were by the stern rail when Hilda Clark fell, or that our presence there has aroused curiosity,' he says softly, 'because if that were the case, someone would have told the captain, we'd have been marched away to a police station for questioning at best and accused of pushing the woman to her death at worst.'

'But we didn't!' Lily squeaks. 'You threw her a rope, you tried to *help*!'

The corners of his mouth turn down. 'I did, didn't I?'

She can't tell what he is thinking. 'Felix?' she prompts.

'Yes. Sorry. Apparently, someone made some vague statement about spotting a party of three, two men and a woman, standing on the stern observation deck before the accident.'

'But that's dreadful, we—'

'Lily, *hush*!' he urges. 'Two points will help us here: one, you and Will actually saw the captain when you came inside, and you told him Will was your nephew.'

She remembers the man she commanded to fetch a glass of water. 'That was the *captain*?'

He grins. 'It was. So he thinks you and Will are together, aunt and nephew in a party of *two*.'

Now she understands. Of course. 'So we can leave quite openly – Will and I – and you can go ashore on your own and we'll meet up?'

'Yes. I'll go first and attach myself to one of the big tour groups. I'll head for the Gare du Nord and wait for you there.'

She already has the Bradshaw's out of her bag and is thumbing through its pages for the large-scale map of Paris when she remembers. 'And what's point two?'

He looks down at his hands. 'Before I came into the salon, I struck up a conversation with a very pretty young woman accompanied by her little son, and she suggested I might like to escort her off the boat when we dock in case she is still suffering the after-effects of shock and is unsteady on her feet.' He sends her a sideways glance. 'In fact,' he adds, 'I think I'd better go back and find her right now.'

He stands up.

For a long moment he doesn't move, but just looks down at her. Then he says softly, 'It's quite exciting, isn't it?' and is gone.

Lily covers her confusion by fishing out the Bradshaw's and committing to memory the route from the left bank of the Seine to the Gare du Nord; far better to memorize it now and not when she is out on the streets of Paris and trying to look after Will as well. 'Back to the Pont Neuf,' she mutters, 'across the river, straight ahead and up the Boulevard de Strasbourg, left at the top and the station will be on the right.' She feels in her bag for the purse of French francs. It is still quite full. *Maybe*, she thinks with a faint smile, *we shall ride in style and take a cab*.

She hears dragging footsteps. Looking up, she sees Will returning from the lavatories. She stitches on a smile and moves over so that he can sit down.

*   *   *

It is bliss to ride and not to have to walk. Sitting in the cab, Will close beside her on the narrow seat, Lily closes her eyes for a few blessed moments. The man and the woman who pretended to be an English couple from Harrow are dead. There is no need to keep peering out of the cab's tiny rear window to see if they are following. She breathes in and out a couple of times, then tries to take a deeper breath but the pain over her left ribs stops her. She tries to suppress the involuntary gasp, but Will has noticed and is looking at her worriedly.

'It's nothing,' she says with a smile, 'just a very minor injury from when we climbed the railings.'

He shakes his head, his expression full of guilt. 'I have led you into such peril, Miss Raynor,' he mutters.

And she says calmly, 'Such is the nature of my job.'

She knows it is foolhardy to let herself believe the danger is past, but nevertheless it seems excessive to take the usual precautions as they walk into the Gare du Nord, and she and Will stand on the forecourt quite openly as they wait for Felix. Will is staring anxiously out into the busy street, jumping violently each time someone shouts or a cart or carriage draws up too swiftly outside the station.

'Where *is* he?' he moans after about seven minutes of waiting.

'He'll soon be here,' Lily replies. 'Don't forget that we found a cab quickly and arrived here in a very short time. Felix may be on foot or have taken a different route.'

She hopes this will be a satisfactory answer and Will won't ask again, but that, she thinks with an inward sigh, is not the nature of chronic worriers, and presently Will mutters, 'He should *be* here by now! Something's gone wrong, I *know* it has!'

Lily takes a surreptitious look at her little silver fob watch. It is now over twenty-five minutes since they parted company from Felix. Will's growing agitation is infectious, and she is starting to think she can see men in long black overcoats lurking behind pillars. Then from outside comes the sound of pounding feet and the sharp, shrill note of a police whistle.

'It is without a doubt nothing to do with us,' she says very firmly.

But Will is jumping with nerves. 'We ought to purchase our tickets!' he says, almost in a wail. 'If Felix is fleeing from a pursuer, it'll be best if we can go straight on to the platform as soon as he appears!'

It is a sensible suggestion. She wishes she had thought of it herself. Briskly she strides over to the office and purchases three one-way fares for the boat train to London. The moment when the clerk slaps them down on the little tray and she scoops them up is surprisingly sweet.

The train leaves from platform two, according to the chalked board beside the ticket office. Glancing over, she sees that it is already there.

The departure is in ten minutes.

She is just sharing this information with Will when abruptly the noise level from outside increases sharply. Amid the general commotion there are a couple of screams, and more piercing whistles. Men are shouting, police and railway officials running outside to see what's happening.

And then Lily spots Felix.

And suddenly, acutely, she has a sense of imminent danger.

Her mind starts to race, thoughts flying so fast that she feels dizzy.

Felix is walking calmly and steadily, apparently in conversation with the elderly man beside him only she's sure he's not really . . . *it's just an act*, she thinks wildly, *a pretence, because the police and probably the two men in dark overcoats are following him and they know who he is and he's trying to lead them all away from Will and me to keep us safe and out of harm's way but that means he's putting himself in danger, terrible danger, and I don't want that – oh I can't have that – because I'm just discovering how much he means to me and—*

Felix looks up, catches her eye and jerks his head towards platform two and the long, elegant line of the boat train. The locomotive is building up steam, and a huge white cloud engulfs the long platform. Lily grabs Will, hurries him through the barrier, flashing their tickets, saying hastily to the guard

that the third one is for the man there following on behind
them – 'Him! Yes, *him!*' pointing wildly, and Felix gives a
laconic wave of his hand to identify himself – and then flying
on, through the steam and Will is opening a carriage door,
they are clambering aboard and doors are slamming, a whistle
blows, the train begins to move and then Felix is there – *oh
thank God thank God* – and calmly sitting down beside her
and saying, 'Sorry I was late. The police were trying to find
a man of my description, and I had to take a few detours. I
managed to evade them, I think. You weren't worried, were
you?'

And surely, *surely*, he must hear the weird little squeak in
her voice as she says, 'Oh, no, not in the least!'

The train pulls into Calais in the early evening.

Felix is on his feet as they slow to a gentle stop. He glances
at his two companions, who are gathering their bags and
perched on the edge of their seats. He is worried about Lily,
but trying not to alarm her by making it obvious that he is.
She is pale, her eyes are ringed with grey and from time to
time she presses her hand to her side. He knows exactly when
she was injured, and he knows it is his fault because he took
the decision to climb the railings and she had no chance to
protest because he was already dragging her up behind him.
Gazing out along the platform, reminding himself of how to
get from the station to the quay – not that it's necessary because
large signs in both French and English clearly mark the way
– he is cursing himself for being so stupid as to forget that
what is a relatively easy physical task for a man is virtually
impossible for a woman in a close-fitting jacket over a corset
and yards and yards of skirts and petticoats.

She doesn't complain, he thinks. *She's clever, brave,
resourceful and probably the least fussy woman I've ever
known.*

And he knows the sense of safety that all three of them
were feeling on the train journey from Paris is an illusion.

The two Germans known as Mr and Mrs Clark may no
longer be a threat, but they are by no means the only or indeed
the smartest of their pursuers. Discounting the French police

– and it's foolish to do so, even if he, Lily and Will are just about to board the cross-channel packet – there are also the English authorities. And, by far the most dangerous and sinister, the two men in long, dark overcoats.

The train has stopped. Doors are being flung open and a station master is shouting '*Calais! Calais!*' in a penetrating bass voice.

Turning back to his companions, Felix says cheerfully, 'Last leg just ahead. We'll be aboard the steamer very soon, and back in England by morning.'

Lily is on her feet and smiling bravely. Her face is very white. He reaches out to take her leather satchel – surely, he can at least help by carrying it for her – but she won't relinquish it.

He jumps down on to the platform, offers her his hand – she does accept that – and, with Will beside him, they head towards the barrier.

Out on the Channel, the sky is inky blue, clear and dotted with stars. Felix has insisted they have supper, although Will is too sick with nerves to do more than pick at his lamb stew and Lily says she isn't hungry and has only managed some bread and cheese. Both of which make Felix feel like a glutton as he works his way through *hors d'oeuvres*, the main course (the same lamb stew), cheese and a chocolate pudding. *But I shall need my strength*, he tells himself, *especially since my two companions' bird-like appetites will mean theirs is diminished.*

They leave the dining area and find a place to sit in a reasonably luxurious lounge looking out at the night. The lights have been dimmed, and quite a lot of passengers are asleep. Will is sitting beneath one of the lamps, sketching. Glancing across, Felix sees that he is drawing Lily, and for some reason he finds this very touching. Lily has her eyes closed; he hopes she will manage to sleep.

He leans back, making himself more comfortable.

His body relaxes.

He is wondering if his racing thoughts and his sense of imminent danger will allow him to have a few hours' sleep too when someone sits down beside him. Glancing up, he sees a slim man in well-cut, expensive-looking coat and trousers under a heavy woollen cloak, his slim feet in highly polished black boots. A courteous and cultured English voice says, 'I do hope I am not disturbing you, but I am travelling alone, the bar is deserted apart from a quartet of Frenchmen who turned their backs very firmly when I tried to engage them in conversation – much to my shame I'm afraid I don't speak French – and I do find these night crossings somewhat . . . ah . . . somewhat nerve-wracking.' He gives a little self-deprecating laugh. 'Stupid, I know, but I find a good cognac eases the fear, and since I was brought up not to drink alone, I wonder if a fellow Englishman might take pity on me and share it?' He is holding up a bottle of Five Star and two brandy balloons, a tentative expression on his handsome face.

How does he know I'm English? Felix wonders.

He instantly answers his own question: he has seen this man before. He was sitting nearby when Felix, Lily and Will ate their supper. He would have overheard them.

As if the slim man has sensed that Felix is weakening, he holds out his free hand. 'Raleigh. Brice Raleigh.'

'Felix Wilbraham.' Felix shakes the man's hand.

Raleigh makes himself comfortable, then opens the bottle and pours two good measures of cognac, handing one to Felix. 'What shall we drink to?' he asks cheerfully. Felix puts a finger to his lips, indicating Lily. 'Oooh, sorry!' Brice Raleigh says in a stage whisper. 'Mustn't wake the little lady!'

Grinning, because he knows exactly how Lily would loathe being called a little lady, Felix clinks glasses and takes a sip of brandy. It's wonderful: warming, calming, reminiscent of good times and open fires. He glances at Will, sitting several rows away under the lamp, still drawing, and wonders if he really can relax his guard a little. Both his companions seem to be all right, for now.

He takes another, larger sip.

After perhaps an hour of Brice Raleigh's company, Felix is wondering what the etiquette is for ridding yourself of a man who has just been generously sharing his finest cognac with you because the man has turned out to be a crashing bore with an apparently very small brain and an even smaller tolerance of strong spirits. Raleigh is loose-mouthed and giggly now, leaning against Felix and gesticulating so wildly with his brandy balloon that quite a lot of it is now splashed on his once-immaculate black boots. Felix is mildly surprised at Raleigh's level of inebriation; he wouldn't have thought they had drunk that much. Well, he certainly hasn't. He is too aware of his responsibilities to Will and Lily to get drunk. He looks at her yet again – still asleep – and Raleigh appears to follow the direction of his glance.

'I'll leave you now,' he says, mouthing rather than saying the words. 'Best if we all try to sleep before we dock at Dover.'

The sensible words are marred by the hiccup in the middle of *Do-ver*.

Time passes.

Felix dozes, then jerks awake again and gazes out into the night. Thankfully there has been no sign of Brice Raleigh, and now that the man has taken himself off, Felix can remember little about him. He tries to recall what they talked about, but it's all rather a blur.

Possibly he drank more of the cognac than he meant to . . .

He gives up. Looking out again, he can make out the lights of Dover, far ahead. There isn't long to go now, then the steamer will be docking and they'll be hurrying off to catch the early train to London.

There's surely time for a short nap. He leans into the corner and closes his eyes. The rhythm of the steady swell sends him to sleep.

EIGHTEEN

The boat train pulls in to Charing Cross just after ten o'clock the next morning. They are weary and dirty, and Felix is trying to remember when he last put on a clean shirt.

Will is reacting to the furious bustle of London as if he has just been dropped in one of Plato's circles of hell. Felix is about to ask Lily what she wants to do with him when she steps out into the scrum on the station forecourt and summons a hansom cab. 'We are going back to my house in Chelsea,' she says firmly to Will.

'But—'

Lily isn't listening. Grinning, Felix watches as she hauls herself on board, pulls Will up behind her and takes their bags from Felix. 'Will you follow us?' she calls down to him.

'Soon,' he replies. 'First I'm going back to the flat for a change of clothes.'

She nods curtly and tells the cabbie to take them to World's End Passage, the riverside end.

Felix strides out on to the Strand and hops on a bus; Lily has just commandeered the last cab in the rank and he is too impatient to wait. As the lumbering conveyance stops and starts its way down the Mall, around Parliament Square and along to Victoria Street, he makes himself relax and enjoy the ride. Too soon – for he has slipped into a rather pleasant half-asleep, half-awake state where nothing much seems to matter – they are in the King's Road and it is time to get off.

He walks swiftly, turning off to the left into the network of little streets between King's Road and Royal Hospital Road. The modest first floor apartment which is home is in a run-down old house with more than its share of charm in Kinver Street, and it belongs to Marm Smithers; Felix has the smaller second bedroom at the back. He unlocks the street door, sprints across the black and white tiles of the hall and up the stairs, and before he can put his key in the lock of the inner door, it opens and Marm, his face full of anxiety and his hair on end from where he's been running his hands through it, says, 'You're back! Oh, thank God!', and immediately hauls him inside and slams the door.

'Whatever is it, Marm?' Felix demands.

But Marm isn't listening. 'Where's Lily?' he cries. 'Is she safe?'

'Yes of course she is, she set off for Hob's Court in a cab and is undoubtedly home by now and surrendering herself to the tender ministrations of Mrs Clapper, who will—'

Marm has dragged him through to the living room and shoved him into his chair beside the hearth, sinking down into his own chair opposite. 'Be quiet, Felix,' he says sharply. 'Listen.'

'But what's happened?'

'You and Lily have fallen into something you can't begin to understand,' Marm says gravely. 'You're probably right and Lily *is* safe, for now, but only because they won't know she's home.' Alarm spreads through his face and he cries, 'Oh, dear God, we must *hurry*!'

'I'm not going anywhere till I've had a wash and put on clean clothes,' Felix says firmly. 'And while I'm doing that you can tell me why you're in such a state.'

'It was Lily coming here before she set off for Paris that set me thinking.' Marm is leaning against the landing wall and talking to Felix through the open door of his bedroom, where he has stripped to the skin and is vigorously lathering himself with warm water and soap. 'That tale of young Wilberforce Chibb being accused of murdering his father always struck me as odd, and then, when there was a report of a very similar death in an institute tucked away in the wilds of Brittany, the whole business turned downright suspicious.'

'How did you hear about the death in the Institute?' Felix asks.

'Young man, I'm a journalist,' Marm says sharply. 'Ears ever alert, eyes always open on the world and all that. Besides,

Lily told me the whole story, just as she'd heard it from this wretched Phyllida Westwood woman. Once she'd gone haring off to join you in France, I primed a couple of contacts to pass on all relevant information, and to keep their eyes open for anything new. When I heard about the young Englishman – *your* young Englishman, poor Wilberforce Chibb – being wanted for the murder in the Institut Hugues Abadie on the feeble grounds that he'd killed his father in the same way, my instincts told me something was seriously amiss.'

'Because you didn't believe Will – Wilberforce – was guilty of his father's murder,' Felix says. He is shaving, and all at once the turn of the conversation has made him extra careful with the open razor he is holding against his own throat . . .

'Quite. I made a few very discreet enquiries of my own, and almost immediately, I had a visit from my old friend Sutherland.'

'Do I know him?' Felix asks.

'No. Hardly anyone knows Sutherland.' Marm clears his throat. 'It is not his job to be *known*,' he adds very quietly.

'You mean he's—'

'*Sssssshh*! No need to spell it out,' Marm whispers. 'Suffice to say Sutherland only emerges from his bunker in Whitehall – only it undoubtedly isn't in Whitehall – for matters of extreme urgency that touch against the – er, the *body* that it is his duty to protect. To, ah, to keep from harm. To defend from malice in all its forms.'

'Marm, you're talking in riddles.'

'That way is safer,' Marm says darkly.

Felix has hurriedly dried himself and is now dressing, pulling shirt sleeves over still-damp arms. His left shoulder is a lurid rainbow of colours and gives a sudden protest, so sharp it makes him cry out. Brushing away Marm's anxious enquiry with a brisk 'Dislocation, but Lily saw to it,' he takes his second-best coat and trousers out of the wardrobe, ties a cravat and puts on his boots. 'Ready,' he says.

Marm nods. He already has his coat on, and now he picks up his hat, shoves it on his head and says, 'Then let us waste no more time.'

*   *   *

At 3, Hob's Court, Lily and Will have been greeted at the door by a very agitated Mrs Clapper. 'Oooh, I'm that glad to see you home, Miss Lily!' she says as she hurries them inside. 'Such goings-on, and that Mr Smithers here at all hours of the night and day demanding to know if I have any idea where you and Mr Felix are and if I've had word from you, as if you'd write to *me*, I told him, you being Abroad on Important Business,' – Lily can hear the capital letters – 'and me just the cleaner and—'

'Very much more than that, Mrs Clapper,' Lily puts in.

Mrs Clapper nods absently. 'That's as may be, but then he asks *her*,' she jerks her head towards the upper floor and Lily knows she means the Little Ballerina, 'if she's seen anyone hanging about outside when she gets in so late of an evening and she comes over all hoity-toity and tells him to mind his own business and he gets cross and then she starts on *me*, if you'll credit it, and says I've never liked her and I'm always trying to find occasions to put a knife in her side – not a real one, of course, she didn't mean that, I'm sure – and the upshot of it all and cutting a long story short, she's gone.'

Lily leans back against the wall. Will is staring at her anxiously, and she gives him what she hopes is a reassuring smile. She is trying to assimilate what she's just been told, and the most crucial part of it is that Marm Smithers has been desperately anxious to get in touch with her and Felix.

She knows she should be addressing this urgently, trying to discover more, hurrying off to find Marm. But all she can think about is that the Little Ballerina, who has been an egotistical, selfish, ruthless, rude and smelly nuisance pretty much since the day she became Lily's tenant, has gone.

She's *gone*.

Lily spares a moment to give a silent cheer, then drags herself back to the present.

'Mr Felix has gone to his apartment now, Mrs Clapper,' she says calmly, 'and I expect both he and Mr Smithers will be here before long. In the meantime, this is Mr Chibb.' She indicates Will, who makes his courteous little bow and murmurs, 'How do you do?'

Mrs Clapper blushes and mutters, 'Nicely, ta,' then, adding

her usual standby at all times of distress, disaster and social unease, adds, 'I'll make a pot of tea and fetch some of my gingerbread, shall I?'

'Yes please, Mrs Clapper,' Lily replies, 'and I shall need a large jug of hot water upstairs in my room as soon as you can manage it, please.'

'I've told that Mr Chibb he can wash in the scullery,' Mrs Clapper says up in Lily's room a short time later. She is tutting over the state of Lily's underclothes and laying out clean linen and a fresh jacket and skirt on Lily's bed. 'Heaven only knows what you've been up to, getting yourselves in such a state and your good clothes all filthy and needing careful washing and that, as if I didn't have enough to do, and I'm not going to ask because I don't want to be told!' She shakes a reproving finger at Lily, who is standing in nothing but her drawers and trying to cover the huge bruise over her left side with her arm. In no condition to defend herself, she says meekly, 'Sorry, Mrs Clapper.'

Mrs Clapper has finished; she takes a last critical look at Lily, picks up the filthy clothes and says, 'Now I'd better go and see what sort of a mess he's left in my scullery.' With a sniff of general disapproval, she stomps off down the stairs.

Lily emits a long, slow breath.

But she is not fooled for a moment by her housekeeper's cross words. She knows full well that, as Mrs Clapper always does, she is disguising distress, worry and kind-hearted sympathy under the cover of anger.

And, quite suddenly, Lily feels tears well up in her eyes.

Some time later, Lily, Felix, Marm and Will are sitting round Felix's desk in the outer office. Introductions have been made, and Mrs Clapper has brought the promised tray of tea and gingerbread, then excused herself to 'carry on with seeing to upstairs'; there is a powerful smell of bleach wafting down from the Little Ballerina's former quarters and sounds of many large items of furniture being moved about. Marm glances at Lily, eyebrows raised, and mutters, 'What on earth is she *doing* up there?'

'My tenant has left. Mrs Clapper is turning out the rooms,' she replies shortly. From the smell, she strongly suspects that Mrs Clapper is fumigating the entire first floor . . .

Marm nods, then raps gently on Felix's desk. As they turn to him, he says, 'I – er, I am sorry, young man,' – he is addressing Will – 'but I would like to speak to Miss Raynor and Mr Wilbraham in private.'

But Will shakes his head. 'If it is about the murders, Mr Smithers,' he says with dignity, 'then I have a right to know what you have to say because it's me who stands in danger of being hanged if I can't prove my innocence.' He looks at Lily, then at Felix. 'But then you probably don't believe me, any of you,' he adds, the edge of hysteria creeping into his voice, 'and you want to talk about me behind my back because you're going to decide how to go about having me arrested.'

Lily is about to speak but Felix catches her eye and shakes his head.

Marm looks at Will for some moments and says quietly, 'That is not true, Mr Chibb. I wished to talk to Miss Raynor and her associate alone because there are matters here that I do not fully understand, and I was hoping they would have information that would elucidate the situation so that it could be presented to you in its entirety. However, if you wish to be present, so be it.' He stops, holding Will's eyes. 'As for not believing in your innocence, *I* do. I think you have become embroiled in an elaborate conspiracy, and that the unscrupulous have used the false accusation that you killed your father to make you the scapegoat for the murder of the poor young man in the mental asylum.'

'Louis,' Will says softly. 'Poor Louis. He was my friend. I would *never* have killed him.'

'I know,' Marm says. He smiles at Will; a particularly sweet expression, Lily thinks.

She has never thought of Marm as an overtly sentimental or demonstrative man. He lives for his work, he shares his flat with Felix rather than a wife or intimate companion, he is unprepossessing to look at and habitually turns a brusque, cynical face to the world. She knows the true nature of the man beneath the carapace, and so does Felix, but she doesn't think many other people do.

But something quite strange is happening there in her outer office. Right before her eyes, the worried, fearful frown that Will has worn almost all the time she and Felix have known him seems to be crumbling away. His facial muscles relax – she can see now that he is a very handsome young man – and the thin body he has been holding in such rigid and, surely, *painful* tension for so long seems to be yielding. He stares at Marm, and it seems as if his lips form a silent question. Marm simply sits there quite still, watching.

Then as Will lurches towards him, Marm gets up, opens his arms and Will – Will who tries to avoid human contact – falls into his embrace. He drops his head on Marm's shoulder, and as Marm rests his thin hands on Will's back, the young man breaks down into deep, gut-wrenching sobs.

Lily senses movement; Felix has come to stand behind her.

'Poor boy has been holding all that emotion in for a long time,' he murmurs. Then – and she can hear that he is smiling – 'How odd, that it should be Marmaduke Smithers, jaundiced, detached, irreverent and, to an observer, totally devoid of sentiment, who allows him to let it out.'

Lily feels a lump in her throat. 'I'm glad someone has,' she mutters back.

Presently Will recovers his equilibrium and apologizes for his storm of weeping. They all tell him not to worry, it's only to be expected. He resumes his seat, and now he, Lily and Felix are waiting while Marm gathers his thoughts.

'Before I tell you what I have found out and the tentative conclusions I have reached,' he begins, 'I would like you three, if you will, to tell me your own observations and how you interpret them. You, after all,' – he looks round at them, holding each pair of eyes for a moment – 'have the advantage of first-hand experience; I am only able to put together the pertinent facts and come up with a plausible, if unlikely, conclusion.' He turns to Will. 'You knew Louis best. Would you like to tell us about him?'

Slowly Will nods. 'Yes. I would.' He hesitates, then goes

on: 'He was twenty-two, a few years younger than me. He was born somewhere in Germany that I've never heard of, although Louis said it was in the Bavarian mountains and very beautiful. His father was a duke, or something – titled, anyway – although Louis did not speak of him much and I don't think they were close. His mother died when he was born. I told you that, didn't I?' He looks at Lily, then at Felix. 'Our early childhoods formed a bond between us. His mother was dead, and I wasn't allowed to know mine because she'd been shut away in the asylum and my brother, my sister and I weren't permitted to mention her.' His cheeks have flushed, and Lily picks up his old resentment and his enduring pain.

'Louis's full name was Louis Eduard Leinengen Saalfeld,' he goes on. Lily sees Marm give a swift, abrupt nod, as if something suspected has just been confirmed. 'Nobody at the Institute used our full names, but I was curious about why everything concerning Louis was so shrouded in secrecy and I sneaked a look at his notes.' He gives Lily a furtive, guilty look as if expecting an admonition. 'He was raised entirely at home, with a nurse and then a governess as well. He knew such a lot,' Will goes on, 'and when I said as much one morning when he'd been telling me about the political situation in eastern Europe and went on to list the gods and goddesses of ancient Greece, he told me he'd had a very good tutor.' He smiles. 'Poor Louis, he said it was his dream to visit Greece and see Mount Olympus and the Acropolis for himself, but he knew they'd never let him.'

'Because of his delicate health,' Marm says softly.

'Yes!' Will sounds surprised. 'How did you know?'

'I think,' Marm says slowly, 'that your good friend Louis suffered from a debilitating and incurable condition. I suspect that those who had the care of him shut him up indoors, banned any sort of rough play and boyish activity, kept him at his studies and, in his leisure time, prescribed reading, jigsaw puzzles, endless games of Patience and activities such as stamp collecting.'

Will's eyebrows shot up. 'He had a very fine stamp collection!' he gasps.

'It was a lucky guess,' Marm says modestly. 'Such are the

pastimes of the invalid child, and that, I am certain, is what Louis was.'

'What was wrong with him?' Lily whispers. She thinks – is almost sure – she knows. She can still picture Will's drawing of his friend Louis . . .

'Before we come to that, there are other pertinent factors,' Marm says quietly. 'Let us consider the manner of poor Louis's death. He was, I believe you said, Lily, found at the foot of the stairs in a great pool of blood with his throat cut.'

'Yes, that's what I was told,' she agrees. 'And his hands and forearms bore wounds too, and they had also bled profusely.' She can hear Miss Westwood's voice in her head, and, with hindsight, she reflects how dispassionately the young woman spoke of such horror and wonders why this did not occur to her before.

Blood.

A weakling who had to be kept from any sort of lively activity.

A mother who died at birth.

'Louis Eduard suffered from a specific condition,' Marm says softly. 'His mother was a carrier of it and passed it on to her son. Women like her do not commonly suffer as men do, although any cut or wound can lead to prolonged bleeding, and the perilous process of childbirth can be particularly hazardous.'

'I have nursed women like that,' Lily murmurs. 'And I've seen baby boys die because the bleeding from the cutting of the umbilical cord could not be stopped.'

'Yes,' Marm says sadly.

Silence falls.

Lily waits. She can almost hear the words before Marm utters them.

'There is a family,' he says eventually, 'well known to us all, in which it is generally believed that this distressing condition is widespread.' He raises his head and looks around, at Will, Felix, finally at Lily.

'It's haemophilia,' she whispers. 'And the family . . .' She doesn't go on; even here, with only the four of them present, it feels wrong to perpetrate the persistent gossip.

'Yes,' Marm agrees. 'The family.' He looks at each of them, then goes on softly, 'Although never actually admitted, it is believed in this country that the Queen is a carrier of the condition, that one of her sons has the disease and that at least two of her daughters are also carriers, for there have been instances of the Queen's grandchildren dying from excessive bleeding following accidents that they ought to have survived.' He sighs. 'It appears that haemophilia runs relentlessly through Queen Victoria's entire family.'

Lily feels as if the world has tilted slightly. 'Then are you saying,' she asks, 'that this man, this German man called Louis Eduard who was an inmate of the Institut Hugues Abadie and tucked away in a remote Breton forest, is a son of the Queen?' She is utterly astounded, and also highly sceptical.

'No, dear Lily,' Marm says. 'That would not be possible, for Victoria was already our crowned queen when the first of her children was born, and there are always witnesses when a reigning queen gives birth in case someone tries to replicate the Warming Pan Scandal.' Seeing blank looks, he explains: 'Mary of Modena, wife to James II, had been unable to conceive for five years, and when she finally gave birth to a son, in June of 1788, there were rumours that the infant was a substitute, smuggled into the birth chamber in a warming pan, no true son of the King and therefore not the rightful heir.' Briskly he shakes his head. 'But enough of tales out of the past: suffice to say that the births of our present Queen's children are very well-documented and recorded and it is simply impossible that another, unrecognized son exists.'

'So who *was* Louis Eduard?' Lily whispers.

Marm shrugs. 'I have no idea. It is not important, anyway. What *is* important, and crucially so, is who some very unscrupulous and influential people *claim* he is.'

'And who is that?' Felix asks. He adds, with discernible impatience, 'Come on, Marm, stop drawing it out!'

Marm smiles. 'Sorry. Journalistic trick, to postpone the final revelation until the last moment. But before I go on, please be warned that this is nothing but speculation and rumour. I heard it from a friend of mine who moves in the deepest and darkest of deep, dark government departments concerned with state security and—'

'Sutherland,' Felix says softly. Lily glances at him questioningly, and he adds, 'Marm mentioned him earlier.'

'Sutherland, yes,' Marm confirms. 'He and I had enjoyed a particularly indulgent Christmas many years ago, when we were callow young men inclined to boast of our professional successes, particularly while in our cups. I had just repeated to him a particularly scurrilous and succulent secret about one of our more glamorous actresses, and I was confident I would be awarded the golden cardboard crown we had manufactured for the winner of our little competition for the juiciest piece of gossip. But as I reached for it, Sutherland murmured, "Not so fast, old pal!" and then he told me.'

He stops, and for a moment his gaze appears to turn inwards. Lily, watching intently, very much hopes he is not going to change his mind and not reveal his friend's secret after all . . .

He isn't.

'Take your minds back, if you will,' he begins, 'to the pre-dawn hours of a May morning in 1819. The place is Kensington Palace, and the specific location is the bedroom of Marie Louise Victoire, the wife of Edward, Duke of Kent. The death in childbirth two years earlier of the much-beloved Charlotte, daughter of George IV, has ended the Hanoverian succession, for none of the King's many brothers and sisters had produced a living, legitimate heir. One had ten children by his mistress,' he goes on, eagerly leaning forward and well into his stride, 'another was widely believed to have fathered a child on his sister, but of the dozen or so siblings who survived to adulthood, none had succeeded in their primary royal duty. What became known to the vulgar as the Royal Race began, and the brothers of the King—'

'What about the King's daughters?' Lily interrupts.

Marm flicks a swift hand. 'Given up as childless years since,' he says dismissively. 'The royal sons, as I was saying, set about marrying suitably fecund women and trying to beget a child as fast as possible. The Duke of Kent selected the widow of a German prince who had already demonstrated her credentials by the production of two healthy children, a boy and a

girl, and almost a year later, here she is in the small hours of
this May morning, giving birth.'

'To the little girl who is now our Queen,' Will says. He
looks shocked, Lily observes, as if such talk of deeply intimate
matters is not decent.

Which, she muses, it isn't.

'As we know,' Marm is saying, 'the baby born on that May
morning was to become our Queen; her legitimacy and her
right to be our monarch has never been questioned.'

'Nor must it be now!' Will says hotly. 'That would be
treason! You mustn't go on, Mr Smithers, I won't hear this,
it's not right and—'

Felix puts a light hand on his arm. 'Let Marm finish, Will,'
he says quietly.

'Thank you, Felix.' Marm closes his eyes for a moment,
then says, 'Let me remind you that this is a rumour, told to
me by an irresponsible, scandal-loving young man who was
very drunk and also badly wanted to win a foolish competition
by outdoing his friend in the height of the tall tales they were
exchanging.' He pauses, looking round at the three intent faces
of his audience.

Then, slowly, softly, he says, 'What Sutherland told me that
Christmas night was that the baby who was christened
Alexandrine Victoria, and who has been our Queen since 1837,
was not the only baby born that morning, for she was one of
twins.'

Together Lily and Felix say, '*Which* one?'

Marm grins. 'Glad to see you are keeping up,' he observes.
'Alexandrine Victoria was the second, born some thirty-nine
minutes after her elder sister. They were said to be identical,
although that can be no more than a little extra colouring to
the story.'

'This elder twin died,' Lily says. 'She *must* have done,
otherwise . . .'

And Marm echoes softly, 'Otherwise. Quite.'

Will has not understood. 'What? What are you telling us?'
he shouts wildly. 'Louis was a *boy* – a man – and anyway he
couldn't have been born in 1819, he'd have been more than
forty and he was *twenty-two*, I *told* you!'

Marm sends him a quick look of sympathy, then turns to Lily. 'In response to your statement, dear Lily, the elder twin was skinny, frail and weak. Or so Sutherland's story went,' he adds. 'It was the opinion of those present that her altogether more robust sister had taken the vast majority of the available nutrients as they grew side by side *in utero*. Moreover, the older sister was making no sound and had bled heavily from the navel, and, believing her to be already dead, those in attendance bundled up the corpse in the bloody sheets and hid it away. When presently she emitted a feeble mewing noise, she was immediately christened by the nurse; baptism by a layperson is recognized by the Church if death is assumed to be imminent. They called her Marie Augusta, and she was swiftly and secretly removed while those present attended to the second twin, already lustily bawling with a small but powerful pair of lungs.'

'And then Marie Augusta died?' Will persists.

'She had deformed limbs and a twisted spine,' Marm says. 'It was fully anticipated that she would die within days, if not hours, and when these dire expectations were not fulfilled, she was smuggled out of the palace and shortly afterwards out of the country, to be cared for in a modest country house deep in the Bavarian mountains. It was thought better, so Sutherland said, to ignore her entirely and concentrate solely on the stronger twin, so that when the weakling died – as was still expected any day – her death would pass unremarked and unrecorded because the very few who knew about her would assume she was already dead.'

He stops, looking round at his audience. None of them speaks.

'They thought she was simple-minded,' he goes on softly. 'It was easy to forget about her, shut away in her big house in the mountains, and in time, everyone did. Confounding expectations, she lived through infancy and childhood. She would sit silently, engaged on some quiet task, and they took it for granted that her mind was blank. It wasn't; Marie was taking note, working things out for herself. With the onset of – er, of womanhood,' – Marm flushes slightly and looks down – 'her health deteriorated further, for the regular loss of a great deal of blood undermined her already feeble constitution. And then,' he goes on, his voice strengthening as he returns to safer topics, 'confounding every single expectation, Marie fell in love with a duke who was fifteen years older than her and she insisted on marrying him. Those who had the care of her told her repeatedly and in no uncertain terms that she was totally unfit for wedlock and most certainly should not contemplate pregnancy and childbirth, but Marie loved her duke, she married him, she insisted she knew best and she became pregnant. Or so she claimed, although they told her it was impossible, that it must be a phantom pregnancy like that of Mary Tudor. It became clear, however, that she really was with child, and the baby – a boy – was born on 7th July 1860. But Marie had been damaged during the birth, she began to bleed and the flow could not be stopped, and the doctor and the nurse stood helplessly by and watched her die.'

'That baby was Louis?' Will whispers. 'My friend Louis?'

'The child was christened Louis Eduard,' Marm says quietly. 'Given Marie Augusta's true identity as the elder child of the Duke of Kent and his wife, she should have been crowned Queen of England. Had that happened, Louis Eduard would have been heir to the throne and, with her death, would become the rightful King of England.'

He frowns, as if something has struck him. 'Louis Eduard,' he says thoughtfully. 'Eduard, of course, is the German version of Edward. Edward, Duke of Kent, was Queen Victoria's father and so would also have been the father of the elder sister. If, of course,' he says with a wry smile, 'there had been an elder sister, which of course there was *not* because it is all no more than a fanciful tale . . .'

He pauses, eyebrows raised to see if anyone is going to say anything.

And after a moment Felix says, 'If Marie Augusta was the rightful Queen of England, then Queen Victoria wouldn't have been crowned and her children would not be who they are.' He frowns, thinking. 'Her daughter Vicky might still have married the Emperor of Germany and her son would still be Frederick's heir, but he could no longer claim that his grand-mother was Queen of England, because she wouldn't be.'

Marm nods. 'And, for a young man who from early

childhood has insisted that he be given the respect due to a grandson of the great Queen Victoria of England, and who has been striving for years to be more British and more royal than his blue-blooded English relatives, what a blow it would be to discover the truth: that his mother was not the daughter of a queen, and his grandmother, as a younger sister, was outranked by her elder twin.'

'And what would he have said when he found out about Louis!' Will cries.

There is quite a long silence. Then Marm says, 'You can see, I am sure, why the most secret of secret government departments in both England and Germany were utterly determined to make quite sure that neither the Queen, the Kaiser or any of their children ever *did* find out.'

'And the most certain way to do that,' Lily says slowly, 'was for the young man in question to be removed to somewhere so well-hidden that he couldn't be found. Then, once he was out of sight and out of mind, to have him quietly disposed of.'

'And for the death of a mysterious foreigner in a Breton asylum to be kept very quiet,' Felix adds, 'and, just in case word should ever leak out, to put the blame very firmly on someone else.'

Will, who has been looking from one to the other of them, a puzzled expression on his face, nods solemnly. Then suddenly he gasps, goes very white and says tentatively, 'Me. *Me.* Oh, dear God . . . you mean *me*?'

And all three of them nod.

NINETEEN

The heavy silence is interrupted by a knocking on the street door; it is not forceful, but insistent. Lily hears Mrs Clapper go to answer it; *she knows Felix and I are busy*, she thinks absently.

And she hears the clear, remembered voice say crisply, 'Miss Phyllida Westwood to see Miss Raynor, and it is rather urgent so as quickly as you can, please.'

Lily spins round to stare at Felix but he is already moving. He grabs Will by the arm, looks at Marm and jerks his head towards Lily's inner sanctum, and the three of them go quickly and quietly through the door and draw it almost closed behind them.

Lily sits down at Felix's desk. She tries to steady her breathing, smoothing her hair and opening a random file. When Mrs Clapper taps at the door and says, 'That Miss Westwood to see you, Miss Lily, the one who was took bad last time,' she smiles calmly and says, 'Thank you, Mrs Clapper, please show her in.'

And as she watches Miss Westwood glide smoothly into the office, she is thinking wildly: *how did she know we were back?* Straight away she answers her own question: *because we have been watched for most of the way and she knows pretty nearly everything.*

Mrs Clapper has come to stand beside Lily, and now she leans down and mutters, 'Poor young lady doesn't look any too bright today, either – I'll make a nice cup of sweet tea and bring it in along with some more of that gingerbread.'

'Thank you, Mrs Clapper,' Lily replies. 'Please, Miss Westwood, sit down.'

When Mrs Clapper has gone, Miss Westwood seats herself and says, 'I believe, Miss Raynor, that you have been feeding me untruths.'

Lily feels her fast heartbeat increase. 'Really?' she says with feigned surprise. 'In what way, Miss Westwood?'

'In many ways, but specifically when you reported that Wilberforce Chibb had been killed falling from a train. Now I accept that he did indeed fall off a train, as did you and Mr Wilbraham – or perhaps I should say you jumped? – but Wilberforce was not killed.'

There is silence as they size each other up.

Then Lily says conversationally, 'One thing puzzles me rather.'

'Just one?' the woman says, the irony heavy.

'When you engaged my services,' – Lily ignores the comment – 'you were extremely well informed about the Chibbs and about the real Phyllida Westwood and her family, and I find myself wondering how you acquired such detailed knowledge?'

The woman is smiling. She does not answer.

'Of course,' Lily muses, 'my good friend Marmaduke Smithers – I'm sure you know all about him – found out most of the facts that you in your Miss Westwood guise mentioned, simply from his own files and careful record-keeping. As to the more personal details, perhaps you made a friend of the real Phyllida Westwood and pumped her for information? Will says that Phyllida is naïve and not very clever, whereas my impression of you, on the contrary, is that you are sophisticated and highly intelligent. I do not doubt that you would have fooled Phyllida as easily as you fooled me.'

'Why not call me Agatha Trevelyan?' the woman suggests. 'It is, naturally, no more my real name than Phyllida Westwood – who is, as you rightly surmise, something of a simpleton – but I detect that you are not keen to go on calling me Miss Westwood.'

'I am sure you are not going to tell me who you work for and what you are up to,' Lily says, 'so *I* shall make a beginning, and say that I am aware you are the hub of a web of agents, both British and German, men and at least one woman who do your work out in the field and report back to you with everything they discover, then await instructions as to what to do next.'

'It is wheels that have hubs, not webs,' Agatha Trevelyan says mildly. 'But in essence you are correct. And yes, our own government's agency has indeed been working with our German brethren, for this fanciful, foolish yet annoyingly persistent tale that I am sure you have now been told cannot be allowed to endure any longer. For myself, I am in the service of a department whose sole purpose is to protect this country's royalty; not only their physical safety but also their reputation and their standing.' She pauses. 'It is quite unthinkable, is it not, that anybody should dare to question the right of a crowned and anointed monarch to sit upon their throne? I am sure you will agree that the merest whisper of any irregularity must be crushed; stamped out as ruthlessly as the first tiny flames of a forest fire.'

First tiny flames, Lily thinks. But she has the impression that Louis Eduard had been an in-patient for some time . . . Then she understands: what prompted the agency, whoever they are, to put the plan into action was not Louis Eduard's arrival in the Institute but Will's. A man locked away because he was accused of killing his father with a razor was just the person on whom to hang the similar slaying that rid the agencies of two countries of the central figure in a persistent and dangerous rumour that refused to go away.

She hears again Miss Trevelyan's intriguing reference to crowned monarchs and their rights, and she is just about to bring up the question of Louis Eduard Leinengen Saalfeld's identity when she seems to hear a voice in her head saying quietly, *No*. And, her mind leaping so fast she can barely follow, she understands that this information is crucial to the matter; she would do better to withhold it. For now.

'Your German brethren did not live up to your high standards, Miss Trevelyan,' she says levelly. 'They killed an innocent man in Pont-Aven, wrongly identifying him as Wilberforce Chibb on the very slim grounds that the poor man had been given an old canvas bag that had belonged to Wilberforce. And later they—'

'I am sure it would give you pleasure to detail all their

failures, Miss Raynor,' Miss Trevelyan interrupts smoothly, 'but let me save you the trouble. I was aware that the couple known to you as Mr and Mrs Joseph Clark from Harrow were – ah – unsuitable for the assignment long before they reached Pont-Aven, and it was no surprise to learn that they had blundered. Not only did they shoot the wrong man,' – Lily hears a hint of anger in the cool voice, even though it is tightly controlled – 'they also failed to discover what *you* did, which was Wilberforce Chibb's next destination.' She smiles, and Lily notices that what on any other face would be a pleasant expression is, on hers, chillingly sinister.

Miss Trevelyan leans forward. 'After Pont-Aven, the Clarks had exhausted what little usefulness they had ever afforded us, and we were working blind. Why, had it not been for your most helpful little messages, Miss Raynor, we should have been at a loss to know quite *where* young Wilberforce had gone!'

Lily stares back into the brilliant bluebell eyes.

'Do you know the fate of these two people you dismiss so ruthlessly?' she asks softly.

Miss Trevelyan shrugs. 'They died. In Paris.'

'They had managed to find my companions and me,' Lily says. 'No doubt you will say that watching the trains at Gare Montparnasse was no great feat of ingenuity and the only thing they *could* do, but the fact remains that they were there, they spotted us, they followed us doggedly all the way to the Seine, and when we managed to board a river boat and they did not, they had the courage and the resourcefulness to find a skiff and give chase, and it was in attempting to board our vessel that they both lost their lives.'

Miss Trevelyan has been watching Lily while she says this, an expression of slight distaste on her face. When Lily has finished, there is a brief silence. And Miss Trevelyan says, 'It is a dangerous game.'

'Who *are* you?' Lily bursts out. 'How can you be so cold?'

Miss Trevelyan sits perfectly still. 'I do what I do because I believe it is necessary,' she says. 'You may or may not know, Miss Raynor – although I take the view that a woman in your profession should make it her business to know – that in this country there has been an intelligence branch of the military services since 1873, and the work they do, although it remains almost entirely unknown, is *crucial* to the safety of our country. The Metropolitan Police, too, are now developing a section which will take on responsibility for matters pertaining to national security and intelligence, for, as the worrying conditions in Ireland indicate, the state will always need protection from acts of subversion and—'

'And these great machines of the state had to roll into action to murder one poor, sick young man in the depths of Brittany who did no harm to anybody, purely because of this ridiculous rumour that he was the son of some totally fictitious elder twin sister of our Queen?' The hot words pour out of Lily. 'And as if that wasn't bad enough, put the blame for the murder firmly on another, equally innocent young man?' She is shouting now, fury driving out any sense of caution. 'For shame, Miss Trevelyan, or whatever your *blasted* name is!'

Even before she has finished, Agatha Trevelyan has leapt up so violently that her chair has toppled over. She is holding out her hands, palms outward, in alarm, hissing: 'Hush! *Hush*! Miss Raynor, keep your voice *down*!'

Even as the chair is crashing on to the floor, Felix is already erupting into the front office. His eyes on Lily, he says, 'What was that? Are you hurt?' and she can see that even as he asks, he is taking in what has happened.

'No. Felix, I'm fine,' she says, 'she's—'

He has spun round to Miss Trevelyan. 'Why are you on your feet?' he shouts. 'Don't you dare draw a weapon, you devil!' He is moving forward, eyes on the woman, and he grabs hold of her by the shoulders, twisting her so that she is standing in front of him facing Lily, and wrapping his arms round her to stop her making any move to delve into her bag or a pocket for a hidden gun.

Outside in the hall, someone is poised to make a move . . .

When Mrs Clapper admitted the person she knew as Miss Phyllida Westwood, the latter contrived to leave the street door on the latch.

One of the two men in dark coats who picked up the trail of Lily, Felix and Will in the south is still a guest of the French police, awaiting a lawyer sent by the British government who will quietly explain to those who need to hear why one of their agents was in a railway carriage with a handgun, apparently hauling a woman on to his lap in order to assault her.

His partner has quietly let himself into 3, Hob's Court.

He hears Lily's clear voice revealing that she – and presumably her two companions – know much of the truth and have guessed the rest. Anticipating the worst, he reckons that Wilberforce Chibb did not escape or die in a fall but has accompanied these two unexpectedly dogged enquiry agents of the World's End Bureau back to London. Where, no doubt, they will soon arrange for him to have legal advice in order to clear his name.

If they have not already done so.

Slowly, stealthily, the man creeps into the outer office and across the floor towards Felix. In his hand is a gun levelled straight at the back of Felix's head.

Lily, who spotted him as soon as he crept in through the office door, has frozen. At least, her body has frozen; her mind is frantically informing her what will happen to Felix if she makes any sudden movement.

But now Felix is staring at her, concern filling his face. 'Lily? What is it? You *are* hurt. What did—'

And then the man in the dark coat is right behind him, grinding the barrel of the gun into the base of his skull. He is not as tall as Felix, and slowly he exerts pressure with the gun to drive Felix to his knees, forcing him to release his captive. Bending forward, he rests his free hand heavily on Felix's shoulder to make him stay there.

'Very wise to let her go, sir,' he says. His voice is quiet and accentless. He looks up at Lily. 'We shall be leaving now, the lady and I. You'll forget we were here, naturally, and then nobody need come to any harm, either now or later.'

But he is not the only person to have heard the crash of Miss Trevelyan's chair.

From out in the scullery, Mrs Clapper not only heard it, but was also startled by the sound of Felix shouting.

Now she too is tiptoeing across the floor of the outer office, almost exactly in the footsteps of the man in the dark coat. But she isn't holding a gun: in her two strong hands is the old oak tea tray bearing cups, saucers, sugar bowl, plates and squares of gingerbread, with a jug of milk, another of hot water and Lily's grandmother's large, heavy silver teapot, which is full of freshly-made tea.

Lily is staring at Mrs Clapper as fixedly as she just stared at Felix. She meets her housekeeper's eyes. Tries to send a message: *be careful, he has a gun pressed to Felix's head.*

Mrs Clapper gives a very faint nod.

But she can't have picked up Lily's frantic message – so silly to expect she could! – because she has not paused in her slow, stealthy progress.

Now she is right behind the man bending over Felix.

She braces her narrow shoulders. The powerful muscles in her thin arms, developed from decades of hard work, flex and bulge. She raises the tea tray and its heavy load, higher and higher. And when it is as high as she can lift it, she brings it crashing down on top of the head of the man in the dark coat.

The gun flies out of his hand.

The deafening noises come hard and fast now. The smashing of china, the splash of a large volume of falling water, the great bounce of a heavy silver teapot on the hard floor and, preceding them all, the crash of a very solid oak tray on the crown of a man's head.

Then, after an instant's shocked silence, the near-boiling water in the teapot and the jug permeates the man's coat, the scarf, the jacket and the shirt. The man starts screaming and he doesn't stop.

Five minutes later, all is calm again.

Marm and Will had come racing out of Lily's inner sanctum as soon as the man in the dark coat began to scream. Now Marm is sizing up the situation with admirable alacrity; he announces calmly, 'I will fetch help for him, and summon the police for them both.'

'Yes, good,' Felix says. He is standing over Lily as she

crouches beside the fallen man, and he has a firm grasp on Miss Trevelyan's arm. Mrs Clapper is sitting in Felix's chair. She is still holding the tray.

'Take Will with you, Marm,' Lily says without looking up.

Marm glances at Will's shocked face. 'Yes. Come on, young man,' he says bracingly, and marches Will out of the office before he can protest.

The outer door bangs shut.

Miss Trevelyan stares pointedly at Felix, then quickly jerks her head towards Mrs Clapper. Felix, understanding, pushes her very firmly down into the spare chair kept for visitors and goes over to the housekeeper.

'Thank you, dear Mrs Clapper,' he says. Gently he picks up her free hand and, bending over it, kisses the knobbly knuckles.

'*Oooh!*' she exclaims.

'Go and make yourself a strong cup of tea. Plenty of sugar. Sit down and stay there till you've drunk it.'

'But what about all this?' Mrs Clapper says in a horrified whisper. 'Water, milk, sugar, tea and my gingerbread, all over Miss Lily's floor, and it's a real *mess!*'

'It could well be a life-saving mess,' Felix says. 'We will clear it up later. Go on, Mrs Clapper.'

She looks up, meets his eyes and slowly nods.

He watches her walk away. He's pretty sure it would embarrass her hugely if he ran after her and hugged her, which is the only reason why he doesn't.

He goes to stand by Lily again. She is still busy with the scalded man, pulling the tea-soaked garments away from his blistering flesh. 'How is he?' Felix asks.

'Burned,' Lily answers shortly. She sounds, he reflects, as if she doesn't have quite as much sympathy as she might.

Into the quiet, Miss Trevelyan says, 'Of course, you realize it is fairly pointless to have asked your friend Mr Smithers to fetch the police.'

Lily's only response is a soft exclamation of disgust.

So Felix says, 'Presumably because if they arrest you both, as I hope they do, it will only be a brief and minor inconvenience because word will go up the chain of command

and you'll be free again by this evening, or tomorrow at latest.'

Miss Trevelyan considers this. 'Tomorrow, probably. As I am sure you will appreciate, Mr Wilbraham, the department has other, more important concerns.'

'In their eyes, naturally, you were following orders and have done nothing wrong,' Felix says coldly.

'Quite,' she agrees.

There is an unpleasant note of smugness in her voice. Felix wishes there was something he could do to remove it. But since punching her doesn't really seem to be an option, he does nothing.

And the four of them wait, three in silence, one moaning quietly in pain, for the police and the doctor to arrive.

TWENTY

The case has good and bad consequences.

The worst of the bad ones is that, despite Lily and Felix having saved Will from being executed for another man's crime, someone else dies for it. One of Marm's European contacts, put on the alert by Marm, digs out a small item in an obscure Breton newspaper which mentions the death of a man who escaped from a carefully anonymous Breton institution.

Felix brings the article into the office one morning.

'The man was known to be violent,' he reads from the article, translating as he goes, 'and had attacked and killed a young German man being treated in the same institution. He had stolen a meat cleaver, with which he was threatening the local police officers who were courageously trying to restrain him. He injured three, one gravely, before he was overcome.'

'Do you think he escaped the night we stayed in Paimpont?' Lily asks. 'And that was what set off the alarms?'

'Convenient if it was,' Felix says sourly. 'Whoever he was, the poor fellow was made the scapegoat that Will was meant to be. With Louis Eduard's murder tidily accounted for, no more investigations will take place. *Ever*,' he adds bitterly.

'It's not *right*!' Lily exclaims hotly. 'The man who escaped no more murdered Louis Eduard than Will did, yet the real killer will never be arrested, never stand trial, never pay for what he did.'

'No,' Felix agrees. He sighs. 'If ever we had the chance to question him, he would probably say exactly what Miss Agatha Trevelyan said. *I do what I do because I believe it is necessary.*'

Lily nods. Then says vehemently, 'Dear God, she was so insufferably *smug*!'

They look at each other, and for the first time during their endless discussions of the case, both of them smile.

* * *

The second bad consequence is that, only a few days after Miss Trevelyan and her dark-coated (and badly burned) companion disappeared from Lily and Felix's lives, never to be seen or heard of by either of them again, the World's End Bureau receives a cheque. In the accompanying unsigned note, it states that the sum is in full and final settlement for the Bureau's services in Europe and includes a bonus for swift resolution.

It is an *enormous* bonus: there is one more nought on the end of the payment than Lily was expecting.

The Bureau's bank accepts the cheque without question. Lily and Felix have no success over trying to trace its source. Marm can only come up with the vague suggestion that it is probably some obscure and largely unknown government department.

Lily and Felix decide to accept the money. But, knowing as they do that the bonus is for keeping their mouths shut, they both feel soiled.

One morning in the office, when Lily is scratching her head over the accounts and Felix has just remembered he hasn't watered the pot plants, she looks up suddenly and says, 'Who do they think she was if she *wasn't* Victoria's elder twin?'

Felix, who had been discussing the same question yesterday evening with Marm, says, 'Funny you should ask that just this morning. Marm has come up with something.'

She throws down her pen. 'Why didn't you *tell* me?' she exclaims.

He grins. 'Well, I've only been here for a quarter of an hour. And these plants really do look thirsty.'

He can tell by the look on her face that she's debating whether or not to throw something at him. Her hand hovers over her little ink pot, but she restrains herself. 'Go on, then,' she orders.

Felix comes to perch on the edge of her desk. 'Marm was in the library's research section all yesterday, and he finally unearthed the tree of an impoverished family with vague claims to minor nobility who live somewhere in Bavaria. Marie Augusta was the middle one of five daughters, and she was married off to a much older man who went by the name of Heinrich Louis, who was duke of somewhere nobody's ever heard of called Meininberg. Or something.'

'And they had a son?' Lily demands.

'Yes. There's something else,' he adds as she opens her mouth to speak. 'Marm traced the maternal line back more than a century to a family who lived in a remote Alpine village with a small and largely enclosed population. The condition now known as haemophilia was widespread among them.'

Lily stares at him. After quite a long time, she says very quietly, 'Which version do we believe?'

And he shrugs.

Among the good outcomes is the appearance of the new, happier, more confident and steadier man that Will is quickly becoming.

For the present he is staying in Marm's flat, crammed into a tiny box room behind the kitchen. Marm has taken charge of the young man's affairs, and the first thing he did was to find a very good solicitor. After some skilful manoeuvring by this clever man, Will has been declared innocent of any residual charges concerning his father's death, and, as sole heir, the house in Rye and his father's substantial estate now belong to him. He has written to Great-Aunt Eulalia in the Spa Hydro de St Roc, generously offering to restore what was once stolen from her, and she has replied with gracious thanks and said that although she will consider coming for a visit, she does not think it likely that she will permanently exchange Aurelie-les-Bains for Rye.

However, he has already said, more than once, that his main concern is to look after his sister and do whatever he can to improve her poor state of health and her sadly restricted life.

Marm has confided to Felix that the engagement to the real Miss Phyllida Westwood has been quietly dissolved.

'Did she mind?' Felix asked Marm.

Marm grinned. 'According to Will – who I'm happy to say is developing a very nice, subtle sense of humour – the lady listened in apathetic silence to his confession that, bearing in mind his recent troubles, he did not consider himself fit to be her husband and so is releasing her from her promise.' He chuckles. 'Will said she displayed – and these were his exact words – *a singular and not very flattering indifference.*'

Marm Smithers has remembered Lily saying rather tersely that the Little Ballerina has left. He calls on Lily late one day, and it becomes apparent that he feels partly responsible, the final row between Mrs Clapper and Lily's former tenant having been sparked off by Marm's presence.

Lily protests that she doesn't blame him in the least, and she is delighted to have seen the back of the woman (the Little Ballerina departed owing a week's rent, but Lily is taking the loss stoically).

'Nevertheless, I should like to help,' Marm says firmly. 'Assuming, dear Miss Raynor, that you wish to let the middle floor again?'

'I'm afraid I must,' Lily confesses.

Marm beams. 'Splendid. Then I may be able to help. I know of two women for whom the accommodation would be perfect. They are scholars; intellectual, lively-minded. One is a librarian and the other a teacher, and both studied at university, one at Cambridge, one at Oxford, although they were not, of course, allowed to take degrees.' He frowns. 'At present they are residents in their London club, although it is not ideal because the accommodation is cramped and neither as quiet nor as private as they would like.'

'Because they need to study,' Lily says, nodding sagely.

'Er – quite.' Marm lowers his eyes. 'The club's rooms are all small singles, each furnished with a narrow bed, a small wardrobe, a desk and a chair, and those few items take up all the space.'

'There are two large rooms on the middle floor,' Lily says. 'One is presently arranged as a bedroom, with a good-sized bed, and the other as a sitting room, with sofas by the fireplace and a table and chairs, although it would be easy to fit both as bedrooms with a desk for study, and . . .'

She has been intrigued by Marm's growing discomfiture. Understanding grows and suddenly she knows exactly why he thinks her middle floor, hidden away within a private house, would suit his two friends so well.

She feels her cheeks grow hot.

She thinks carefully, then says, 'Of course, if the ladies decided to take the rooms, it would be entirely up to them how they arranged the furniture. The middle landing would be their domain, and Mrs Clapper would do as much or as little in the way of housekeeping as they chose.'

She is quite sure she is not imagining the wave of relief that is flooding through Marm.

'Thank you, dear Lily,' he says softly after a moment. 'My friends' names are Dorothea Sutherland and Bernice Adderley, although dear old Bernice hasn't been called anything but Bunty by those who know and love her since she was about six.' He is smiling a gently reminiscent smile.

'*You* are obviously fond of her,' Lily observes.

'Indeed I am. She's my cousin.'

'And Sutherland . . .' Lily raises her eyebrows. Surely it would be too much of a coincidence to come across another, unassociated Sutherland?

Marm drops an eyelid in a wink and says softly, 'Let us just leave it at that, Miss Raynor.'

A month later, Will is poised to go down to Rye and move permanently into Old Saltway House, where his sister Alexandra has been happily finishing the final preparations.

Lily knows that, before he leaves, she must speak to him in private. Accordingly, one afternoon when Felix is off investigating a potential new case and Marm is out of London, she goes round to Kinver Street, where Will, delighted to see her, sits her down and makes her a cup of tea.

As soon as they are settled, she says without preamble, 'Will, why are you so obsessed with drawing those cats?'

He looks at her for a long moment. She wonders if she has distressed or offended him; his expression is hard to read. Then he says, 'I have stopped drawing them.'

She thinks that is all he's going to offer.

She waits.

Then he leans back in the chair and, smiling gently, says,
'Nobody ever asked me before. They all got worried, then
annoyed, then irate when I kept on. But nobody said, what *is*
it, this cat with a man's eyes?'

Lily waits again. Then she prompts gently, 'Well?'

He closes his eyes. There is pain in his face, as well as
distress and growing horror. Then, still with his eyes closed,
he says, 'One day when I was travelling home from school
for the holidays, I was involved in a dreadful railway accident.
A locomotive ran off the rails in a tunnel, the driver was
crushed, the train ran straight into a stationary one and then
everything caught fire.'

She breathes, 'Will, how frightful,' but she doesn't think he
hears.

'There was a man in my carriage. Earlier – before it
happened – the man looked up once or twice and smiled.
He had a nice smile, and kind eyes. When the collision
smashed the world apart, a sharp-edged piece of metal tore
off somewhere on the locomotive or the tender and it came
flying back through the broken carriage, spinning like a
huge discus. It caught the smiling man under the chin. It cut
his head clean off.'

Lily puts her hand to her mouth, stifling the gasp of horror.

'The boy that I was then,' Will continues, his voice taking
on a dreamy tone, 'heard something bouncing along the
carriage towards him. He felt this something bump against his
legs. He thought it was a football; one that had been played
with on a wet day so that the leather was soaked and the ball
was very heavy. But when he – *I* – looked down, it wasn't a
football at all.'

Lily watches and waits.

'In the orange light of the hungry flames,' Will's dream-like
voice goes on, 'I saw someone looking up at me. It was
the kind man. Under the dark eyebrows, his light hazel eyes
were wide open in surprise. Strangely,' – he frowns – 'the
face was *still* wearing that smile.' He looks up and meets
Lily's eyes. 'Which was really weird, considering the head
didn't have a body anymore.'

Lily whispers, 'But why did you have to draw the cats?'

Will smiles, a sad, reflective expression. 'Because before he was decapitated, the smiling man had been burned; wreathed in smoke. It marked his face with a strange black and grey brindled effect, just like a cat's whiskered muzzle. He *was* a cat, I thought he had turned into a cat,' he adds earnestly, as if keen that she understands. 'But he still had human eyes.'

Late one evening, Lily lets herself out of the back of the house and makes her way down to the basin where the boats tie up.

Tamáz greets her with the usual warmth. They drink their tea, she describes her French travels, she tells him how she kept the witch's bottle on its chain round her neck at all times.

'And here you are, safely home again,' he murmurs. He is looking at her, and she does not quite recognize the expression in his eyes.

They talk for some time, then she gets up and he sees her to her rear door.

She turns to look at him as they say goodnight.

That expression is back in his eyes, she thinks.

And now she realizes he looks sad.

Felix is in the office early the next morning. He is full of everything he's been finding out about the new case. Lily invites him to bring his tea into the inner sanctum and settles down to listen.

She watches him as he speaks. His face is alight with enthusiasm, and frequently, as he so often does, he makes her laugh.

She is paying careful attention to the somewhat complex details he is explaining to her. Thinking that it sounds like an intriguing case.

Nevertheless, a small, detached part of her mind is informing her that she is very, very happy.